*A Novel*

# JASON DIX AND THE AMAZING EPHEMERAL ETHEREAL PIXIES

## C J BALLAY

D1260460

# Jason Dix
# and the
# Amazing Ephemeral
# Ethereal Pixies

C. Joseph Ballay

Katie Lowery at Clear Voice Editors

Thank you to those special people who gave me the courage to complete this book.

The characters hereafter are entirely fictional. Any deviations from historical truths are entirely artistic license.

# CHAPTER 1

## A DAY IN SCHOOL

*Friday, October 27, 2017*

And so the sun rose in the East, the skies were a crisp, morning blue, and Mother Nature had no reservations about starting another beautiful fall day as she cast her brilliant rays of sunshine down upon the town of Carrollton, a suburb of New Orleans.

The day was quiet and peaceful, and there was a sense of ease in the air. These pleasant traits generally afforded one a prescient feeling of tranquility; such was the norm of the languorous days along the banks of the mighty Mississippi with minimal expectations for deviation from such qualities. In fact, no deviations from anything other than ordinary were expected on most days, including today. However, it would be remiss to say that all shared in the same sentiment. On this given day, one who would not agree was an adolescent who went by the name of Jason Dix, who could not help but be annoyed by his ever-increasing vexatious situation that seemed to have no resolution but time. At this early eight o'clock hour, he sat in a hard, wooden desk in classroom 134 with his arms folded firmly across his lithe chest as his visage projected his true feelings. It was clear that he was growing increasingly irritated by the resonating cadence of a monotonous, predictable, black-and-white machine: a clock. Its clamor seemed louder than his instructor, whose voice was muted as he rambled on about various species of plants over the incessant scribbling on the green chalkboard.

"Now class," he began. The drone of his voice was as soporific as irritating. "I would like you to open your text to page fifty-three and try to follow along. The information may seem a bit long-winded and verbose for your grade level, so please pay close attention. If you have forgotten your text, please raise your hand." He focused on a rather small boy afflicted with progeria who was seated at the front of the class and dressed in a rooster costume.

"Barry, especially you. Please follow along."

"O-okay Mr. B-Bill." The young man spoke with an extreme stammer but worked diligently to express himself. Giggles from the back of the class were silenced by their instructor's stark gaze. Bill could never understand why parents of children with disabilities would dress them for ridicule.

Jason, however, gave their snickers zero consideration, knowing their laughter to be in jest. Unbeknownst to the authoritative school figures, Barry was the leader of a brigade of black marketeers who specialized in prohibited foodstuffs and trinkets. Anyone found to be seriously making fun of the boy would be blacklisted with a mere snap of his fingers. The items in his raggedy knapsack were a complete mystery, however, since he was careful to always keep it near his person.

Finding it particularly hard to focus on school this morning and nearing a hypnagogic state of dreaminess, Jason's gaze was fixated on the annoying clock inconveniently perched at the head of the class. He shook himself awake when he found his head rocking to-and-fro in sync with its cadence, as if he'd been in a trance. The clock's obstreperous banter was proving to be a true menace; the monochrome apparatus fixed to the front wall directly above the chalkboard was severely in need of lubrication. Its second hand's perturbations consisted of a click, clatter, and click as its hands marched clockwise, circling round, round, and round, circumnavigating a white disc of time. A tick followed by a tock would have been better and more aligned with the sounds one expects a clock to make, and for this reason, Jason felt he had the right to be annoyed; the clock's clattering seemed confusing and not at all like a clock. Like time, the clock continued to get the best of him. Jason was well aware that his discontent should not have been directed at the clock, as there was

really no reason to blame it. After all, it was just perform-
ing its assigned duty as the class's timekeeper and was
incapable of self-repair. He could accept that his annoyance was misdirected; he was actually quite cross with
himself for allowing a simple clock to annoy him to such
a degree, but even more so for not having had the fore-
sight to arrive to class earlier and tweak the time forward
a bit, lubricate the clock, or provide some means of rem-
edying the situation. Removing it, replacing it with a
digital timepiece, or even fixing it would have been a
breeze, but now that class had begun, his instructor
would never allow him a moment to retrieve and repair
the wall-mounted apparatus. He was stuck, and class
clicked and clattered on.

And so time laboriously and ever-so-slowly tick-tocked
forward for the young Jason Dix, age fifteen, grade 9, of
average height, weight, and otherwise average physical
attributes for a boy his age. He was thin with a light
complexion, straight, brown hair, brown eyes, and glasses, and he was dressed in khaki shorts and a black-and-
gold fleur-de-lis T-shirt. He sat at his desk near the front
of the class feeling bored, growing progressively dispirit-
ed as his teacher scribbled on the chalkboard and he
awaited the magic hour of nine.

The class was rather sparsely appointed, and the sole
items atop each desktop were a notebook, a pencil, and
Darwin's dissertation, *The Origin of Species*, an overly
verbose yet somehow highly esteemed, mandatory read-

ing assignment from the class's overbearing and self-as-cribed omnipotent instructor, Mr. Bill. While Jason found the book itself quite boring and his instructor even more so, he had a true aptitude for the scientific arts. He had read the abridged notes of Darwin's work and the Wiki-pedia pages for discordant views, including those for or-thogenesis, Lamarckism, and contradictory theories of devolution, along with Rupert Sheldrake's Theories on Morphogenetic Fields.

Instead of listening to his instructor's wearisome voice, he dreamed of two warring factions, as if they were box-ers in a ring of a Pay-Per-View special. *On the right side of the ring, we have our fighter Mr. Evolution, a.k.a. Nat-ural Selection. Weighing in at 180 pounds, he is an ape . . . no, a neanderthal . . . no, a human! Folks, he's a-changin' before our eyes and boy does his brain work like lightning! And on the left, we have the evil Mr. Devolu-tion. This lumbering human . . . no wait, neanderthal . . . no, he's a flipping ape! He's limber for his size, weighing in at 100 pounds with mass-specific muscle performance out of sight! This will be a good one, folks: brains versus brawn.*

He enjoyed imagining the heavyweights on the subject of evolution pounding Mr. Bill, if only to get him into the ring. Jason was more than ready to mount a rebuke of the subject matter if called upon. It was no secret to anyone in the class that Bill, for some reason, did not like Jason to the point of bullying him by frequently calling on him to answer some obscure or hypothetical question in an attempt to catch him unprepared and therefore cause him embarrassment. Prepared for assault, Jason was ready for any debate, as evidenced by the oddsmakers (Barry, the black marketeer) giving him a ten-to-one advantage over Bill. Jason was held in esteem by his classmates, but out of coolness and succumbing to peer pressure, he often feigned lassitude for the subject matter, and after the disputes, he would deny all self-pedagogical endeavors if he had appeared to be knowledgeable on any bit of the subject. Despite Jason's brazenness with Bill, he somehow always excelled in science.

Fed up, Jason tried sitting, then slouching, then sitting upright before slouching again, elbow up, elbow down, elbow sideways, head up, head down, neck flexed then extended. There was just not a comfortable position to be found as he moved his skinny backside back and forth, all the while staring at the godforsaken clock that continued to taunt him in his assigned, highly uncomfortable, brown-gray, wood and metal school desk, row two, seat B, in room 134 of Carrollton School. Yet despite his aggravation, class continued, drawn along by the monotone jabberwocky of their vapid instructor. His monotonous cadence coupled with the irksome discord from the clock quickly sucked the life force out of everyone in the class. Click, clack, tick, tock. No one seemed to be taking notes or paying attention.

Jason fought to keep his eyes from succumbing to the class's contagious slumber, longing for nine, then the school's noon dismissal when he would be set free for fall break.

Finally, Jason had enough. Class was just too boring, and he was not willing to wait for Bill's first strike. The turmoil created by the clock and the monotonous blabbering created a tempest in Jason's head, and so he blurted, "Mr. Bill, the clock sounds ill! Might we remove it so that we can better hear your wonderful lecture? I mean, how long do you think we will have to listen to that confounded clock?"

A single laugh was heard from the back of the class as the other students held their breath in awe, their mouths agape at the manner in which Jason brazenly spoke to Bill. Macey Mae stared at him, her eyes like saucers, and she said, "Shut up, Jason. You'll get detention! Where will that get you? You'll be stuck in this hell."

Jason was undeterred. "I, no *we*, cannot listen to its annoying cacophony a moment longer. It's driving us mad! It's hard to adequately soak up the information you are feeding our young minds. We are sponges at our age, you know, but all we can hear is a clock sickened by some sort of ailment. Might it be typhus, the plague, or some sort of vile virus from the swamps outside New Orleans? Perhaps you've brought an ailment over from the Westbank? Perhaps all it needs is love, sir. Like John Lennon said, all we need is love, Mr. Bill." More laughter erupted from somewhere to his rear. "Perhaps there is a clock shop or clocksmith nearby, or perhaps it can evolve into a digital clock. That sad apparatus may need CPR." The remainder of the class let loose a raucous laughter that drew Bill's ire.

Mr. Bill did not even bother to turn to face Jason but continued nonchalantly scribbling on the board. "Keep your eyes focused on the board and stay sharp. There'll be no further interruptions, Mr. Dix, or we'll have an immediate pop quiz. I bet your classmates will be pleased with you then! I'll have a few questions for you in a moment, or perhaps we should wait to discuss it with your father. Is he not around to teach you some discipline? Truth hurts, doesn't it? You have so much to learn, and the simple banter from a clock, even if it is in need of maintenance, should not be enough to ruin your day. There are others in this world besides yourself." The giggles from the back of the class had all quieted, and Jason thought he heard his teacher mutter, "Insolent fool. Get over it, you spoiled brat. Yellow-bellied pansy."

Jason brushed off the rebuke without response. In his eyes, the only positive thing about his currently assigned seat near the head of the class was his placement one row from his best friend, the only boy in school with perpetually tanned skin, jet-black, curly hair, and thick, black eyebrows: Zach T. Russoni. Zach was nearly asleep, staring blankly ahead with heavy eyelids, chin perched atop his forearm, which rested on his desktop. He was dressed in a makeshift gondolier shirt, red scarf, and roughened jeans. Though Italian-looking today by design, his true pedigree was English-Spanish with a hint of Creole, the latter endowing him with a year-round, golden tan. He looked a few years older than most of his classmates, and for reasons never fully explained, he used his mother's maiden name. Jason assumed it had something to do with a father-son bond that never quite developed as a result of an age-old, sour subject involving his father's business partner, Merl, and Zach's mother. Zach swore he couldn't remember the details of bitter feelings, but he knew it wasn't good.

Zach's long legs were stretched out into the aisle, and the floor surrounding his chair was in shambles: his cowboy boots, muddied from the walk to school, had deposited a good deal of grime onto the pristine, beige laminate floor. Zach's father was Mr. Sims, the school's enigmatic martinet and neat-freak principal who, as of late, had developed a split personality and assumed a self-imposed assistant janitorial role. Jason envisioned a confrontation should he pop into their class; he seemed to have it out for Jason, and Zach's mess would somehow be his own fault.

Zach's head was turned toward Jason as he rested it atop his forearms. He mumbled, "Jason, cut it out. I'm not ready for a quiz. I haven't read a thing. This stuff is so boring." Zach's long, black locks nearly covered the entirety of his face.

"You know your father will kick your butt if he finds out that you're not doing your assignments. Why didn't you call me? I could easily have explained it to you."

"Look, you may find science interesting, but I think it stinks. I'll take arts and crafts any day of the week. Theater. Any class but science. Why can't it be like last year when we were in eighth grade? I may not remember much of that class, but it had to be better than this. The school council never should have let this guy teach this class; he's an idiot. They're all a bunch of idiots. I guess that's what we get for letting a Westbanker teach here." He closed his eyes again and nuzzled back into his forearms. "C'mon, leave Bill alone. I cannot take him today. Just let me sleep."

"Wake up. What are you doing later, after school?"

"Like right after?"

"Yeah, right after."

Zach lifted his sweaty face off his forearms, straightening a little as if he were becoming more lucid. "Well, if you'd let me get some rest, I plan to pack and maybe see my girlfriend if I'm lucky. But you know all that. Why ask such a silly question? We talked about the trip already.

17

I'm not looking forward to our sixteen-hour drive tomorrow. There's always too much construction on I-10. Like I'm excited to sit in traffic all day."

"But aren't you going to see your mother again? That's got to make you excited, right? Maybe she'll move back here; god knows we need her. The school library hasn't been the same since she left. You should be stoked. I would be stoked. Anyway, do you want to come over to my house after school? We don't leave until tomorrow morning anyway. PlayStation, some Madden football? C'mon, my dad won't be home until late tonight. We'll have the run of the place."

Zach's tone increased sharply. "Dude, for the umpteenth time, my dad will kill me if I don't get home to help out. Our house is wired, and you know how he is. He'll know what time I left school, he knows how long it takes me to walk home, and he knows what streets I take. In any case, I have a long list of chores to do and my dad has play rehearsal until nine, some English or Spanish preacher thingy. At least, that's what I've heard."

"At Le Petit Theatre?"

"Yep. You haven't noticed the way he's speaking? He's already made it quite clear that he expects me to get things ready. He's been rambling about practicing his lines and dressing as a monk, I guess?"

"Come on, don't be a pansy. Just come for an hour or two. He'll never know. You have all night. He'll never catch you."

"Bull, Jason. We're supposed to leave at like six o'clock tomorrow morning. He's on edge anyway, hoping to see mom maybe. He'll absolutely kill me if I screw this up. It's not like there's anyone else to help."

"What about your brothers and sisters? Can't they help?"

Zach was accurately referred to as a slouch, but at least he was the most useful slouch of his siblings. He had five brothers and sisters in total, none of whom were capable of thinking of anyone but themselves.

"Not only do I need to pack my stuff, but I've been put in charge of food and beverages too. I've got to wash out the ice chest, go shopping, and Arlis asked me to cut his hair."

"Tell him to go over to Ricouard's. I'll pay for it. Dude, if you don't come over, you'll be the biggest pansy in the world. I'll buy dinner."

A thunderous, mercurial boom from Mr. Bill overpowered the room, startling awake those who had fallen asleep. "Silence! Strike one, both of you! Have you two no courtesy for others? No interruptions!" Bill did not even take the time to turn to face the two interlopers, but he was unwilling to accede to their rude shenanigans. Laughter from the back of the class crescendoed and then diminished. Jason knew that he had only two more strikes to go before Bill would issue a detention, which would be horrible on the last day before the break. Jason would surely be in trouble with his dad, but Zach would be buried beneath the jail. He would keep Zach out of harm's way.

Zach whispered, "Don't worry, I'll deal with him later. This is so boring." He laid his head back down on his desk and closed his eyes, mumbling, "I'll mention him to Dad again."

Bill paused for a moment, allowing a brief respite as the din of the room quieted. His obese, piggish sides jiggled as he drew a Punnett square on the chalkboard, sweat permeating his underarms and back, tracking down to his large buttocks and stretching across the seam of his pants.

Next to the series of squares, Bill had written, "Phylum species: Pisum sativum."

By the sea of vacant faces in the class, attention was far, far away from the chalkboard.

Jason was miserable. He fidgeted a bit longer as his mood grew increasingly sour. *First the clock, now this boring and utterly useless lecture. I can't learn from you, Bill. I can't speak with anyone. Room 134 is nothing short of a pernicious prison. Why can't time just speed along? What a royal waste of time!*

This month's lessons—Charles Darwin and his theory of evolution, and Bill's take on how it relates to Mendelian inheritance—were Boring with a capital B! The class had been, today and every other day, uninteresting. If there were a benchmark to measure the rate at which the students retained information, Bill would fail miserably. The resounding opinion in the class was that life would be better if Darwin took a wrong turn at South America or if Bill had just given them a few days off. Yawn after contagious yawn emitted from the sleepy, uninterested adolescents. Personally, Jason thought the subject would be interesting if presented properly, but it was just too complex for Bill. After all, what did he know about taxonomy, alleles, and the like? He was nothing more than a blabbering oaf.

And so, quiet and miserable, Jason anxiously awaited a misstep on Bill's part so that he could correct or prod him in the midst of his lecture. It would surely drive him mad and may even cause two more strikes and detention. To see him come unhinged would be worth it.

"If one takes into account the works of the esteemed Gregory Mendel, one can see that inheritance of favorable genetic alleles in a population over time selects for certain traits. This is in agreement with Mr. Darwin's theory of evolution. Favorable traits will have a better chance of being passed on to subsequent generations. Mr. Mendel's experiment with over five thousand pea plants helped forge our understanding of inheritance patterns."

*Ding.* Through the open classroom door and nearly out of Jason's line of sight, he could hear and slightly view the sliding doors of the school's single Otis elevator.

"Take for instance this Punnett square. By now, you should all be well familiar with this square, and I will be testing you on its use the day you return from break." Those still awake let out an audible sigh at the thought of a test the day after break.

"Oh, brother. Look who is getting out of here early," Jason jealously said under his breath as he nodded to the doorway. "Some kids have all the luck."

"H-h-he always g-g-gets special treatment," Barry said.

According to Jason, the elevator was reserved mostly for the "lazy faculty unwilling to use the stairs," and rarely served students in need of assistance. The Otis dinged again. Out rolled Jim Fisher, a boy who had recently sliced his foot on a bit of glass while playing softball barefoot in the schoolyard. He wore a large, black boot and pushed himself around on a knee scooter, expecting sympathy and a lightened workload from his teachers. Unfortunately for Jim, his querulous attitude more often aggravated even the most tolerant of students and faculty.

22

Usually, at some early part of the day, that suck-off was able to weasel out of his remaining classes and go home early. No one in school felt sorry for the boy, a rather petulant individual who was supposedly a "chip off the old block." It was supposed to be a secret, but the entire student body was aware that Mr. Sims gave Jim such sweeping freedom in an effort to avoid a potential lawsuit while sufficiently placating the family so that they would continue to contribute benevolently to the local theater. Jim's father was an attorney and councilman serving the Carrollton district and was known to be quite litigious. Mr. Sims thus afforded the lad unlimited access to the school's conveniences, including the elevator. The resonating squeak of the passing cycle, in Jason's eyes, punctuated the unfairness of the entire educational system. When the sound passed, the silence of the empty hallway gave way to the continued hum of Bill's instruction and the banter of the clock.

Looking for any other means with which to keep himself occupied, Jason stared through the classroom's expansive windows. He drifted away into reverie, lost in the brilliant, dreamy blue sky that beckoned him outdoors, the same outdoors he would meet graciously for fall break in mere hours. It was too apropos that the blue sky and crisp, fall air were so rudely interrupted by the school's metal doors slamming closed in the hallway, a departing gift from that jerk, Jim.

The ruckus shook Jason back to reality. The drone of Bill's banter was interrupted by the muted clap of erasers and a large plume of chalk dust created by his friend, Bobby Malone, who had been gifted with eraser cleaning duties. Bobby, likely hiding under the sill, could not be seen, but the plume he created was prodigious and clouded the windows. Jason knew he was probably goofing, just throwing chalk dust into the air while banging the eraser against the class's wall. *He would be lucky enough to have pulled eraser duty today*, Jason thought. Something was just not right with him; the kid was a whiz, lived in the library, and should be in some honors class somewhere. Instead, he was outside screwing off, likely because some teacher gave him the duty to get him and his ADHD out of their hair.

Bobby's cacophony continued uninterrupted until it was finally overpowered by the comforting sounds of a small seaplane's approach, followed by the caw of a mockingbird in a tree outside the window. The bird's shrill call carried on for reasons only birds could understand, but perhaps it was mad at Bobby's dust cloud or maybe it was just making fun of the kids stuck in class. *Tick, tock, click, clack, caw caw.*

The elevator's pealing chime announced its return, yet no one emerged as Jason careened his head to investigate who else could be getting out early. Jason had the eerie feeling of being watched, the hairs on the back of his neck on edge, but no eyes could be seen upon him. No classmates seemed to be staring in his direction, Bill was in his own world as he blathered on about dominant traits, the hallway was clear, and the clapping of the eraser persisted. Jason kept watching for someone to reveal themselves in the hallway, but as the minutes passed and that someone proved to be no one, Jason attributed the elevator's arrival to someone on a floor above knowingly or inadvertently mashing the first-floor button.

First period marched on, minute by slow minute by slow minute, as the noisy second hand of the black-and-white clock coupled with Bill's droning drew his eyes forward again. At long last, the minute hand hit number six, subtracting one more minute from his wait. *Click, clack, tick, tock.* Boring, boring, boring, boring. It was now Friday, eight thirty in the morning. Just 210 minutes stood between Jason and freedom.

Bill had written on the board. "Homework! Species examples, give thirty in total. Quercus? Pinus? Salix? Taxodium?"

For a brief moment, Jason thought he heard someone shouting for Zach from the hallway, but nothing came of it. Perhaps it was some sort of auditory hallucination or hypnagogic, cognitive breakthrough brought on by the persistent chatter and his sheer boredom. What could be seen of the hallway and elevator remained vacant. Zach was asleep. The cloud of chalk dust was huge.

Unable to restrain himself any longer, Jason's hand shot up. "Excuse'm, Mr. Bill? Did you hear that?"

Someone in the back of the class issued a loud, wet fart, and uproarious laughter ensued.

"Excuse'm Mr. Bill. I need to use the men's room. For the record, that fart was not mine, sir."

Mr. Bill continued mumbling, failing to acknowledge the laughter or Jason's contraction.

"Oh my gosh, it smells so bad I can almost taste it!" Someone coughed dramatically.

"Excuse'm, Mr. Bill. I have a serious question. Can I ask you why Mr. Darwin looks like the guy who does the science report on channel six, Mr. Wedgwood? We have a picture of him in our book." Jason held up the inside cover of his book and pointed to Charles Darwin. A few classmates in the back let out cackles of laughter.

"We'll have no more blabbering nonsense," Mr. Bill said, not even giving Jason the courtesy to look at him, his lack of acknowledgment meant to abase the rude outburst.

"But he does, Mr. Bill. Mr. Bill, can I use the restroom? Nature is, in fact, calling. And for the record, I was not the farter."

"You absolutely may not. Restroom breaks shall be saved for just that: breaks. Now be quiet and pay attention like the rest of the class."

"But the rest of the class is asleep, sir. Take a look around. They're bored stiff."

"Strike two!"

"Look, I really need to use the restroom. It'll only take a minute or two. Please, Mr. Bill, I'm about to pee myself. Give me a strike three if you wish, but I need to use the men's room. I promise to hurry right back. Please. Come on, please. I'm not joking this time. It's about to get messy."

Zach mumbled incoherently without taking his head off his forearms. "Let him go, sir. We don't need the mess or the stink."

"Be hasty and only you. No monkey business. I'll be timing you. And by the way, I will proceed with the lesson in your absence. Instruction will not be curtailed on account of your bladder. You will have to rely upon your classmates for any information you miss." Bill turned back toward the chalkboard and continued writing. "Go."

Bill was not about to deviate from his lesson plan; in fact, he never deviated from his lesson plan. His lumbering waist jiggled in motion with his arm, movement rippling through the abdominal and axillary fat that pressed tightly against the obnoxiously colored, ill-fitting, polyester pant and shirt ensemble meant to represent the livery of a fast foodie. He continued scribbling, outlining the genus and species information for a series of amphibians as noted in Darwin's travels on the HMS *Beagle*. Jason slid out of his desk and rapidly dashed out of the class before he had a chance to change his mind.

He turned left in the hallway, and then took another immediate left past a large sign that read, "DIX FOR FRESHMAN PRESIDENT," which was affixed to the wall above a half-full library cart that included his recently returned copy of a large book entitled, *Useless Facts and Tidbits You'll Never Need to Know (New Orleans Edition), Volume I.* Near the ceiling, wires poked out of the wall, part of the first installment and currently nonfunctional, Orwellian video monitoring system for the school's hallways: GECO—Guarding Education COvertly. There were rumored to be about thirty-four more cameras waiting to be installed, all designed specifically to monitor each student's whereabouts throughout the day. Farther down the hall, the door to the interminable library construction project was covered in clear construction-grade plastic, and work-related refuse littered the hallway, including numerous boxes for the new computer section. The entrance to the library was impressive, even while under construction; one of the deep-pocketed donors had paid for the facade to look centuries old with

28

thick stones and ornate carvings. If time spent were an indicator of quality, the interior would be even nicer than the entrance. To his right, MEN was stenciled on one of the tan bricks in the hallway above a perpetually non-functioning water fountain.

Jason ducked into the men's room and headed for one of the stalls. The room was like so many others, the usual white tile, white porcelain sinks, and gray stalls.

"Well that's unusual."

Jason stopped short as he noticed the graffiti on a mirror above one of the sinks. Using bright red lipstick, someone had written in cursive hand, "Stay home. It's a trap." The message was underlined twice for emphasis, and the author had left their signature in the form of a kiss in lipstick. Jason paused to think about the message. The penmanship seemed oddly familiar, but he dismissed his suppositions knowing them to be more than improbable. *It must have been a girl sneaking into the men's room. Why would a boy bring lipstick from home? Maybe it was Bobby; he was out of class, after all. I wouldn't put it past that brainy kid. He has an odd sense of humor, was out of class, and has loads of time now that the library is closed. But again, why? And to whom is the message directed? If it were Bobby, he had no way of knowing I'd have gone into the restroom. If it was meant to be funny, they had failed miserably. It doesn't matter anyway; we'll*

*all be on break soon, so who cares. Noon can't come
soon enough.*

Jason looked in the mirror, speaking aloud as he tossed
his hair. "Whoever you are, I agree with you. School is
but a trap—a trap designed to drive me mad with that
noisy clock."

Jason surveyed the stalls, glancing under each before deciding on which to use. He discovered that the farthest
stall door was closed and locked from the inside, but Jason was not about to interrupt the occupant. Such an intrusion would be way too weird and the likely impetus
for a perverted rumor. Perhaps the perpetrator of the graffiti was hiding inside. The more he thought about it, the
more certain he became that it couldn't be Bobby. There
was no way that egghead would risk adversely affecting
his GPA with a suspension. Although he was curious, it
would seem too strange to begin a conversation with
whomever sat in the closed stall, so he kept his mouth
shut and entered another to take care of business.

*Oh well. This day will end soon enough. You just need to
stay quiet and keep yourself out of detention.* His brief
interlude was interrupted by the familiar sound of jangling keys approaching, a sound unique to Mr. Sims.

Jason nudged the bathroom stall door closed with his
rear, not wanting to be confronted when peeing or having

to explain his classroom absence. He hoped that Mr. Sims's presence would be fleeting.

"Zachary Trevor Russoni, is that you?" Mr. Sims's English accent could be heard outside in the hallway.

Jason chose not to answer, hoping that Mr. Sims would just keep walking. As he finished relieving himself, the jangle of keys became louder and could be heard along with the whistling and singing lamentations of Para Que Quiero un Corazón:

"Porque si dicen que el amor es lo mejor que existe, a mí siempre me ha hecho sufrir, mi alma se resiste. Y ser herido otra vez no creo que lo aguante a veces pienso que es mejor no tener corazón."

Jason finished and zipped his pants.

With the cessation of Mr. Sims's singing, the sound of running water started and then stopped. After the motor of the paper towel dispenser activated and a towel was torn off, Jason heard a knock on his stall door. "Mr. Dix? Mr. Dix, is that you?"

"Well I'll be, it's Principal Sims." Jason opened the stall door to face the dark-complected and muscular principal with horrid breath, crooked, yellow teeth, and a poorly glued false mustache. Today, as on all other days, he was clad in his usual khaki uniform, but unlike the days that had come before, his skin was painted bright green in celebration of the Halloween festivities.

"Umm, sir? This is a bit weird, wouldn't you say? Your singing, I mean; it's rather unique today. And umm, you look like a lizard. How did you know I was in here, sir?" The electric toilet flushed itself. Jason checked his zipper and shuffled past Mr. Sims to wash his hands at the sink.

Sims always seemed to have it out for Jason. Since he wasn't sure which of the principal's capricious personalities would surface, he tried to remain polite. Mr. Sims followed Jason with his eyes, looking askance at the youth. A full head taller than Jason, Mr. Sims stood to the side, allowing a moment of awkward silence to pass.

"Sorry I'm not in class, Mr. Sims. Nature was calling." The principal didn't move or speak but continued staring suspiciously at Jason. "I'm . . . is there something I can help you with, sir? You realize that we're in the men's room, right? Zach tells me that you're practicing for another play. That must be exciting." Jason looked at Mr. Sims in the mirror as he finished washing his hands.

"Weird would be the errant misdeeds that perpetrated this crime, Mr. Dix." Mr. Sims tapped on the graffitied mirror and stared at Jason as if waiting for an admission of guilt.

"Was it you, Mr. Dix? You are an impetuous young man by your very nature. I think this insolent act may have ill

32

effects on your campaign for office, not to mention the odds of you spending any time with my son." He wiped a bit of the lipstick off the mirror, smelled it, then applied it to his lips as if to taste it. His thoughts momentarily seemed pensively elsewhere as he looked away; an amoristic reverie blanketed his eyes. He looked odd, unlike himself, his eyebrow raised and mustache tilted as he stared blankly.

"I'm not quite sure what I've done to rub you the wrong way, sir, but whatever it was, I sincerely apologize. I can honestly say that the graffiti was here when I entered, scout's honor," Jason said as he raised two fingers. "I had nothing to do with its presence on the mirror. You're welcome to turn my pockets inside and out; you'll see that there is no lipstick to be found on my person."

Snapping out of his trance, Mr. Sims said, "Let's see your pockets then. I'll call your bluff. Turn them out. Perhaps the item is hidden; after all, I expect that you're smart enough to toss it out the window or to bury it deep in the refuse bin. Did you forget that this is costume day, Mr. Dix? Trevor may not have the best costume, but at least he participates. Why are you out of class, anyway? You should be in Bill's science lecture, I believe. Truancy from an important lesson and with no costume? Shorts and a T-shirt—what are you, dressing up as a teenager? You have such a wonderful imagination! Or are you too good for costume day? Are you lacking in school spirit? Not a great quality for a boy who is running for president. You know, your instructors did an awful lot of planning for costume day."

Jason turned out his pockets, proving them to be empty with the exception of his cell phone. "My father and I truly forgot about the costume, Mr. Sims. I meant no offense. Didn't you hear that there is a storm approaching? We have quite a lot of things on our plate."

"I would think you are old enough to be responsible."

"But wasn't the costume listed as optional? And yes, I'm in science with Mr. Bill. My classmates and I were all nearly asleep; Bill is so boring. Believe me, I'm not missing anything. Ask Zach; he'll concur. In any case, I asked to go to the restroom, and Mr. Bill allowed me to leave if I promised to make it quick. This is a restroom, and I urinated. That's it. No graffiti for me! The message on the mirror was here when I arrived, sir." Jason was growing irate at being falsely accused. He was not willing to rat out the occupant of the last stall, and Mr. Sims did not seem to notice the closed stall door.

"Back pockets, please. Did anyone skip class with you? Don't be a hero, Dix."

Jason turned around to show his empty rear pockets, "No, sir. It was only me."

"Did your accomplice do this? Perhaps an inquest is in order. Might I interest you in detention?"

"No."

"Aha! So you *did* perpetrate this crime. Who else is out and about?"

"Sir, that is a trick question and I take offense at your insinuations. I had nothing to do with the writing on the mirror. But if you're looking for the perpetrator, I did see Jim Fisher in the hallway earlier. Perhaps you should ask him. He was dressed up as a cripple today, like he is on most other days, but I guess he just has costume day every day of the week. He seems to be out of school awfully early." Jason's remonstrance was forceful. After all, why was he being singled out? *Is it a crime to use the men's room?* He conveniently neglected to mention that Bobby Malone was also out of class and likely wandering the halls.

"Jason, I've got my eye on you. This had best not happen again. Now get back to class." Mr. Sims wet a paper towel and cleaned the remainder of the lipstick from the mirror.

"But I didn't do this, so how can I prevent it from happening?"

"Back to class." The two exited the bathroom, and as Jason turned to leave, Mr. Sims said, "Mr. Dix, something seems awry today. I haven't quite put my finger on what you boys are up to, but if you're planning a prank before the holiday, I advise that you cease and desist. Zach has quite a bit of work scheduled tonight."

Mr. Sims marched Jason back to class, not saying a word thereafter. *That's odd*, thought Jason. The thick copy of *Useless Facts and Tidbits You'll Never Need to Know (New Orleans Edition), Volume I* had been on the cart just moments ago, but now it was missing. *Someone else must be out and about.*

Mr. Sims stood outside the classroom and addressed Mr. Bill from the doorway as Jason took his seat. The lumbering Bill didn't miss a stride, his adipose jiggling in sync with his frantic scribbling on the board. In his typical fashion, he didn't bother to look at Jason or the principal, but kept his eyes glued to the chalkboard.

"Bill, I've found one of your wayward students in the men's room under suspicious circumstances. Perhaps you need to keep a better handle on your class. And if any of you ladies in class are missing a tube of lipstick, please see me after school. Bill, remember: I'll be holding detention after school if you have any takers."

"Yes, sir. I think Jason has a bit of catching up to do. And Mr. Dix, if I can have your attention, I would think the subject to be of profound interest to you. I hope you had a nice vacation. I've made sure to mention a number of items that cannot be found in *The Origin of Species* during your absence, and they are sure to appear on the next test. Perhaps our studies on taxonomy, genetics, and inheritance patterns are too advanced for you."

Jason was infuriated but remained silent.

Bill continued on, seemingly immune to any happenings other than his chalk scribbling on the chalkboard. Without any attention given to him, Mr. Sims rather obnoxiously cleared his throat. "Zachary Trevor, clean the area around your desk before departure. Is that clear, mister? If you don't comply, I'll be seeing you in detention today just like anyone else! You'll receive no special favors from your father. I'm not here to clean up after each and every one of you."

A less-than-eager peep was heard from Zach as he opened his eyes and peeled his face off his forearms. "Yes, sir."

"I'll be back to check on this later. By the way, Bill, have you seen Ms. Somerall?" The question was clearly rhetorical, as Mr. Sims did not wait for a reply before heading in the direction of her classroom. A few of the girls in the back of the class giggled at his question as if they were in on some piece of juicy gossip.

Bill continued scribbling, completely oblivious to anything in his periphery. The chalkboard was getting crowded, but he always seemed to find enough space to keep writing. He scrawled, "The STRUGGLE FOR EXISTENCE. Modern evolutionary synthesis."

"Class, open your book to Chapter Three."

The blank and helpless expressions on the faces of his classmates told Jason that nothing interesting had taken place in his absence.

Zach succumbed to sleep again as his head bobbed up and down like a chicken or the crazy lizard Jason had seen on a *National Geographic* show. Finally, his head flopped atop his forearms, his torso sprawled across his desktop. Jason imagined Zach's countenance to be like some sort of crazy, Italian, crossbred mammalian-lizard (Italio reptilia) with his tongue half out and his eyes jumping around under his lids. He snored and snorted as drool ran out of the corner of his mouth and onto his desk and book. Hilarious. No one other than Jason seemed to notice or care, including the teacher. Who would notice? At this point, nearly half the class was asleep, most of whom also had drool running down their cheeks, and the other half were doodling and passing notes every time Mr. Bill turned his back. Clearly, Bill had not taken the Captivating Your Students 101 class. Perhaps he could naturally select himself on to the next class.

"And when Darwin wrote . . ." The blabbering continued and Jason's mind wandered.

He tongued his lower lip to check if his fever blister had fully healed — nope. Plenty old enough for acne, he thought that perhaps a pimple was coming to a head on his hairless right cheek. Although his voice had already begun changing, he was still waiting on his beard. *Maybe if I shave the peach fuzz on my face, the hair might just grow in faster and darker? I heard somewhere that eating black olives can put hair on your chest. What natural advantage could that bring? Would my eyebrows grow back if I shaved them? Perhaps there is some natural advantage to having no hair. Who was Darwin, anyway? No sane person would set out on a voyage into the unknown for such distances, risking life and limb. For what, to write a book? I guess it's no different from our quest to the moon or Mars.* He did not have to perseverate long; his mind was made up. If blasting off to the moon would get him out of this boring class, he would do it. *Where could I get an application to space camp? Anything is better than sitting in this boring class.* Since it was the last day before break, he could have set some mice loose or put a fart cushion on Bill's chair. Maybe, if he were lucky, someone would pull the fire alarm or order a delivery pizza to class.

The elevator chimed, but again, no one appeared to get off or on. Perhaps the elevator, equally as bored, was going up and down of its own volition. Jason thought that if he were an elevator, he wouldn't just remain stationary. Wouldn't it be fun to go up and down all day? Maybe that would get old too. Poor elevator. Misunderstood.

His thoughts meandered aimlessly, and he dreamed that he and his classmates were dressed in black-and-white striped uniforms, prisoners shackled and chained to their desks as punishment, forced to endure the dull, monotonic drone of their warden: the drippy, morbidly obese, vapid, polyester-clad science instructor who stunk to high heaven. He then began to imagine their jailer as Mr. Bill the Aneuploidic Potato Head, walking around and waving his stubby arms, having evolved by natural selection from his grandfather, a simple potato called Señor Spud. If he could only stick some toothpicks in him and suspend him over a jar of water, he may grow roots just like a potato.

And *poof*, the pounding of the erasers ceased. The plume vanished as the hypnotic clock's hands finally reached their target hour: nine o'clock. The bell rang simultaneously with the clock's final tock, and what was once a sleeping class now moved like lightning to clear the room, minus Zach who remained asleep and snoring. Mr. Bill never broke his stride, continuing his monotonic yammering, unmindful of the bell's dismissal.

Jason led the mass exodus, flicking his light brown hair out of the way of his black-rimmed glasses, which he pushed up the bridge of his nose. As he passed Zach's desk, he flicked his friend's ear to startle him awake before he zipped out the doorway. "Tonight, my place. Be there! See ya later, suckas!"

Hustling out into the noisy hall, he nearly collided with Bobby, who was coated in white chalk. *No detention today and so long to first period! The remainder of the day will be a breeze.*

Jason's second class was on the floor above, so he hustled up the staircase through the throngs of his schoolmates, took a right, and entered room 234: Nutrition and Health class. Passing the threshold, the sweet smell of lavender permeated the air, emanating from a lit oil lamp. The scent put him at ease, a marked contrast from rancid Bill. The pealing ding of the elevator preceded the school bell's ring as second period's hour allotment began.

Jason was excited for this class, as were the other male students, singularly due to their instructor: a smoking hot, lithe, thirty-ish, blonde teacher, Ms. Jessica Somerall, who matriculated into their teacher pool this year. She was strikingly beautiful, and routinely dressed in yoga pants and some sort of hip, tightly fitting Parisian blouse ensemble. Today's Halloween attire proved no different, as her shapely frame was squeezed into a red spandex catsuit and her blonde hair was pulled back into a neat ponytail. Even the toes on the ends of her perfectly shaped feet were painted a bright red to match the bright red fingernails on her perfectly shaped hands. She may have been dressed like the devil, but to Jason, she was an angel straight from heaven.

Today, as always, she smelled like expensive herbs, unguents, lotions, or perhaps the magic potions used by many women to make themselves more appealing and attractive. To say that her beauty was captivating was an enormous understatement. Her Texas drawl was dreamy and her toned physique and perky breasts insinuated that she was a paragon of health. A serpent tattoo wound its way up her delicate left arm, wrapping around her in a way that many of the boys envied. She was exciting, well educated, articulate, and seductive. To put it in biology terms, she was uniformly agreed to be a classic specimen of the species *Womana perfecta lotta*. She possessed a collection of qualities Jason thought not to be found in most of the other women of the city (much less the teachers in any school), and so he expected her time to be limited. Every moment with her was precious. Some rich guy was bound to sweep her off her feet and whisk her away forever.

In Jason's eye, she was too perfect to be stuck teaching a bunch of pimple-faced teenagers; surely she must have some dark, unforeseen qualities, or perhaps she was hiding from past indiscretions. The gossip brigade (i.e., most of the girls in school) had started a number of rumors, including that she was teaching while earning her master's degree in psychology, independently wealthy through malevolent business endeavors, in the habit of dating

42

'bad guys,' using an alias (the embroidered initials PA on one of her satchels was highly suspicious), or that she had moved to New Orleans to right some family wrongs. Jason knew these rumors to be bunk, as she was living in the guest house of his father's business partner and life-long friend Merl, who had nothing but glowing things to say about her. Her relationship with Merl was likely the reason she paid more attention to Jason.

Merl had once let it slip that Ms. Somerall was actually quite educated, having spent time at a prestigious univer-sity in England. Jason made the mistake of mentioning this factoid to a classmate, only to have the gossip brigade run with it and start a rumor that she was dating Mr. Sims, the only congruent piece of information being their mutual love of England. After all, both Mr. Sims and Ms. Somerall enjoyed tea together in his office now and then! It was only natural for the hormone-crazed stu-dent body to embellish on her relationships. These ru-mors made Zach a bit angry.

Regardless of why she was at Carrollton School, Jason enjoyed her class and her presence. The girls watched her with dreamy eyes, longing to look like her, and the boys all had an obsessional limerence. For the concupiscent, pubescent males in the class, the favorite running joke was about who she was in love with amongst their lot. They all fought to gain her attention, asking question af-ter question, waving their hands high in the air or even shouting their answer when she called on someone else, their actions nearing hooliganism. Her legendary beauty even drew the attention of the parents; Jason's father had recently painted the portrait of a woman purported to be Jason's relation and hung it on their dining room wall, but the woman's facial features were strikingly similar to Ms. Somerall.

In any case, Jason took the first open seat. Ms. Somerall didn't have seating assignments as stringent as block-headed Bill. The clock at the head of the class was mercifully noiseless.

"Psst!" Jason leaned over to his friend Jimmy and whispered, "Who let him in?" He motioned to a muscle-bound, long-haired, mustached meathead who looked as though he stepped right out of the 1970s. To make matters stranger, he was dressed identically to Bill, and consequently, just like the workers at a local fast-food joint. He had tattoos running up the inside of both arms. "What's the 411?"

"I dunno. Dude's from Algiers. Somebody said he's Bill's friend. All I know is that he was here when I walked in. What a meathead, right? What is he, a Lucky Dog sales-man? Do you think that he's wearing a costume or is that his natural way of dressing? Maybe Macey's right; maybe Somerall likes bad guys."

Jason struggled to contain his laughter. "He must shop with Bill because he and Bill look identical today. I cannot even describe how horrible first period was; what a waste of time. And what's up with Zach's dad? He's obsessed with Somerall. You should've seen him in first period. He stood at the door of Bill's class for the longest time before asking about Somerall and just wandering off. Anyway, where are you going on break, Jimmy?"

"Dunno." Jimmy shrugged. "No plans. I'll likely just be stuck at home. Where do you think she's headed on break? Wherever it is, I want to go too!"

"I don't know, but I wish it were with me. I'd cancel with my dad in a heartbeat. She could be my chaperone, anytime, anywhere."

"Me too! Do you think we could pop by your dad's partner's house sometime? Doesn't he have a pool? Do you think she'd be there? Can you imagine her in a swimsuit?" Jimmy exaggeratedly bulged out his eyes and stuck out his tongue like a cartoon wolf.

"He does have a pool, but I'll have to come up with a good excuse. It'd be worth it, though. By the way, that guy looks like he could kick all of our asses with both hands tied behind his back. He's a beast."

"Yeah, I know. He's been just sitting there, staring ahead like a zombie since I sat down."

"Do you think that Macey was right?"

Ms. Somerall interrupted the boys, her smooth voice dripping with flirtation. At least, Jason imagined that it was. "Boys, let's quiet down now as I turn on the telly."

Jason and Jimmy blushed and quieted instantly at her request. Glancing to the rear of the class, the muscle-bound jerk was staring directly at Jason and cracking his knuckles, leering as if he had ESP or superhuman hearing. Both young men swiftly turned back toward the front of the class, straightened in their chairs, and quieted, each swallowing the lump that had developed in their throats.

The man's presence would not have been such an issue, but all school volunteers went through a rigorous screening process and were vetted by numerous teachers and administrators before setting foot on school property. Given all the craziness in schools in recent years, Mr. Sims and the PTA were quite strict on who was allowed on campus. They even went so far as to demand that the GECO video system be installed to monitor the grounds and hallways. Surely Mr. Sims knew this beefy stranger was in the school, though Jason had a hunch that the man had not been vetted and was not legally supposed to be in a classroom full of minors. Regardless, no one dared to say a word, given his size, though they all whispered amongst themselves.

Jason was making a mental note to ask the proper authorities about him when Ms. Somerall spoke. She looked directly at Jason, as if reading his mind. "Everyone, may I

46

please have your attention? Larry, who is a good friend of mine, will be observing our class today. I expect that no one will tattle on him." She winked at Larry and then at Jason. She turned the lights off overhead and began the movie.

"Jeezum, I hope he's not taking her place when she leaves. If he's her protégé, we're in deep trouble."

"You said it. We'd all be in trouble. But I think he knows more about steroids than nutrition anyway."

Jason hoped that the meathead was only an acquaintance. If those two were an item, Jason suspected that he would guard her like an overprotective animal. He would think less of Ms. Somerall for allowing such behavior. And Lucky Dogs? Ugh! Just the thought of one made him want to puke. *I mean, how many cockroach hairs are allowed in a hot dog these days?*

Ms. Somerall brushed past Jason as she moved to close the blinds, her sweet smell teasing his nose. She took a seat at her desk and opened a large red book as a movie titled *Farm to Fridge* commenced. It was no secret that Ms. Somerall was a card-carrying vegan and routinely sought to recruit new disciples to her vegan faith; this movie was surely more propaganda, and her use of the film was a transparent ploy to convert the student body to veganism. Although Jason had a massive crush on her and her figure was just as good if not better than any of the women selling exercise equipment on television (score one for veganism) and he would do anything to impress her, he vowed to keep his position on meat unchanged. He vowed to continue eating hamburgers, oysters, shrimp, steak, chicken, and any other manly proteins. The film was nothing but another ploy to brainwash youth, and so his smoking hot, vegan teacher would just have to find another young mind to brainwash. He would not become her vegan disciple.

Before long, there was a knock on the door as Mr. Sims poked his lizard head into the class, his amorous eyes lightening when Ms. Somerall acknowledged him. He conspicuously tried to whisper but had to raise his voice to be heard over the movie, drawing more attention. "So there you are. I've been looking for you all morning. Tea?" He noticed the meathead at the back of the room ominously cracking his knuckles, and then he saw that all eyes in the room were on him. He tugged awkwardly on the collar of his shirt and said, "Oh, I see that you have company and your class has begun. As you were." He slunk away, and his rapid footsteps could be heard dissipating down the hallway as the volume on the television intensified.

"Well, that was a bit odd."

"You know what the gossip brigade has been saying about those two. Nobody better mention this to Zach."

Time seemed to fly by, and before long, the clock struck ten. Ms. Somerall paused the television and turned on the lights, and the students departed to their next classes.

"Goodbye, Ms. Somerall. I hope you have a good break."

"You too! Au revoir, my cute little students. A week will seem like eternity."

Jason bounded through the door, into the hallway melee, and toward his next class: ancient history with a twist. The class, taught by a young, early twenties hipster, Steve Winwood (no relation to the musician), was at least enjoyable. He was as nuts as he was flamboyant, and no less so today; he was dressed as a full-fledged knight, complete with broadsword and heavy chain mail. He somehow even smelled like cooked meats and mead. Mr. Winwood had only been teaching at the school for three weeks, but he settled in straight away as if he'd been there for years, filling his room with odd artifacts and a terrarium brimming with arachnids and reptilian species. The former history teacher, Mr. Jennings, departed under odd circumstances. The gossip brigade told the tale of a love gone bad, but no one knew for sure.

This new guy was crazy in his own way with a forgetive imagination, convinced that a more advanced society from another planet preceded our own. He shared fact after historical fact to support his convictions, cleverly spun until they no longer resembled the truth. His long words, abusages, and solecisms befuddled even the most attentive student. In the past three weeks, Jason had identified Winwood's four main quirks: he was a bit of a control freak; he believed that much of history should be "tweaked" to better fit our needs, and the world would be a better place if he were in charge; he liked Bill, which defied all reason and logic; and he had the uncanny ability to just vanish at the end of the day, into the elevator and *poof*!

Clearly, the principal had not thoroughly vetted Carrollton's newest hire and had no idea what baloney and neologisms he was feeding the class. Despite his lunacy, Jason liked Mr. Winwood because his convivial attitude made the subject matter pop-off-the-page interesting, using "my dudes" with an faux Italian or French accent and role playing his lessons instead of offering a dry lecture. He was hip, loved to teach, and most importantly, he was just fun to listen to. Jason was able to absorb the information with little effort. Mr. Winwood clearly knew a lot about a lot of things and loved the subject matter. In only three short weeks, his lesson plans spanned history, including seminars on an antediluvian society called Atlantis; Crete and the Minoans; Egypt; Mesopotamia and Mesoamerican cultures, including the Mayan peoples, their God of Time, and the colonies of this great early civilization; Constantinople and the architecture of the Basilica Cistern, winding a twisted path to the Romans and Helike and the destruction of the famed Library of

Alexandria by Julius Caesar; the Doges and ancient city of Venice; the knights and feudalistic societies of Europe, including an erudite, Jesuit priest who had a sunflower-powered clock (many of the kids tried to correct him, asking if it was solar-powered); a magical land in a Mayan text akin to Valhalla, Heaven, or Jannah, with its entry tangibly located somewhere in the Yucatan; and most recently, a documented storm in the middle of the South Pacific. He always spoke about how all of history relates to the parallel universes that exist to our parallel "ids," controlled by supernatural spirits. The man even went so far as scheduling a field trip to Mayan ruins to prove his point, sending home permission slips. As if any sane parent would allow their child to fly from New Orleans to Mexico City to Villahermosa, not to mention the two- to three-hour drive to Palenque! He was odd, no doubt about that, but the way he made it all relate and jive meant that class was fun. Maybe he just needed some medications? Jason doubted his tenure would be long, and based upon the rumblings of his father and the other PTA members, he suspected that Winwood wouldn't be around after the fall break. Class went off without a hitch.

As a fuzzy, politically correct way to help the students bond before their break, afternoon classes were canceled and a mandatory pre-Halloween social event was scheduled to take place in the school's auditorium. The festivities were replete with all the ice cream, hot dogs, pretzels, and other foods high in carbohydrates and trans fats that one could eat. None of the students wanted to attend mostly because Mr. Sims and Bill would be there.

Most of the student body shared Jason's opinion of Mr. Sims: that he was a mean-spirited, stern fellow who was capricious and unstable. Zach was cool and popular, so everyone assumed that he must take after his mother. Mr. Sims's lisp and crooked, yellow teeth grossed people out, particularly given his habit of spitting as he spoke. The joke amongst the students was that his cockney slobbering (i.e., woolly dental disease) would shoot from his maw and end up all over the food, a thought that was outright disgusting. In fact, the petite and adorable Macey Mae swore he coughed up a bit of spittle onto her mac and cheese while scolding her for her improper use of a fork in the cafeteria.

He also had the odd habit of wearing an all-khaki uniform on most days of the year, exactly like the school's real janitor, Marvin. Subsequent to his wife's departure, he compulsively whistled and sang sad Tejano music throughout the day to lament her loss. As for the student body's aversion to Bill, well, Bill was Bill. No further explanation is needed as to why Bill was not welcomed by the students at the social. When Jason had last laid eyes upon him, he had eaten at least five hot dogs with ketchup and chili that had dripped down onto his expanding blubber gut.

The uselessness of the supposed "bonding session" was best illustrated by Jason's sole interaction with Mr. Sims, who said, "Mr. Dix, I haven't forgotten about your graffiti. Next time, you *will* be caught. Despite your relationship with my son, I will not offer you any special treatment."

"Understood, Mr. Sims. But again, I had nothing to do with the graffiti and I would appreciate not being treated as the perpetrator of a crime of which I have not committed."

"Well, Mr. Dix, I'll have my eye on you."

The day wore on, but finally, the big hallelujah arrived. As the school bell rang at noon, bedlam erupted. The rabble in the schoolyard quickly scattered after the usual handshakes, back pats, and hugs were shared. The break was here, at long last! Jason was exiting the schoolyard and waving to his friends as the last of the school buses pulled out of the parking lot when he spotted Ms. Somerall. She was shaking hands with Mr. Winwood, who had changed out of his knight costume and had a large text tucked in the Burberry satchel slung over his shoulder. The letters CB were stitched on the satchel's side.

"Goodbye, Steve. Have a great break. I'm sure we'll meet again soon," she said with a wink.

"Remember our little competition over the break. May the best person win. I've got my eye on you, Jessica. I just hope that neither of us gets hurt." He returned her wink.

What are those two up to? Jason had to pass her in order to exit the schoolyard.

The last of their exchange was lost to the motorcycle's exhaust. *Blub, blub, blub, blub.* She climbed onto the back of the Harley Davidson and shrugged her shoulders, answering the meathead, who presumably asked her what that was all about. As Jason turned to follow Mr. Winwood, he seemed to have vanished.

Ms. Somerall caught sight of Jason. "Have a great break, Jason!"

"And you as well, Ms. Somerall. Be careful on the back of that bike. There are quite a lot of potholes, and some are pretty deep. You are in New Orleans, after all!"

"Don't you worry." She winked. "Is that a chain you're wearing? It's cute." Her attention caused Jason to blush, inviting a growl from her muscly friend. She rolled her eyes and barked at him. "We're going, OK? I just wanted to say bye to a student. Chill out."

"Oh, it's just my house key. It's pretty heavy, though."

"I see that. Well anyway, have a great break. Don't lose that key; your dad mentioned it to Merl, so it must be important! I'll see you soon enough." Wearing a half face shield painted to resemble a demon and her red spandex bodysuit, she patted the meathead on his shoulder and they shot out of the schoolyard, her hair flowing in the wind.

*Hmm, why did she mention the key?* he thought. *Thanks, Dad! What could she possibly see in that Westbank bozo of a guy? And what did she mean by "soon enough?"*

Jason exited the schoolyard and stepped into a tranquil, Carrollton fall day, relieved to finally be on break.

# CHAPTER 2

## THE PLOT BEGINS

*Friday, October 27, 2017*

Jason took his usual route home, no different from any
other day, and headed toward Audubon Park. The brilliantly blue sky and crisp weather were so perfect that Jason had a prescient feeling of excitement, ready and anxious to start his fall break adventure. He was really looking forward to the father-son time they had planned; the
time together would be awesome. Given his mood, he
had a bit of pep in his step, eager to get packed and ready
for departure.

Loads of activities were planned. The upcoming week
would be a true man's week; he and his father were destined for an adventurous vacation in the Texas Hill Country and west Texas. The two had decided on the itinerary
together months ago after scouring numerous magazines
and pamphlets. The trip promised some great bonding
and new experiences. Jason had been working his tail off
in school to make his dad proud of his academic and

sporting achievements, his small way of showing his appreciation. By Jason's estimate, he had truly earned this trip after having put forth a tremendous amount of effort in school: he was receiving above-average grades, leading the pack in the election for class president, and placed second in the district swim meet. By the same token, his father had been up to his ears in work, spending most of his time away from home. Both needed the time off, but more than anything, they needed the time together. As luck would have it, Zach and the rest of his family were also traveling to Texas and their paths would likely cross.

His usual way home took him left onto Carrollton Avenue and then left onto St. Charles Avenue. He nodded to numerous meter maids, their hair brightly colored and highlighted in a manner more becoming of a doughnut topping. They were ever-so-happily writing parking citations in front of mansion after mansion decked in Halloween paraphernalia, with spooks, hobgoblins, witches, and jack-o'-lanterns. He cut through Audubon Park, under beautiful arbors of majestic, moss-laden oaks, through manicured gardens, past a quartet practicing jazz in one of the peristyles, past riders on horseback decorated with advertisements for Cascade Stables, past a homeless man who always seemed to be lying on the same bench, and past the plaque for the Buffalo Soldiers. He stopped for a moment to reflect on their strife and admire the majestic Bedford limestone facade of Tulane University and the spires and rooftops of Loyola University rising above the oaks.

Jason loved the park and its activities. He and his father occasionally rented horses for the afternoon or played tennis on the back courts near the Children's Hospital. The courageousness of past New Orleans residents, particularly the Buffalo Soldiers, played a part in shaping the history of the Wild West. With such majesty surrounding him, he hoped he would amount to something of historical significance at some point in his life. He felt that there was no room left for adventure in the modern world, only politics, and politics seemed less than virtuous. He could imagine those locals called to duty in 1866, galloping on horseback through what is now a park but was likely a swampy, overgrown field surrounded by small oak trees at the time.

His reverie was sharply interrupted as he inadvertently stepped backward onto the bike path, narrowly dodging a woman on rollerblades wearing a Green Wave T-shirt with earphones. The park was full of joggers and cyclists exercising during their lunch hour or off early for the weekend, dogs bounding to-and-fro, and the playful magnificence of waterfowl on the lagoon, all enjoying the gorgeous afternoon.

Eager to get ready for his trip, Jason continued through the park, past a couple sharing a picnic basket on the lawn, and past Temple Sinai before exiting the park and turning right onto Calhoun Street. He meandered along the ill-maintained sidewalk, through the patchwork of swaying shadows of tall oak and maple trees. A cool, crisp breeze swept down the street as if magically conjured, sending a chill down his spine as hundreds and hundreds of helicopter maple seeds twirled aloft, a dazzling display of nature in motion. It was the kind of day that made him feel alive, and if the day's weather were foretelling, it would be a perfect week. Life was good. No, life was great! Equally as important, the good weather conditions meant that their flight to San Antonio would be smooth.

He was in sight of his front door when his cell phone rang. The ringtone was uniquely his dad's, and his father's bearded face and trademark Hawaiian shirt appeared on the screen. Jason adjusted his glasses and answered the phone on the second ring. His dad towered over him at six foot two, and despite his thin and non-muscular build, he had a commanding presence.

Jason answered excitedly. "Jason's phone, home of the 'I'm ready to get the heck out of town and start vacation.' Dad, how goes it? And before you ask, yes I'm almost home—I can see our house—and I'll be finished packing before you get home. School let out a bit early today, remember?" No immediate reply was heard. Jason stopped walking. "Hello, Dad? Hello?"

Jason's father, Alfred Dix, had a peculiar habit of waiting a moment before speaking. Jason could picture him, his feet propped up on his desk, leaned back in his chair, his office phone mashed to his ear.

"Jason, I'm glad to hear you're almost home. I'm just checking in. Does your molar still hurt? You were complaining yesterday. Listen, I have my calendar in front of me and I'm going to make an appointment for you with the oral surgeon this week, or at least the first available opportunity. I may have to call in a favor. I think it may be time to consider getting your wisdom teeth removed. If we don't, your teeth may start to shift, and I know you don't want to have braces again. By the way, did you ever find your retainer?"

"Dad, I'm fine. It would be best to schedule the extraction around the Christmas holiday, so I don't have to miss school. Besides, we have a vacation and need to get going."

"Do you have your key, son? I know you're almost home; I saw your location in the park. And hey, how was that kook Winwood's class? Is he still teaching? Is he still going on about organizing a class trip? I've been meaning to speak with Zach's father. I think we have a bit of a job for him."

"Dad, I don't think he wants to speak with you. Remember Merl? Yeah, I know I'm not supposed to know about that. And yes, Dad, my key's on a chain around my neck. Remember what you told me: 'The next time you misplace the key, I'm going to put it on a chain around your neck!' Well, it's around my neck. And yes, Mr. Winwood's still there, but no, the notion of a field trip is past tense. I don't think you need to speak with Mr. Sims."

"Please don't lose the key, son. It's hard to replace and nearly one of a kind. There's no one in New Orleans who can replicate it. Don't worry about Winwood; I gather that his tenure is going to be short. I take it you still enjoy Ms. Somerall's class?"

"I'm not complaining, sir. And lose the key? Impossible, Dad. It's not going anywhere. But why have such an expensive lock, anyway? I mean, wouldn't it be easier to get one that I can get a key made for at the hardware shop? Anyway, what time will you be home? I was thinking of going to Langenstein's and getting takeout for dinner tonight. That way we don't have to cook, and we won't make a bunch of leftovers that will spoil. Oh, I've been meaning to ask, does Merl have a pool?"

"Well, yes. That's an odd question. Why do you ask?"

"No reason."

Another long silence came from Alfred's end of the phone, a pause lasting perhaps a bit too long even for his dad; maybe Jason had expected it deep in his subconscious, but Alfred's prolonged hesitation was his general preamble to bad news. A feeling of disappointment began to cloud Jason's mind. *Something always seems to pop up and take priority over our one-on-one time*, he thought. From past experience, he knew that these unforeseen and last-minute changes only meant one thing: the trip will be indefinitely postponed, and Jason would be expected to be fine with it. This fall break would wind up like all the other so-called vacations—remaining at home, finding ways to pass the time with a week of vacation and no schoolwork, alone and bored. *Yard work, here I come*. It's not as if he and his father didn't make plans, it was just that things always seemed to fall apart at the last minute. This was neither the first nor would it be the last time his dad would bail on him.

"Dad, are you still there? Dad?"

Alfred's voice was hesitant. "Jason, look. I hate to . . ."

A yellow minivan taxi emblazoned with the emblem "Dragon Wagon Taxi" sped by, blaring heavy metal music. It nearly bottomed out when it hit a pothole hidden in a shadow. It set Jason on edge. He clenched his teeth and interrupted his father mid-sentence.

"Pops, I'll be waiting for you at home. Bags will be packed, and I'll have dinner waiting." Jason spotted a Life Is Good sticker and a half-ripped Kinky Friedman for Governor sticker on the back of the van with Texas plates before it disappeared from view down Magazine Street. Jason thought, *Whose name is Kinky and why would anyone vote for this person?*

"Jason, I know it's important to you, but . . ."

"Aw, c'mon Dad! I know you're busy and all, but not again! Why can't we go, just this time? I mean, really. We've spent all this time, literally months, making these plans. I've worked so hard this year. You know Zach and his family also have a trip to Texas planned. I was so looking forward to the trip. You and I talked about it. The flights are only an hour and a half; if we need to get back quickly, we can. It's not like we're flying halfway across the globe. Why schedule these trips and get my hopes up if you're never going to follow through?"

"I know I promised, but I have been swamped this week and there is a tropical depression in the Gulf. Turn on the television when you get home. Mayor Landrieu was just on the news saying that he may be calling for evacuations in a few days. I just cannot leave certain matters to the staff. We've got orders coming in and with the threat of a tropical depression or hurricane headed our way, we're rushing to finish a few things before the holiday season. If the storm hits, it will set us back, god forbid like the flooding after Katrina. I guess I should have expected it, but you know how the weather can be. I'm sorry, son, but I'll have to make it up to you."

Jason persisted indignantly, "Really? I mean, this is every time."

"Jason, c'mon. I can't control the weather."

"But Dad, it's every single godforsaken time!"

"Watch your tone, son."

"Why can't this one time be different? Why can't I be your priority for once? We're supposed to be headed off in a few hours for a trip billed as 'guaranteed excitement and adventure,' but no. Instead, I'm guaranteed to have a boring, boring, boring week. I've been busting it hard in school. You said, 'Jason, do well in swimming and I'll reward you.' And what did I do? I took second place in the swim meet. 'Play an instrument,' you said. Well, how about band? 'Son, you should run for class president.' I've done what you've asked of me, so why can't we go? I mean, they're likely to call an evacuation anyway, so why not get out of town? Just think of it as early evacuation, per the mayor's orders! No workers will be in the backyard this week. There'll be nothing for me to do. C'mon, Dad. Please!"

"I'll make it up to you, I promise. Just hear me out. You will have your excitement and adventure. It just may not be in Texas this week. We'll talk when I get home tonight and we'll plan another. I have something else in mind. But in the meantime, why don't you set your stuff down in the house and head over to Ricouard's Barber Shop and get a haircut. Just tell Jimmy or John to put it on my tab. That'll be one less thing we need to take care of before you go back to school. Your hair is getting a bit long and shaggy. It'll give you something to do before I get home this evening. And be sure to ask them to quit fixing up the place. It's losing its ambience."

"Haircut? Dad, I don't want your lighthearted banter now. I want us to spend time together, but all you're capable of thinking about is work. Are you trying to distract me? Don't insult my intelligence, Dad. Come on. Besides, isn't the trip paid for?"

"Jason, I already told you no. Do you really think that I would incommode us both if I didn't have to? I simply cannot go. I'm sorry."

"What about that outing you have set up with your friend, that adventure guru guy, Arthur the Adventurer? That guy on TV. Are you just going to bail on him too? You might as well call him and tell him that he shouldn't take you seriously. Isn't there a whole group of us scheduled? If you can't go, why can't I get Aunt Florine to take me? Can't she drive down from Fort Worth? She said she would the last time she was here, remember? She said, 'If your dad can't take you, I will.' You pulled this same bogus excuse last New Year's and Thanksgiving and summer break and the fall break before. It's seriously every

65

time, Dad. Are you really trying to offer yet another lame excuse?

"And why do you cover so much for that deadbeat partner of yours? He's never around. What does he do for you, anyway? Hasn't he been divorced like five times? The guy's never going to grow up. You said it yourself just the other night: 'He's nothing but a playboy gadabout!' Remember? I do—I had to look up the word. Maybe he's rubbed off on you after all these years. I bet he's never taken any of his kids on fall break, much less know their names. And why does he have to be putting up Ms. Somerall of all people? You may look up to him because he sailed around the world and he's done some crazy things in his time, but I sure don't. The guy is a wreck. If he hadn't slept with Zach's mom, maybe Mr. Sims would like me!

"C'mon, Dad. I am really looking forward to this trip. I need it. Just this time, please!" Jason pleaded emphatically.

"Son, you need to watch your tone with me. I understand your frustration, but I will not speak to you when you're using that tone of voice. And don't forget that Merl is your elder. Do you understand me? He has a number of commitments from ages ago and he does a lot for both of us. Maybe one day you'll appreciate this. Do you understand?"

"Yeah."

"Excuse me?" Alfred's tone was harsh.

"Yes, sir."

Alfred's tone softened. "Look, I know you are frustrated, and you have the right to be. But you cannot be serious— your pedantic Aunt Flo? Are you kidding? She's an English teacher, not an adventurer or thrill-seeker. The last time she traveled with us, you swore up and down never to do so again. Remember all her vocabulary lessons? The quizzes? You know you would have zero fun with her. She'll spend all week correcting your grammar."

"At least traveling with her would be better than staying home alone. What about Uncle Ralph? If I get him to agree to it, would you be OK with me going with him?"

"I'm sorry, but no. The airlines have not allowed the last-minute substitution of passengers on flights since 9/11, and Florine would have to get here from Fort Worth and last I checked, the flight was full. Not to mention that Florine hates hiking or camping or really anything outdoors, and Ralph . . . well, Ralph's Ralph. There is no way to get Ralph on the plane with you. Walking around in a cave would give them both a heart attack. That pugnacious SOB from the Ninth Ward would be swatting at everyone and everything before he set foot in a cave, and you know how he gets if he doesn't have his afternoon drink. He could never drive from San Antonio to west Texas, let alone drive you there from New Orleans. Look, son, I'm sorry. I really am. I'm gonna make it up to you. The weather out in west Texas is going to be lousy anyway."

"Dad, c'mon. *Please?*" Jason tried to plead his case one final time. "The same thing happened last time. I was stuck at home watching TV. Remember? I was stuck watching reruns of your favorite goofy sitcom DVDs. I watched so many that the only ones left were *Murder She Wrote*, and those are Boring with a capital B. I've been busting my chops at school, and you promised. All my friends are leaving town. If I had known you were going to bail on me again, I would have gone with Zach. It's not like they'd notice one extra kid. There's no one to hang out with; it'll be a ghost town around here. Maybe I could go with Bobby. They're going to shore up that camp before the storm. I'm sure it'll be OK if I call." Jason's conversation was interrupted by the chime of an incoming email titled, "Historical Simulations Meeting (by popular demand), November 8th."

Alfred cut him off. "Jason, I do not want you to head down to Buras or Venice or wherever that camp is with the storm approaching. His family is from the Westbank of all places. Bobby is a nice kid, and yes, I sort of know his dad, but I haven't spent enough time with his family to know if they can be trusted with my kid. Didn't he and Bobby get stuck on Bretton Sound last time?"

68

"Dad, I've met him. C'mon, you let me stay over at their house before. His dad may be a politician, but he seems like a nice guy. And he told me they're headed to a camp near Jean Lafitte Park, not way out on the Sound. Bobby's a good kid, so his parents must be good to have raised him right, right? He's practically guaranteed to be our valedictorian."

"Lafitte? Politician, pirate, or whatever, it doesn't matter. From what I remember, you can only get to his dad's camp by boat and across the Mississippi, not Jean Lafitte. I know where all of this is headed, and with all the fog lately, I just don't feel that it's safe. Even Henry Peterson, that looney riverboat pilot who lives down the street, mentioned how dangerous the fog and the high river were making river traffic. They had to open the spillway last week. I know you're disappointed and I'm sorry, buddy. I promise I'll make it up to you. C'mon, the Saints play the Bears on Sunday in the Dome; we're sure to win. I'll get some tickets for us, and maybe we'll go skiing over Mardi Gras. I just can't get out of town right now. You'll understand one day when you're a bit older.

"So, for now, I'll plan on seeing you this evening. We'll discuss all of this more then. Maybe we can head down the coast to Destin or 30A for a few days next week if the storm fizzles out. If the weather is right, we'll go sailing. I love you, but I just can't leave today. And don't worry about Langenstein's; there are some pastries on the counter and Popeyes fried chicken in the fridge. I'll stop

at the supermarket tomorrow. Why don't you order yourself a movie . . ."

The line went dead. With the phone's battery at less than
one percent, Jason was left staring at a black screen.

He foresaw the inevitable, boring week ahead. *Why even
bother making plans? They just get canceled. Period!
Life is not fair. This break is going to stink, just like all
the others.*

Jason pretended his dad were still on the line. "Dad, can I
ask you this: what if I had a mother or there was a
woman in your life? Would you always be so eager to
change plans? Would you brush me off at the last
minute? You're the only man your age I know without at
least a girlfriend." He knew the phone was off, but his
snide outburst at least made him feel better. He shoved
his phone back into his pocket as the bursting pipes of a
Harley Davidson motorcycle passed a few streets over.

He stood still for a moment to reflect on his misfortune,
just enjoying the wonderful sky, the falling helicopter
seeds, and the cool air. Everything seemed to be headed
in the right direction until, WHAM! Out of the blue, his
father bailed on him, all because his loser partner could
not run the business during a storm that may or may not
hit the city. He should have wasted a bit more time in the
park. Frustrated and disappointed, Jason was tempted to
throw his phone as far away as possible, or perhaps just

70

smash its face into a million pieces on one of the oaks, but reason got the best of him. While breaking it would provide a brief sense of satiety or relief, it would accomplish nothing, and then he would have to face the reality of being stuck at home minus a phone. What good would that do? He couldn't exactly call his father and say, "Yeah, hey Dad. Remember our conversation? Well, I was pissed so I smashed my phone. How about some dough so I can buy another?" *Yeah right, like that would ever happen.* He would be stuck with no way to call his friends and no way to waste his time. Such a senseless outburst would only cause his father to make him earn the money to replace the phone, which would take longer than fall break.

*Oh, well. Ho-hum. You'd better get yourself ready for another tremendously boring week courtesy of your father and that slouch, Merl.* With a more measured step, Jason continued onward, his walk home now more a of a burden.

He slowly ambled the remainder of the way home. He passed an empty cable truck featuring the company logo: "ACME Cable: Taking You Out of the Dark Ages." It was parked in the street in front of his neighbor's house, and the technician was likely installing some extravagantly priced, Orwellian devices billed as technological advancements for the home. Jason stepped up his home's inclined, cement path under majestic oaks, past countless lizard and frog figurines, through the ivy-covered, leaf-strewn yard, to the front door of his large, English-castle-styled home: 13 Calhoun Street.

The yellow taxi passed again, presumably searching for an address, and this time, its sticker sarcastically taunted Jason.

"Yeah, right. Life Is NOT Good!" Jason used the gold, ornate key around his neck to unlock the front door.

Finding the house cold and empty, his emotions flared and he began to weep inconsolably. He yelled into the void, "Gosh Dad, every single time. Can't you put me first just this once?" He pounded on the front door in a fit of rage; no one was home, and so it made no difference if he made a racket. Finally, Jason wiped away his melancholic tears and removed his key from the door's ornate lock. A resounding clunk reminded him of the emptiness of their home as he pushed the heavy front door open with his shoulder and let himself into the large, cold, spacious foyer. The heavy door closed with a resonating *kaboom* and locked automatically as lights synchronously illuminated the entry. The house was silent.

Jason sarcastically shouted, "To the nobody that's here, I'm home. Glad to see you today. We get to spend the entire week together, great big house. Get ready for boredom. Congratulations! You can thank Dad for the pleasure. It's just you and me for an entire week."

The home was large and cold like a museum, the foyer decorated with multiple large, polished suits of armor standing at attention around the periphery, placed as if to intimidate. Automatic lights flickered to life as Jason made his way past a meandering, white marble staircase and elevator. Lining the walls were dark, mahogany shelves on which sat a plethora of expensive antiquities and artifacts from different periods of history, labeled with plaques denoting their year of origin, including multiple marble busts. The largest bust, labeled C. Wheatstone, was sturdily mounted in a golden cabinet with a double lock, off-limits to anyone but his father.

Jason cut through the impersonal, white marble formal dining room, replete with fine china and silvers and adorned with paintings in both old and new styles, including the one of a woman who looked very much like his teacher dressed in a golden, flowing gown. "Hi, Ms. Somerall. Glad to see you again today." He stepped over a common house gecko scampering to get out of harm's way as he headed into the kitchen. Tossing his knapsack onto the white tile counter next to a mound of pastries, he plugged his phone into a charger.

On the chalkboard next to the massive stainless Sub-Zero refrigerator was written, "oryh brx," followed by an illustration representing A'l(a) Di'x(i) as a Mayan glyph.

Under the illustration was a list of various unguents, salves, and energy drinks they planned to purchase on their trip, and a taped mockup illustration of the grand grotto planned in their backyard.

"Yeah, right." He took a piece of chalk and angrily struck through his father's cryptic words, instead writing a big "BS" next to the original message. He grabbed a Topo Chico out of the refrigerator, popped it open, and took a swig of the effervescent water. *Remarkably good. I can only imagine the amount of fizz there would have been if I'd opened it at a higher altitude in Texas.*

He didn't really feel like getting a haircut, so he headed into the living room, passing large picture windows that overlooked a verdurous backyard with azaleas and iron plants growing under the windows. The backyard was a wreck; surrounding the base of a large oak tree were numerous holes, and lumber was piled everywhere. In the middle of the yard, an immense mound of dirt sat adjacent to the beginnings of a large hole, currently filled with roots from the oak. Eventually, the hole was destined to become a swimming pool, vast grotto, and elaborate waterfall system. To the rear of the yard near the garage was a white greenhouse, sunflower garden, his father's small art studio, and a flowering arbor. No workers were present, as evidenced by the presence of the soft cadence of frogs mixed with the stridulations of cicadas. The ginormous stone house beyond their fence was dark and appeared uninhabited. Jason imagined that the house was empty, its inhabitants probably lucky and off on fall break.

The living room stood in stark contrast to the backyard and was in its usual order. Their maid, Flower, must have been through the house this morning as the room smelled like Pine-Sol. His father's vinyl records were neatly stacked by the phonograph on the counter, the throw pillows were precisely placed on the large sofas, and the coffee table materials were neatly arranged. He could expect to find animals created from towels atop his bed along with a small piece of chocolate, and all the toilet paper rolls' loose ends would be folded into a point. Their maid's touches were great, but her little accoutrements meant nothing to him now that he was a prisoner in his home for the week.

Jason plopped down onto the soft, brown leather sofa and listened to the silence, hearing only the faint sound of the overhead ceiling fan and the muted backyard symphony. *What now?* he thought. *Zach will be out of town. Can't go with Bobby, who will probably just be studying all week like he always does. I'm not sure that there's anyone else that I'd want to hang out with. Well, Jason, looks like you're stuck. Just plain stuck.*

The spray of the sprinkler system striking the picture window glass broke the monotony of the ceiling fan's drone as he switched on the television with the nearby remote control. What would he do for the week?

On the coffee table laid the standard fare of coffee table picture books, plus a yellow-and-black copy of *Magic for Dummies*, a book on King Arthur's court, Alexander Dumas's *The Count of Monte Cristo* (his favorite), some unusual books on word ciphers, pangrams, and other word puzzles, and a few pamphlets for the now-defunct trip with famed adventure guru Arthur the Adventurer. Near the end of the table was a binder with the beginnings of his dad's work to trace the Dix family genealogy. Jason set the television remote within arm's reach, then picked up the pamphlets and laid back onto the leather sofa, kicked his feet up, and adjusted his pillow to make himself more comfortable in the deep cushions. He wiped the chalk off his hands and onto his khaki shorts, adjusted his glasses, and began to read and imagine the trip that had slipped out of his reach. "No spelunking for you, Jason Dix. No spelunking for you!" Their first adventure was supposed to be a hiking and amateur spelunking trek in the Texas Hill Country, but instead, he'd be exploring the channels on his TV.

He switched the television to the news channel and saw the face of the mayor prattling on about hurricane preparedness. The next channel featured some random game show, interrupted by the obnoxious Ronnie Lamarque (nothing to do with Lamarckism), a local car peddler and wannabe celebrity singing about his car dealerships. Next he found a morbid documentary investigating air disasters, and then another, equally disturbing show documenting a tragic earthquake on a remote, South Pacific island. The digital clock to the right of the television read 13:20 in bright, bold, red numerals. His phone chimed in the other room. *To heck with it. I'm stuck here for the week. I don't want to talk to anyone.*

As he was closing his eyes, he caught sight of the same gecko in his periphery scurrying along the baseboard below the television. "Have a good day, little buddy. How do you deal with boredom?"

# CHAPTER 3

## THE BOY IS HOOKED

*Friday, October 27, 2017*

Jason awoke to the flickering of lamplight feeling dazed as if he'd been asleep for a few hours. He lifted one eyelid and then the other. His head was stuck between the deep cushioning of the sofa, the fan blades spinning round and round directly overhead.

"Did I doze off?" he said, speaking to no one in particular as he felt the sweaty hair at the nape of his neck.

He looked around. By the deepening gloaming, it was likely a bit late for a haircut. Ricouard's was surely closed. *No worry*, he thought, *I'll have all week.*

"Jeezum, what time is it? I must have slept for hours."

Jason lifted his head further out of the cushions and peeked to the right; he must have slept hard because he had to peel his sweaty forearm off the sofa. The digital clock next to the television was flashing Thursday, 13:00,

1960. The lamp atop the credenza flickered, as if power were being intermittently interrupted.

"Beautiful blue skies to this? Maybe Dad's right and a storm is coming. I hope the Sewerage and Water Board is ready this time around. Flooding, here we come again." He took a deep breath. "Well, I guess I needed the sleep. I wonder why the power would go out; maybe a branch knocked out the line or maybe someone ran into a pole again. Note to self, check down the street." He shrugged. "I guess I'll just have to go outside to see if the neighbor's lights are on." He noticed the clock again. "That's weird, I don't remember the clock displaying the year. Maybe 1960 is the default setting."

Just then, the television screen flickered and flashed brightly to life, illuminating the room with an accompanying buzz. Across the screen were myriad vertical SMPTE color bars, and the speakers blared a 1kHz resonating tone. The screen crackled, flipping vertically several times, reminiscent of a 1960s analog television set. Finally, the vertical synchronization improved, and the screen stabilized. The words, "GRABBING YOUR ATTENTION," were stretched across the screen. The collage slowly dissolved to reveal a beautiful blonde dressed in a resplendent, colorful gown, the cut right out of ancient England. Her head was decorated with flowers and a makeshift straw hat as she twirled in a field of flowers before an arbor and large castle. The volume steadily increased as she softly called his name like a fragrance on a smooth breeze. "Jason, oh Jason. That's right. Look over here, Jason." The annoying tone had been replaced with the music from a lute.

"What the heck?" Shock was written across Jason's dumbfounded face, his mind markedly confused by the circumstance. Even more odd, the woman bore a striking resemblance to a young lady in one of the paintings hanging in his dining room, and therefore to Ms. Somerall. He stared at her with singular intentness as she twirled round and round, reminding him of the telegenic Julie Andrews in *The Sound of Music*, her arms gracefully fanning like a ballerina. "Do I know you? Is that you, Ms. Somerall?"

"Testing, one, two. Testing, one, two. Mr. Dix, wake up. Mr. Dix, wake up. Oh, hi there! I see that you are finally awake." She winked and waved alluringly. "We have so much to discuss about your future, and what a future it is, or maybe it's a past. Quite the precocious boy you are." Her silky voice and glowing face were striking. The camera zoomed in for a close-up of her eyes and then her mouth.

She enunciated every word precisely, speaking with clarity and urgency. "Jason, I need you. Will you help me?" She spoke directly to him in some sort of hyperrealistic dream, her voice cutting in and out.

"What the heck's wrong with our cable? Wait, are you in the cable truck out front? The guy next door must have screwed up. That idiot." Jason searched the room for a camera or microphone but came up empty-handed. "Who let you in? Was it Flower, our maid? To whom it may concern or to anyone listening, we do not want any Orwellian devices in our home! You do not have my permission and Flower had no right to let you in. Stop all recordings now!"

Jason rubbed his eyes and took a long minute to focus on the television screen, trying to make sense of the senseless. The whole event somehow reminded him of the annoying clock at school. *Wait until my father hears about this*, he thought. There was a squelch and some feedback on the television before her pitch changed from pleasant to a poorly produced auto-tune effect, murdering any semblance of a Rodgers and Hammerstein's conception. She noisily adjusted what looked to be a lapel microphone.

"Do you realize how rude and annoying this is? Is this some sort of reality TV that involves the audience? You look vaguely like the picture of a lady we have in our dining room, but whoever you are, give it up. I don't like the idea of being watched in my own home, and furthermore, you need to get your technician to remove whatever device is hidden in our home. We did not and will not order or pay for any of ACME Cable's services. I saw the van out front, so don't try to deny it. You have clearly confused us with one of our brainless, couch-potato neighbors. Now turn yourself off and stop intruding on my privacy. Perhaps try the Moores next door; I'm sure they'll buy your garbage. That's where your truck was parked, after all." Jason lay back on the sofa and stared at the ceiling, expecting his delivery to be rude and sharp enough that the castigation would encourage her immediate departure. But she just smiled. The television remained on and brightly illuminated.

A few silent moments passed and Jason realized that she was unremitting. He sat back up and threw the pillow off the sofa in frustration. The sky beyond his windows was dark and fireflies were swarming in the backyard. He flicked his bangs out of his eyes and stared at her directly, resting his forearms on his knees and leaning forward. "Did I ask you to leave me alone or did I ask you to leave me alone? What is really going on here? What time is it really? The charade needs to stop this instant. It's over and done. I'm finished with this ruse."

"What time do you want it to be? Would it really matter if it were one p.m.?"

"Well, as a matter of fact, it would. There's a storm coming. Now look, I really DO mean to be rude, so leave me alone. Come and get the device. We are not interested in whatever it is that has been placed in my home, and if the lady earlier today OK'd it, she did not have the authority.

She was just the maid. I think she only knows about two dozen words in the English language."

"Jason, I thought that a boy of your caliber would be interested in action and adventure, in making a difference in this world. Was I wrong? Would you prefer to stay at home and be bored all week, having a pity party for one? What was that you told your father? 'Oh, *wah*! Daddy, I want to go on an adventure.'"

"No. That's not quite what I said . . ."

"You have an opportunity, young man. From what I have gathered about you, you are a leader. You have aspirations of becoming president of your class. But perhaps I've judged you incorrectly. I was going to be nice about it, but if you don't have the grit, we'll have to do this another way."

Jason could not recall speaking with his father about any new services or devices, nor had any of his school friends mentioned anything like this. The television screen flickered a few times before flashing off and on again as if meant to annoy.

"Thank you for leaving . . ." Before Jason could finish his sentence, the television blared back to life, tuned to the opening sequence of *Magnum, P.I.*, featuring mustachioed Selleck, the rosso Ferrari 308 GTS, and the chopper over the sea. Screeching to a halt, the action sequence abruptly cut to a blue screen with glowing text that read, "YOU ARE NEEDED! I AM NOT LEAVING." The fanfare of a trumpet sounded.

"Not again. C'mon, leave me alone. Dad, I swear if this is a joke . . ."

Jason looked around the room, expecting to be the patsy of a hidden camera prank. He rubbed his eyes again and pinched himself. "Ouch! OK, I'll bite. Come on out, Dad. I guess your call earlier was a farce. Does this mean we're going on our trip? If not, this is all so frickin' redunculus—that's ridiculous cubed. If you're paying for this silliness, you're getting ripped off. The only thing you really got me with was the window tinting." Jason was careful in his tone; if this was all a precursor to a great surprise, he didn't want to act completely asinine and eschew his father's charade.

The video feed featured a close-up of the lanugo hair on her cheek, and then the shot widened to show her entire angelic face. Her voice was now euphonic, and she said, "The sound quality is better, is it not? More inviting?" She danced in her colorful dress, spinning in the field, her raiment ballooning out as she twirled round and round. She threw maple seeds into the air and they whirled around her on the wind as the camera pulled back to a wide shot, a lake to the side and a castle in the background. The camera took a position above as the long shadow of whomever was filming could be seen. She was not alone.

Jason hopped up from the sofa and sneaked around the room, jumping to open drawers as if trying to surprise the hidden cameraman.

"All right, Dad, enough is enough." He peeked under shelving, inside cabinets, and investigated every room of the house, looking for intruders or hidden devices. "Where's the camera? Are you at the TV station? I know a cheap green-screen effect when I see it. Enough is enough. I get the joke and this is getting old. Hop to it. If we're going to make it to the airport, we'll need to get moving. Great joke. I appreciate it, but let's go. Kudos to you, but it's time we get moving."

The entire debacle was starting to look like a cross between an old Fellini film and a Monty Python skit. His dad had a habit of watching the unusual, which often included art films and retro game show reruns late at night. If he were not the subject of a joke, this had to be a dream, right? But his dreams had never felt so tangible, and he'd never realized that he was in a dream when it was still happening. *Could this all just be a dream?* He searched the sofa, table, and living room floor, but the television remote was missing. He got down on all fours to look under the coffee table. "That's strange. I'm sure the remote was on the table when I fell asleep."

The woman was staring at him again. "What are you doing, Jason? There is no need to look for a hidden apparatus; I am in control. Come and speak to me directly. I was going to save this surprise for when we met in person, but we don't have the time. I am not just any woman. I . . . I . . ." She struggled to find the words. "I am your mother."

Jason's head swiveled immediately to the screen, his eyes like saucers.

"Don't look so surprised! Why would Alfred paint a random woman and hang her on your dining room wall? He was painting me. That's me, your mother, in my younger years. I guess the joke's on you now."

"Not funny, lady. You've gone too far. It was funny at first, but now I'm angry." Jason's cheeks were suffused with a bright red glow as his eyes squinted in disdain at the sore subject.

"Oh, is that your mad face? Am I supposed to be frightened? You will not even leave your home. Some adventurer you are. You'll soon realize how our lives and your reality are forever intertwined."

"It's time you shut your pie hole, you shrew. I'm not going to listen to your stupid mendacious rant a moment longer." Jason rose to mash the power button and the channel button directly on the television, but it remained

86

powered on and the station unchanged. "C'mon Dad. Come out, come out, wherever you are. Bringing my mother into this is a step too far. Bags are packed, I'm done. I don't care if I'm being insolent. This woman is rude." He unplugged the television from the wall, but the screen remained illuminated.

Her blue eyes were lustrous and mesmerizing, and it truly felt like she was staring right at him, *seeing* him. Something about her eyes reminded him of Ms. Somerall, though there were subtle differences.

"Angry, are we? Trying to dismiss me? I thought you were the one seeking adventure and excitement. Well, you'll find neither in your home and on your sofa. Some rebel you are. I thought you had more guts than this, but I guess I was wrong."

"What's your problem, lady?"

"Like you, Jason, I am interested in time, which is something we both need more of. May I interest you in my watch, Mr. Dix? Watch the watch. Look at this beautiful chronograph." She was captivating as she swung a golden pocket watch across the screen like a pendulum. "That's right, follow the watch. Back and forth, back and forth. Tick, tock, tick, tock. I find it quite soothing. Don't you? Look at me, Jason. Stare into my eyes."

He had to admit that the watch was soothing, but his mild curiosity turned to confusion when she began chanting a series of odd incantations to accompany the rhythmic swinging of the watch. "Bonum est quadraginta annis, Tempus Fugit. Bonum est quadraginta annis. Tempus Fugit."

"This is downright ridiculous. Cut it out, OK? First I just thought you were odd, then you were aggravating. But now you're just being weird. Enough is enough, cut it out. Cease and desist. Leave. Go away or whatever. I give. How are you doing this? Who put you up to this?" Jason felt like an imbecile speaking with the television; he was resigned to playing the fool.

"Mr. Dix, now stop your chatter. Do I see a degree of distrust in those beautiful, sleepy, brown eyes of yours? Don't be afraid; I'll cause you no harm. After all, I am just on television. I just want to watch you, to look at you. What will it take to have you come to me?"

"Get lost, lady."

"Come now, Jason, can't you play along with the game?"

"What are you talking about?"

The woman composed herself and took a deep breath. "Please, just give me a few minutes, for I have not seen you in ages. My, how you've grown. You know, I have been watching you from afar. First grade with Ms. Marcum, second with Mrs. Bonnet, let's see, T-ball with Coach Ragas. All the most important events of your life, summed up, recorded on video, and stored on your father's computer. Today, my relationship with you is finally changed. If you have ever wanted to make a difference in this world, now is the time. I am far away, confined to an island, and I need your help. Your help—only you can save me." Her voice sucked him in as if she were a mesmerizing mermaid or seductive siren, a mythological creature known for luring unwary sailors to their demise.

The watch swung back and forth.

"Snap out of it, Jason." He swatted himself across his face. "What are you doing to me, lady? Why do I feel this way?" Jason's head started to swim. "Why are you doing this? If you really know me, prove it. Show me something real. Stop lying!" Jason tried to reason his way out of the trance, but he could not. The pendulous motion of the watch was too soothing.

Tick, tock, tick, tock, tick, tock.

The predictable cadence was profoundly comforting. The only other sounds to be heard were the light hum of air blowing from a central air conditioner vent overhead and the faint whisper of the ceiling fans. Even the symphony of insects had quieted.

"Jason, my dear Jason, I understand your hesitation and disbelief. After all, I probably wouldn't believe me either. Perhaps there is a way for me to prove myself. How about this: ask me any question about your past, and I'll answer correctly. Something about you and your life that no one else would know. Fair enough?"

"You mean like what's my favorite color or food? C'-mon, anyone can get those sorts of answers from social media."

"No, I was thinking of specific dates and times. A mother's intuition should be good enough."

"OK. But if you lose, you'll scram?"

"I promise. But if I am correct, you have to come to me."

Jason thought about it for a moment. "August 11, 2015, specifically, between the hours of 9:00 and 10:00 p.m." He folded his arms across his chest with a look of smug satisfaction. He was certain that he'd won. "Bye bye, then."

The television flickered and refocused on her face. "You snuck out of your bedroom window and hopped in an Uber to meet Shelly Langenstein at Angelo Brocato's for ice cream. It was a Tuesday, a school night. She had butter pecan and you had their famed torroncino. You had your first real kiss that night at a little round table. You were wearing khaki shorts, a blue, collared shirt with a crawfish emblem, and white sneakers. Your father found out about your rendezvous when the Uber account alerted him about the fare, and you were in a bit of trouble when you got home."

Jason was startled. "OK. Maybe you heard that from a friend of mine. How about July 6, 2015? Where did I go with my dad that morning?"

Again the screen flickered. "It was the Monday after a long, holiday weekend. You and your father had to bail your Uncle Ralph out of the pokey after he got too inebriated and tried to fight a guy for his The 9th Ward Ain't The Betty Ford T-shirt from Mimi's in the Faubourg. He still owes quite a large indemnity for the damages to the place. Your father claimed the shirt as a keepsake."

She adjusted her microphone and used a more serious tone of voice. "Listen, you and I can waste time all evening with these silly games, but in your heart, you know that I am who I say I am. I need you. I need your help, son. You are the only one who can help me. One day, it will all make perfect sense, but for now, let me tell you a bit more to help you understand." The watch continued its pendulous rocking.

"I have been held captive on a strange and beautiful island in the South Pacific, but it's not just any island—far from it. I can assure you with absolute certainty that your

91

father has no knowledge of my communications with you at this moment, nor would he want you to speak with me. I'm sure he would disavow everything that I will tell you. He knows this island all too well. I can see in your eyes that, deep down, you know what I'm telling you is true. This is why I look familiar. I'm your mother, the same woman whose portrait hangs in your dining room. You have the means to correct our situation with that key around your neck."

Jason felt all the color drop out of his face. He never knew his mother, never even knew she was alive, much less expected to be introduced to her in this manner. He'd always been told that his mother died in childbirth. To fill the void, his father has had a few on-and-off relationships, some more long-lasting than others, but he never remarried. Jason wasn't sure why his brain felt so twisted and malleable, why he acquiesced to each and every word from her mouth. How did she know the details of his life?

She continued, "I may as well tell you the whole truth and let you decide your own fate. The man you call Alfred was once a peccant sailor on the run. He was marooned on our sleepy island, but again, this is not just any island. I am on the Island of Tripe, and he came here in 1960. He destroyed our home, the island's commonweal, and displaced our leader before vanishing into thin air . . . or so we thought. He called himself Beau Champs, and he is responsible for what we call 'The Change.'

"Perhaps he was tricked into his misconceptions or even his depraved indifference, but the man you believed to be your father has hidden a great many things from you. And now he hides in another time and place, pretending to be what he is not. I'm sorry, my love, but he is not your real father. You are so clever and smart; I can't believe that you've never questioned why he bails on traveling all these years. Always canceling trips? He's got to be spooked."

"Spooked?"

"Yes, he must be afraid that someone will find him and make him pay for the harm he has caused to so, so many. Ask him if you wish. Give him a call and mention the Island of Tripe and just watch the reaction it evokes."

"But why did he do the awful things you say he did? It's just the two of us here. There are no secrets. My father doesn't have a mean bone in his body."

"So you think! Who knows why he did what he has done? Regardless of his motives in his younger days, his actions brought about the demise of our tiny island, causing immeasurable harm to everyone here. I will prove it to you. Maybe he has changed, but he has yet to try to correct history. If we meant so much to him, why would he remain silent about his youth? Why hasn't he returned to right his wrongs? Unconscionable. What would a reasonable person infer about the choices he's made?"

93

A bright light flashed on the television, and the image changed to a field full of creatures, mostly warthogs, standing on their hind legs and fighting with swords. Clanks and twangs pealed from the swords, screams and howls spewed from their exasperated mouths. A bright, electrical arc reminiscent of Tesla's plasma globe enveloped the hogs as they fell to their knees.

The screen went dark. With a bright flash, the pocket watch returned, smoothly swinging in its rhythmic, tick-tock cadence.

"Jason, you're looking a bit clueless. Has Alfred really kept his history from you? I had guessed that you were just complacent, that you knew at least something, but now I see I was incorrect. Tell me, did he never offer some inkling of his history to you as some bedtime fiction? 'Once upon a time, there was an island?'"

Jason shook his head no.

"No? No mention of a beautiful land behind golden gates, for instance? Crossed keys like these?" She held up an illustration of two crossed keys. "Your father, or whatever I should call him, escaped our island in October of 1960. There is no written historical account of the terror he wrought, so I have no way of proving anything I am telling you. Victors write history, Jason, and he was the victor. I bet Alfred didn't even have the guts to tell you that he robbed you from me. Did you ever wonder where you came from? Did he not mention the French Revolution?"

"What are . . . you're making absolutely no sense. If he left in 1960, I would be in my forties, no, fifties. And what does the French Revolution have to do with anything? Are you talking about the painting of Bastille Day hanging in our dining room?"

"You're a smart kid. How can I explain this without sounding insane?" She looked away, clearly searching for the right words. "OK, here goes.

"Once upon a time, many eons ago, the height of civilization was destroyed and civility dissolved. The world became dark. I do not mean black; I mean a complete loss of technology. Humankind was plunged back into hunter-gatherer existence. This continued for a really long time, not years, but eons. The world was abandoned by those who retained knowledge.

"Finally, an altruistic population agreed that the world needed to be pulled from the darkness. These great people, the Viracocha, had spread themselves far and wide across the earth. You can see them for yourself; the Viracocha are depicted in many historical accounts, dressed in feathered headdresses. Their illustrations can be found dating back thousands of years, and all around the globe: Egypt, Central and South Americas, Mesopotamia. In every great era of civilization, the Viracocha were there.

These magnificent people aimed to pull the world from the darkness by traveling through time and spreading knowledge on astronomy, free will, medicine, engineering, technology, law, and so much more.

"Our little island was blessed with their presence. This is a large world with many to teach, and we recognized that their time in any one place was finite. So we selected a leader to rule our island, a man of the people who was fearless and strong. This great man had a lengthy history of dedication and selflessness, so the Viracocha bestowed their ancient knowledge upon him. Our people lived in peace and prosperity for many years.

"And then your father arrived. With extreme avarice and greed, he overthrew our great leader and initiated a violent reversion to earlier times. His actions inflicted ignominious grief upon all who remained on the Island of Tripe. The Change was an ugly time in our people's history."

She took a moment to compose herself, her look turning stony. "I must reiterate that Alfred Dix is not your true blood, Jason. You should feel no guilt for any of his actions. You are a victim of him, just as we are. Your father stole our knowledge, reversed our progress, and destroyed our lives, locking it all away behind a hidden gate with two special locks. Worst of all, he banished our leader.

"The man you call 'father' has been lying to you. He is the sole reason for our island's destruction. We have yet to figure out exactly how he did it, what future power or arts he may possess, but what I do know with certainty is that somehow you and that key around your neck are fundamental to the restoration of our civilization."

Jason broke from his trance. "Answer me this, then: if you are my mother, why now? Why reach out now? Plus, I may be sleepy, but your math does not make sense. I should be in my fifties, but I'm only sixteen. How do I know you are who you claim to be? We've never met! Prove it to me! Prove it to me! Why would I ever believe anything you say? This is insane!" Jason's emotional turmoil overwhelmed him as he thrust his head between his hands and pulled on his hair. "How do I know you're not just some crazy, sick woman playing a joke?"

"Calm. Calm, my son. I will try to explain. Just give me a few more minutes. Lift your head up and take a breath. Listen to me. Time provides all answers."

Tick, tock, tick, tock. Jason stared into her mesmerizing, cerulean eyes as the gold pocket watch continued its persistent oscillations, drawing Jason's eye closer and closer to the screen.

"It took me quite some time to find you. When Beau left our island and took you back to the States, he first moved you from the 1960s to the 2000s. I know it sounds im-

97

possible, but he traveled through time. This was part of the knowledge imparted by the Viracocha. Have you read Einstein's theory of special relativity? He was just ahead of his time. Moving through time made it more difficult to find you, of course, and explains your age discrepancy. I mean, you two could have gone practically anywhere. Just think about the vastitude of possibilities: the year 2000 or 3000, or even back to the Renaissance or the Stone Age. The sky's the limit, right? Well, that's not entirely true. He couldn't have just gone anywhere, but at least within the confines of expected values because he used his watch and not the elevator . . . oh, never mind, too much information. It has taken me years to come to my minuscule understanding.

"In any case, I had to consider where and when he would pick, where he would take you and at what age would I find you. What town or city? Boston, Paris, Helsinki? Heck, Buras, Louisiana, for all I knew. Some rural, one-stoplight town? To make matters more difficult, he changed his name. So now we have a single male with a child taking up a new identity in a new time—you can see why I had such difficulty locating you.

"Fortunately, thanks to the Internet, the world has become a little bit smaller. After his online search for the island and its current political climate, we were able to track him and find you. I know a few computer experts at Google who analyzed search queries, evaluated demographic data, identified static IP addresses, and then searched the metadata for a few specific accounts, and *poof*: single man with a single male child. There were a few, but not many searching for the Island of Tripe. It's not exactly a popular search query. I guess I'm just lucky he never married or it would have taken more time. Still, I wanted to be sure, so I've been observing from afar: watching you at school, at the park, with your friends. I knew it had to be you, and here we are. I finally get to see my boy after all these years."

"Why not come in person? Like, ring the doorbell. 'Hi, Alfred. Can we talk?' Or, 'I'm here for the kid.' Perhaps you could have consulted with an attorney. Oh, what the heck am I saying . . ."

"I've been held captive for a number of years, and even if I were free, I would have been prevented from seeing you. Besides, if he were cornered, what action would he take? Run? Fight? Would he harm you? Hide again? The only way I thought I could safely communicate with you was this television channel and from afar. Come on, Jason, if your father knew I was speaking to you, he would find a way to keep you from me. We need you here. You have the power to free me and countless others. I wanted you to understand how you fit into this puzzle. You need to look at me, look into my eyes, son.

"Weren't you just lamenting your lack of adventure? Well, here's your chance! Don't turn your back on me, your mother, after so many years of being kept apart.

Don't shy from adventure. This is your shining time to make a difference in the world. I want you to come see this wild island for yourself."

She spoke lovingly in a soothing, motherly tone. "That's right, come to me, my sweet boy. I'll prove that I am who I say I am and that your past is what I have stated. What do you have to lose? Your vacation has been canceled, has it not? You were literally crying and pleading for excitement and adventure, and now I am offering them to you. Our plight is real, and we need your help."

"Really?"

"There are several items placed in your home that will make a believer out of you."

"But how did you . . ."

"Don't worry about how I have access to your telephone conversations or how I know that you're supposed to travel to Texas or that you were supposed to get a haircut earlier today or even how your plane ticket is upstairs in your desk drawer. I'll explain these details in person, but you must come *alone*. That means without Alfred. You can't tell anyone else. Agreed? Only you? This must be a solo trip. You are special, Jason. You can and will make a difference in this world. I must warn you, though: you must not tell the man you call your father or anyone else about this, or lives will be in danger. You do not understand how much damage has already been done. And you must bring your key."

Her elocution became solemn. "I do not expect you to believe me without proof, and it's proof I intend to give you." The watch continued swinging. "Jason, trust me, look at the timepiece. Would you like to help your mother? Would you like to right the wrongs committed by your father? Would you like to make history?" Her perlocutionary pleadings continued.

Jason's eyes grew heavy. He succumbed to the peaceful feeling washing over him and closed his eyes, focusing on his mother's voice. "Yes."

"Then you must trust our plan. Trust your mother. It is imperative that you leave now. Make your way to the island. Your presence and the key that you keep around your neck is all I require. You must find the gate with double locks. Two crossed keys. Stay strong, young one, as your journey will be filled with peril. There are those who will be intent on capturing you. Remain vigilant and cautious. A plane ticket and money for travel have been placed in your top desk drawer. Call a taxi and make haste to the airport, my son. We will meet again soon, though circumstances will mandate discretion. When you open your eyes, you will immediately depart for the Armstrong International Airport. You have been booked on the last direct flight to the Island of Tripe, on Pan-World Airlines. Haste, my son, act in haste. Do not, I repeat, do *not* mention this conversation to anyone, including your friends, teachers, and especially Alfred. Is that clear?"

"Yes, mother."

"Go, my love. You must go."

The beautiful woman dissolved into waves on the screen, and Jason blinked out of his trance.

Without a moment to lose, he dashed through the kitchen to grab his satchel before bounding upstairs to his bedroom. He opened his desk drawer to find a golden, first-class ticket clipped to his passport.

*Tripe Airlines—A Five-Star Alliance Member of Pan-World.*

*Boarding 6:47 p.m., October 27, 2017*

*Departure 7:10 p.m., October 27, 2017*

"FIRST-CLASS ACCOMMODATIONS TO THE IS-LAND OF TRIPE" was written on a card with embossed, script lettering, along with a sticky note: "Do not forget your passport!" A stack of twenty-dollar bills was set neatly beside his travel documents.

The clock on his desk read five thirty, so he needed to get moving. Time was of the essence; he would be lucky to make the flight.

Pocketing the ticket, his passport, and the bills, he emptied his gray satchel onto the closet floor and providently grabbed his black, lucky towel, a few chocolate bars off his desk, and a phone charger, stuffing them in. He threw a few extra sets of clothes haphazardly into his already-full floral suitcase that he'd packed for his Texas vacation, then he tucked a pillow under his bedspread and tousled the sheets to make it look like he was sleeping. He ran downstairs, lugging his knapsack and suitcase, grabbed his cell phone off the charger, and called a taxi. If he used Uber or Lyft, his father would be alerted, lesson learned from his rendezvous with Miss Langenstein. When he opened his front door, the yellow taxi with the Kinky Friedman sticker pulled up to the curb with miraculous timing.

Jason skipped down his path as the front door slammed shut. He opened the back hatch of the taxi, threw his knapsack and suitcase inside, and then climbed into the backseat. The driver was a scruffy, olive-complexioned fellow with a serpent sleeve tattoo. He was puffing on a cigarette as he languidly turned to face Jason. "How old are you?" he asked in a heavy Persian accent. The ACME Cable van passed, heading in the opposite direction.

"Armstrong Airport, and quickly, please. I don't have much time," Jason barked like a seasoned pro. "Can you get going, please? I really don't have much time. I don't want to be rude, but I'm late for my flight."

The taxi driver's phone began to ring. To Jason's annoyance, he was slow to answer the call.

"Well? Are you going to answer the phone?"

"Does your father, I mean, parents know where you are heading?" He answered the flip phone and spoke quickly. "I can't talk now, I have the kid, I mean, I have a passenger. You better pay me." He slammed the phone shut and threw his cigarette butt out the window.

"What does it matter? I look young for my age. By the way, you shouldn't smoke, and you just littered when you threw your cigarette out on my lawn. What if you were to catch the place on fire? And of course my father is aware of where I'm going; who do you think I'm meeting?"

"I was just asking. I have kids myself. I'd hate for you to be running away from home, you know? My son is a bit independent, like you. Kids these days. What am I saying—look where you live! Young highness, how do you propose to pay the fare?"

"Does this answer your question?" Jason flashed his roll of twenty-dollar bills.

He was pinned against the seat as the driver accelerated away from the curb, barreling down the bumpy street. Jason looked out the rear window, where he thought he caught a glimpse of a pedestrian who looked strikingly similar to Mr. Winwood, "Hey, I know that guy. There goes my teacher . . ."

The driver hit every pothole as he zipped up Carrollton Avenue, then merged west onto I-10. Jason texted his father: "Going 2 hang with some friends, maybe get a haircut," but he didn't check to see if it was read or even delivered before turning off the phone to save battery. He wasn't sure if any charging stations would be free near his gate.

Without further conversation, the two expeditiously zigzagged in and out of traffic through Metairie and Kenner, and then onto the main thoroughfare to the airport's concourse. They pulled alongside a truck with a New Orleans Iron Works emblem; the man lollygagging in the driver's seat had toenails painted in Mardi Gras colors and a dragon tattoo on the foot he had hanging out the window, while The Hawketts' "Mardi Gras Mambo" blared, completely out of season.

Jason paid his fare and grabbed his bags, negotiating his way around the colorful toes hanging out the window and making his way past the skycaps hauling luggage. Through the bustling crowd, he could see the ticketing counter for Pan-World Airlines. He entered the massive, marble atrium as the horrendous cacophony made the overall gestalt of the place pandemonic. *So ironic*, he thought. *This place is named after Louis Armstrong, but the acoustics are so terrible in here!*

He crossed the atrium and verified that his flight was scheduled for an on-time departure. It would be close, but if he weren't held up at ticketing, he should make the flight. He hadn't considered that they might not let him on the plane without an accompanying adult, but it was worth a try. *Too late to turn back now!*

"Excuse me. Excuse me," he said as he pushed through the throngs of families leaving for fall break.

Although there were quite a lot of people in the terminal, the Tripe Airlines first-class queue was sparse, so Jason had carte blanche with respect to service. Feeling the jealous gaze of others in line, he strutted to the first-class lane, separated from the others by maroon-roped stanchions and red carpet, and stood behind the black line marked on the floor. As Jason stared at the airline's logo, he realized that he was viewing a hologram, transforming from Pan-World to Tripe Airlines. *Fancy*, he thought, *must be a good airline.*

"Next in line, please," announced a tall, buxom, stunning, blonde attendant.

"Good evening, miss." Jason shuffled his suitcase and knapsack to the weighing station at the counter.

"Sir, I can take that for you. How may I help you?" She smiled from ear to ear, her teeth gleaming white.

He stood at about breast height and had to look up when speaking to her. He politely handed her his ticket confirmation and placed his sole suitcase on the scale. The item was easily below the fifty-pound restriction.

"Oh, I see that you're making a special trip. Tripe Airlines, a valued member of our Pan-World Five-Star Alliance, serves over 100 destinations, domestic and worldwide. You have chosen a rather distant hub; must be a special event this week." She printed out his boarding pass and attached a luggage tag to his suitcase.

"Actually, I think I may be meeting my mother."

"Well, that's as special as it gets! And you're flying first class, too. Sir, do you have any other items to check? They are required to be less than fifty pounds each, but first-class passengers are allotted two free bags." She winked at Jason to let him know that he could break the rules a little if necessary. "Meal preference today? Steak or chicken? All beverages are complimentary."

"Just one item to check." Jason checked his watch and continued nervously, "Ma'am, the thing is that I'm all alone. My family made it here before me; I had to hurry from school and had to take a taxi alone. Do you think I'll make my flight? Departure is scheduled for 7:10 and it's already 6:45. I've raced to get here as quickly as I could, but traffic was horrendous. There are so many people leaving for fall break that I'll never make it through security in time. It's more crowded here than I expected."

"I'll need some identification, please." She didn't seem the least bit concerned about the crowds or his worries. "Well, with everyone traveling for fall break, this is one of our busier days of the year. Meal preference?"

Fumbling through his pockets, he fished out his passport and mumbled, "Oh, chicken, I guess. I really hope I can make it. I'm meeting my mother for the first time. I just can't miss the flight; I have so many important things to do this week. I've never been to the Island of Tripe. Have you?"

"Actually, I know it quite well. It's an amazing place. Normally, regulations prevent me from passing you through without an adult." She lowered her voice and looked around conspiratorially. "But given the circumstances—meeting your mother and your first-class status—I think I can make an exception." She put a finger to her lips surreptitiously. Grabbing the suitcase from the scale, she affixed a departure sticker, placed it on the conveyor belt behind her, and handed him the corresponding claim ticket.

"Keep this handy in the event that your luggage is lost. You'll make it in no time, I just know it. And Jason . . ."

He interrupted her. "Please, I understand the rules, but I need to make it to my plane. My father should already be at the gate. I'd hate for him to come back through security looking for me."

She flashed her pearly white teeth in a Cheshire-cat grin and picked up her walkie-talkie. "I need assistance escorting a minor to the gate."

"Enjoy first class. I hear that the service and refreshments, particularly the cola of all things, are fantastic in first class."

An airport security guard appeared from out of Jason's periphery. The attendant tucked his boarding pass into his passport and passed the bundle across the counter. Jason noticed that his boarding pass featured the same script lettering as the note he found in his desk. He was about to comment on the coincidence when he thought he spotted Mr. Winwood across the terminal.

"Hey, I know him. But he was just walking on my street. How could he . . ."

"Excuse me? You had a question, sir?"

"Oh, it's nothing. I thought I just saw one of my teachers. No big deal; it was someone else."

"Can you please help this young man get to his gate on time?" the attendant said to the security guard.

"Yes, ma'am. I'll make sure he gets aboard safely," the tall man said.

Jason caught a brief glimpse of her tattooed forearm as her sleeve momentarily rode up her arm. The tattoo was exactly like Ms. Somerall's, the taxi driver, and the foot hanging out of the truck: a serpent.

"Thank you, miss."

"This gentleman will help you reach your gate on time. Have a great flight, Mr. Dix. I hear the Island of Tripe is beautiful this time of year. I'm sure you'll enjoy your stay and your fall break. It will no doubt be eventful."

Jason whisked through security and boarded the flight without incident. Not even a second glance was given as he handed the boarding pass to the gate attendant, who ushered him to his seat like royalty.

Finally in his seat and ready for departure, Jason turned his phone back on and composed a video message to Alfred, explaining his dissatisfaction with their ruse of a relationship and where he was headed. After confirming that the message had been delivered, he immediately powered his phone off and uttered a sigh of relief. It was 7:09 p.m.

# CHAPTER 4

## FINDING A WATCH

*1963*

Our story commences on the Island of Tripe, a UNESCO World Heritage site. The isle was a fragment of the former continent of Zealandia, one of a smattering of islands comprising an archipelago, located just south of the equator, about 4,000 miles off the western coast of Peru. This island, relatively unknown to the outside world with minimal write-ups in travel journals, is and was merely a punctate refugium of the long-lost continent of Zealandia. The island was so remotely located in the far reaches of the South Pacific that it went relatively unnoticed and was perpetually wanting in first-world accoutrements, consequently kept behind the times and in an anachronistic state. Things had changed in recent years with the growing influx of air travel and a certain American billionaire, who brought the island a more touristic appeal.

The island was of interesting character. It was rather circular when viewed from above, measuring a diameter of roughly thirty-two kilometers across. The apex of the volcanic mountain that stretched from the center of the island into the heavens was blanketed year-round by a lenticular cloud cover. Its official elevation was 2.563 kilometers, but the height was always subject to discussions amongst inkhorns regarding derivatives near Pi.

The island's topography varied wildly. The northern two-thirds could best be described as quite wide-ranging, with plentiful elevation changes, a rocky coast replete with coves and inlets, and the mountain. All told, this portion of the island featured over 600 microclimates, enabling innumerable and variegated flora that grew from soils of differing compositions, including a base of karstic limestone in some areas and volcanic scoria in others. Curiously and to this day, the southern third of the island was uncharted, as exploration of this portion of the island has been forever forbidden for reasons unknown to all. Thus, a description of its terra incognita remained impossible to substantiate and the area is consistently dismissed from conversation. UNESCO, the World Trade Organization, The United Nations, and numerous other international governing bodies passed strict laws and treaties that forbade trespassing in the southern portion of the island for reasons never to be elaborated upon. Despite the technological miracles of satellite imagery, the southern third was permanently covered in a uniform, ultraviolet, obscuring haze, rendering any attempts at mapping the entire island fruitless.

The residents of the Island of Tripe were largely settled to the northeast in the better-soiled, lush, and verdurous jungle. The main Tripe township, Tripe Airport, and Tripe Marina were nestled amongst the abundant wilderness near the coast, though a few outposts and smaller granges dotted the mid-island landscape. In the far reaches of the northwesterly corner of the island, the landscape was rocky, volcanic, and barren. As a result, the land harbored few inhabitants; a single township, the Westbank, housed the dregs of the island's inhabitants, those who had been banished from polite Tripe society.

It was on this odd, remote island that Dr. Patricia Gail Atwood, a striking, five foot six (five-eight with boots) woman dressed in blue jeans, cowboy boots, and a breezy blouse sat atop the hood of her blue 1956 Chevy pickup truck. She had backed it into the antemeridian shade of a fragrant group of rainbow eucalyptus trees along a dirt road, Lowerline Street. From her perch, she overlooked her planned worksite, a depression in the earth known as the Grand Cavas Cenote, an enormous sinkhole on the eastern side of the island.

A scowl was written across her face as she anxiously tapped her foot and drummed her fingers on the hood of the truck. Her other hand twisted her ponytail as she waited impatiently for the work to begin.

She was a beautiful, thirty-four-year-old woman, pic-turesquely gifted with prominent blue eyes, long, flowing, blonde hair, and a face highlighted with prominent malar bones. Her perfect proportions and other superficial gifts were overshadowed by an even greater amount of intelligence, manifested in her fiery, feverish, astute demeanor and august mannerisms, her back straight, her chin high, and her mind lost in frustrated thoughts as she watched the two men trampling around her site. It was upsetting that the morning's delay was due to government bureaucracy and the selfishness of a single politician. Her nerves were on edge, due in large part to the singularly ridiculous and quite unexpected reiteration of the government's uselessness and the council's inability to produce anything but quagmires of legal mumbo jumbo. She was accustomed to getting her way, and she generally had the ability to make everyone she encountered acquiesce to her demands.

Earlier that morning, eager to get to work, she and her crew had arrived before her permit's scheduled seven o'clock start time to prepare. Not one to waste time, she immediately gave her crew their marching orders. She sent the bulk bustling out of the bed of the truck and down a rocky declivity to the base of the Grand Cenote below, where they were to begin the hard work of clearing foliage before measuring the grids needed for the planned excavation and search for relics. The notion that they would be committing an egregious crime never crossed her mind, as they were in the middle of nowhere, far from any residents who might take issue with the hustle and bustle. She kept two of her men up top and tasked them with the rather laborious but mundane job of obtaining wood, a simple enough task as they were in a forest.

To her dismay, however, her plans were halted shortly after arrival due to an unannounced visit by an acrimonious, headstrong council member who seemed to have a beef with her project and the audacity she displayed in not following the law. He bellowed, "My job is to enforce the work permit to a T!" his voice resonating in her clenched jaw.

She only had herself to blame; it was her fault for not being on guard, and she had learned the lesson well. Upon his arrival, she let her guard down to excitedly explain her plans in an ingratiating manner, expecting his congratulations or words of encouragement in finally getting this project started. After all, in addition to the excavation, her agreement with the council was that she was to restore the Grand Cenote to its former grandeur. Instead, she was handed a thankless castigation and mordant rebuke of her selfless and undisciplined attitude as he brusquely reminded her that she did not own the island. Not only did he dress her down in front of her workers, but he also shoved a strongly worded epistle into her hands.

Eventually, the feverish conversation led to his promise that her work would cease if her excavation permit were not properly displayed, citing Article 19.3 Subsection 42 of the archaeological and excavation bylaws. To make matters worse, the council member noticed that the two brutes had not only begun working before the permitted time, but even more egregiously, were caught red-handed illegally chopping down a coveted patch of rainbow eucalyptus trees for the lumber she requested. The discovery of the newly created glade produced a verbal haranguing so contemptuous that the crew thought her health to be at risk.

The council member avowed to halt all work and press charges should her work permit not be properly displayed immediately. And so, due to her carelessness, her workers' conspicuousness, and the unnecessary quagmire of legal nonsense, she was unable to start work. She sat. And sat. And sat with forbearance, drumming her manicured nails and tapping her boots on the hood and fender of the truck, trying to remain calm as she waited for her two buffoons to finish setting the requisite signpost into the earth so she could display her permit and begin to seek out the precious pocket watch (or any other items noted in her codex). She made a mental note to address the council regarding the whole debacle. It had cost her the entire morning to get a copy of the permit and requisite post from town. Even more ridiculously, not only did her permit need to be displayed, but it needed its own special post from that very council member's store (a point that questioned his ethics), which didn't open until ten o'clock. She would have to complete a commutation form for their destruction of trees when she returned to the township.

"What a jerk," she muttered. His reprimand had caught her by surprise; most of the island's native population adored her, treating her as a denizen who diligently worked to remediate their dilapidated island, preserve their history and precious relics, and offer benevolent psychological care to the island's population, and all at no charge. Who was he to barge in and act in such a callous manner? It was her time, not his, spent in countless hours of therapy sessions to mollify those in need of psychological care, teaching coping skills to help them endure the grief, guilt, and trauma they experienced after the island's Change. She had expected the usual special dispensation given her broad altruistic efforts, so his mordant rebuke was even more unexpected. The island owed her a debt of gratitude, and a simple dig was the least that should be offered in thanks for her services. And thus, with no time for indolence, she remained irritated about her forced stagnation.

A calming, cool breeze blew across her face and bent the surrounding colorful foliage as she took a few more deep breaths to calm her frayed nerves. Never one to sit idly by, she took advantage of her inertness and reflected on the situation. If life were a bell curve, lately, she was falling more to the left, where life's slings and arrows rained down. By her account, a swing to the right should surely be forthcoming.

It seemed like only yesterday when her mother would rock her in her lap on their front porch that overlooked the Rio Frio, the warm, Texas breeze blowing. Together, they would look out upon the vastitude of hills and wildlife as Patricia listened to what she thought to be fairytales. It was pleasant to recall such comforting days of old, and she felt the tension in her body dissolve. The stories her mother told seemed like mere fictional accounts of men from another time, but they made more of an impression than she cared to realize. She recalled her mother's lifelike accounts of men donning feathered garb and traveling through time with knowledge that far exceeded anything that was known at the time. Perhaps it was myth, but her mother was assured of their reality. Patricia was now closer to this connection than ever before, and this was not the time to lessen her zeal for discovery.

The sound of banging shook her from her brief reverie. Having finally acquired the requisite supplies, she watched two maladroit imbeciles taking turns violently pounding the post into the rocky, limestone earth, the post head near splinters and on the verge of separation. Left alone, the bumbling duo would likely hurt one another, and then she would have yet another mess to clean up. What else could she expect from two monstrous anthropoid warthogs with biceps the size of tree trunks, pugnacious demeanors, and brains the size of walnuts.

Patricia hollered, "Now c'mon, boys. Larry, you can't get so close to Billy when he's swinging the mallet. You're going to get knocked square in the head."

"But Larry won't give it to me. It's my turn to swing. Why does he get to have all the fun?"

"Yes, I will, but you don't swing it correctly. Here, then. Let's see you do it, if you're so strong." He shoved the large mallet into Billy's hands.

Bill slammed the mallet onto the top of the splintering post, driving it yet another inch into the earth as he and Larry continued their velitation.

"Did somebody fudge when completing the application? I thought you two had skills. If you keep whacking it so hard, there won't be any post left and I'll have to send you back to the Westbank. You both checked the box for post driving skills, but I have yet to see them demonstrated. C'mon now, you know I'm already in trouble and if either one of you gets hurt, this project will be canceled. That's quite enough horsing around."

To keep calm, she bit her lower lip and focused on the dancing patterns of light created by the truck's specular, blue, glittering hood that reflected the sun's rays to illuminate the forest's canopy. The two inveterate buffoons were buffoons before The Change, and therefore, they were buffoons after The Change. No matter how many years of life they had left, they would remain buffoons. The only reason she hired them for this dig was her past acquaintance with Larry and her sympathy for Bill. She was cross with herself for succumbing to such emotional thoughts. She'd clearly had a lapse in judgment when she hired the pair, who continued banging on the post in their trademark careless manner.

Swatting an unseen insect from her face, she slid off the hood. "How about you boys gather up some of the lumber and the supplies in the back of the truck and run them down to base camp. That post looks deep enough." She pointed to the truck bed with her thumb as she walked to the post with the permit in one hand and a hammer and nails in the other.

At her request, the two warthogs obediently dropped the mallet and proceeded to the truck to gather materials.

"No, no, no . . ."

They looked inquisitively at each other, clearly not understanding the problem. Their acrid smell overpowered the delicate eucalyptus nearby.

"Do you think I can lift that?" She gestured to the large mallet, and both beasts shrugged their shoulders. "Can you put it in the back of the truck, please?"

Larry grabbed the mallet and carried it in an obsequiously kyphotic manner past her and placed it gently into the truck bed, causing the truck to sink an inch or two. Despite their gargantuan size, she clearly ruled the roost.

"Now, you two get a move on. They'll need some help down below." The two headed down into the cenote to join the others.

At long last, Patricia nailed the permit to the signpost, spitting on it for good measure. "That should take care of the matter," she said to no one in particular.

*The Island of Tripe hereby grants Dr. Patricia Atwood the right for excavation at the base of the mountain, in the Grand Cavas Cenote. Anything found therein is hers to keep.*

*Signed, Peresitene Patitur*

A cool, soothing breeze blew across her face again, giving her a momentary respite to reflect upon even deeper memories and the circuitous path that led her to this point. The morning's unexpected setback had irritated her more than she had expected.

Dr. Patricia Atwood had always been a complex individual. Precocious as a child, she had possessed persistence, ingenuity, adroitness, and zeal, all mixed with a great blessing of beauty that continually drew luck to her side.

Her venerated life was replete with instances of talent as her natural intelligence and inexorable work ethic landed her accolades as early as grade school. After high school, she received full-ride scholarships to several prestigious colleges. She pursued the fields of psychology and antiquities and graduated summa cum laude, having made noteworthy scientific achievements and multiple acclaimed publications. Her efforts were rewarded to such a degree that her accession seemed, at times, guided by a higher power. And with each such accolade or milestone, she developed a certain phronesis that guided her toward increasingly lofty goals. If she were successful today, this would be her greatest achievement to date, but it all started with a bit of luck.

Upon completion of her doctorate, she was drawn to begin further postdoctoral work studying ancient civilizations (particularly Mayan) under the tutelage of famed professor Zeringe D. Montegue, PhD. Late one night, she inadvertently surprised him in his office as he toiled under lamplight, and he let slip his efforts to decipher a Mayan text thought to have been destroyed centuries ago by conquistadors. The text featured odd references to past civilizations and technologies, and, by his interpretation, it claimed to be a tangible path to extreme enlightenment. Intriguingly, the people and items depicted in the text seemed to mirror those in her mother's accounts and nighttime stories, though she kept that detail to herself. Despite his trust in her and their growing relationship, his dissimulation would not allow her to examine the large, red, leather-bound tome, and he would give no elaboration on the subject when questioned. Shortly thereafter, she devised a plan to obtain the codex. In the end, Dr. Montegue was a man to whom she truly owed nothing, yet owed everything, a lonely man who was a sucker for her beauty.

If successful, today's excavation would be the culmination of her years of efforts. These efforts began one fateful evening seven years ago when she tried to obtain the text as her own. Her endeavors led her to the island and her pursuit of the codex's truths. On this particular night, having patiently nurtured their relationship for months, she finally drew the unsuspecting Professor Montegue and his volume of Mayan glyphs into her coy and coquettish arms amidst the university's library stacks. He could no longer restrain his amorous feelings for her as he howled and pleaded for her love. He believed the two to be alone, but as he made his advances upon her feint of innocence, the mindful eyes of university security were upon them. He had brought his personal volume of Mayan glyphs and illustrations within a satchel for their rendezvous, as per her persistent request. In the shuffle of his arrest, the satchel was lost or purloined by persons unknown.

As Professor Montegue was marched out in handcuffs, he suddenly succumbed to a fit of apoplexy on the steps of the library and died shortly thereafter. He was symbolically terminated days later, and given the professor's notoriety, the situation was quickly publicized. The ensuing media circus felt so dire for Dr. Atwood that many thought she would dismiss any further educational endeavors and shy away from public view. On the surface, that is just what she did; she left the institution under the pretext of post-traumatic stress and received a hefty financial settlement for her silence and departure.

The truth, however, was a different story. The entire sordid affair was planned, and her subterfuge was greatly rewarded with the book that she had affectionately termed the Montegue Codex, a lifetime of Professor Montegue's notations scribbled within the text's margins and passim. The settlement she received from the university allowed her to finance her future studies and investigations. No longer was she subject to the mythoclastic generalizations of ancient times, publicly available works, and dead-end leads. Dr. Atwood now had concrete information in her hands that suggested the possibility of a lost knowledge. The stories she remembered from sitting on her mother's lap were finally within reach of being found again.

Her mind was enkindled with the possibilities of an alternate or superior race with abilities out of the ordinary and exceeding our current level of technological advancement, as was described in the text. Whether the accounts in the illustrations and undecipherable glyphs were fictional or historically accurate was not yet known to her, but her most plausible path forward was to follow the clues left in the book. The first breadcrumb she followed, two young men in a sailboat, led her to the South Pacific Island of Tripe and to her current archaeological endeavors.

Dr. Atwood dropped the hammer and nails into the bed of the truck and turned as she heard Art's voice from down below.

"Professor! Professor!" Art, one of the more educated and articulate warthogs, called out from the cenote. He had helped her intermittently with brute tasks since The Change.

"Dr. Atwood, come and take a look at this!" His gargantuan form could briefly be seen at the base of the pit through the swaying foliage. He stood in the Grand Cavas Cenote, which was not so grand at present. A once ineffably beautiful cenote, in the three years since The Change, it had been used as a mere construction refuse pit. Neglected, it was now overgrown with vegetation.

"I think we've found something. It appears that we're digging in the right place!"

"Coming right down. Give me just a minute." Patricia hastened her pace, trotting down a switchback, down the rungs of a rusty ladder, and to the base of a culvert where

Art was waiting. Upon clearing enough plant life, the extreme, derelict nature of the depression became clear.

Art stood at least two feet taller than Patricia. "By the look of some of the debris I've come across, I think the airport construction trucks dropped some of their waste above us. Look at this," Art said as he pulled out a few small pieces of brick, rebar, and the mesh used to hold cement together from out of a shallow hole. "Lucky no one stepped on this."

"Someone must have just backed their trucks up to the edge and tossed this stuff over. Art, I want you to focus on the water's edge and into the cavern. By the looks of the topography above, any runoff from the forest and the mountain would head in this direction. And in the water there, I'll need you to use the sieve and pan. Even the smallest of items are important. Remember, no item is too small. Oh, and don't forget to teach those two oafs a thing or two." She gestured to Billy and Larry.

"Will not forget, ma'am. Once we get these frames in place, I'll get right on it."

"What are we looking for, boss?" barked Bill, who stood idly beside Larry and his shovel.

Dr. Atwood said, "Just listen to Art. I think I'll go take a look around in the cavern while you finish setting up.

And watch out for these two, Art," she gestured to Bill and Larry. "They're liable to hurt someone."

Art went back to work with the others, giving orders and recording measurements in his field notebook as Patricia surveyed the area.

Navigating through the thick foliage, she pushed through branches and vines as she made her way to the edge of the Grand Cavas Cenote where she could take in its splendor. She stood in awe of the indescribably beautiful scene before her as a light breeze blew across her face. Composed perfectly with a vast multitude of shades, the cenote could have been painted by one of the masters. The beach comprised nearly translucent, pink pebbles that sloped down into a bright azure, almost glowing lagoon with crystal-clear water that lapped gently near her feet. The cavern was as tall as its mouth was wide, fifty, maybe one hundred feet high, and near the center of the ceiling, a small, likely man-made oculus allowed the bright, midday sun's rays to enhance the mist that hung tranquilly in the air. The gray walls of the cave were dotted here and there with a colorful array of verdant lichen and plant life. The cave's waters led off in many directions and disappeared from view.

And so she stood, ingesting the splendor before her as the boisterous beasts remained at work beyond the cave. Other than a slight, hollow sound of a drip, the cavern was quiet and peaceful. She thought that she could momentarily hear the queer and nearly imperceptible clinking of utensils, plates clanking, and food orders being shouted, which was quite odd as they were far from the main township and no one lived in this area.

It was in this idyllic setting, where she and her men panned for antiquities, that her golden timepiece was finally discovered buried amongst the pink pebbles, a timepiece similarly depicted on page after page of her precious Montegue Codex.

# CHAPTER 5

## MOUNTING A CAPTURE

*October 1972*

A portentous, inky gray sky and a sonorous, gusting, northwesterly wind was gaining in intensity minute by minute as a tempest churned toward the Island of Tripe. A storm would be striking soon, both figuratively and literally.

Across this small island's barren northwestern landscape, an eerie green, purple, and gold smoke arose, dotted with lofting embers that had billowed from an abundance of pores and fumaroles in the volcanic earth. The seemingly endless smoke spewed forth, twisting and churning, fighting to rise amidst the howling winds, captured by unseen vortices and rising and dissipating high above the tall cliffs that overlooked the rough, glowing Pacific Ocean. The smell of rain filled the air as storm clouds whisked across the sky, intermittently dropping their loads as the storm's outer bands thrashed overhead.

In these inclement circumstances, a lone, green gecko dressed in overalls and a hard hat stenciled with number thirty-four popped his head out of one of the higher fumaroles near the cliff's edge. He had a job to accomplish: seek, observe, document, and report.

He first checked the safety of his surroundings. Finding no gulls or other birds of prey nearby, he lifted his body out of the depression, stretched his back in a manner peculiar for his species, dusted himself off, and gathered his small satchel. It wasn't as if he were afraid of the gulls, he just thought it best not to tempt their inherent desire for gecko meat on this particular day.

Since the coast was clear, he peered down over the rather sheer face of the cliff in the direction of the rookery of a township known as the Westbank. The churning, salty sea below him ebbed and flowed, crashing against the shore. He looked around for inhabitants, but it was apparent that the declivities and stairways from the cliff and outcroppings down to the town below were deserted. No one seemed to be about; perhaps it was a calm before the storm, so to speak, but in his experience, it was too calm for the Westbank. In the tumultuous sea below, the glow of microscopic plankton mixed in neon, phosphorescent, whitewashed swells to create a luminous display of colors as the waves crashed themselves against the roughened cliff's promontories and surge-swept reefs below the township. The methodical violence of the beautiful display was almost deafening. A gam of whales just off the coast seemed excited, lobtailing and slapping into the wash with no apparent or premeditated rhythm.

The little creature fought the winds and kept his footing as he fumbled through his satchel, digging for the supplies he would need if he were to remain inconspicuous. He needed to get closer. He needed to be sure.

He withdrew a pair of audio binoculars with one hand and clasped his hat tightly against his head with the other. He wrapped the binoculars' strap around his neck as he stepped back onto the leeward side of a rock, the torrential wind making it difficult to get situated. Raising the telephoto lenses to his eyes, securely fastening the ear bud into his left ear, and adjusting the microphone's parabolic windscreen, he stepped back into the gale and turned his equipment toward the Westbank. About a furlong away, he could see the dwellings well enough through his lenses, though lightning sporadically bleached his view as thunder clamored and a ruckus erupted from nearing clouds. As the rain began to pour, he adjusted the telephoto lens to a higher power and swept his narrow field of view across the town, abode by abode, down oblique walkways cut into the rock faces. With the exception of a few sporadic flickers of light left on in the windows, there was no movement in the town. The only apparent sign of life was the distant cacophony of a few hungry gulls riding the wind gusts out at sea, braving both the storm and the gam of cetaceans. None of the town's inhabitants seemed to be home; there was not a single movement amongst the thousands upon thousands of masoned huts and makeshift shanties. The Westbank appeared empty.

And so, he waited, getting more drenched by the second. Something must have held up his charge on the way from the airport. In time, he spotted some activity, or so he thought. It was near an illuminated neon light; a sign for Urban North beer shone like a lighthouse guiding him to the amphitheater's entrance. He adjusted his binoculars and zoomed in for a closer examination of Westbank's only round-the-clock tavern, Harry's Bar, which was famously open 24/7, 365 days a year. If any place in the town would be busy or bustling with life, the tavern was it. The little gecko was well acquainted with the tavern because, since The Change, the nightlife offered was legendary and the tavern was often full of crapulous escapades, barroom scuffles, and weekly, pop-up entertainment. No one on the island really cared what happened at Harry's as long as it didn't cause problems on the rest of the island. After all, what happened in the Westbank stayed in the Westbank. The patrons of the tavern didn't matter one iota to the island's elite, and so abuses throughout the Westbank were ignored.

Without warning, the front door of the hut flung open and a hairy, obese, anthropoid warthog dressed in a gaudy, striped outfit ran out the door, his lumbering fat rolling as he zipped his front trousers and pulled up his rear as he ran up an adjacent walkway. The lumbering beast disappeared from his narrow field of view, but the gecko kept his sights on the establishment's door as it slammed closed in a gust of wind. No further activity was seen.

The little interloper waited a few minutes longer as he let his lens wander. Exploring the area where the absconder had disappeared, into a rock face about fifty meters from the illuminated sign, he spotted a portion of cliff face that was imperceptibly different from the others. While most of the edges and walkways extended just a few feet into the rock face, this larger depression cut much deeper, masked by a single juniper that grew out of a barren rock and obscured the difference in depths between the two faces—a parallax of sorts. Through his parabolic audio device, he could hear the faint beating of drums. Having worked the area many times before, he was aware of the camouflaged entrance with the nook brilliantly disguised to be easily overlooked were it not for the faint illumina-tion outlining these subtle differences, the well-worn path leading up to this portico in the cliff, and the bits of con-struction detritus at the entrance. This would be the spot to watch; the chieftain should be arriving soon.

The winds continued their sonorous tirade as the distant sounds of drums echoed off the rock. As if on cue and with a flash of lightning to highlight his appearance, a lone figure adorned in a tan cloak with a golden sash emerged. He was momentarily lost behind a stretched trammel net and the large pile of rubble and construction debris (Westbankers were avid fishermen and skilled tradesmen). The creature's face was hidden in his shadowed veil, making his face and lips difficult to read as he efficiently scaled the path toward the nook, favoring his left as he leaned into an illuminated staff with a slight hobble.

The gecko fumbled with his audio apparatus, turning the volume up to hear what he could despite the wind. His English accent was nearly inaudible, but it was clear that the asperous voice was perturbed. "Blimey, Atwood, I swear that if your methods fail to direct me to the former leader, there'll be heck to pay. I mean we've been digging and squandering from the airport day in and day out, and for naught. Perhaps you need to put forth a bit more effort, Melvin. You—what have you done? You seem to be the one who has gotten us into this mess. And for what —revenge? You're being used. Shut your mouth; no one asked you to come! As for the imbeciles, they had better be waiting for me and standing at attention!"

Approaching the juniper and the hidden opening, the creature suddenly disappeared from view. The little gecko, whose duty was to observe and report, scampered back down his hole, knowing that the meeting had begun. He navigated the twists and turns to his destination at the top of the auditorium.

Shimmying through the portico, the cloaked figure's mannerisms became more controlled and austere, readying for his performance. He marched decisively down a series of dimly lit steps, synchronizing his footing to the loud cadence of the drum, emerging at the center of a moderately sized, circular, alabaster anteroom decorated garishly with random items, such as mismatched lighting fixtures and directional signs marked as belonging to the island's airport. Visually chaotic, the room could best be described as a refuge of sloppy workmanship with bits of caulk, stone chips, mounds of wet dirt, and muddy footprints covering the floor, and mortar and grout seeping out from the seams in the walls. While perturbed, he was never surprised, expecting nothing more from those who reside on the Westbank. And if the room's untidiness were not enough to produce disdain, the acrid, noxious smell profoundly irritated the senses. Outside, the wind and sea air kept the town's stench to a minimum, but indoors, one could grasp the full force of the malodors: the musty, repugnant odor of wet fur, stale beer, burning timber, and ash. He had a particularly sensitive sense of smell, and this rancid combination made him shudder and wretch. He thought to himself that the place needed a good cleaning and to be shellacked with Pine-Sol or any strong, antibromic. But all of this would have to wait; the boy would be landing soon, and his people would need to be in position. It was time to ready his men.

Through an illuminated stone hall where red flames glistened and danced in ornate and garish golden candelabras, an illuminated path led through a parabolic arch and into a much larger and warmer cavern. It was from here that the acrid smell wafted as silhouettes moved in time with the rhythmic tautophony of drumbeats that echoed throughout the enormous cave system. To the left, a haphazardly created, elliptical archway was their current directive, a rectangular tunnel currently cordoned off with rope and a yellow construction sign. The torches gently flickered to illuminate the tunnel as a damp, cool breeze whipped through it. Affixed to the wall, a white poster board bore the words, "Library Express" with a crudely drawn arrow pointing down the hall. Next to the poster, a fake permit had been tacked up, a declaration of unionization along with a government certificate delineating the requirement that work be conducted by companies owned by unrepresented minorities. Power cords extended from a single wall outlet down the corridor and into the darkness, past debris and construction rubble scattered about the arenaceous, roughened floor.

The figure took a moment to adjust his cloak and sash. He dusted his shoulders before dramatically thrusting his garment's hood farther down over his face. "Hum," he exhaled, then increasing his volume, he belted a solfège of "Do, Re, Mi, Fa, Sol, La, Ti," working his diaphragmatic and abdominal muscles, pleased that the resonance in the room made his voice seem larger. He cleared his throat multiple times, dusted his shoulders again, and pulled the cloak even further over his face. Readied for the show at last, the histrionic figure chose the path toward the warm and rutilant light and strode through the illuminated arch and into the large, open cavern that functioned as the Westbank's auditorium.

The drumbeats stopped instantaneously. The stench remained.

Unbeknownst to anyone at the ceremony, the gecko observed his every movement from a nook hidden in the recesses of the ceiling.

The theater was enormous. The stage's proscenium featured a sole microphone, and the curtain behind it was a ragtag amalgamation of cloth scraps. In the center of the room, a large fire pit billowed green, gold, and purple smoke and embers that rose to a distant ceiling somewhere in the darkness above. In front of the fire, in the orchestral pit, heavily muscular warthogs dressed in scant, tight, white loin cloths, their skins slick with various unguents, held drumsticks at the ready to pound on empty buckets. Around the periphery, statues, artwork, and items nicked from the island's airport and other public spaces were illuminated by the plethora of candelabras.

He shed a slight tear at the enrapturing sight. His plenary powers and her plan were coming to fruition. Before him were hundreds upon hundreds of warthog soldiers clad in Roman battle garb, others in construction gear, and some who were obese and stuffed into gaudy, striped fast-food outfits like prodigious sausages. They all stood in cramped attention at the empty stage, waiting for his speech. Order in this group was clear, denoted by sashes and position in the crowd, with the most ardent, elite, paludamentum-clad leaders in the front, the motley plebeians in the middle, and the construction and fast-food workers crammed in the back. In elevated balconies sat the female attendees, caretakers, and the young.

He was playing to a packed house. The enormous room fell silent as he entered, the only exception the crackle of the raging fire and the hiss of fervid coals. He had spent weeks on strident, rhadamanthine disciplinary tactics that were apparently paying off.

As he stood at the entrance, ready to walk onstage, many could not restrain their heightened fervor, turning in his direction and breaking ranks to get a glimpse of their leader, their exalted Messiah. The grumble of their excitement could be heard, "Oh my, its him. Look who it is. Our Messiah!" The exclamation of exaltation persisted like a wave nearing the shore, ready to break. It was mostly the fast-food workers breaking ranks; the odors wafting from their direction reeked of beer. *More discipline will be needed with this group*, he thought.

After pausing for effect, he pushed his way through the crowd as their din escalated into a susurrant murmur. He knew these heathens were in awe of his presence and revered him as a demiurge, a savior, a means to escape their forsaken life. Their obedience and gratitude were expected; he was granting them his presence, after all. As he continued forward, the crowd reverently parted, as if frightened to make contact. He methodically made his way up the steps and walked to center stage as the audience began their thunderous applause. He stood before the microphone, tapping it to confirm that it was hot.

"Saul, Saul, Saul, Saul, Saul!" The rhythmic chanting of the attendees had whipped them into a bellicose fervor as they chanted and hooted for their exalted leader, chest bumping, fist pounding, and creating an echoing racket.

Reluctant to lessen the spectacle, which he quite enjoyed, he raised his arms and illuminated staff upward, slowly letting the fervor rise to the occasion, then quickly dropped them to silence his audience, the hush only broken by the frightened cry of a startled child in a lower balcony. The child's mother shushed him, her cheeks red with embarrassment as a rumble of disdain for this outburst could be heard spreading through the crowd.

He spoke severely to the masses of his loyal followers. "Silence!" Turning to the child, he softened his tone and said, "You have nothing to fear, little one. For the rest of you, your time has come to redeem yourselves. Our time is finally here."

The crowd began screaming frenetically, "Saul, Saul, Saul!"

"Silence, please. Afford me your attention. Silence."

His voice was disciplined and authoritarian, its cadence slow and exacting. Clearly superior. Definitely British, even Shakespearean.

Facing the biddable masses, he cleared his throat before adjusting his voice to a lower octave and enunciating his words clearly, like a preacher. "I have an important task for each and every one of you. You are all special in my eyes. Others on the island may consider you to be scum, low lives, but you are mighty Westbankers! Where would they be without you? I see your value and celebrate you for it! Be on your toes; your brethren are depending on you.

"I stand before you today to confirm that history has been set in motion. Our visitor will be arriving soon, the son of the man who caused your change. At this very hour, he is on a flight bound for Tripe. The time has come to regain the honor so unfairly taken from us, to free ourselves from our prison. You have been stuck in this exile for far too long. The island is yours; no longer will you be stuck in the Westbank, looked down upon, loathed by those who think themselves to be better than you!"

Fanatical cheers erupted from the crowd.

Staring into the eyes of his audience, he precisely timed the cadence of his apodictic polemic for maximum theatrics. He was to be their savior. They were convinced.

He raised and lowered his arms again. "This weekend marks the anniversary of the day your former leader, your father, was banished and held in exile. Why else would he leave you? Your status was unfairly demoted. You were once rulers, and you've devolved to pigs not worth a mere farthing! Our kind once flourished on this island, took what we wanted. We had RESPECT. You're now banished to this west bank, a godforsaken desert, begging for scraps and eking out a meager existence with lower wages and more work than the rest of the islanders. Where would they be without each and every one of you? Do you have a pension? When was the last time you had a paid vacation? What succor have you? I'll tell you: zero! Never since the day of The Change. Our lives began to end the day we became silent about the things that matter. I'll be your brains, your guide, your shining light, and we *will* forge our way back into the annals of power." Foam spewed from his cloaked mouth as his fervor whipped the audience into a frenzy.

Gaining some composure, he said, "It is our time to step into the spotlight. We will ravage the inhabitants of this island to obtain our goals, if necessary. Keep those East-bankers in holding if need be. Torture them for information. Feed them some of your vilest foodstuffs and drink. With the boy in our pocket, we will procure the location of your once-exalted leader, and he, he, he . . ." his voice peaked, "he will lead us all back to salvation! We'll do whatever it takes—for our kin! We will rise back into the power we deserve!

"When I stepped into the room next door, it was immediately evident that our demolition crew has made great headway over the past week. We are close to our goal. In order to achieve our goal, the Ancient Collection must be located. The Library Express is nearing completion."

The masses began clapping and chanting their affirmations again. "Saul, Saul, Saul, Saul!"

The cloaked figure quieted his audience. "None of you know the true history of how Beau Champs and Merl Linstein brought reproach upon your families. Those two are mine! I want them. How did they punish us? I'll tell you: through deception, trickery, and greed. Beau's son will be on the island soon enough. We will capture him and use him to achieve our lofty goals. His father will have to negotiate with us to secure his release." He slowed his cadence to a more exacting and cajoling tone. "But you are all so big and strong. You could easily tear most things apart. Will you?"

A resounding "Yeah!" echoed through the auditorium.

"No, you will not! I need him captured alive. You cannot and will not kill him. We need him alive. Look at me. I want you all to look at me and listen. WE NEED HIM ALIVE. Understand? When we have what we need, you can use him as you will. When his plane arrives, he will be held for me. You know your roles, and I expect you to stick to the plan. It all begins with the fast-food workers in the airport concourse, so be ready. No more beer from this point on!" A grumble was heard from the rear of the crowd. "The boy's father will undoubtedly follow and meet his fate. He could use a good bruising!"

The crowd again began whooping and hollering.

"Shush! Many of you have witnessed the power of magic given to me by our ancient ancestors. The gathering storm is nothing more than a glimpse of what is in store. Once the child and his key are in our control, there is nothing that can stop us from regaining our power. Every last one of you will be held accountable for our success, just as every last one of you will reap the rewards we will gain."

He nodded to the drummers as a rhythmic procession grew in parallel to the crowd's swelling emotion.

"It is time to strike out and fulfill the duties I have en-trusted in you. If you should fail, consider your status as Westbankers forever unchanged. Today is our day of reckoning, our chance to reverse The Change. Today is our day of destiny!"

In his mindless excitement, one of the warthogs clad in a hard hat and tool belt blurted, "Show us your magic, boss!"

"My most trusted followers, come with me." With a swoop of his robes, he exited the stage behind the curtain, followed by the hustle of the obsequious front-row sycophants and a few drummers. The drumbeats intensified as the crowd roared.

The gecko scampered back into his depression, back to the jobsite to report his findings. He had seen enough. All was going according to plan.

Saul, along with approximately a dozen of his most devout disciples and a smattering of drummers, moved outside to the top of a barren cliff, the rough, phosphorescent sea below. The day was growing darker, the tempest nearing.

In a melodramatic scene, the cloaked figure raised his arms outward and upward as the wind howled and smoke billowed around him. His cloak blew as a gust whipped past, adding to the overall eeriness of the ceremony. In his left hand was his staff, a wooden contrivance with a gilded head and glowing jade stones. He raised it above his head, as if commanding the heavens.

Clouds passed rapidly overhead and brief rays of light broke through the murk. Distant lightning strikes added to the surreal feeling.

As the wind howled, a few of the larger warthogs walked slowly forward, protecting their sacerdotal leader in a semicircle, blanketing him from the elements. The drumming continued.

He screamed to the heavens above. "From the ancient verses! Iko iko wan dey. Jock-a-mo fi no wan an dey. Jock-a-mo fi na ney."

The watching followers rocked back and forth in time with the drumbeat.

"Jock-a-mo fi no wan an dey. Jock-a-mo fi na ney. May the heavens open and the rain fall."

The drummers genuflected in approbation of their leader. Gradually, in succession, they began their requiem, "Jock-a-mo fi no wan an dey. Jock-a-mo fi na ney. Jock-a-mo fi no wan an dey. Jock-a-mo fi na ney."

The surf pounded below. The winds whipped and whistled above. The smell of fresh rain cut through the saltiness in the air. Lightning blazed across the sky.

"It is time to execute our plan. I will be with you, watching you. In heart and spirit."

Instantly, the enigmatic creature vanished in a puff of smoke.

# CHAPTER 6

## RUN

*Friday, October 27, 2017*

Flight 411, a large red-and-white 737 aircraft, was making its final descent onto the Island of Tripe at 9:30 in the morning. Jason had been traveling for no less than fourteen hours and was more than a bit fatigued. The flight had been rough, encountering turbulence over the Rockies and again as they made the long trek west over the Pacific Ocean. Two movies, two in-flight meals, and countless sodas made Jason feel desperate for a bit of exercise. He could use a good run or at least to stretch his legs. His teeth felt shaggy; a good toothbrushing and a towel bath would go a long way toward making him feel human again.

Reflecting on the events of the past day, he realized that his departure may have been—no, definitely was—a bit hasty. Perhaps he shouldn't have been so headstrong, perhaps he should have waited to discuss the situation with his father; perhaps he should have remained at home. Not an impetuous person by nature and generally obsequiously respectful toward his father, he was not quite sure what had gotten into him, why his mind seemed ready to run. Alfred would demand a reasonable explanation, which he rightly deserved, but no rational reason could be furnished. Jason's mind was confused and cloudy, and his stomach was in knots. The fact that he had run off on an adventure left him flabbergasted.

Still, questions abounded. Was Alfred really his father? Was the woman on his television really his mother? His father never talked much about her. Surely the voice of reason would suggest trusting the man he called Dad for as long as he could remember. The baloney about time travel had to be just that—baloney, an overzealous imagination wanting for adventure. But the tickets, the money?

The intercom chimed, followed by the overhead voice of the captain. "Ladies and gentlemen, in a few minutes, we will begin to prepare the cabin for some turbulence. It looks like we'll make it in ahead of the storm, but the descent will be bumpy. The seatbelt sign will remain illuminated and I'd like to ask you to remain in your seats with your seatbelts fastened. Flight attendants, please stow your service items. Thank you."

Jason was not keen on flying and had already felt nervous about crossing an ocean. The announcement made his stomach churn. It seemed quite odd that none of the airport attendants had mentioned a storm. Surely the FAA would not have let the flight take off if there was bad weather, but what did he know? He focused on the television screen fitted into the leather seatback in front of him as he made sure his tray table was stowed and his seat was upright. The massive thunderheads could be seen through the windows, lightning flashing amidst the mountains of clouds. There was nothing good to watch on TV; every last program on the entertainment system was a rerun.

Adjusting his blanket and twisting the knob above, a stream of cool air blew across his face. Nervously, he tested the strap across his waist; his seatbelt was secure. A lump rose in his throat and butterflies flitted in his stomach as he tried to close his eyes and ignore the increasing turbulence.

"Please, just let me fall asleep. If I live through this, I promise to never ever run like this again." He repeated this mantra as his sight became wavy like he was falling into a cheesy television dream. *My living room sofa would be more comfortable*, he thought. *Think happy thoughts and take a deep breath.*

Just as he was dozing off, he felt a tap on his shoulder.

"Excuse me. Would you like a refill, Mr. Dix? More soda before we land? I think you'll develop a taste for our famous island soda," the smiling, arthritic stewardess said as she filled his cup.

*She is not very comforting.* He took a big gulp and then mercifully dozed off.

"How long was I asleep?" Jason asked the stewardess who was again tapping him on the shoulder. "Sure, I'll have another cola. What is it now, number thirteen? Am I going for a new record?" Jason mumbled in a sleepy stupor.

The cabin was getting weirder by the minute. Who was the obnoxious woman in the seat behind him dressed in a 1950s floral dress with an exposed, pink petticoat? She snorted and turned in her sleep.

"Drink up, Jason. Drink up. There's plenty more where that came from."

"Thank you, ma'am." She finished pouring the Tripe Wake Up cola and added a swizzle stick and cherry to garnish the mix. Jason guzzled down the cola in one large gulp.

Right across the aisle, a wrinkly old man with a tattooed neck was gnawing on his thick, almost claw-like fingernails. *Is he serious? How disgusting.*

The buxom, heavy-set lady two rows behind Jason with bright red hair was playing Sudoku. She kept tapping her pencil on the armrest and looked in Jason's direction. *Aggravating.*

No other kids in first class.

Feeling woozy, he dozed off again.

Jason awoke at the start of the descent, finally feeling more rested. He raised his chair to an inclined position and gathered his faculties. It took time to get reoriented, yawning and stretching, readying his body for arrival. His stomach was upset—too much soda. As much as the stewardess pushed that Tripe cola, you would think she was being paid by a dentist.

Powering on his cell phone, he connected to the in-flight Wi-Fi and his device began to chirp and ping.

Nothing like an irate father. *Gulp.*

As he read the messages, Jason wondered what in the hell he had done. His father was stuck in traffic, so despite his best efforts, he had missed Jason's flight. Upon arriving at the airport, he had purchased another ticket for the next flight to the island, but he had a connection at LAX, which would delay his arrival. As explained by an explicit text message, his instructions were as follows:

1. The person you spoke to was lying. I am not sure who she was (I have my suspicions), but she is not to be trusted and I can absolutely guarantee that the woman on

television who tricked you is not your mother. You are being gravely deceived. I will fill you in when we are face-to-face. There is quite a bit more to this story than you know.

2. I want you to look for the COMPETENT ADULT that I will have waiting for you at the airport. Listen to him! Until I am by your side, he has been granted an immediate and irrevocable tutelary responsibility. His name is Art. You can't miss him. He's an old friend and right now, he's very ugly—really! The password is Topo Chico (you left the top on the counter).

3. Do not speak with strangers (except Art).

4. Cogitate on what you have done wrong. You will have plenty of time to think about it, because when we get home, you are grounded. Under no circumstances are you to leave the airport property!

5. We will leave as soon as I get there. DO NOT LEAVE THE AIRPORT.

6. Most importantly, DO NOT ACCEPT FOOD OR DRINKS FROM STRANGERS, NO ONE OTHER THAN ART! Wait for him if he is late!

7. And last, DO NOT LOSE YOUR KEY!

Wi-Fi service was lost as the plane entered a series of turbulent clouds. Jason powered off his phone and hand-

153

ed his cup to the stewardess as she collected the last of the rubbish, her cart rattling into the galley. The turbulence was nauseating and the thunder was only increasing. The weather quickly grew grimmer, and the plane banked hard in its speedy descent. A loud boom rattled the cabin from some unseen location in the gathering storm. The ailerons adjusted the angle of the plane's descent, and suddenly, they broke through the lowest layer of clouds. The emerald-green, lush forest with jagged peaks and rocky terrain rose high up through the jungle flora. It was breathtaking.

Out of the corner of his eye, Jason spotted a glimpse of what looked like the tail of a gecko lizard heading into the overhead bin across the aisle. Turning to look, nothing seemed to be out of the ordinary. His fitful sleep and anxiety about his dad must be playing tricks on his mind. Jason gripped his armrest, eager to land.

*Saturday, October 28, 1972*

A green haze illuminated the cabin as the aircraft continued its approach to the runway. The interior of the plane seemed to take on a slightly different appearance, and even the sounds of the engine changed pitch. Through the porthole windows of the aircraft, the earth grew larger and waterfalls could be seen spewing forth from within rocky faces, descending into a mist toward the valley below. When the plane banked left, Jason could see a thin haze shrouding the valley as the water displayed an incredible, almost magical array of colors. Terracotta rooftops could be seen among the shimmering greenery. At long last, the flight was nearing its end.

The plane leveled, the wheels emerged from the fuselage, and with a final turn, the plane met the rising earth. The aircraft touched down rather softly, violently reversed its thrusters to slow its speed, and expeditiously made its way across the cracked cement taxiways to the terminal. With a British accent, the copilot introduced himself over the crackly intercom, thanked the passengers for flying Tripe Airlines, and then gave the local time and weather conditions, which included impending rainfall due to a developing low-pressure squall. A complete lack of other aircrafts parked at the terminal told Jason that Flight 411 was the sole arriving aircraft.

Through the window, Jason watched as a less-than-graceful, hunter-orange-clad ground crew member semaphorically directed the plane to its final positioning at Gate 4B before a gantry began closing in on the cabin door. Was it his imagination, or was the ground crew really, really ugly? The copilot made it clear that they had arrived ahead of the storm, then brought the plane to an abrupt stop. Jason stayed put, knowing that he would have to wait for his luggage and then seek out the adult sent by his father and wait. He'd have a good shellacking within the next twenty-four hours. There was no need to rush.

The moment the debarkation light dinged, the cabin roused to life. The elderly, arthritic stewardess became increasingly nimble and helped Jason get his baggage down from the overhead bin, moving on to help someone else, lifting nearly double her weight in baggage. Noticing Jason gawking, she said, "Don't you just love the island climate? It works wonders for one's joints. Have a good time, Jason."

"Thank you, ma'am."

"We appreciate your choice to fly Tripe Airlines. Have a great day! I hear the concourse has loads of great treats." She winked surreptitiously and then ducked into the forward galley.

Surveying the cabin for any loose items, Jason caught a glimpse of something odd. It was *so* odd, in fact, that he found himself knocking and shaking his head as if to rattle his senses. *Ah, yes, a long flight, too much caffeine, and not enough sleep.* Across the aisle in seat 4F, a striking and familiar woman was gathering her belongings. She looked to be in her early thirties, had amazing blue eyes and blonde hair, wore an aqua, western-style summer dress, western boots, and had the same serpent tattoo down her left arm as the taxi driver and airport attendant. She held a gold pocket watch and was checking the time. If one could dream up a stereotypical rock star, she would be it. Oddly, she sort of looked like the woman from his living room television encounter and vaguely like Miss Somerall.

*Should I introduce myself? No, you fool, keep quiet.* She was so gorgeous that he couldn't take his eyes off her. The tattoo was nothing unusual in this day and age, but he thought he got a brief glimpse of a tail, like a reptile, as it tucked itself under her dress. Had tattoo parlors begun placing prosthetic vestiges? Ear hoops, tongue rings, sure, but tails? Maybe more sleep was needed. Embarrassingly, she caught Jason staring at her rear. He had no decent explanation to offer. A tail? Perhaps he had merely seen her designer bag. Could the sunlight coming through the cabin window have produced an optical illusion? After all, this was first class.

Jason chanced a glimpse at her derriere, where the tail popped out from under her dress as if to say, "We've finally made it, thank goodness!" before tucking itself back under her dress. She caught his gaze and smiled before reaching to gather the last of her belongings from the overhead bin. Jason looked away, mortified.

Wow, she really had a tail like a reptile! His logical side knew the notion was preposterous, but he knew what he saw. Daring to steal one last look as she disembarked, he saw that she had an aqua, western-style dress and cowboy boots—but no tail.

*Oh well. The flight must have done a number on me*, he thought. His stomach remained a bit uneasy; perhaps it was due to jet lag, but a more likely culprit was the cola. Something to eat would sooth his trembling stomach and perhaps straighten his thoughts. If he was seeing tails on beautiful women, he must need sleep. The cabin suddenly became a bit musty, and he felt a bit claustrophobic as he waited for his turn to deplane.

"Thank you for flying with us, Mr. Dix," the captain said as Jason debarked. Oddly, his name tag read like something he'd see in a scientific textbook; his official Tripe Airlines badge said, "Gymnogyps californianus."

The stewardess popped out as he deplaned. "Mr. Dix, if you're hungry, I hear that the concourse ice cream is the best on the island. I just thought I heard your stomach rumbling."

"Thank you, ma'am." He walked through the gantry, past the check-in podium, and took a right toward the baggage claim. Under the plaque with an image of a suitcase with an arrow to the baggage carousels, a chrome sign was posted that read: "Due to recent thievery of airport belongings, this area may be monitored or recorded." *That's surprising. There's even crime here on this remote island.*

As airports go, the place had a retro but still hip, neoteric vibe. It was spotless and smelled of Pine-Sol, and aside from a few lighting fixtures that were missing from the

158

walls, the terminal was well cared for. An old departures/ arrivals sign sat beside a large, stone statue of a head with an associated descriptive placard: La Venta, one of many archaeological relics scattered about, none of which piqued Jason's attention. No other planes seemed to be boarding or debarking.

*I need to retrieve my luggage, but not before I settle my stomach. So I guess ice cream it is, then. Where oh where can I find some ice cream?*

Jason powered on his phone and attempted to call his father, but he had no cellular service and the phone's battery was at less than five percent. *I'll just have to man up and take my punishment. Jason, Jason, Jason. How do you get so carried away with your crazy ideas?* There would be no respite from his father's fury; he was sure to be punished for the remainder of the school year. The pit in his stomach was growing. He couldn't help but wonder where Zach was at the moment—probably crammed into the back seat of the station wagon somewhere between New Orleans and San Antonio, carsick as always. And Bobby? Jason could only guess. He hoped he wasn't stuck at his camp if the hurricane hit New Orleans; his father was just nuts enough to try to weather the storm.

As the lady from 4F passed on her way to baggage claim, her presumed tail ruffled under her dress. Jason focused, trying to examine her curves to ascertain if any of her accoutrements looked taillike, but she only carried a multi-

159

colored canvas knapsack with a PETA slogan: "Animals are not ours to eat."

A vegan rock star, maybe even hipper than Ms. Somerall.

Food vendors were scant and scattered sparingly along the concourse. Jason remembered his father's instructions, but he was truly in need of sustenance. Without many options, he chose the refreshment counter that was decorated with a large ice cream cone. What harm could a little ice cream do? Perhaps food would provide a momentary reprieve from his qualms.

"That's odd," Jason said as he stared at a framed poster that featured an illustration of a darkened portico with two crossed, golden keys and the words, "You are in the right place." He thought back to his conversation with the woman on television and realized that he'd seen the same key illustration on his home's elevator button and the school's, too.

*Is that the same illustration? The obscure so brazenly framed in color on the wall? I thought this was a secret.*

Jason shook the confusion away and approached the kiosk that was decorated with an ice cream cone and a sign that read, "Ice Cream, You Scream, We All Scream for Ice Cream." At the register stood a six-foot-tall, gargantuan individual with atavistic facial characteristics remarkably like a warthog. He lumbered beside his colorful ice cream cart, wearing an orange-and-red, vertically striped shirt and pant ensemble, unkempt, with adipose tissue and coarse hair screaming to pop his buttons. The cart was not unlike the ice cream or Lucky Dog carts back home.

Jason neared the vendor. He thought he could smell the odor of beer. "This shop looks like some of the vendors back home." *Must be a chain*, he thought, *but gosh, the vendor could win the ugly award.*

"Where's home, young man?"

"New Orleans, sir. In the United States."

"Well, today is your lucky day, Mr. USA. We have some of the best ice cream on the Island of Tripe, brought to you by one of the island's world-famous creameries. Can I interest you in a scoop or two? Always fresh and always delicious, at least that's the company's motto, anyway. We take US dollars, by the way." The vendor awkwardly moved the napkins around on an adjacent counter, feigning busyness and seemingly a bit nervous. Jason thought that a plug-in air freshener would do wonders for his profitability.

The lady from 4F stepped onto the escalator and descended out of view, winking at Jason when she turned.

"I have a bit of a queasy stomach. Flew all night. Perhaps something plain?" Peeking down the concourse, he weighed his options. "Yes, I would definitely prefer something plain."

The hoard of passengers who had been stuck behind Jason in coach were debarking and now marching toward baggage claim. Jason hadn't thought about it earlier, but it seemed odd that no children were on his flight, and even more surprisingly, one of the passengers looked astonishingly like Mr. Winwood.

The vendor opened the retractable, stainless lid to reveal an array of delicious colors. "Well, we have vanilla, rocky road—my favorite—chocolate, double chocolate, and strawberry. If you don't see anything you like, we have many more flavors in the cooler in the back. Perhaps a gelato or sorbet? Psst . . ." he whispered, cupping his mouth, "we also have Topo Chico." The cup sizes and cost were taped to the front of the cart.

"Just vanilla, sir, a medium cup, please. Is your name . . ."

"Name's Bill. Sprinkles? Regular, waffle cone, or cup?"

"Bill, you say? Are you sure? Cup, please."

Another vendor with the same atavistic look worked at the pretzel counter across the way. The pretzel peddler, better described as a beast, was staring intently in their direction. *The whole family must work here. Ugly bunch.*

"Can you tell me your name again, sir?"

"I'm sure you'll love our ice cream. Umm, it's Bill. One medium vanilla cup coming up. By the way, did you say where you were from?" His nervousness was increasingly evident as he clumsily fumbled and mishandled the cup and scoop. "Sorry, I've got a bit of a tremor. Take propranolol, you know," he said, laughing. "No worries, one scoop on its way."

Bill dipped the ice cream scoop in water before scooping a large dollop out of the bin, plopping it into a cup as the last of the passengers passed by. Otherwise, the concourse was silent.

Jason's intuition told him that something was off. *Did I hear him incorrectly? Topo Chico was the password, but he's not Art. Just wait for the price. Just wait for the price.* The preoccupied vendor was seemingly trying to lure him, but why? *How dare he? Well, I'm not going to take the bait.*

"Wouldn't want to drop the cup," gesticulated the maladroit Bill, thrusting his arms up in a bunglesome, toast-like fashion. "That'll be five American doll . . ." The cup of ice cream flew out of Bill's hands and careened over Jason's head.

163

"Nice, Bill. You ever play football?"

"Well, that was the last of the vanilla. How about helping me lift a new tub of vanilla from the cooler?"

"Are you serious? Look, there's plenty left in the bin. What do you mean you're out?"

Jason felt heated breath on the nape of his neck. Turning, he dropped his knapsack onto the floor to confront the pretzel vendor, who was now standing directly behind him, the feel and repugnance of his warm, malodorous, beer breath a bit too close for comfort. Jason could see the last of the passengers descending the escalator, emptying the concourse. The three were alone.

Immediately, the pretzel vendor pounced on him with open arms, hollering, "Topo Chico!" He swept Jason up in a bear hug, lifting him off the ground.

"Help! Quit it, you freak!" Jason fought back with all his might, furiously kicking and writhing. "Pervert! Put me down. I said, put me down!"

The vendor held fast, leaning back to steady himself and his catch. "Topo Chico, Topo Chico," he repeated, trying to subdue the child.

"Put him in the container, Larry," Bill said while opening the lid to the ice cream cart.

"I thought you weren't supposed to use my name?"

"Help! Put me down! I'm being abducted!"

"Larry, on the count of three, let's stuff him in."

Kicking the massive brute in the shins, Jason caused a sudden change in his grip that allowed him to grab hold of Larry's muscular, hairy forearm and bite down as hard as he could. Somewhere nearby, the flash of a camera went off, but Jason was too preoccupied to notice.

"Aaargh!" wailed Larry as Bill tried to grab Jason's legs.

Not relenting on the writing and kicking, Jason was now truly in need of a good toothbrushing to get the acrid taste of fur out of his mouth.

"Dad!" Jason screamed. He knew that his dad was still thousands of miles away, but he hoped to make enough of a fuss to solicit some help. "Aah! Help!"

At last, Jason was able to squirm and twist out of the melee. Falling to the floor, he rolled between his assailant's legs, grabbed his knapsack, punched the pretzel vendor in the groin, and sprinted through the concourse toward baggage claim.

"I learned my lesson, Dad! I'll never accept food from strangers," Jason blurted as he ran fast and hard. The two attackers initially followed in pursuit, Larry grabbing his crotch in agony, but after only a few paces, Bill pulled a walkie-talkie from his pocket, huffing and puffing, out of shape and out of breath.

Jason sprinted as fast as his legs could muster and made a ninety-degree turn to bolt down the glass and chrome escalator, taking two steps at a time.

Clearing the bottom of the escalator, he dropped to a crouched position, embosked behind a white planter densely packed with philodendrons. Other than the verdant burst of color, the room was otherwise shockingly white. White floor tiles were separated by white caulk, and the alabaster-white walls were free from any designs or hangings. It was clean, cold, and empty. Two white, metal doors behind him led to baggage claim. He waited silently, not wanting to pass through the doors in the event that the brute above had called friends or security over the walkie-talkie. As he was a stranger in this land, he surmised that the vendors' account of events would supersede that of a traveler, and a minor, at that.

He listened. No one seemed to be in chase. The only sound he could hear was the escalator's whir and his own thundering heartbeat.

He waited a few minutes before peering slowly over the top edge of the planter. Through his shrubberied camouflage, he saw no one suspicious, no one searching for him. His heart raced as he remained hypervigilant, eyes scanning every which way. The resonance and poor acoustic quality of the room seemed to amplify his rapid heartbeat; his senses were on edge. He silently slid the knapsack onto his back in the event that he would have to run fast. His stomach rumbled, the run no good for his queasiness; his upset stomach had become increasingly disturbed as the pungent smell of cleaning agents in the air amplified his nausea. He just prayed that his ailment would not be accompanied by diarrhea. He would be cornered in the men's room.

And so, not knowing if he was still being pursued, Jason waited. And waited. And then continued to wait a bit longer before deciding to move on. No one approached from above, no one gave chase, and the doors to his rear remained closed. He was prepared for an ambuscade, doubtful that the two upstairs had simply given up, particularly after the groin kick.

His only real option was to exit through the metal doors toward baggage claim. The airport's temperature had been cool, but he could feel the warm, humid air emanating from under the doors. The smell was different and had a musty quality. *Hopefully, baggage claim will lead outside, where I would have space to run if I had to. I need to follow Dad's instructions and find this Art guy.*

As he was about to stand, the clankety-clank and swoosh of a janitor's keys, dustpan, and broom announced the presence of someone approaching from the concourse above. Jason remained in a crouch as music began playing over the airport's PA system. The clanking sounds of the keys were coming closer, yet no one could be seen.

*Jason, you idiot. What have I gotten myself into? Where the heck am I? Am I dreaming? Is this a dream? Please tell me this is a dream. Please tell me this is a dream.* He pinched himself, only to feel the ensuing pain. It was definitely not a dream.

A silhouette appeared on the wall above the escalator threshold, growing larger as the rattling grew nearer. Finally, a creature's face appeared, followed by his torso and pelvis, the surprise so unexpected that Jason dropped to his knees, nearly unable to grasp the gravity of the moment without fainting. It was a man-lizard! Jason fought to catch his breath, shrinking even further behind the planter. "What the heck?" Dressed in a khaki uniform with a large ring of keys coupled to a belt loop, the anthropoid reptile vaguely resembled his school principal and fledgling janitor.

*Silent as a mouse. Silent as a mouse. I must be going crazy. Maybe I'm ill. Could it be food poisoning? I've heard of crazier things happening. But a janitor? A lizard janitor? This cannot be.*

The lizard man swept and cleaned the escalator vestibule as Jason perched on all fours and peered around the side of the planter.

*Could it be? The song that was played at my birthday party?* The lizard was whistling the tune for "Cielito Lindo" interposed with intermittent singing.

"De la Sierra Morena, cielito lindo, vienen bajando, un par de ojitos negros, cielito lindo, de contraband." The creature sang happily while working, seemingly unaware of Jason's presence.

Listening more closely, Jason discovered that it was the same song that was faintly playing over the PA system.

"Cielito Lindo" ended and "Guantanamera" began as the janitor lizard began to wail, throwing his arms to the sky like a crazed, charlatan, vagabond evangelist.

Jason inched backward, sweat beading on his forehead, not taking his eyes off the janitor. *Quiet, Jason. This day has been weird, every last minute. Maybe you're ill. Meningitis? That's it. You must be on the sofa at home having contracted meningitis. How do I call 911? What the heck is wrong with me?* He pinched himself. *Ouch! Please wake up. Please, just wake up on the sofa.* Moving as quietly as possible, not quite sure what he was seeing or if any of it was real, he tucked himself into the corner, between the wall and the planter. Beads of perspiration were now running down his temples.

It was time to find a well-ventilated place to sit and rest out of the confounded airport. If he could find a hospital or doctor's office, surely they wouldn't turn him away. Perhaps the pungent cleaning agents were making him hallucinate, but that wouldn't explain the plane, the vendors, or the tail. He just kept assuring himself that his dad was on the way, that he would find him, and that everything would be OK. *Dad, where are you when I need you most?*

Unfortunately, the two heavy, metal doors, equipped with pewter levers stood between Jason and baggage claim, and they were formidably closed. *I will make a lot of noise if I try to get through those doors.* Beyond the door, Jason could hear the muted din of a busy place.

*Great. He's going to hear me open them. Why would the airport not leave them open? Who will be waiting on the other side of the doors? A thousand ice cream vendors? What if the janitor is a decoy and they're coming in behind me?*

With a slight limp, the lizard man was defying gravity by walking up one of the walls. Sweeping in a nonchalant fashion, he whistled, twirled, and mouthed along to the song, pantomiming in sync with the music, dancing a traditional Mexican dance.

As sweat poured from his forehead, Jason's dizziness was threatening to overtake him. His shirt was sticky and his heartbeat resounded rapidly in his ears as his stomach churned, twisting and upset. He fought the urge to vomit.

It was time to act. Not knowing if the creature walking up the wall was friend or foe, Jason kept quiet. After his run-in with the vendors upstairs, he wasn't willing to take the chance. It was best to remain inconspicuous. *Jason, it's time to find Art. He should be waiting for you. I bet he's just through those doors, waiting in baggage claim.*

Certain that an ambuscade was eminent (the vendors had to show up sooner or later), Jason inched toward the large doors. Choosing the right door, he slowly attempted to turn the lever clockwise. No movement. He turned it counterclockwise, and although a minute clink could be heard, again, no movement. The janitor turned his head briefly and Jason froze, trying to blend in with the wall as he held his breath and waited for the lizard man to go back to his task.

*Who the heck locks the doors in the middle of the day?*

Crawling to the next handle, he turned the handle about ten degrees before meeting similar resistance. He was growing irate and he'd had enough. He mumbled, "To heck with this!" and thrust all of his weight downward onto the lever. The latch sounded and gave way in a defining CLANK.

The janitor whipped his head around, and within half a second, he was at the top of the escalator, his visage con-torted like some crazed, distempered beast. His body looked poised to jump to the bottom.

"Silence! Strike three!"

Jason heaved open the door with all his might and ran over the threshold, the heavy metal door slamming loudly behind him.

*Gulp.*

He was not prepared for what he saw. It was so quiet that he could've heard a pin drop. It felt like a million eyes were upon him.

*Oh my, how did I get into this mess?*

Around the baggage carousel stood, crouched, fluttered, and crawled at least a hundred creatures, some human-like, some reptilian, others insect, bipeds, quadrupeds, heck, even octopeds. They were everywhere—at the help desk, the counter for the car rental company, and outside, hailing taxis. They were all staring intently at the interloper, and suddenly, Jason felt like dinner—their dinner. Every creature had stopped and turned to face him as he entered the room, like the abrupt screech of a record being jolted. What was once a cacophony of mottled sound and noisome smell was instantaneously silenced; the smell remained.

The woman from 4F stood next to a turnstile with her luggage, her tail in full view. Next to her was a figure that looked like a mosquito with a black-and-white striped pattern, bright red lips, and a proboscis that looked long and sharp. Its compound eyes were staring directly at Jason. "Hi there. My name is Aedes albopictus. Don't worry, I'm not bloodthirsty . . . yet."

Not really knowing what to do, Jason put up both hands and took a step backward. "I mean you no harm," he said, hoping they spoke English.

The mellow sound of "Girl from Ipanema" (the Portuguese version) played on the overhead PA.

"I can't imagine what language you all speak. I'm just a kid. This is all just a big mistake."

The masses seemed to take a collective step forward. A greasy, brown nutria with a high-pitched voice and severe strabismus stepped up to Jason, ardently tapping an index finger or claw on his leg whilst vehemently scolding, "Your father did this to us. You should be ashamed! Karma is a tough pill to swallow."

As if the situation were not harrowing enough, the muted silence was shattered as the metal doors behind him burst open. A dozen or more warthogs, all clad in food-service garb, came pouring through the doorway.

"GET HIM! He bit me, that animal!" the pretzel vendor growled. "Call security! It was a groin kick!"

"This is insane! You're all insane!" Despite the orders from his father, Jason couldn't cope with the madness and needed to get away. He took off in a sprint, past the luggage cart machine, pushing another cart out of his path in haste, sending it crashing into the adjacent kiosk. A sliding glass door opened and he dashed outside. *So much for remaining inside the airport*, he thought. He needed space to run.

"What was up with that guy?" asked a baritone, multi-colored, teenage reptile in a plaid suit waiting for his luggage.

"I'm not sure. I just wanted to shake his hand," stridulated a thin insect who had his hand out in Jason's direction.

"I think he forgot his luggage," barked a pug who was dressed as a baggage handler.

Jason's floral suitcase was lonesomely circling the turnstile.

Jason ran through the glass doors and into the fresh air. The skies were an ominous gray as the storm approached the island.

"Leave me alone! You monsters! Art! I am supposed to find Art! Someone call Art!"

Passing the line of taxis, he ran out to the cement median before coming to a halt. The smell of exhaust, rubber, avgas, gasoline, and motor oil exacerbated his growing nausea. A never-ending line of honking taxis moved like Newton's cradle: stop, go, stop, go. Newspaper vendors were shouting. Traffic policemen with faces like German Shepherds were directing traffic as their shrill whistles coupled with the rumble of distant thunder to escalate the confusion. With all the hustle and bustle, his senses were overwhelmed. He waited for some sort of Fraser spiral illusion to appear and whisk him out of an incredible dream. If only he could click his heels together to get home like Dorothy in *The Wizard of Oz*. He pinched himself again. *This is not a dream. This is not a dream. What do I do now?*

Not knowing where to go, who to meet, who was safe, or where to wait for his father, he decided that hiding was his best option. First, he needed to get away from the airport. His experience at baggage claim had freaked him out too much. He needed fresh air, and maybe a place to doze off, if he could get his adrenaline to subside. He just needed to keep moving, and from the air, it looked like there might be good places to hide in the jungle. Sprinting across the taxi lane, he dashed toward the main thoroughfare.

A taxi's brakes screeched as it nearly struck him when he darted into the street. A newspaper scuttled down the street on a strong gust of wind. A frog-like cabbie stuck his head out of the window to yell, "Watch where you're going! You want to get killed or something?" He stopped his cab abruptly, canted his head side to side and then caught an insect with his long, lightning-quick tongue.

# CHAPTER 7

## INDIGENOUS CREATURES

*Saturday, October 28, 1972*

Nestled within a verdant glade near Tripe's Grand Cavas Cenote, disguised and well hidden among groves of rainbow eucalyptus trees, monticules replete with thick, golden grasses, and fecund flora, was an odd and colorful stump. Atop this particular stump, perhaps the largest in the glade, a small, white, furry moth-human waited patiently for a haircut, eager for a fabulous new coiffure.

"C'mon, An. We need to get going with the cut. You have places to be this morning, remember? Today is your big day; this is huge! Lacey is bound to be up soon, and she'll be on to you. She said . . ."

"I know, Mo. If you're on time, you're five minutes late." An's voice ascended from somewhere below inside the stump. "Your cut won't take me long."

The glade was south of the main township in a rather secluded area off Lowerline Street. It was known by many of the inhabitants as both a home and place of business, as announced with a sign nailed above a hollow, "An's Hair and Weave." To those who knew him personally, they knew the proprietor's registered entity to be "Anura Pelodryadidae Litoria Thesaurensis's Hair and Weave," but that was a bit too long for a hairdresser's signage.

The stump and entire business aesthetic were tacky by most conventional standards and looked like a gaudy, neoclassical Italian painting, like *Dogs Playing Poker*, adorned with golden rope, artificial turf, purple venation, and a hodgepodge of curated refuse, including decrepit marble columns and a sticker on the floor that read, "No Taxonomy without Representation." In the center of the stump sat a single white, metal lawn chair with a red umbrella and cupholder attached. Waiting in the cupholder was an iced drink, frothy and beautiful, that held an identical but smaller decorative umbrella, both umbrellas twisting in the occasional gust of wind. Panoramic speakers disguised as rocks wafted the sweet sounds of an early version of Alessandro Alessandroni's "Montmartre" through the air. The moth indecisively flipped through a magazine, examining hair styles in the modish pages of *Hair and Weave: A Men's Magazine*, a publication with minimal circulation at best.

This was An's place, a green-spotted reptilian-human, who was only six inches tall. He climbed onto the top of his gaudily ornamented stump with his forelimbs gesticulating his every thought, mumbling to himself in a heavy

Italian accent in mostly incomprehensible jargon that illustrated the nuances of the island's language and variable lexicon.

"Coming, coming! Sorry, Mo, I'm just glad you get to see me today. Move it here, move it there. Put it back. And on and on and on and on and on. What's the world devolving into? That's a joke, Mo. You can laugh. C'-mon, today is going to be a great day!"

"I suppose Lacey put you to work?"

"Yes! 'Help me out a bit with decorating.' She says it so cute, you know. Redecorating. Re-redecorating. Re-re-redecorating. She gets a new mirror and what do I do? I hang it on every wall in the house. Upside down, sideways. You know how women can be. She's just like the mirror. Look at me, look at you. Move this, move that. But Mo, never fear . . ."

"I'm not rushing you."

"We have loads of time. You're gonna look good, no, *great*! You are going to look great after this cut today. I'm tellin' ya, the ladies are gonna love it."

There were other stumps scattered throughout the glade, but none were quite as grand; at least none had the same degree of pizzazz or joie de vivre as An's establishment. If one were to examine his mien from any distance, it would be instantly obvious what a happy lizard he was, smiling ear to ear as this was a special day to him. This odd, grinning reptile was festooned in a golden mantlet, white boxer shorts pulled over his corpulent umbilicus, and a worn pair of brown cowboy boots that were desperately in need of polish. The notability of this particular day was such that he had defied his normative schedule of improper punctuality, had risen early, eaten a healthy breakfast, performed ten laborious push-ups, showered, and was ready to begin work. To be at work on time was quite a substantial feat given his usual tardiness and discordance with schedules. To the casual onlooker, the stump fit the happy reptile and the happy reptile fit the stump.

An walked to the chair and sat with his chest inflated, ready to conquer what was to be a vivifying and historic day. He began by polishing his silver, gleaming shears and golden comb before stretching his fingers, cracking his knuckles, and stretching his back.

"Next!" He announced in a rather bland, impersonal manner.

"Hey, this style number thirty-two may be the winner!" Mo said, pointing to one of the cuts in the magazine.

"No, no, I've got a much better style in store for you today. How's the new library coming?"

"You know, An, you've really outdone yourself today. I just know you are going to ace *la prova del remo* today! Ace it, I tell you. I can feel it. I am in your corner!"

"What are they saying down by the stream?"

"Oddsmakers have it thirty-to-one in your favor of passing on your first go. Like I said, there are quite a few of us rooting for you. I am so honored that you asked me to attend with you. You look so dapper today, I must say." Mo assumed his usual position in the barber's chair.

"Yes I do, Mo, and yes I will. Now scoot your derriere a bit more posteriorly. How's the locksmith business holding? Any word from the council on when the excavation will start? Bless her soul." An reverently hit his chest and pointed to the sky.

"Focus on the positives, An. Did I mention that I plan to be your first customer when you start your new job? I can't believe it! You're going to be a union man. I hear that the benefits plan is really incredible, not to mention the fully funded pension. No decisions have been made about the library yet, and the lock business . . . I don't mean to broach a touchy subject, but I had to drop off a key to your father for the airport. VERY expensive looking. Is he moving?"

"No one's mentioned it to me. You know I ain't seen him in ages. You know how it is between us. We'll see.

181

Maybe we'll mend, maybe we won't. Life's too short for me to worry about him all the time. How's the airport?"

"Sorry, I did not mean to mention him. Today, we need to focus on you and the exam. You'll do great! No, better than great! You'll do GRAND! Airport? From what I hear, things just keep disappearing. They're sure to catch the culprit eventually. For goodness' sake, we're on an island. Who would be such a fool?"

An felt that he was pushing the limit on sartorial etiquette on this day—a trend setter, an influencer, sitting out-doors, only half dressed (and in some clothing intended for the opposite sex), sipping his drink, and intermittently combing Mo's white fur.

Italian music floated on the breeze as the heavens above announced the approaching storm, with clouds whisking along as An began the cut. It was generally consequent to a storm that Anura was busy, and this day was proving to be no different. Being so busy put him in exceptionally good spirits. In fact, the correlation between busyness, inclement weather, and Anura's happiness was so great, he only needed to listen to the weather forecast to know when a storm was to be expected and hence when he would be busy, and therefore in exceptionally good spir-its. None of the fervor demonstrated by his clients in their thirst for haircare made sense to him because he did not use fixatives to keep hair neat in high wind. Storms would mess up hair, but hey, it paid the bills, so who was he to complain or discourage clients? The excitement was based on an implicit hope for a change with any approaching storm, and his clients wanted to look good in case the change back to normal was impending. His list of scheduled clients was always long and distinguished as the forecast developed toward a tempest, but today he had time for only one: his best friend, Mo.

From a distance, one would think An to be Italian, given his broad gesticulations and general physiognomy, but his accent and annunciation was pure Brooklyn or New Jersey (or perhaps Marrero, Louisiana). His stainless shears danced in a graceful ballet as snippets of white fur flew through the air, and he paused only for the occasional sip of his drink. It's not often one sees a humanesque reptile hairdresser in the wild going wild. You could say he was a busy bee today, but he was not a bee. In fact, he ate them. Since The Change, he was a lizard, specifically, Anura Pelodryadidae Litoria Thesaurensis.

Mo said, "I agree. Let's focus on more important and happy things, like the exam. Think of the loads of clams you'll earn. You'll be making dough on both ends—stormy and clear weather. But I guess you do have school tuition next year for the little munchkin to plan for. In the meantime, you should think of giving some of us less fortunate clients a break on your pricing."

"Ha! Get real, Mo. I don't want to focus on the exam right now; it's bad luck. If I ain't proficient by now, when

183

will I be? Let's change the subject. I've memorized, memorized, and rememorized. If I'm not ready now, I'll never be ready. Now, what was I saying yesterday? Oh yes, there is no way that the Yankees were going to beat Philly. USA! USA! USA! Where did you drudge up that story? I mean, look at us. We're stuck here in the South Pacific, locked away from the world. There's no way you were in the Bronx. Your imagination is something else. I know moths who migrate, and you're not one of them. We need to figure out how to bottle that imagination of yours. It'll sell!"

"I'm tellin' you, it was not a dream, but if it was, it was the most lifelike dream in the history of dreams. Picture the scene: I had flown into the stadium and the crowd was going nuts. It was packed wall to wall with people, popcorn and hot dogs passed round like there was no limit. Well, I was minding my own business when some schmuck in a purple sweater tried to swat me, then a white ball came flying past me. It was bedlam, I tell ya. Oh, did I mention that the library hasn't made any progress? I told you that right?"

"Yeah, you did. Leave it up to the council and ain't nothin'll get done. You mark my words. Zip. Zilch. Zero. 'Hi, I'm from the government and I'm here to help.' Yeah, right. You can take dat to the bank, Mo. Anyway, I'm glad you had your wits about you that day, even if it was just in your imagination. Stuck on this island, I tell ya."

An took a long swig from his beautiful drink before continuing, "Yeah, yeah. Anywho, about New York—I heard
all about de home run race. You're not the only one who
reads. DiMaggio! Hey, you think HE hit the ball that
swatted you? What year was dat?"

Mo said, "It was '48, May 14. New York by three. The
home run race was one of Arty Fleming's Jeopardy!
questions last week."

"I don't have time for that daytime television hocus-
pocus. Some of us have work and studying to do. Anyhow, you were stuck here on the island back then, only
old enough to be in diapers. You never saw no Joe
DiMaggio. You ain't got a clue, I mean not a clue. You
used to have all the time in the world to read about him in
one of them library books with all of your numbers and
ciphers and statistics. You know, that's one discipline I
just can't get. It was a dream, Mo, 100 percent a dream.
It's a good story, but you need to get a grip on your times.
Look up something recent. No one'll believe that you
were in Yankee Stadium back in '48.

"If I can give you a piece of advice, it'd be to stick to
what you're good at. You need to think before you speak,
don't just blurt out some nonsense like it's an irrefutable
fact. Just because you memorize baseball facts and statistics here and there don't mean you can pull one over
on me. I was born during the day, but not yesterday, Mo."

"An, did you hear who's playing over at the stream this weekend?"

"No, who's dat?"

"Knee Deep, Knee Deep." Mo tried to imitate a frog sound. "That's us! Get it? Ha! It never gets old, I'm tellin' ya." Mo clucked to himself as his fur shook. "An, you're the best crooner around."

"Your stridulations aren't that bad either!" An belted out, "Don't know why there's no sun up in the sky. Stormy weather since my gal and I ain't together, keeps raining all the time." An took a theatrical bow and said, "That's ol' Frankie Sinatra, Mo. I've been working on it. Plan to use it for those romantic customers."

"Pretty good. Pretty good. It'll be a hit. You need to become a minister and marry folks on your gondola. It would be a hit!"

"Maybe I need to change some of the lyrics like, 'There's no sun up in the sky. But you're in my chair so I'll cut your hair.'" An paused and moved his eyes to look behind him. "Did you hear that? Oh, never mind."

"An, I think your song will be a hit, but you need a catchy chorus. That's where I come in. Da do ron-ron-ron, da do ron-ron."

"Thanks but no thanks, Mo."

"I'm tellin' you, I was there. I remember it like it was yesterday."

"Don't kid yourself, you ain't never been off this island."

"But I am willing to travel, An. I am willing to travel. You know, us two, we could use some adventure. How about one of the other islands? Just you and me. We could make a boat. Hey, not to change the subject, but how's Lacey and the kid? Getting along OK?"

"Like I told ya. Re-re-re-redecorating. She'll be up in a bit. She's into baking these days. I'm hoping she'll be heading into town later. We need more fabric for another outfit."

All who knew An knew that there were some eccentricities and oddities in his family unit, and thus the decoration, business, and his persona were acceptable to the denizens forming the neighborhood committee. The committee included An and his family, three field mice, a dozen gerbils, three squirrels, and at least a million mosquitoes, some of whom were on the menu for An. As a result, the mosquitoes were a bit chicken-hearted and always voted in favor of Anura's requests.

An's immediate family included his lovely, svelte wife, Lacertilia (Lacey for short), and son Roden, a five-month-old, adopted gerbil from a neighboring clan. Roden now had a full head of hair and a hankering for gathering rubbish, a known gerbil predilection that caused no concerns as his parents loved him ever so dearly, though his compulsion left Lacey cleaning house much of the time. The gerbil family had initially put up a fight over his adoption, but luckily, An and Lacey were able to complete the process after arguing, "For goodness' sake, the child's mother had six. What's a man gotta do to help someone out?"

An's choice of stump, situated in the Garden District, was located in one of the nicer and more fertile glades on the island, and most importantly, it was hidden and safe. The canopy of the colorful rainbow eucalyptus offered protection from above. There were not too many predatory birds, and the ones who did live on the island ate mostly from the sea. Additionally, local laws prohibited any carnivorous misdeeds since The Change. But to further ensure the residents' safety from the occasional malevolent bird, the neighborhood committee had implemented an early warning system. If an unfamiliar bird flew into the treetops, it would trigger their warning system, causing the instantaneous scamper of those on the stump. If anyone saw anything hazardous or out of the ordinary, they were to scream at the top of their lungs, take cover, bury their heads in the dirt, or hug a friend and say their goodbyes. Their system was far from foolproof, but fortunately, attacks were few and far between. Today, many birds were perched in the treetops, but not to hunt. They needed shelter from the approaching storm. The trees were swaying back and forth with increasing ferocity. Thunder rumbled in the distance, and from their vantage point, they watched the clouds zipping past the mountain through breaks in the swaying foliage.

Lacey appeared from the spiral staircase, dressed in a resplendent, yellow fall dress that blew in the breeze as she immediately began to clean up his shears, combs, and other supplies strewn haphazardly around his workspace, loading them into his gray canvas knapsack that was already bulging with a thick book.

"Honey-dear, can't you see that I'm in the middle of a job? We have an important customer visiting us today."

"It's just Mo, honey. No offense, Mo."

"None taken."

"We need to pick up your tools before the storm. And look at the time; you're going to be late for your big day." She crossed over to his chair. "You can cut his hair anytime. Time to go on down and get into your uniform. I am so proud of you for sticking with it." She kissed him on the cheek and looked into his eyes. "You're the first in our family to achieve such an honor. I've already thought about remodeling and decorations with your big pay increase."

Mo scooted forward as An folded up the umbrella and snickered under his breath.

"Now, Lacey, honey-dear. Let's not get ahead of ourselves."

"Mo, thanks for going with him. You keep him straight, OK? I'm counting on you." She gave Mo a friendly peck on the cheek. "How's the library coming?"

"Library's closed, still under construction. No one has called for a locksmith. What else is there to do? How's Roden?"

"Oh, he's fine. If we could just get his room decorated, we'd be in good shape. Yours truly has a bit of work to do. The boy just won't stop with the wood shavings. We make him a nice, new bed, and the next day, wood shavings. Oh well. He just went down for a nap." She gently prodded her husband. "An, you know . . ."

An cut her off, a bit embarrassed. ". . . if you're five minutes early, you're already ten minutes late, right honey? I appreciate the help. We were just about to get moving."

Lacey obsessed over punctuality. "Oh hush, An, you know I'm just looking out for your best interest. You two get a move on. And by the way, dear, look at this." She held up the front page of *The Island Daily Times* and read the headline. "Be on the lookout for Jason Dix, wanted felon. Reward $10,000."

"His face looks familiar. There's something about him," he said with a shrug. "Just act naturally. Criminals can smell fear, you know. If we see him, just act naturally."

"Act naturally?"

"Look here, Mo."

Lacey continued, unappeased, "He must be somebody to warrant that kind of money. It looks like we've got a biter on the island. What are they teaching kids nowadays? It's parenting. Our little Roden may make a mess, but at least he knows not to bite others. Here, take this in case you have some downtime and need something to read." She folded the paper and placed it into his knapsack's side pocket.

An glanced down at the folded paper and said, "Thanks, dear. We'll be on the lookout. If I see him, I'll give him the old one-two chop," feigning a skillful karate chop. "That kid could use a good haircut and we could use the moola. His bangs are atrocious. Love you, honey," he said, giving her a parting peck on the cheek. "Mo, give me five minutes. We'll get something to eat on the way. You're still coming?"

"I'm on a diet, so I'll pass on the food, but I wouldn't miss your performance for the world. I just can't wait to see you fall into the brink. Now that'll be a sight for sore eyes. I hope you know how to swim," Mo said, chuckling.

"That's drink, Mo. And might I say I have such a beautiful drink." He held his drink up high. "How about a toast? 'To those like us and those who want to be like us.'"

Lacey cut in. "An, you're missing the point. We don't have drinks."

"Mo, you would think that an assistant librarian turned locksmith extraordinaire would have a better understanding of the English language. Listen, just because you pay me to cut your hair . . ."

Lacey interrupted again. "Go change, An. I'll keep Mo company. And keep it quiet; your son is sleeping. Don't forget your book, but please bring it home. You know it cost an arm and a leg. I'll meet you at the stream at 6:00 p.m. sharp."

"Yes, ma'am." An submissively descended the spiral staircase to don his gondolier attire.

# CHAPTER 8

## OFF TO SAVE JASON

*Friday, October 27, 2017*

Alfred Dix downshifted as his front tire struck the curb on Calhoun Street. He gunned the accelerator to excite his silver 1960 Porsche 356B up the acclivity of his driveway and under the shade of the majestic, moss-laden oaks. He parked the vehicle in the garage, a fuzzy, green tennis ball on a string barely touching its windshield, then he shut down the engine and reached up to close the garage door using the automatic controller. A few of the potholes in the street had gotten larger; he made a mental note to call the city.

He rolled up his driver side window, smiling a broad smile as he collected his thoughts before climbing out of the car. No different from any other day, he nonchalantly walked through the room's side door as the rattling garage door reached the pavement. Everything looked to be in place, but his sixth sense suggested that something was askew; he felt as if he were being watched. The garage was in order with the exception of a few leaves that needed to be swept. He closed the garage door behind him and walked across the flagstones in his work-ridden backyard, acorns crunching underfoot. He tried to keep a stern face, but his sixth sense was still alerting him that something was off. The hair on the back of his neck stood at attention. He was sure of it: someone was watching.

He stood still and silent, surveying the work that had been done in the backyard. It was hard to see in the gloaming, but he paused to take account of the state of things, along with what could be seen of the neighboring houses. Aside from a gecko scampering along the brick wall of the garage, nothing moved. No one seemed to be in the art room or the greenhouse. There was a bit of work to do in the backyard, but otherwise, nothing looked out of place. All seemed normal—too normal. A gentle breeze rustled the treetops as maple leaves gently fell around him, twirling in the breeze. A few birds could be heard cawing to each other.

He blurted out, "Jason, I'm sorry I had to bail on you again," but the backyard was silent.

Alfred expected Jason to be a bit peeved, and he was ready for a verbal haranguing the moment he stepped foot in the house. He would have to find something fun to do with him in the coming week. He even tried to phone ahead to mitigate some of his anger, but the call had gone straight to voice mail. He tried calling Ricouard's, but no one answered, the phone just rang and rang. He surely wouldn't have run off with Bobby.

He took his keys from his pocket, opened the back door into the utility room, and went through his usual ritual of removing his sport coat, hanging it on the coat rack, and setting his gray satchel atop the counter. The tote nearly landed on a small gecko that scurried through a break in the sheetrock.

"Jason, it's me. I'm home." He wandered into the kitchen. "Jason?"

He still sensed that someone was watching.

"Alexa, play Louis Armstrong." The chime of the activated device was followed by the soft swelling of jazz.

*Oh, the shark has pretty teeth, dear*

*And he shows them pearly white*

*Just a jackknife has MacHeath, dear*

Alfred spied Jason's handiwork on the kitchen chalkboard and the Topo Chico top left behind on the counter. He deposited the top into the refuse bin inside a cabinet before turning on the rest of the kitchen lights and heading for the living room. Wandering past the picture windows, the room seemed to be in order except for a single throw pillow on the ground in front of the sofa, the pamphlets for Texas scattered on the coffee table, and a smidgen of chalk on the leather sofa. The house was silent minus the hum of the fan overhead and the jazz drifting in from the kitchen. Perhaps Jason was asleep upstairs.

He yelled, "Jason, come on down. Let's talk. I'd like to explain some things. C'mon, like I said, the storm is approaching and I just can't leave. Look, I'm optimistic that we can get away next week."

Not a peep from Jason.

"Jason! C'mon down. Let's go get a bite to eat. I don't want you to be mad at me." His realization that there was a big problem happened in slow motion.

*The cement's just for the weight, dear*

*Bet you Mack, he's back in town*

As he picked up the throw pillow from the ground, Alfred spotted the clock. His heart skipped a beat and he began to perspire. The red, illuminated dial was blinking 13:00, 1960. In that moment, he knew Jason was in serious trouble.

"Jason! Please don't play games with me! I'm sorry about bailing!"

Alfred quickly dug into his pocket and retrieved a jeweled pocket watch, checking the time. Dashing out of the living room, he ran through his home's lower level and then up the stairs, taking them two at a time.

"Jason!" He yelled loudly, his sense of unease and urgency escalating. The house was silent.

"Jason!" Alfred tore through Jason's room—empty. He threw back the comforter on the bed, even searching under the box spring before checking the closet. His suitcase was gone. He checked the remaining rooms upstairs, looking in the closets and under the beds, but it only confirmed what he already knew: Jason was gone.

Picking up the telephone, he called Ricouard's Barber Shop. "Jimmy, it's Alfred. Yeah, I hope you're doing well. Hey, by chance is Jason around? I asked him to come see you for a haircut this afternoon. No? Oh, he's not been by. OK, I see. Sure, if you see him, please ask him to call me immediately. Yeah, I know it's about time for me to come in. OK. Yeah. Well, I don't quite have the time right now. You'll have to tell me about the dog another time. Please, just have Jason call me." Alfred disconnected.

He walked back into Jason's room as he felt his phone vibrating in his front pocket, reflexively retrieving it to answer a message from Jason. Panicked about what Jason's absence meant, he reflected on his past and his old

197

persona, Beau Champs. Perhaps he had placed too much faith in the boy.

## 1960

What was that strange clicking sound? Click, click, click . . . click, click, click . . . click. It stopped as abruptly as it started.

Blankets were haphazardly strewn atop a woolly and bearded young man as he opened one eye then peeled open the other, curious about the origin of the odd sound that had awoken him from his sleep. His deep-set and dark brown eyes, bushy eyebrows, sun-leathered skin, high cheekbones, and thin build gave him a striking countenance one would consider appealing. Unable to immediately discern the source of the noise, he stared inquisitively up at the wooden ceiling of the dormitory; a spider was spinning its web in one corner, past the slowly rotating, out-of-balance blades of a rocking ceiling fan. Merl had slept in the same room night after night and was accustomed to the building's creaks and groans, but not this sound; this was new. His mind and ears were keenly tuned and he knew something was awry. His sonorous friend in the adjacent bed didn't budge.

The unfamiliar clicking sound resumed outside his door; from his cozy position in bed, it sounded like it was coming from the forest. Curiosity tickled his mind as his consciousness pushed aside what remained of his hypnagogic dreariness to listen more carefully.

Down the hall, as the last of security headed out for the night, he heard their keys jangle as they went through their usual routine of closing up shop. "Last call, lights out! Time for bed. Lights out! Time for bed." Merl heard the guard lock the front door and considered that perhaps he had just misinterpreted the clicking sound.

And so he rolled to his left decubitus position and curled up to get comfortable, expecting the sound to have passed. However, only moments later, the clicking outside resumed, a sound unlike any to which he was accustomed. Merl was a disciple of curiosity, and his growing proclivity for the unusual left him desperate to determine the source.

"Psst, Beau! Do you hear that?"

Beau was a tall rail of a man. He lay in the adjacent bed and did not rouse.

"Come on, you lazy fool. Wake up," whispered Merl. Beau, clothed in his issued set of floral Tripe Security Force pajamas, was sleeping an arm's length away, sprawled across the bed with covers strewn halfway over his body and drool leaking from his mouth onto his sad excuse for a pillow. Despite Merl's call, he did not budge; he was not one to be intrigued by unusual happenings and was always the less adventurous and more pragmatic of the two. Merl contemplated shaking Beau but dismissed the notion until he knew more about the sound. It was imperative that he remain silent as the walls in the building were thin and the others would naturally be curious if they heard any nighttime activity or presumed mischief. If they were up and about, someone would rat them out. He also knew that Beau's answer to his request for nocturnal adventure would be a resounding "no" because the punishment for violating curfew would be severe. They had been busted twice in the past month, and the next reprimand would likely separate the pair of roommates. Besides, Beau was a rule follower and didn't appreciate being dragged into Merl's shenanigans.

A minute or two later, the clicking resumed; the cadence and timbre of the sound were odd, unlike any sound made by a person or device.

"To heck with it." Merl resolutely shot out of bed and threw on his tan cargo shorts over his underwear and floral Aloha shirt, leftovers from a life of freedom. Curiously, he tiptoed to the door and peered through the blurry and condensate-laden glass onto the damp porch. Their building was part of the work camp south of the airport, so it was expected that all would be quiet and still after work hours. The porch was deserted and there was no movement in the darkness outside. What could have made the sound? He pushed the draperies aside a bit more and wiped away some of the interior precipitate before cupping his hands around his eyes to peer deeply into the dark forest canopy across the dimly lit yard. Nothing seemed askew. A loud madrigal of frogs, cicadas, and locusts assured him that despite their visual absence, the dark forest canopy was alive. The occasional light from a firefly fleetingly flickered amongst the foliage, momentarily adding some illumination to the night. Then suddenly, with a different cadence, the clicking resumed from somewhere near the mountain, louder this time and seemingly more directed toward Merl. Again, it stopped after only a moment. The whisper of the fan and Beau's slight sonorous breathing were the only other sounds; no one else in the camp seemed to be awake, and there was no movement in any of the adjacent rooms.

Merl remained silent as he gingerly opened the back door and stepped a foot outside. The light breeze was pleasant but did little to quell the heat and humidity, and his perspiration was running in streams down his back. He could never quite understand why the front door remained locked at night when all the back doors were left open; if they just left all the doors and windows open, they could get at least some degree of ventilation. With his curiosity piqued, he was nearly out the door and onto the porch, each step prohibited. He expected at least some movement from Beau, but the slugabed was back in a deep slumber and could be heard breathing heavily, the forest sounds functioning as his soporific. By Merl's estimate, it must have been around midnight, but he had lost his timepiece and couldn't be certain.

Having waited long enough for Beau, Merl tiptoed back to his bedside, stepping over the creaky floorboards, and quietly shook him, covering his mouth with a hand to keep him from blurting out upon wakening.

"Beau, wake up. Let's go." Merl licked a finger and stuck it into one of his ears.

Beau pawed at the air. "Tell Grammy that I'll be down for dinner in a minute. I'll have the meatloaf."

"Shh. Seriously, wake up. It's me. It's important. Someone may be sneaking out, maybe an escape. Something strange is happening tonight. Didn't you hear the clicking?"

Beau opened one eye and then the other as he came to recognize his friend. They could hear the fan and the cacophonous forest symphony, but no clicking.

"What are you saying?" He rubbed the sleep from his eyes and lifted his head. "What is it? Why would you wake me from such a pleasant dream? Do you know where I was?"

"Yes, you're right here in this bedroom. Now get up, you bum. Didn't you hear that? There's a strange clicking sound outside the door and in the direction of the trail-head. C'mon, I need your help. Let's get a move on."

"Are you serious? Let me sleep, you woolly fool. It's just nature. Listen. I just hear the cicadas. You're waking me for a freaking clicking noise?" Beau tried to turn to the opposite decubitus position, but Merl held his side.

"C'mon, I have a feeling something important is going to happen tonight and I want you there. Someone else may be out. The clicking is unlike anything I've heard before; the cadence is just not right."

"Leave me to sleep." Beau rolled onto his side and closed his eyes. "All you'll do is get us in trouble. Aren't you supposed to meet up with that librarian you've been ca-vorting with? You don't need me—three's a crowd."

"Shh, this has nothing to do with her. Something is up. Let's see what's going on. C'mon, this may be our big chance. What if someone is trying to escape? C'mon, please, just this last time."

"Merl, quit it. Are you seriously going to feed me this blarney again? Look around and take a smell. There are no roses. Get real. There's no way off this godforsaken island. We're stuck here unless a miracle or savior ar-rives. What's the point of going out? All we'll accom-plish is a reprimand. Do you want to split us up? I'd rather forgo the wrath of that jerk, Bauman. We were screwed the moment our boat ran aground and we landed in this dreadful prison. So leave me be. Sleep is more important to me and I have to work breakfast in the morning. Unlike you, I don't get to take naps during the day. You are the smart one, but I have to work in the cafeteria serving the usual assortment of delectable viands to these arrogant fools; they're just a bunch of pigs. They stuck me in the dining hall with Ralph yesterday. He's not that bad, but the pugilistic SOB can be pretty demanding, and if those jerks Bill and Larry strike me once more, I may just pop. I don't get breaks, remember? You wanted the easy job and you got it, so there you go. I don't mean to incommode you, but you can go it alone this time. Thanks but no thanks, so long, and have fun doing whatever it is you get into. I need my sleep and now I am going to close my eyes. I am going back to bed to dream of wonderful things that have nothing to do with this godforsaken Island of Tripe. By the way, I was dreaming of lasagna. That's right, I was in an Italian kitchen, eating a real lasagna with meat and cheese. Oh, and will you turn up the fan? It's a bit hot in here." He rolled away from Merl and shut his eyes.

Merl whispered, "It's hot because you're wearing long-sleeve pajamas, you oaf. Take off some clothes if you're hot." Beau remained stationary. "C'mon, I need you. Something was out at the trailhead, I know it. I just want to check it out and then we'll come right back to bed. My first mate, just this one more night. You can sleep tomorrow night." Merl pulled on one of his legs, unwavering in his insistence that Beau be part of the adventure. Beau knew Merl's apodictically unwavering personality would be undeterred, especially by any thought of recourse against their captors. And so, knowing that the sooner he acquiesced, the sooner he could get back to sleep, Beau reluctantly slid his feet into flip-flops and slowly sat up at the edge of his bed.

"Alrighty, you asked for it. Let's go get this out of the way. I will prove to you that nothing is awry and that all is well on our magical Island of Tripe. If a few of the others are running about, so what? Why should I care? There's no way out of this place. They are wasting their time unless they build us a sailboat. You know this. Get it through your thick head already. Do you remember what happened four months ago, when we tried to wave down that passing ketch?"

Beau was all too aware of Merl's curiosity and wanderlust. By this point, his nighttime excursions were a well-established habit, some of which were rumored to be a rendezvous with a certain paramour from the nearby township. Beau's job was always to cover for Merl, coughing loudly to cover the sound of Merl opening the door as he slipped away into the forest. By Merl's account and always denying any interest in a tryst, he would hike in the moonlight to a secluded location and look up into the refulgence of the night sky, free from any light pollution, gazing into the heavens that were

colored like an artist's rutilant palate with stars as numerous as the grains of sand on a beach. He expounded that
it gave him a sense of freedom and reminded him of
watching the heavens at night from their sailboat; it was
true that when the two sailed, he would stay up all night
just staring into the vast ocean of sky. Beau was not as
cavalier as Merl, mostly due to his discordant views on
sleep, desiring slumber more than adventure, as adventure led nowhere time and time again.

On this night, Beau reluctantly acquiesced, and the two
silently slid out the door and onto the porch.

Merl whispered, "I heard it over there by the trailhead."
He pointed to the caliginous forest.

Across the meadow and shadowed in the tree line, a
rocky path cut through the forest from the mountain and
edged its way into their encampment. A signpost at the
junction offered directional information about the trails
and a white truss held complimentary information sheets.
Near the junction, they glimpsed a flicker of light as they
sneaked to the porch's edge.

"Hey, did you see that? Like I said." Another brief flash
of light illuminated the trailhead.

"Yeah, what is it?" Beau wiped the sleep from his eyes.

"I don't know. I know there isn't electricity over there. It must be a flashlight. That's why we need to go and check it out. See? I told you!" Merl continued whispering. "I'm telling you, someone's out there. What could they be up to?"

Beau rubbed his eyes, not used to being awake at this hour. "Who cares? This is a waste of time."

Merl thought he saw the same flicker of light further up the trail. "Look toward the trailhead. It just moved or maybe there's more than one."

Both squinted into the inky darkness. Merl was insistent and said, "Must be signaling with a flashlight. The guards would not be so quiet. Look at that, it seems to be moving, almost like dancing. There's a rhythm to it. I don't see how anyone could make that happen."

Beau did not want to get caught. "Shh. Keep it down. Whoa! Look!"

The light flickered and danced to a series of clicks, whisking along the trail in thirty-foot arches, the position changing in an irregular fashion. Were they being taunted? No other light could be seen.

Merl lifted his leg over the porch railing and Alfred followed in his pajamas, both setting their feet onto the dewy grass.

Merl whispered, "Quiet from here on out, let's sneak up on whoever it is. They'll owe us big time for not turning them in."

The two crept across the grass, attempting to make as little sound as possible as they approached the trailhead. The unidentified object continued its sporadic movement and clicking. Merl, desperate to get a glimpse of who or what was producing the light and sound, kept his eyes fixated on the light. Beau, on the other hand, was not as engaged, following closely and sometimes colliding with Merl's rear. As they drew near, the light's direction changed, dancing up the rocky path and above sabulous, earthen stairs that led up the trailhead and toward the island's mountain.

The two continued their slow creep, passing the signpost and advancing up the acclivitous trail. The higher they climbed, the better their view of the horizon and a few noctilucent clouds below the vastitude of the shimmering heavens that dimly illuminated the night. As if by luck, a shooting star sliced across the sky in a dazzling display.

A few meters along the path, the stairs became mere outcroppings, varying in width and height; some of the path was naturally created, but most was by human design. Merl, an adept climber and wide awake, was easily able to negotiate the step's differences. Beau, on the other hand, was lanky and lacking the same degree of athleticism. Thus, he had a much harder time, particularly in slick flip-flops and pajamas, and his fatigued senses were neither interested nor keen. Having traveled the path countless times, both men knew there to be a good number of steps of varying heights before the ground plateaued to a red granite path, much of the trail shadowed by trees and foliage.

"Beau, hold on to the tail of my shirt."

"How much longer? I did not sign up for a confounded hike. This is ridiculous. Can't we just say someone was out and call it a night? I can hear my bed calling me."

"The path gets steep here. Follow closely and watch your step. Let's make it to the top, take a look around, and if no one is there, we'll head back down. We're almost there."

The pair negotiated the darkened path as the grade sharply increased; worn from many years of use, the stairs were damp and slick with algae from the natural springs that trickled over the path and into the stream set in the valley below. Beau had one hand on Merl's shirttail and the other on an old, decrepit, wooden railing.

"Keep your weight on the stairs and place each step carefully. Like I've told you before, the railing is weak. Don't trust it."

The two continued on, Beau panting as they passed stone statues from some past civilization that abutted the path and seemed to eerily keep their watchful eyes on the intruders. The path curved, following the ascending rock face up and left, skirting around foliage. The sounds of the susurrous flow of a mountain stream in the valley below increased above the jungle's symphony.

The flicker of light continued clicking and jumping from side to side, teasing them forward as it bobbled and glowed dimmer then brighter. It shot off toward the tree line, then over the gorge, then back to the path ahead in wide arcs.

Merl trekked methodically up the path, surefooted although the soles of his feet were slick from the damp, lichen-covered rocks. Beau was increasingly upset as sweat dripped down his back; his wet pajama bottoms aggravated his ankles. He was exhausted, cranky, and his nerves were frayed. He knew someone would notice his dirty pajama pants and he would have to explain why they were so dirty. It was a bad situation all around.

The two found themselves on an especially wet portion of the path in order to avoid the overgrown brush, and suddenly, the path took a sharp left turn and cut up the rock face at a steep angle. While navigating under and around shrubbery, the light multiplied from one to two, two to four, and four to thousands, all advancing directly toward the pair, momentarily blinding and disorientating them. The clicking sound was so loud that it overwhelmed their senses.

Beau's fall was instantaneous. The safety railing crumbled in his hand and the rock gave out underfoot, causing him to fall sideways over the cliff's edge. Instinctively, he grabbed for Merl's shirttails, which just resulted in both men falling over, somersaulting down through the jungle foliage, twisting, turning, and tumbling over rock and mud, unsuccessfully trying to grab hold of anything to stop their fall before they plunged into the icy, limpid water.

"Merl, where are you? You good-for-nothing scoundrel, I told you this was a bad idea!" Beau spat and struggled to keep his head above water, trying to catch his breath.

"We need to stick together. There are rapids up ahead. Hold on to me and don't let go."

The two bobbed like corks, spitting and gasping for air, instinctively grabbing and holding one another as the current picked up speed, rushing them away into the dark jungle. The constant twisting of the river and the sprays of water distorted their view as the mountain grew ever more distant. They fought the current in a battle for their lives. Through the treacherous rapids, the water was violent and voluminous, and they plunged down the river valley at a breakneck pace, whipping and spinning like two rudderless dinghies. Smashing into nearly every boulder along the way, they were tossed around like rag dolls, both struggling to keep their heads above water. Suddenly, they were weightless, plummeting feet first over a giant cataract, landing in the heavy spray of a deep plunge basin. The violent water pounded over them as they were thrust beneath the surface, pushed to the bottom in the maelstrom.

Beau and Merl fought to survive, both forced to let go of the other. It was every man for himself. They swam with everything they had, trying to break free of the current pulling them to the bottom, spinning and churning, over and over. Hypoxia was taking hold as the frigid, blue water darkened and the two were pulled to the bottom of the river.

Suddenly, a blinding light flashed as the men were tugged through thick algae and plants, through a breach in the river's bottom and into a scaturient aquifer, passing through tunnel after tunnel. Then, just as life's end appeared imminent, the two were shot out of the water and onto a stone landing where they lay gasping and coughing, trying to fill their oxygen-depleted lungs with air.

Slowly, the two regained enough lucidity to realize they were still alive, laying at the distal tip of a stone quay in a cavern with dazzling, azure water and a ceiling covered in roots and vines. Nearby was the half-sunken skeleton of a brig sloop and their long-lost sailboat with its broken mast and cracked hull. Across the narrow waterway from where they lay sputtering and wheezing, they spotted a temple with an intricate clock and an elevator that stood open, the light above illuminated green.

Across the open lake and above a lonely stone dock, a derelict sign for "Alibaba's Watches and Gemstones" flickered on and off.

# CHAPTER 9

## TRAVEL TO THE EXAM

*Saturday, October 28, 1972*

With air travel making the far reaches of the globe increasingly accessible, by 1972, Tripe Island's isolationism had been supplanted with tourism and its requisite accoutrements. The shift was welcomed by many locals, as the island's revenue stream and means of taxation had dried up after The Change and the collapse of the island's once-vibrant textile industry. With the needed influx of cash, most visitors were welcomed, even as some of the island's cherished bohemian flare was lost to a more commercialized, anachronistic construction of the township with newer buildings developed for boutique hotels and food vendors. Such development was consolidated mainly in the northeastern corner of the island. In time, the island's economy became wholly reliant on the service industry.

To increase their attractiveness to the tourism industry, the island heavily marketed their many unique features, much like the Galapagos or Easter Islands had. Rich in history, the island featured innumerable, diverse fauna that had developed in relative isolation for thousands of years. Archaeological digs, taxonomy studies, and their associated recreational endeavors frequently took place on the northern portion of the island. Any request for exploration of the south, a UNESCO World Heritage site, was quashed by both local and international courts. While some of the island's flare and personality were lost to tourism and development, the subterranean realm remained relatively untouched.

Below the island's terra firma, a twisted maze of waterways remained hidden, though they were easy to find if one knew where to search. The system comprised numerous subterranean streams and cenotes of varying sizes that were used by the locals for recreation and a reliable means of transportation, but the system was never disclosed to the tourists. To placate the tourist bureau and help draw revenue, a few of the larger and less important cenotes were opened to tourists in modern times. The more historic and ecologically delicate areas, like the Grand Cavas Cenote, were preserved and remained hidden.

To use them, one only needed to know where to look: follow the signs. The entrances were cleverly disguised, and industrial-looking placards featuring maps of the system were posted for newcomers, those with cognitive impairments, or those just interested in cartography. This system ran south to north, though north was difficult to discern when underground. The northern routes were more easily accessible and thus more frequently used, flowing in a south-to-north direction. There were a few streams running in the opposite direction, flowing southward, but these were few and cost more to use. For a small fee, a gondolier could be hired to transport patrons in either direction, but never past the mountain to the southern third of the island, and never in the cenotes frequented by tourists. The gondoliers were habitually late, so it was hard to count on their services.

The southern system was completely off-limits, period, and no known map existed to diagram its routes. All the cenotes and subterranean waterways on the island were anchialine systems, radiating out from the base of the central mountain to the sea or from the sea to the mountain. The utility and safety of each stream depended on rainfall totals and tidal flow and were subject to abrupt changes. Disclaimers were added to the placards in infinitesimally small print, and at the entrances to some of the cenotes (particularly the ones without the standard placards), green, octagonal signs warned, "Travel at your own risk," in red print. One would expect the signage to work well, and it did for the most part, but a colorblind species of mouse was unable to read the signs and brought a class-action lawsuit against the agency that maintained the streams. Some beautification committee members once tried to do away with all the signage, but their complaint was thrown out.

The system was highly influenced by Mother Nature. When favorable, "green" conditions existed, the rivers were open for recreation and travel, but when the flow was moderately to severely dangerous and red conditions were present, access was prohibited. In addition to the color system, two additional safety systems were implemented but were not yet fully operational. An air-raid-like siren sounded in the event of impending tidal surge, and a state-of-the-art CCD video system monitored traffic through the streams. However, due to the complex nature of installation, only a few of the cameras were functional. The Subterranean Utility and River Authority (SURA) maintained the system, signage, and usage. SURA employees were employed by the government and worked only two hours a day, maximum eight hours a week. The island's nepotistic slug population had a monopoly on the job. There were a lot of slugs in government, all from the Limacidae family.

To use the system for anything other than recreation, travelers were required to hire a gondolier. The local 526 Union had a monopoly on transportation and their system was not free. Money, or something with equivalent monetary value, must be deposited in the turnstile to gain access to the system. The money was split between the union and the slugs, but the system often lost money due to freeloaders who didn't pay. The lost revenue and the cost of the upgraded video system were a strain on the system, and hence, some of the services and notices were not up to par. The revenue shortfall would be addressed by an upcoming referendum. A charitable event, affectionately known as "Slug Fest," was held to keep the system afloat until the referendum could pass.

On this day, Anura and Mo were traveling to the Grand Cavas Cenote, where the Gondolier's Examination was administered semiannually. It was just a short and easy jaunt from An's home.

An walked proudly, ready to take the exam. He carried his book in hand, and over his shoulder, he slung his gray knapsack filled with shears, hair dyes, combs, and other grooming equipment. Lost in thought, he thumbed through his large volume of *A Complete Guide to Gondoliering*, second guessing himself as he walked.

To any islander, his livery was clear. As per Lacey's instructions, he was dressed in a white-and-blue striped, long-sleeve shirt and blue pant ensemble reminiscent of a classic Italian gondolier. He could hear her voice echoing in his mind as he approached his exam: "If you dress the part, you are the part."

Mo, his usual, gay self, jocularly lofted himself up to ride the gust of wind as the two passed an illuminated sign that read, "Green." The wind was picking up as the treetops swayed and the occasional drop of rain fell.

An was clearly nervous as he frantically thumbed through his book's pages, barely stopping on any one page long enough to take in the information. When he was nervous, he made small talk. "Can you believe the weather today? Of all days!"

Mo knew him well and could feel his tension building, so he tried to placate his friend. "An, you're just going to be terrific! I know you're nervous, but don't you worry, not one bit. You're going to do great. The way I see it, if Ratu, that ugly one who lives just outside town, let's see, his wife is Sciurinae, big bosom and wide hips . . . well anyhow, if *he* can pass, anyone can pass. You'll do just fine. I know you have memorized most of that book. You've put the time in. You're ready for this. Hmm, it surprises me that the signage is green; looks like foul weather today," Mo said as he tried desperately to keep steady in the growing gusts that tossed him to-and-fro.

"Argh, how am I supposed to know what a prow head is used for?" An raised both of his hands to his head in frustration. "How would this knowledge make me a better gondolier? Oarsmanship? What the . . ." An's nerves were unraveling more with every step he took toward the exam. "C'mon, Mo, quiz me. We'll be there soon. My book's going to get wet." An tucked the volume into his satchel.

To be invited to test for gondolier status and take *la prova del remo* was a great honor; to pass the test and become a gondolier was, according to the gondolier's union, a life-time achievement, particularly for an applicant with no family ties in the union.

"I'll be happy to quiz you if you have flashcards. But it's not like I know the information. Why didn't you bring your waterproof knapsack instead of that one? You know it's going to rain, and you're bound to get water in the boat. If you ruin that book, Lacey will have your head. How many pages is that thing, anyway? Pretty heavy, yeah?" Noticing the change in An's facial expression, he shifted his tone to be more sanguine. "C'mon, An. You're going to be great! The best-est best ever!"

An stopped short. "Mo, thank you for trying to lift my spirits. What do you think of my voice, my singing?" He began to belt. "I think it's pretty gooooooood! I want to be a gondolieeeer!" Burp. "Singing is one-third of the exam, after all."

"Yeah, I think you've got a great set of lungs. I've always said that. Answer me this: how could you be the lead singer of Knee Deep, the best band on the whole island, without a great voice? If the test is a singalong, you'll easily pass. Just wait and see, you'll knock 'em dead this weekend just like you will at the exam today." Mo's hair was getting discombobulated in the wind. "Hey, when we get back to your place, can you straighten some of this fur?"

"If I straighten it, I'm gonna charge you again." An smiled and continued to lead them down the arenaceous declivity.

"But I already paid you twice this week!"

"I don't control the weather! Sure, Mo. Sure."

Through a number of switchbacks, the two wended past a derelict signpost and down a foliage-ridden, rocky incline toward an ineffably beautiful cenote. Through the cavern's entrance and across a pink-pebbled beach, they could see a tranquil lagoon and self-illuminated, azure river with an oculus in the cave's ceiling. Multiple turnstiles lay before them, their size varied for the size of the user, positioned equidistantly from the walls of the cave's opening. If one chose to be a cheat, they could simply walk around any one of the turnstiles and through the entrance, but this duplicitous behavior was frowned upon. Furthermore, An was unsure if hidden cameras were trained on the entrance. It was rumored that the subject of ethics was a recent addition to the gondolier test. He decided it wasn't worth the risk. It was unclear how many were expected at the examination today, but he was clearly the first examinee to arrive. *Lacey would be proud.*

The site was prepared for the exam; dozens of black gondolas were pulled onto the pebble beach and a few were moored in the lagoon alongside the floating pier. Strung between two creosote pilings on bright yellow rope was a banner written in simple, sloppy handwriting that read, "EXAMINATION."

An was finally feeling optimistic. "Well this is it; we must be early! At least we're in the right place and ahead of schedule. But where is everyone? You would think there would be some people here by now, at least an instructor or two. What time is it, anyway? Mo, hand over some clams so we can get in, will ya? Let's get ready. Maybe there's some useful information or hints for the test on that board over there. I bet I'll have my pick of the boats. You know, like first come, first served. Lacey, I love ya!" He pounded his chest with a fist and pointed upward.

"An, I paid you for the haircut and that was all I had. For goodness' sake, I'm not made of moola. I'm an assistant librarian. In any case, I'll be paying you twice: once for the cut and again to the local 526."

"C'mon, Mo, there's no pocket in this get up. It's not like I can just barge in; the slugs may be watching us on the camera. Treat everything like a test, that's my motto. My nerves are fried anyway. Sheesh, I should have worn my other pants with a pocket; I don't think I even have my wallet. Gosh, I hope I don't need a photo ID." An fumbled through his satchel, visibly nervous.

"Lower the cost of my next cut?" Mo laughed good-naturedly. "You want to be a hairdresser or a wealthy gondolier? Just think of the pension you'll get. Soon you'll keep loads of money in that satchel of yours!" The two made small talk for a few more minutes before depositing the necessary funds into the turnstile. The counter clicked to 1 as An entered, and 2 with Mo. They hesitantly entered the cavern, their voices echoing throughout the massive chamber. They were alone.

An yelled, "Hello? Hello? Is anybody home?" His voice echoed through the nooks and chambers, but there was no reply. Other than Anura and Mo, the cavern was deserted, and the only sounds were from the flowing river, pebbles crunching underfoot as they walked, and a drip from somewhere in the cavern. An thought he could hear the sound of plates clanking and voices in the distance, but that seemed improbable.

An stared contemplatively out over the lagoon. "Mo, the sign was green when we walked down here, but the rain is coming. Do you think the test was postponed? Maybe the sign changed after we passed, or maybe the signage itself was a test. Maybe I've already failed. We were not supposed to come down here in a storm. I don't see anyone else around or even headed this way. There are no footprints or anything! Maybe we need to go check back up at the top."

"You're being paranoid. How could we see footprints in the pebbles? Maybe you're the only one taking the test today. I can't believe it's only a stone's throw from your home. How convenient is this? You'll be able to work at home, and then presto, pop down here to pick up some shifts. I once knew a guy who worked so far away from home that he was sometimes gone for like a week at a time. Look on the bright side: you'll get to sleep at home every night!"

"This place sure is big." An kept up the small talk as he walked across a plank and onto one of the smallest piers. An approached the announcement board, hoping to find an explanation for their solitude.

"An, do you ever wonder what we would be doing right now if we hadn't experienced The Change? There wouldn't be any of this."

"Not a day goes by that I . . ." An stopped short and backed up to look closely at the board. "Mo, what's today's date?"

The board clearly read: "Gondolier exam, Stage 101: 10/29/1972 @ 13:00.

"I knew something wasn't right! See, look here." An pointed to the board, deflated. "The exam is *tomorrow* at 13:00, not today. What am I to do? Lacey, god bless her intentions, but in her never-ending haste to be punctual, she must have written down the wrong date. Instead of arriving ten minutes before the scheduled time, we are a day early—a whole twenty-four hours! So much for the celebration tonight, Mo. Then tomorrow the tempest will strike and the exam will surely be postponed! How long before the next exam? It's semiannual—will I have to wait another six months? And what are we to do about the Knee Deep gig? We'll have to reschedule and I'm sure the rest of the guys will be fuming."

"Aw, don't get so upset. It's just an honest mistake. When life gives you lemons, what do you do?"

An was silent with a dejected scowl on his face.

Mo tried to cheer him up. "You make lemonade, that's what you do. You can't change this, so use it to your advantage. How about we get you some extra practice? Just look at all of these beautiful boats floating here, not being used. We have a few hours before we have to meet Lacey, and surely you'd be OK borrowing one for practice. There's no sign that says you can't. See?" Mo widely panned an arm through the space before helping himself to an éclair from a white doughnut box left on a café table under the announcement board.

"Mo, you don't know how long that éclair has been sitting there. What if the cream's gone bad? I do NOT want you getting sick all over me and the gondola. Frankly, it's disgusting."

Mo shrugged. "I'm eating alfresco, An. Did I ever tell you about the time I was in Venice, Italy? I was crossing the Rialto bridge as this gondolier was approaching. I was well above the Grand Canal when . . ." Mo stopped mid-sentence as he thought he heard an explosion in the distance. "You hear that?"

"Thunder, Mo, thunder. Haven't you looked at the weather report? I'll bet you ten clams there will be more."

"Let's make the best of this extra time. No one will care if you practice a little. Think of all the great gondoliers in history. You'll be the next king of Barataria."

"And what happened to the king?" Both had seen the play when it had been put on some months ago.

"OK, forget that analogy. But the gist of what I'm saying is that no one ever made it big without practice. Tomorrow, or whenever the exam is held, will be your lucky day. We'll come back, no sweat, only this time with more practice under your belt."

The two chose a sleek, black gondola and climbed aboard; Mo eased into one of the passenger seats, placing a red-and-white ring buoy around his neck. With the prowess of one accustomed to such a position, An took a proud stance toward the stern. Hoisting an oar, he expertly used it to free the looped mooring off the decking, placed it in the forcola, and began to navigate around the other gondolas and moorings. Picking up speed, he rowed into the main subterranean channel. "This feels great! You really think this will be OK, Mo? It's not considered cheating, right? I don't see anyone else around, but we both know there are cameras."

"If I were your instructor, I'd give you extra credit for being here a day early and practicing."

"Well, thank you for being honest, Signor Esaminatore. I guess I'll take your recommendation and raise you one. You need to pick out a song. You'll get to see all facets of gondoliering today."

"An, you're doing it! Whoop, whoop! You're fantastic. A natural, I'm telling you. You have a knack for this job. You're going to be the most famous gondolier in our island's history. You'll be rich! Now take me down that river to the left. Presto! Rapidamente! An, take us away for an An-venture—pardon the pun."

"You're pushin' it, Mo. Keep it up and you'll be in the water."

The two headed into an underground river as the boat scuttled along the stream and into the depths of the waterway system. An began singing, "Il tempo passa e il sol, già sorto a levante, torno the Island of Tripe, e ho voglia di cantare!"

# CHAPTER 10

## COCOONED

*Friday, October 27, 2017*

Jason's departure created quite a shift in Alfred's plans. Immediately upon his realization of his son's whereabouts, he hastily canceled all of his upcoming business endeavors while zipping to Louis Armstrong International Airport, throttling his Porsche to the redline. Traffic was miraculously light, so he reached the airport just in time to catch the last flight out to LAX, where he would have a better chance of finding a flight to Tripe or a neighboring island. He was aware that curious eyes were upon him, but it didn't matter.

The flight to Los Angeles was uneventful, and he was fortunate enough to procure a seat on the last flight to Tripe that very evening, Friday's Flight 605. Given the favorable winds, the pilots were able to make up some time in the air, so his arrival time was expected to follow Jason's by about two hours. He was not worried about the passenger manifest; he already knew the flight was doomed.

After a long, boring flight, Alfred's plane was finally making its final descent onto the Island of Tripe in the midst of a growing tempest. The copilot frequently recited the local weather amidst gusts of wind, and all the passengers on board Flight 605 were growing increasingly anxious. Far from the mainland and over the open ocean, they were as good as stuck with no other safe options; they would have to weather the storm and land.

"Ladies and gentlemen, the turbulence is a bit more than expected and we have switched over to manual flight controls. It looks like the ride will be rough from here on. The seatbelt sign will remain illuminated for the remainder of the flight, and all food services will be canceled. Please make sure your seat belts are securely fastened and your items are stowed. We expect to be landing shortly. Flight attendants, please take your seats. And to whomever lit a cigarette in coach, please remember that smoking on flights is prohibited and a federal offense."

The pilots had their work cut out for them. He could feel the plane slipping and the rudder working hard to prevent a roll as they passed through cloud after cloud. An eerie, ominous, green smoke began to fill the back of the coach cabin.

"Ladies and gentlemen, we've been instructed to remain in a holding pattern. The current weather conditions on the island are expected to pass . . ."

*October 28, 1972*

As the plane passed through a cumulonimbus cloud, Alfred could feel the fuselage shudder as winds suddenly increased. The aircraft hit a massive pocket of turbulence and the intercom went silent. One of the flight attendants bolted for her seat, her hands pawing at anything she could grab as she desperately attempted to remain upright. The unsecured beverage cart slammed against something in the galley, and as the plane pitched further onto its side, cans of Wake Up cola rolled down the aisle.

The coming events seemed to pass in slow motion.

The resonant buffeting of machinery under the fuselage was replaced by a menacing grinding noise. The screams of fear grew even louder when oxygen masks dropped out of their overhead compartments, gravity highlighting their bank as the masks dangled steeply toward the windows on the left side of the plane. The plane's bank became steeper and steeper as the ocean flashed intermittently through the clouds, followed by glimpses of the island. Bright lights flashed through the windows. Passengers were slammed into their seats, and the unbuckled few were thrown around the cabin like rag dolls. Complete disarray, madness, and panic ensued.

Alfred gripped his armrests and closed his eyes, only to open them when an overhead bin popped open, spewing its contents in his direction as he reflexively ducked to prevent a certain concussion. Many passengers were sobbing and pleading for their lives, and others were desperately grasping for their oxygen masks. He tried to duck as another suitcase came flying through the cabin, but it struck him squarely across the side of his head and nearly knocked him unconscious. He knew what recourse he needed to take.

In a daze, with the plane on its side and a crash imminent, Alfred reached into his shirt and extracted a glass vial on a silver neck chain, labeled "Last Resort" with a skull and crossbones. He yanked on the chain and broke it, his hands shaking as he ungracefully removed the brown glass vial's crown-shaped cap. Raising the vial to his lips, he took a deep breath and drank the oily tincture in one gulp.

Alfred dropped the vial and immediately began to choke. He clawed at his throat, finding it hard to catch his stridorous breath as he felt the spicy oil's caustic flow running over his tongue, past his palate, and into his esophagus.

As the mixture reached his stomach, the laryngospasm passed and was replaced by intense abdominal pains. Like a burning hot branding iron inside his stomach, the ensuing abdominal pain was severe, like being twisted

231

and ripped apart from the inside. He found himself screaming, writhing in pain in opisthotonus, wide awake as the plane plummeted toward the earth. As the sheer terror in his fellow passenger's screams intensified, his metamorphosis and pain accelerated. As his body began shrinking, his lap belt no longer offered him any protection and he couldn't reach the armrests for an anchor to moor himself to. With the plane in free fall, he was pushed into the seat, his weight shoved into his spine. Time slowed to a crawl; a mobile phone the size of a large house passed overhead in slow motion and gargantuan pieces of paper, planetary liquid droplets, and other monstrous refuse floated like dandelion seeds in the cabin breeze. His auditory perception became distorted as the pitch of the cabin noise slowed and deepened, like a record being played at half speed.

As his pains intensified, his stomach suddenly ballooned outward and his abdominal musculature began wave-like contractions as if he were giving birth. A glassy, translucent substance formed on his abdomen, analogous to the aril that coats a seedling. Grabbing his abdomen, he screamed but could not hear himself. His overall size continued to decrease and he felt his weight lightening. Floating. Weightless. Helpless. He drifted upward in the microgravity, striking the colossal, illuminated stewardess button overhead as the crystalline structure began encasing his limbs.

Alfred twisted his head as a megalopic effect distorted his view of the cabin, the environment becoming increasingly larger. The process, known as ensporulation, was nearing completion. The crystalline, aril lattice now completely enveloped his body, clouding his vision with a frosted blur. Microseconds before a thundering explosion decimated the plane, he was completely encased in a soft cocoon the size and shape of a maple seed. His pain was gone.

Any deep rumbles were silenced as a white light as bright as the sun flashed and blinded him. Intense heat and a red blaze followed—flames. His world turned pitch black, gradually lightening to shades of gray as he wafted up through the black smoke and soot.

Out of the smoke, he floated through the hot air, out and over the wreckage and into the storm's gale, the wind lofting him, cooling him, and protecting him, carrying him to safer ground as he spun round and round like a helicopter.

He landed softly on the moist soil of a distant glade, under the leaves of a large plant and hidden by tall blades of golden grass. He looked around, trying to gain some semblance of his bearings, and spotted a flat, golden-brown stump with some sort of red parasol on top. He was trapped. Unable to fight his soul-crushing weariness, he closed his eyes to rest.

*** 

The group of warthogs clad in hunter orange comprised the ground crew at the Tripe Airport. In gleeful silence, they watched Flight 605 explode into a massive fireball over the island. In unison, they genuflected in approbation of their leader and began their rote requiem: "Iko iko wan dey. Jock-a-mo fi no wan an dey. Jock-a-mo fi na ney. Iko iko wan dey. Jock-a-mo fi no wan an dey. Jock-a-mo fi na ney." Beau Champs was finally dead, a mere requital for his past misdeeds. Saul was unaware of their sabotage but would surely be proud of their success. They lumbered away to inform their superior.

# CHAPTER 11

## JASON ESCAPES

*Saturday, October 28, 1972*

Flummoxed, with no semblance of normalcy and a clouded mind, Jason pushed himself onward under darkening skies, a seemingly diegetic character stuck in a fantasy world. This had to be a dream.

*Just need to keep moving forward. Just go forward. You're not going crazy; you must be crazy. Why can't I just wake up on the sofa? Must find a place to hide, to wait. Dad will be here soon enough and all will be OK. Need shelter from the storm.* Refuge was needed, time to gather himself. Forward seemed his best option.

After successfully escaping baggage claim, Jason rounded the nearest corner and burst across a busy avenue, cars screeching to a halt as he zigged and zagged through traffic and made his way to the opposite curb. The streets were crowded, but he didn't perseverate on anything or anyone, singularly focused on forward motion. His vision was myopic and tunneled, his hearing was muffled, and voices seemed distant, hollow, and echoic. His heart raced at a dizzying pace; he was febrile and beginning to perspire. Gray, cobblestone streets outlined by lateritious sidewalks seemed to welcome him, and like an airport approach lighting system, the mortar between the bricks and cobblestones produced a luminous, golden hue that pulled him forward. *Follow the rabbit, follow the rabbit.*

Turning left past a collage of storefronts, he ignored any onlookers and the leery eyes of billboard personalities with their shiny, white teeth, odd appendages, and colorful plumage. He stumbled forward as his gait grew more and more ataxic. Feeling disconnected from reality, Jason paused before a reflective storefront window to feel his face and appendages and assure himself that he was still himself. And so stood a boy, the resemblance exact. Not sure why his mind compelled him to keep moving forward, all he knew was that he needed to reach the red-and-white building down the road. The storefront was like a magnetic tractor beam and his body had become ferromagnetic, the unseen force pulling him and drawing him ever closer. His gut told him that the building would be a safe haven.

*Must escape. Must escape. That's where Father wants me to wait, I can feel it. Father! Father! Help me! I'll never go alone again.* He panted as he wove down the sidewalk, feeling the stares and glares from onlookers all around him. "Leave me alone, you animals, you monsters! Away!" Every creature was a foe to him. The world was twisting, the thought of the Fraser spiral starting again. *There's no place like home. There's no place like home.*

"Hey buddy, need a ride?" a frog-like creature with a Hispanic accent asked. He drove a purple and gold lowrider truck complete with a neon-glow undercarriage and flames painted on the side. The license plate read, "PLAYA."

"You don't look so good, muchacho." The air shocks violently raised and lowered the front section of the truck. "I can take you to the enfermería, amigo."

Jason ignored the offer and gravitated to the red-and-white shop across the intersection. Patrons could be seen through the large picture windows, sitting on stools with their backs turned. The place looked like an old soda shop with writing on the windows advertising the various sundries inside, the language a patchwork of English and maybe Arabic, familiar yet unfamiliar. Somewhere in the recesses of his mind, Jason had some vague recollection of one of his dad's medical books on the foyer shelf that was written in a similar language.

Most mesmerizing was the oversized, red-and-white striped, slowly twisting pole outside the shop, like a barber pole or candy cane. It was hypnotic and looked oddly delicious at the same time. At the pole's apex sat two intertwined pewter snakes that resembled the caduceus seen in doctors' offices. "Apothecary" was parabolically engraved over the doorway in raised, chrome lettering, but when he shifted his position, the words changed like a hologram to read "Ralph's Diner."

With the mindset of a zombie, Jason lumbered across the intersection and pulled the door open as two patrons emerged from the shop, keeping their distance from this stricken dishabille. The second patron held the door open as Jason staggered inside, his lower half failing to keep up with his torso as he fell onto his elbows on the counter. The place smelled like bacon, eggs, and fried chicken.

As soon as his bottom touched the stool, a waitress was upon him. A stereotypical waitress, complete with pink skirt ensemble, southern accent, and curly, pink beehive hairdo, straight out of the sitcom *Alice*, asked, "What can I do for ya, hun? Are you new to the island? I don't 'member seeing you here before. Are you one of them turistas?" Her voice was momentarily muted by the passing of firetrucks and ambulances with sirens blaring.

"Water please, ma'am. I don't know what's come over me. I don't think I'm supposed to be here. Umm, is that ambulance for me?"

"Name's Flo. Hun, you actin' funny. And don't you worry a bit. Did you take the Wake Up? And child, look at me, you don't need no ambulance. Ralph," she hollered over her shoulder, "fire trucks and ambulances passin'. Better turn on the radio."

"What? What do you mean?"

Turning back to Jason, she said, "Is this the first time you drank the cola, the Kool-Aid?" She spoke in slow motion, her gleaming, white teeth magnified and protruding out of her mouth. "Did ya, hun? Well, welcome to 1972 on Tripe Island. Where ya from?"

Jason's perspective shifted and undulated; it was as if he saw the world through a fisheye lens. He leaned his head back, trying and failing to focus his eyes.

Calling over her shoulder, she yelled out to a stocky, unshaven man who Jason estimated to be about five and a half feet tall. The man was clad in a dirty apron and a dirty white tee, and his balding head was covered with a white sailor hat. His flattened nose suggested that he'd lost more than a few boxing matches. The cook glanced up from his screaming-hot grill when Flo called his name.

"Hey, Ralph, you may need to come on out. I think we have a newbie. His name is Jason Dix, look in the paper."

"How do you know my name?"

"Well hun, you're gonna need a lot of learnin', but for now, you just grab yourself a seat. You just don't look

239

well, I tell ya. How 'bout some eggs and toast? You come to the island for some craic? I learned that-there word in Ireland. Know it, hun? This ain't no small-town girl you're lookin' at."

"Just toast, please. I'm not sure what craic is, ma'am."

She wiped the counter clean with a damp rag and then placed a jar of Soothing Strawberry Jelly, a clean plate, and two pieces of toast soaked in the jelly before him.

"On the house, eat up. Coffee, hun? You just keep your tush on that seat. I think you and Ralph need to have a little chat, but not before some of this jelly's soothed your nerves. Are you one of them adventure seekers? Comin' here to ride the waves with the storm a-comin' and all? Surfin' it, hun? From the US of A, are ya?"

"I landed about an hour or two ago, I guess. Hey, does this island have a warthog problem? This vendor at the airport was so ugly, I swear he looked like a warthog. And at baggage claim, the passengers looked like animals and insects. I'm telling you, my head's not right. I really may need that ambulance. I thought I was coming here to meet my mother, but I think I've been duped. Then I get here and there's all this craziness, I don't know what to make of it. I just want to go home." Jason started to nibble on the food.

"Raaalph? He's askin' about the warthog. You got the paper today? You better come on out here. Said he was here to meet his mama. I think it's him on the middle of the front page. We've got ourselves a bona fide celebrity! Ten-thousand-dollar reward! Man, somebody wants him *bad*."

The jelly was working. Instantly, his flushed face cooled and the knots in his queasy stomach loosened. A swinging door opened from the kitchen as Ralph, the owner and head cook, ambled to the counter holding a newspaper, smiling ear to ear. Jason caught a glimpse of the headline on the front page of *The Island Daily Times*.

"Your surname is Dix?"

"Yes, sir."

"What about your father?"

"Alfred?"

"Well I'll be. I just knew it would be you. I didn't know what name you and your father would take if you made it off the island. Talk about a pair of cojones; your dad has them! I always thought he'd use Dix. We came up with the name in a card game. You know your pop used to work for me in the kitchen? I'll be, so your name really is Dix? There's no denying it; you made the papers already today."

"Yes, sir, my name's Dix, sir. Thank you for the toast, sir. Did you know my mother? Was I really duped?"

"Not a lick, never heard of her, and never a mention from your father. It was always so strange that your father wound up with a kid but not his gallivanting friend. Now he was slick. I mean *slick*! Strange times they were, strange times. Look at you, though; you're growing into a young man. A strapping young lad you are. Fleur-de-lis, yeah?" He pointed to Jason's shirt. "Nice. Saints fan, are ya? Tied game last week versus San Fran. You see it?" Ralph patted Jason on the shoulders. "You know, the last time I saw you, you were about the size of a loaf of bread. Seems like just yesterday when Beau was asking for help. Did he ever tell you how I started in this business? That he worked in the kitchen for me for a bit? Well, not this particular kitchen, it was south of here. But then, *poof* . . ."

Quickly and without explanation, Ralph shoved the paper in front of Jason, hiding his face from the front window. Ralph stared directly at him, pencil in hand as if he were taking an order. Seconds later, a sounder of warthogs passed by the diner, Bill the bellicose ice cream vendor leading the pack.

Scanning the main stories, Jason spotted a photograph of his face biting a hairy arm. The photo accompanied the lead story: "Be On the Lookout for Jason Dix, Felon. Reward $10,000." The story portrayed him as a violent, barbaric monster, and photos depicting him in various disguises ran at the bottom of the page. Jason read the first few lines in which he was portrayed as a monster. The sidebar story featured a glowing headshot of the woman across from him on the airplane, with the title: "The Salubrious Dr. Patricia Atwood Returns to Tripe."

Jason watched the warthogs in a mirror behind the counter before focusing on his photo and the women from the plane. For some reason, he wasn't as fearful of them as Ralph was, even though he had good cause to be.

Jason pointed to her photo. "That's the woman. That's the woman who tricked me into coming to this island. She's the one who was on my television, dancing around in a field. She's the one who told me that Alfred is my abductor and not my real father."

"Atwood? Really? She's been digging things up around here for ages. She does travel a lot, but golly. What would she have to do with . . ." He momentarily lost himself in thought. "Anyhow, warthogs were passing. I'm trying to protect you. With that kind of reward, they'll be after you. Hell, who wouldn't, right? If I hadn't made a deal with your father, I'd think of turning you in myself. What I could do with $10,000. They've already got you on the front page of the paper. You're going to be captured if we don't act fast. It's best we get moving."

"They grabbed me and I was just trying to protect myself. A beast of a pretzel vendor tried to wrap me up, and an ice cream vendor, Bill, helped him. Atwood, the woman on the front page of the paper, was the one who tricked me into coming to this island. I'm certain it's her. What does she want from me? Why didn't she speak to me on the plane? When my father gets here, I'll sort all of this out."

"I know, I know. You're frustrated, I get it. But it's going to be your word against hers, and you're already charged with a felony. Biting is a serious crime on this island. Why would anyone believe you? You're an outsider, and she's beautiful and beloved by the locals."

"What was that you said?" Flo nudged Ralph.

"She's nowhere near as beautiful as you, hun. Listen, Jason, you're clearly not thinking right. They gave you the cola, but you can't do anything about that now. You must save yourself. Atwood can't be the only reason you're here on this island. There has to be someone else. I've never known her to have a mean bone in her body. Listen to me, boy, this thing goes deeper than you think. You have history here, more than you know. Let's stop focusing on why and who, and start thinking about self-preservation. Those hogs have become a bit more aggressive this past week. The whole Westbank has gone cuckoo. Something must be afoot and that afoot must be you. You've got to listen to me. Wait, tell me again, why are you here? I mean, your father really took a risk when he got you off this island. Why did you come back? Both of you here, for what?"

"I don't know, wait . . . I ran, she tricked me," Jason grabbed his head. "I don't know. I'm so confused."

"I mean, why now? It's only a matter of time before you're caught. Those hogs, they've got pretty good noses. I'm surprised they didn't catch your scent when they passed by. We need to stay focused and a few steps ahead of their game." Ralph grabbed Jason's ear and dragged him into the kitchen through the swinging door when the coast was clear.

"My toast!"

"You'll have time to eat later. I'll give you some advice: remember that pigs are mean. Really mean. Those ruddy you-know-whats will eat anything, and at the moment, you're on the menu. We need to get you somewhere safe. You need to hide, but first, I have to fulfill a promise to your father. With so much money on your head for a reward, everyone will be looking for you."

"Why me? I mean, what did I do? Dad is supposed to be here soon; can't we just wait here for him to arrive? I'm supposed to be waiting for someone named Art."

"Art, hmm?" He rubbed his chin. "I'm not sure where he is. I guess he'll just have to catch up. You don't call me Uncle Ralph for nothin'!" He paused to think for a minute. "OK, kid, there's a bounty on your head. News flash: your father is numero uno on their wanted list. Merl's a close second. We'll get to what your dad and his friend did another time, but it'll take too long to explain right now. I made a promise to your dad to keep you safe. If you're going to make it off this island, you're going to need some help. Now stay put and do as you're told. I'll keep an eye out front. This whole place is going nuts; first Flight 605 goes down and then you pop in."

"Wait, you're not joking, are you? What have I done? Where is my father? Did you just say plane crash? Flight 605? Was my dad in a crash? Like, gone? How do you two know each other?"

"Crash, yes. Gone? Well, that's where things get a bit complicated. Look, trust me when I tell you your father made it. But no time for small talk, we've got to get you moving. I promise to explain when we have time. You need to trust me. Time's a-tickin'."

He walked toward the stove and pulled a lever on its side, opening a hidden passage behind an adjacent shelving unit. His meaty arm grabbed Jason, thrusting him through the portico and into an elegantly furnished room, complete with a pharmacist's desk and lab equipment. Com-

246

pared with the loud acoustics in the diner, this room was muted and even a bit stuffy.

"But my father texted me. He was on Flight 605. Down? Like, crashed or landed?" Jason's concern was evident.

"Exploded, like with a huge fireball. That's what the ruckus outside. You're lucky you made it ahead of the storm. I'll be back for you in a few minutes. There are a few things you'll need, and Barry will help you out. He's a good man, someone you can trust. He's been on this is- land for over a thousand years, or so they say. Trust me, he's seen it all. I rang him when I knew it was you. He'll be up in a moment. I'm going to keep watch out front and see what else I can find out. Your father will be fine." Ralph sat him in one of two green wingback chairs, and Jason placed his knapsack on the floor beside the chair.

Ralph retreated back to the diner. "Listen carefully to what Barry has to say. He's got a bit of a speech issue, a real sesquipedalian. Good with black-market-type stuff. The real deal. Your dad set up this meeting before he left."

"What's a sesquipedalian?" Jason mumbled to no one, Ralph having already exited.

The sight and smell of the room was surreal, no matter one's cognitive state. Settling in for a long wait, Jason examined the room around him. The most noticeable features were the cream shag carpet and an oversized, highly polished mahogany desk. A credenza sat against the wall behind the desk, and the wingback chairs were positioned in front. For a hidden room, the ceiling was surprisingly tall—about twenty feet high. A stunning, crystal chandelier functioned like a prism, blanketing the room in an array of colors. Deep, rich, wooden shelves lined the walls from floor to ceiling; the shelves were practically overflowing with meticulously labeled glass containers of varying shapes, sizes, and colors. The desk and credenza were covered with beakers, mortars and pestles, and a plethora of other sundries found in ancient apothecary shops. Incense smoke wafted from the chars of a smoldering wick set atop a tea saucer. Rolling ladders were fixed to the sides of the shelving units, and an oversized leather chair was pulled up behind the desk. An ancient cash register sat on its own stand to the left of the desk. A large oil painting of a grand battle featuring warring, armored knights and a dashing, allegorical hero hung on the wall behind the desk.

Jason eyed the focus of the painting, the king on horseback. There was something about him that spoke to Jason.

In the far corner of the room, a black, iron staircase spiraled downward. It began rattling in an indicative cadence of a biped making a slow ascent.

"Hello? Who is it? Hello?"

248

No reply.

Like the comb of a Leghorn rooster, a dark, oily, gray mane could be seen rising from the stairwell in advance of the rest of his body. It was an elderly, grandfatherly gentleman, dressed in gray pants, a white, starched shirt, and a long, white lab coat. He grabbed a cane out of an old, green milk jug near the stairwell and limped to the leather chair behind the desk, all the while remaining fixated on Jason. Windsor eyeglasses sat atop his Roman nose, and his spavined rhytid-laden face looked as though it had been weathered by thousands of seasons. His deep-set eyes with elongated lateral canthi were weary but full of wisdom.

"Jason, g-g-gweetings. I take it you've wad the most extraordinary day. Hewo, I am the won and wonly Warry we Wapothecawy." He smiled wide, pausing momentarily as if expecting Jason to answer.

Jason remained silent and in rapt attention; his mouth hung open in a stupor. "Excuse me?"

"I-I-I'm w-w-wetting wold. Wy w-w-wheumatism is willing we." The creature flexed his hip as if for effect before slowly sitting.

He paused again and stared intently into Jason's eyes before speaking. "Wi wonwore weswion. Wes, and wonsiderably well at wat! Wi will wexpwain." Barry began his verbal onslaught by offering a lengthy explanation of how a man named Beau Champs helped to rid the island of its previous leader and caused The Change. Jason remained confused and unable to fully comprehend the elder, whose circumlocutions, protracted and enervated, delved deeper and deeper into a speech replete with rhotacisms and substitutions, afflicted with a stammer as he described himself and the island's notable history. Barry's loquacious, incomprehensible, monotone voice, coupled with the soothing smell of incense and the chandelier's prismatic glistening created a hypnotic atmosphere, all sedatives that lulled Jason into a soporific trance.

For his part, Jason neared slumber. Only a smidgen of Barry's longiloquent speech was understandable, and much to Jason's dismay, there was no mention of any woman, his mother, or the lady on the television. Jason tried to keep himself from falling into a sweven state, his head bobbing as the elder continued using a sesquipedal dialogue that even the most stoic and committed individuals would find incomprehensible.

"You do know my father, Alfred? That's him, right there in your painting." An epiphany hit Jason like a ton of bricks as he pointed: the character in the painting looked exactly like younger photographs of Alfred. "My mother. Do you know her too?"

Barry rambled on about the painting.

"Um, I don't mean to be impolite, but I'm having a hard time understanding you. My father, if that is who you are referring to, never once mentioned his time here. Perhaps you have me mistaken. I think you may be confused. I will admit that the man in the picture does look an awful lot like him, but that must be a coincidence."

It was then that Barry swept his arm into one of the desk drawers and tossed a tow sack onto the desk and explained the contents valuable to Jason having been left to him by his father and, to the best of Jason's comprehension, some compensation owed.

Mercifully, Jason's stupor was interrupted by the peripatetic Ralph, who clamorously barreled through the hidden door with a look of harried emotion. Jason startled back to his baseline state of delirium. The bedlam of a distant argument and the smashing of dinnerware could be heard toward the front of the diner.

He could hear Flo yelling, "That'll be the last time we serve the likes of you lot here. You damn beasts are about to find out what happens when you mess with a grown-ass woman!" Flo's voice trailed off as the smashing of dinnerware became more pronounced.

"Sorry to interrupt, Barry, but it's time for Jason to leave. Remember that smell thing? They're on to your scent, kid." Ralph grabbed Jason, his hand tugging at the back of his shirt.

"We must not worget the wewixirs and wetter, a gift fwom his wather! Wewember to wask wim for wi woney. What he waid with was wot wegal wender." Barry motioned to the sack on the desk as Ralph looked at Jason and shrugged as if in agreement that Barry's speech was immensely cryptic. Ralph grabbed Jason's ear with one hand and the patrimonial tow sack and Jason's knapsack in the other and dragged him back into the kitchen and toward the excitement, quickly shutting the hidden door behind him. By the tone of Flo's voice, a physical altercation was imminent.

"Shouldn't I be heading in the other direction? Like down the stairs?"

Ralph hurriedly camouflaged the passage from which they had emerged.

Turning to Jason, he said, "Son, get in the sink!" He shoved him toward a shiny, metal sink overflowing with suds.

"What? It's an awfully small sink, Mr. Uncle Ralph."

"I didn't ask ya, I'm tellin' ya. If you want to live, get in. We discovered this trick a few years ago on accident. Don't ask me how. This place is turning into a madhouse. The first place they'll look is down the ladder. They'll catch you soon enough if you don't keep moving, and when they do, they'll turn you into pâté." Ralph thrust the knapsack over Jason's shoulder, shoved the tow sack inside, and then closed the fasteners.

"I still don't understand what is going on or why I'm in danger. I didn't do anything wrong!"

Ralph frantically shoved the folded, white envelope into the back pocket of Jason's pants. "You'll be safe where you're headed if you keep moving. Read this when you have a chance. It may help to explain some of what's happening. Your father left it for you. Listen, we've done all that we can do here. You need to get moving or you'll be caught. I'm not sure why you're here or what you have to do with any of this, but I promised your father I'd help you if I ever saw you again. Somehow, he knew you'd be back, and he needed you to see Barry. He must've had his reasons. Now get in the damn sink."

Jason was flabbergasted and completely befuddled. The day had not gone as planned, and in fact, much of it could not begin to be explained. Now he was being forced into a kitchen sink. There was no rhyme or reason for any of this. Jason was perplexed. Was Ralph asking him to hide under the suds and breathe through a straw until the coast was clear, like in a cartoon or old movie? Maybe his uncle was crazy.

"But it's a tiny sink. I won't fit!"

"Get in the damn sink! You're even more hardheaded than your father." He squirted detergent over Jason's head, twisted on the tap, then flipped a nearby switch, turning on what sounded like a garbage disposal.

*Now I'm really in trouble.* "Is there a straw for me to breathe through?" Water swirled around his body as the unmistakable sound of a flushing toilet filled his ears. Ralph's growing hand pushed him down the drain.

"Son, you're just like your father. He had moxie, and so do you. You'll survive. And you don't need a straw." Ralph's voice grew ever more distant. "It's Shrinking Suds."

"You said 'had,' like past tense? Where is my dad?" But before he could hear the reply, Jason was sucked into the drain.

Jason could now say he knew how a billiards ball feels when it's thrust into the guts of a billiards table. He plunged down into the drain, pinging to-and-fro into a dark maze of piping. As he picked up speed, the pipes pulsed red, green, yellow, or blue, like an electronic Simon game, as he struck the sides. "Entrance of the Gladiators" began to play on some unseen PA system.

# CHAPTER 12

## THE TIME OF CHANGE

*October 1960*

The sun was high overhead, baking the Island of Tripe's moist, tropical air into a sauna. Outside the island's newly created and bustling airport, Beau sat in an alcove at a cast-iron table, attempting to blend in as the lone, bohemian wayfarer without appurtenances except for a baby carriage at his side. Any real attempt to remain inconspicuous on this small island was for naught, as his malodor and disheveled appearance—wan, bleary-eyed, and wearing dirty, Hawaiian-print pajamas and tattered flip-flops—made him stick out like a sore thumb. He failed to feel the watchful eyes of an astute, blonde woman upon him.

Beau tried unsuccessfully to redirect the salty beads of perspiration that formed on his forehead, the moisture coalescing and rolling down his tired eyelids and long nose, over his lips, and dripping onto the thin, cotton parchment that lay on the iron table before him. He was too exhausted to notice that his sweat was smearing his notations on the Wheatstone cipher he was quietly working. He kept wiping his forehead with his sweaty, dirty forearm, creating an even bigger mess, threatening to render his notes illegible. Despite his attempts to maintain adequate posture, his tall, gaunt, famished frame drooped like an ill-proportioned, enervated Salvador Dali statue; he remained hunched over the black, iron table, working diligently.

Having been awake for nearly forty-eight hours, his mind skirted the boundaries of delirium and his head bobbed impotently. His imperspicuous plans were growingly unpropitious and foolhardy. His reality had become dramatically twisted and malleable in the span of only a few short days, a reality he no longer understood to be concrete. The reality of life, his life, those on the island, heck, the world over, was far different from his wildest imagination. *What defines reality? The eye of the beholder? From what perspective?* He desperately needed an escape and a means with which to put reality into some form of order, even if it were brief.

He glanced up at the clock in the atrium, which read 12:48; he had only twelve more minutes to prepare. He was at his wits' end, having taken the precautions to interject a modicum of correction to that fateful night when he and Merl fell off the mountain. He had hoped to circumvent the island's part of any further modifications of history. The former leader may have slipped through his grasp, but at least he was only one. He could still be captured and his ills corrected. But for now, Beau needed to proverbially wash his hands of the matter and right his contribution, this island's contribution, at least for the time being. The correction would come now, the leader's capture later.

Surveying his cryptic notations, he checked them for accuracy one final time as the writing continued to bleed on account of the dripping sweat; the smear was rather long but would not affect the message.

He reviewed his actions over the past few days and checked the remainder of the tasks off his mental list:

1. Reach Barry the Apothecary and convince the long-winded patron of his true identity, discuss the best method of egress, decide upon the elixirs necessary for escape, and delineate instructions for their use.

2. Obtain two travel vouchers for himself and the child.

3. Gain possession of the watch and the keys to the elevator.

4. Deposit a few rudimentary elixirs in a tow sack and pay the requisite fees to the apothecary.

5. Finish the letter and brave the airport.

He folded the manuscript to letter size. If his plan back-fired or the child needed to return to the island, his nota-tions and supplies would hopefully lessen his son's future troubles. There was just one thing left to do: deposit the letter before boarding Flight 411. The next few minutes would be critical.

The clock inside his head ticked forward as he waited nervously, needing to complete one final task before he could board the departing aircraft. He checked the golden watch, taking it from his pocket as the second hand final-ly struck 13:00 on Wednesday, October 12, 1960. The large clock situated in the airport atrium concurred as a distant bell tower tolled.

The moment of truth was upon him. He stood abruptly as a crowd of tourists passed, his eyes dancing furtively back and forth. With care and attention, he folded the parchment map and letter, placed them into a crisp, white envelope labeled:

Attention: Jason Dix
c/o Barry at The Apothecary
PO Box 13
Island of Tripe
South Pacific

Whispering into the baby carriage, Beau said, "I hope this finds its way to you if you are ever back on this blasted island. Most importantly, I hope we both make it to our new home. May the twenty-first century be prosperous for us both. Only fifty yards to go." He checked his chronograph one final time before pocketing it again. Raising his clenched fists to his lips, he kissed them for good luck and then withdrew a golden stamp from his pocket. When he placed it on the upper right-hand corner of the envelope, the letter began to glow an eerie, iridescent yellow. He then sealed the envelope and deposited it into a red pillar box labeled Intra-Island Mail.

At his full height, six foot three inches, his shadow was short in the bright, midday sun. He arched his back and stretched one final time, hoping this would be his last day on this most obscure island. Checking the items in his pocket again—a small vial of Real World liquid; two travel vouchers; two ornate, golden keys; one small, glowing, glass sphere; and the pocket watch—his mental check list was complete. Around his neck, he felt the hidden chain and vial of Last Resort elixir, truly his last resort if his plans were unsuccessful. He took the vial of Real World oil from his pocket, poured a small amount onto his callused left finger, and offered it to the suckling child hidden behind the yellow silk draperies that blanketed the carriage. Beau raised the vial to his lips and swallowed the remaining oily mixture, tossing the refuse in a nearby trash bin. Grabbing the handle of the carriage, he hurriedly pushed it into the airport's cool vestibule.

As he walked, Beau whispered to the bustling crowd, "Good luck, and may we meet again. The little one and I will make it, thanks to your brave souls. To all the friends I have made here, please forgive me. I believe most of you will understand." He took one last look at all the unsuspecting locals and tourists.

Pushing the carriage through the first set of glass doors, he withdrew the sphere from his pocket and smashed it on the floor with a firm downward force, stepping on it to make sure all the contents were released. The moment the sphere shattered, a gray gaseous plume clouded the vestibule, effectively barricading those inside the airport from those outside. Confused travelers gazed in wonder, perplexed over the goings-on. Without hesitation, he extracted the watch from his pocket and quickly spun the dial to the year 2003.

While most were unaware of the significance of the events unfolding, a young, blonde woman took the liberty of running after Beau. She found herself stuck half in and half out of the airport doors when the sphere was shattered. She was nearly through the airport vestibule doors when the gaseous plume was released, and she found herself trapped with her derriere outside and torso and head inside. Wiggling and writhing failed to yield her any progress out of her situation.

Frenetic pandemonium erupted as those outside watched the sky changing to soot black with a billowing pall of clouds as the earth began to shake and rumble. Those trying to take refuge inside the airport were barred entry by the grayish green gaseous effusion that enveloped the airport, spreading through its concourses. With a dramatic flash, a massive, nearly translucent dome encircled the airport. Inky plumes of clouds blanketed the entire area as the sky darkened and the wind whipped into a frenzy. Clouds as thick as soot descended upon the earth, thickened with gritty moisture that precipitated on the windows, obscuring the sun and the tempestuous sky.

As the rumbling grew louder, the island's topography followed suit. The landscape was changing dramatically by the second; hills sunk into the earth as others erupted, nature's ancient tectonic puzzle was suddenly adjusted. A second flash illuminated the growing darkness as thousands of shimmering, ephemeral lights shot out of the mountain and disappeared in a southerly direction.

Just as quickly as it had spread, the plume of smoke in the airport dissipated. The patrons trapped inside suddenly froze, statuesque. In synchrony, the hands of Beau's watch and the large airport clock began to spin clockwise at incredible speed. Time became distorted, rushing forward like the rapids of a river. Beyond the vestibule, airport personnel began morphing from 1960s attire into 2000s style, and serpent tattoos appeared on some of their arms. Even the equipment inside the airport began to shift and change; a security checkpoint, X-ray machines, full-body scanners, and metal detectors appeared from nowhere. Through the windows, a plane at the nearest gate transformed from a Boeing 707 into a 747.

People outside the dome were not immune from the potion's effects; in fact, the effect was far more drastic. Most people outside the airport began to transmogrify into creatures fitting a devolutionary representation of their personalities. Those at the lowest level of their devolutionary ladder remained unchanged. Where a human being stood moments before, now stood a congeneric animalistic representation, including anthropomorphic lizards, birds, butterflies, warthogs, and a variety of insects. Some people were transformed according to their profession; meter maids turned into slugs, and police officers became dogs. The woman stuck in the vestibule was affected, but in an incomplete manner; her torso and head remained seemingly immune, while her derriere and arm, stuck mostly out the door, developed a tail and serpent tattoo, respectively. The entirety of the circumstance was unbelievable, and those affected just stared at each other in utter amazement at the sheer implausibility of it all.

So much for Darwinism. Long live Buffon's Law of venerated degenerative evolution.

Beau remained able to function, but he and the child were not completely immune from the potion's effects. His tattered threads were replaced with a white, linen top, white, linen pants, and new sandals. His hair was neatly combed, his face was cleanly shaven, and he smelled like Old Spice.

If the potion proved to be unstable, all creatures would revert back to their initial state, so stopping to take inventory was a luxury for which he hadn't the time. Knowing that he was not yet out of harm's way, his curiosity would have to wait. He pushed the carriage, now a cheap plastic stroller with a Made in China decal, hastily into the crowd and through the airport security checkpoint as he nicked a tan fedora and Wayfarer sunglasses off a nearby mannequin.

Once he had gotten past security, time returned to normal and the airport patrons continued their routines, seemingly oblivious to the preceding events and the change in scenery. Beau knew their ignorance would only be momentary.

Just as rapidly as they had come, the heavy clouds parted, giving way to blue skies over a tranquil island.

Beau joined the shuffling cue at Gate 4B and boarded the plane bound for the States. Trying to force a calm countenance, he took his seat, the baby on his lap. He could be seen through the window of the aircraft, one key in hand as his eyes were glued to the happenings outside.

As if nothing extraordinary had happened, the aircraft taxied and departed just as the dome around the airport collapsed. The airport reverted back to its chronistic place in time, and the patrons inside began to devolve like their brethren outside. The child would be safer away from the island, not knowing what had happened. For now, they needed anonymity.

# CHAPTER 13

## THE THERAPY SESSION

*Saturday, October 28, 1972*

Throughout history, there have been many a rise and fall of empires and cultures, and the guiding light behind the success of most institutions has ultimately been that of authority, whether it be aristocracy, geniocracy, technocracy, or any other. Tripe Island was technically like any other after The Change, with its governance reliant upon authority. However, the current political climate was a bit lax and irresolute due to the events of 1960. It had become a cross between a democracy and meritocracy, and authority rested somewhere between a council and a president. The island functioned peacefully and well enough, but the island's government was not always so. According to folklore, the preceding government was a bit violent—a kleptocracy or kratocracy, depending on your point of view—run by an avaricious and narcissistic leader who developed powers unlike any known to twenty-first-century mankind.

The island's change to a more democratic society was not brought about by some altruistic self-realization, a religious conversion on the part of the previous leader, or even by divine providence, but by outsiders who forcefully removed the leader, his privileged acquaintances, and all associated symbols of his reign. According to legend, the leader was either permanently held in a state of preservation in another time or dimension, or somehow disappeared into the frays of time itself. Any truth to this detail was aligned more with superstition than fact, and the details and certainty of his whereabouts remained less than vague. What was certain, however, was that the lives of his ardent followers were ignominiously affected. In their devolved states, they all became the precariat of the island's society: Westbank warthogs. When the island's populous regressed consequent to their leader's disappearance, he was rumored to have been traded for the island's current degree of civility, lack of culture, and declining base of knowledge. This legend remained a veiled threat that hung over the island should any one person come to power.

And thus, the Island of Tripe's new and current political system functioned in the following manner, according to its ever-evolving constitution. The island was split into twelve voting districts. Each district's residents voted to appoint a single representative (no matter the species) for a term of four years. The Westbank warthog population, having been aligned with the previous leader, were afforded no voting rights and could not function as a government officer of any type—period! The elected representatives sat on the Tripe Island Council and were apportioned to handle various matters important to the island. Every four years, these elected representatives also appointed a non-elected individual with abilities that suited the island's current need to act as ombudsman, president, and principal spokesperson. The president's authority was inherently limited; their role was to shape the agenda and policies of the governing body, and listen to any serious grievances that may be worthy of the council's time. Every district representative worked part-time, with half of the governing body undergoing reelection every other year. The four-year term ruled out many of the insects with projected life spans of less than four years, but they didn't seem to mind the exclusion. It just so happened that the new presidential appointment was to occur next week.

Melvin, the grumpy, parsimonious airport janitor was the island's current president. He was known to be a rule follower and stickler for cleanliness and order. Everyone who passed through the island's airport knew of the superior quality of his work, and thus, he was a reasonably good fit for the job. The aging airport was kept strikingly neoteric as a result of his incessant care and cleaning. He kept it up so well that it not only functioned as an airport, but also as an anachronistic, usable piece of art.

Despite Melvin's orderliness, his appointment was not born out of a generalized admiration, but rather, through an unusual and tragic set of circumstances. His wife, Chamé, the island's beautiful and endearing former librarian, a darling to all who knew her, was killed when the library collapsed. It had been built eons ago, long before The Change, and after a support beam gave way, the entire structure crashed to the ground, crushing her in the rubble. Her death was a profound blow to Melvin's psyche. He was middle-aged, and with the children grown and out of the home, Melvin was suddenly forced into solitude. This isolation led to loneliness and depression, which affected him rather severely. A deep-seated angst sprouted and grew within him. He tried to develop coping mechanisms, a healthy sublimation, with a resolve for cleaning and a respect for order that was dramatic. The Tripe Island Council thought it best to offer him the position of president to boost his spirits and aid in his dolorous psyche. (Plus, his appointment came with the added benefit of keeping the island clean.)

The new role seemed to help, but halfway through his tenure, he began acting out and regressing as more emotional turmoil surfaced. Eventually, the council paired him with Dr. Atwood to work through his megrims. The pairing worked beautifully for a time, and he was making progress, but in recent days, he had become more aggressive. As many expected, he would be dismissed from the job when the next presidential appointment took place.

Dr. Atwood was tasked with aiding his ailing mental health and supporting him through the transition.

As the tempest rolled toward Tripe, Melvin sat behind his large mahogany desk in his starched, khaki uniform, and looked out in a lugubrious trance. He valued order, so his office was sparse and impeccably clean with beige carpeting, a small, beige settee resting against the far wall, a phonograph near the doorway adjacent to a single Ficus lyrata, a credenza, on which sat a picture of him and his deceased wife, and two beige, cushioned chairs. On his wooden desk, he kept a calendar, an electric clock, an intercom, and an orderly pen set. He had been allowed to choose his decor, but soon, it would likely all change at the discretion of the next occupant. He had considered keeping the settee and the plant.

He pensively looked out the large bay windows and across the Tripe township as the storm rolled in, listening to the distant thunder mixed with the faint hum of the electric analog clock that sat atop his desk. The clock's flip could be heard as the time progressed to 2:36, and the windowpanes shuddered with each gust of wind. Manuel de Falla's *Nights in the Gardens of Spain*, Melvin's favorite piece of music, played on the phonograph but was barely audible over the approaching squall. The imponderabilia to reflect upon was vast, just as his presidential decisions had been over the past four years. He thought he had performed his presidential duties well, and he felt melancholy over his growing obsoleteness. He was aging; perhaps his utility was nearing its twilight. And so, he sat contemplating his years with nothing to do but wait. There was no more cleaning needed, as all was in order and the sweet odor of Pine-Sol permeated his space. His scheduled appointment with Dr. Atwood was at three o'clock, so he still had twenty-four minutes.

He sat quietly, drumming his fingers together, basking in the fresh scent as he contemplated his life without Chamé. From the recesses of his desk's top drawer, he withdrew an old relic purloined from the airport's recon-struction years ago: an antique, ornate, golden skeleton key. It was the second time today he fiddled with the item, the first being that morning when he had removed it from a shoe box hidden away in a closet back home. Its re-creation was so exact that for a moment he questioned that he had the correct copy. His inquisitor was vehe-mently interested in the item; he knew it would be advan-tageous to bring it to the meeting.

Questions abounded in his mind. So many things as of late were amiss. Perhaps his charade was going a bit too far. What malefactors could be nicking the lighting fix-tures and sconces from the airport? Who could have pos-sibly removed all the marble and faux alabaster? Why was he subject to so many unexplained lapses in memo-ry? He knew that most creatures on the island could pos-sibly engage in such depredating behavior. It was as if the answers were staring him in the face, but he just couldn't bring them to light. Why was his cloak and sash placed in one of his desk drawers, when he knew that he last placed them in his locker at the airport?

Thunder boomed and lightning blazed across the distant sky, interrupting his bemused trance, the flash highlighting the picture of his wife. The love of his life was deceased; if only he could hold her one last time.

He picked up the key to examine it closely. Its bow was heavy and ornate and featured a brown, centrally placed crest. There was no stop. A leaf-like pattern was inscribed on the key's two bits. He remembered the day when he found its archetype. A portion of the terminal's stone flooring was being demolished near an elevator shaft, and the key had simply been a serendipitous find among the refuse. Attempts to find the matching keyhole in the airport, the post office, and various doorways across the island had been for naught. He could find no lock to fit his key. Because it was quite ornate and beautiful, he thought it reasonable to tuck it away amongst his shoe boxes, knowing that a key of such magnitude had to unlock something of importance. He would find the lock one day, so he decided that it was best to keep the master.

Without warning, the speaker on his desk loudly barked, shaking him from his reverie, the sharp, nasally voice of his secretary abruptly shifting his attention. "Mr. Melvin, sir? There is a group of warthogs from the Westbank here to see you. Apparently, someone told them you wished to visit with them, something about an injustice. They are quite rude and stink to high heaven. Shouldn't we have a dress policy? And I've said before, you really ought to make appointments earlier in the day. I really don't think it's appropriate to schedule appointments so late in the afternoon. I only get government pay, you know. For that matter, my salary is a bit too low to deal with the likes of the Westbankers. Who's going to pay my dry-cleaning bill? Never mind, I may just burn this outfit. Since when do they have a voice?"

Melvin pushed the black lever on the box and worked to keep his voice calm. "Like I've said before, everyone gets a voice. You can send them in, Deloris."

Melvin opened his top drawer and hid the key deep in the back behind a stack of government papers and a book of magic tricks. He shut the drawer and tried hard to remove the thought of the key from his mind. The clock flipped to 2:40; he had twenty minutes to prepare.

To his dismay, he heard a loud rancor outside his door. In less than a second and in rapid succession, two unkempt, lumbering, gargantuan warthogs barreled through the door like feral bulls. Dressed in vertically striped, or-ange-and-red ensembles, their ruckus caused Melvin's phonograph to come to a screeching a halt, the needle scratching across the vinyl disc. Adipose rolls rippled across their abdomens with each step as the acrid smell of wet, dirty fur engulfed the room.

Melvin eyed them abhorrently as the pounding of their steps produced a thinly veiled look of contempt on his face. They were tracking mud across his pristine, beige carpet, and strands of wet fur fell from their bodies. *Great. This room is going to stink for weeks.* He knew the two from the airport; their personal hygiene and respect for order were vile, no matter the location. In fact, a travailing portion of each day was uniquely devoted to cleaning up their refuse, so to add their pigsty to his impeccable office was inexcusable.

"Mr. President, there's been an injustice and it's your job to fix the matter!" inveighed Bill the ice cream vendor. His heated breath could be felt from behind the desk.

"My problem? You're the problem! Just look at my office, the muck on your feet . . ." He gesticulated widely. "How dare you march in here without cleaning yourselves, you filthy beasts! This is the presidential suite. We're not in the Westbank. When you're in the Westbank, you can do what you please, but not here. You're not fraternizing at one of your beer joints. Do you not have any semblance of hygiene? Look at the mud!"

"We demand . . ." Bill paused to think for a moment as he pulled a *Law for Dummies* book out of his pocket.

"Yeah, we demand! What do we demand?" Larry stood at his side.

"We demand damages paid in recompense! As president, you have a tutelary responsibility!" He waved his book in the air. "I've read up on this point of fact! There is legal precedent. We have rights."

His counterpart interjected, "Yeah to what Bill said. You're the one we're supposed to talk to when we got a problem. Well, I've been bitten by a young boy, and it's not the first time. I may have some sort of disease. I may have been afflicted by a case of the mulligrubs! That would make it your problem," blathered Larry the pretzel vendor, pointing directly at Melvin. "This needs the council's immediate attention. If I am infirmed, who is to pay my doctor bills? What about my wages? I demand disability pay!"

"Doubtful." Melvin was not swayed by their size, and he acerbically said, "You two miscreants are not attorneys. You have no authority on this island. You are fast-food vendors, and I am the president. How dare you come into my clean office and point your grubby finger at me? I'll break it if it's not out of my face in three, two . . ."

Larry quickly withdrew his finger.

Unaffected by Melvin's firm tone, Bill leaned over the desk and pointed his own finger at Melvin. "Since you've been elected president, you've always told us to report any issues before we take matters into our own hands. Well, I can't make a living if I'm being stolen from and my friends are being bitten. We want this kid, and we're going to take matters into our own hands to get him. What's a poor ice cream vendor to do? God knows what sort of disease I'll catch now that Larry is clearly ill. Did you know that the human mouth is one of the dirtiest places on the planet?"

Larry interjected, "Yeah, and it was a foreign boy, Jason Dix. He made the paper. You never know what foreigners are carrying these days!"

"First we have to work for minimum wage, and to make matters worse, we're being stolen from and bitten. I hope our workers' comp insurance is paid in full! I'm taking this matter to the council. Habeas corpus if there ever was one!" Bill waved his text in the air. "I demand indemnification!"

"Yeah, we're being stolen from. He ran down the escalator before disappearing past the luggage."

Melvin had heard enough. "Wait, wait! Who instructed you two buffoons to come here? I'll bet you were loafing in Harry's Bar when this bright idea struck. Right? And it's Actus reus you imbeciles!"

"Whatever! Why should that matter? What are you going to do about it? We need you to find the boy!" Bill stared directly at him, eyes steadfast.

"Nothing. I'm going to do absolutely and utterly nothing," Melvin calmly stated. He turned to face the window for a forbearing moment before deciding his position. Rather instantaneously, he decided that he could not be bothered to accede to their rough inquiry. "Look, I have one week remaining in this position. Your issues will need to be taken up with the next president, whomever that may be," he said with a dismissive wave of his hand. "You're going to need a long-term solution, one that I cannot give you. Seek help elsewhere and after the storm."

"But Melvin!" Bill threw his arms up, remonstrating in frustration.

"Have you called the Tripe Main Security Force and filed a grievance?"

"No," they sheepishly admitted in unison.

"You need to work your way up the chain of command. You can't just walk into the president's office and start making demands."

"But you're their boss!"

Melvin silently twirled his seat, his back to the two, pensively staring at the vast expanse beyond the bay window. A minute or two of silence was meant to unnerve his visitors as he struggled to calm himself. He drew upon the forbearance of changing into his alter ego and taking physical action against the two.

"Well?" grunted Bill after the silence continued.

The speaker on his desk blared. "Melvin, do you need me anymore? I'd like to get home before the storm, which is making my bursitis flare, by the way."

Mashing the button on the intercom, he said, "Yes, Deloris, you need to stay until five, as we discussed last week."

"Now where were we?"

Bill barked, "You were talking to the speaker."

The speaker once again droned, "Melvin, I'm glad you only have a week remaining because I see we have another late appointment. I guess we'll just be here all night because I know that I don't have anything else to do in my life, like go home to a family, make dinner, enjoy my time after work, or do anything other than sit in this blasted office for all hours while my boss tries to placate the likes of two Westbank oafs."

"Good god, can you get on with it, you incessant woman?" Melvin's voice was growing more asperous with the hint of a British accent.

"Pardon me, sir. I'll accept your apologies a bit later along with a box of chocolate. By the way, Dr. Patricia Atwood is standing in front of me and is waiting to see you. I believe she has an appointment. Shall I send her in? I bet you wouldn't treat her in the same manner. I guess you'll want me to wait here until after she departs."

"Get her a cup of coffee or tea and make her comfortable. Give me a minute to finish up with Bill and Larry."

Melvin made it clear that he had nothing more to say on the matter, and then kicked the warthogs out of his office. Before his psychotherapy session would begin, he took the liberty of removing the telephone receiver from the cradle, cleaning some of the grime off the carpet, and tidying up his office. Dr. Atwood encouraged these types of steps to avoid interruptions to their session that would cause him to lose focus. He was incessant about cleanliness and order. When he was done, he sat on the edge of the settee, taking a few moments to gather his thoughts and settle his nerves. There was much to ponder.

Recently, Dr. Atwood had questioned his convictions regarding their relationship and his devotion to therapy. She mentioned that he seemed a bit edgy and nervous in her presence, a point that invited Melvin's quick rebuke. He insisted that perhaps she was misconstruing his feelings of adoration and perception of luck, quick to acknowledge and politely aware of his good fortune that someone of her caliber was helping him. After all, what

278

were the chances, given their remote location in the South Pacific? He reiterated that he was not alone in these feelings, as she was beloved by countless others across the island who were in need of psychological help after The Change. Her altruistic efforts afforded her a high degree of acceptance and deference, to the point that many simply referred to her by the sobriquet, "healer."

Had his inquiries invited her restiveness? And if so, what was there to hide? Why had she settled on this small South Pacific island? Why grace him with her presence? Were these not questions that should be asked directly of such a remarkable woman? His inquiries were always met with a bit of circumlocution, and she was yet to provide any proper answers. He was certain that time would reveal her ulterior motives, and now, after months, his intuition was proving to be correct. After all, it was she who alerted him to the boy's arrival at the airport.

He wasn't quite sure what drew him to such a conclusion during their initial meetings. Perhaps her subtle mannerisms had made him suspect that her intentions and motives were misguided. Over time, as their relationship grew, he dismissed such feelings, supplanting them with trust, but recently, his views were devolving. These notions were subtle, hazy, and at times, confusing. It wasn't as if she were selfish; she did far more than most natives to bolster the quality of life on the island. For instance, she had recently donated a number of her praised archaeological finds to the island's airport and other public spaces, which drew tourists and revenue to the island. He made a point to keep the collection incessantly clean as a show of gratitude. It was in these circumstances that their complicated but healthy relationship evolved.

His reverie was broken by a slight click from the intercom. Melvin glanced around his office to make sure nothing else needed to be addressed. He wiped the last bit of fur from his desktop, bringing the rag up to his nostrils. *Only a fool wouldn't love the sweet incense of Pine-Sol. Harry Cole was a genius. Oh, how I love you so for satiating my olfactory apparatus. I think we are ready.* He took a long inhalation of the rag as he held it close before tucking it away in the bottom drawer. He switched off the phonograph and took a deep, inspiratory breath to calm his nerves and regain some of his lost composure.

Pressing the intercom button, he said, "OK, Deloris. Please ask Dr. Atwood to come in."

"It's about time, sir. We've been waiting and waiting. I thought we'd have to send in medical. It's not like we haven't been waiting all day. If I were her, I'm not sure I would have waited, particularly for the likes of you."

Dressed in similar attire from her earlier airplane departure, Dr. Atwood let herself in and shook Melvin's hand. They exchanged their usual pleasantries, and Deloris's rant finally subsided. Without direction, Melvin assumed a supine position on the beige settee, closed his eyelids, and attempted to relax as the sound of whistling wind and pattering rain struck the window glass.

Melvin was the first to speak. "I must say, doc, thanks for the incite at the airport earlier today. I've had to deal with Bill and Larry and their nonsense."

"Airport?"

"It was clever of you to procure the young Champs boy. I cannot imagine how you found him. Did you see the paper? How did you make the connection with his father? Changing his name to Dix, ingenious!"

Patricia quizzically studied for any hint of facial expressions, as she had no recollection of meeting him today at the airport. She wasn't even sure to whom she was speaking: was it Melvin or Saul? He remained comfortably sprawled, his face expressionless with no hint of deceit. This was not the first time an episode of his dissociative fugue led her inquiry to a dead end. It was something to look into.

Dr. Atwood set her multicolored canvas knapsack next to the settee, then adjusted the rheostat to its lowest setting, a cool fifty-eight degrees Fahrenheit, as the air conditioning unit shuddered to life. She dimmed the lights to make the office and her client more comfortable, and given Melvin's poikilothermic metabolism, the lowered temperature caused him to drift into a more languid and docile state. She combed her hair with her fingers, and then opened the door a crack and whispered, "Deloris, you can go on home now, dear. Our session may be a while, and he'll have no more need for you this afternoon. Thank you for your patience, and thank you for the tea."

Melvin could be heard exhaling through his mouth, slowing his breathing, readying himself for what came next.

"Well, it's about time someone showed some respect around here. Maybe Dr. Atwood CAN teach you a few things."

Dr. Atwood closed the door, slid a wedge below it to prevent anyone from entering, unplugged the intercom, and pulled one of the beige chairs to Melvin's side. She could faintly hear Deloris's voice as she left the office. "It's about time someone appreciated me. I just cannot wait for the new president so we can get some things straight. Oh, Dr. Atwood, I thought I . . ." Her voice and footsteps trailed off as she walked through the front door of the building, followed by the sound of a lock and the light jingle of the door's bell.

Dr. Atwood let a few more moments pass before speaking. Melvin's breath was now rhythmically assured. She retrieved a golden pocket watch from her bag. "Melvin, we will begin our session with a brief recital." She began to chant, reading the watch's inscription aloud as she rhythmically pendulated the device before her patient.

"Bonum est quadraginta annis.

Tempus Fugit.

Elementum temporis.

Prudenter uti."

If an outsider were to witness the session, they might say she fancied him. Dangling the golden piece before him, Patricia smiled widely, drawing nearer as their eyes met, dissembling her true emotion by displaying the most saccharine of demeanors. Her long, blonde hair wafted across his face, her scent clean and crisp. Her beauty easily broke through any interspecies differences. She was the epitome of vigor and youth, especially when seen through the languid eyes of a cold-blooded lizard creature.

She spoke in an even, soothing tone. "Melvin, I believe you're getting into the right mindset. I need you to keep your eyes open, your head still, and your attention on the watch. Remember, focus on the watch and slow your breathing. I need you at peace. Let your mind drift into a bliss. That's right, my prized, golden Alibaba watch, the same from last session. Hypnosis again. I think it had a positive effect last time."

"Thank you, Dr. Atwood. Your presence is always so enlightening. By chance is your scent the Yves Saint Laurent Rive Gauche? I think Deloris's periodical had an ad." He enjoyed her smell as his mind was suddenly suffused with many of the wonderful scents he had experienced throughout his life.

She smiled. "I must say, Mr. President, I'm impressed. I've always thought of you as a Pine-Sol man. I was unaware that your talents extended to perfume connoisseur. Thank you for putting your trust in me, and please, call me Patricia. We've spent so much time together; let us dispose of such formalities. I insist. This doctor stuff is for strangers." She coquettishly batted her eyes. "Now, where were we in our last conversation? And did I catch the faint sounds of de Falla's *Nights in the Gardens of Spain* before I came in? Deloris says you've been waiting."

Melvin's speech was becoming more slurred as his metabolism slowed, his eyelids drifted to near slits.

"Now don't fall asleep on me."

His voice became even more languorous as he continued, "Most affected in The Change was my trenchant sense of smell. I knew you'd arrived when you walked through the doors downstairs. And yes, that was de Falla." Melvin smiled a broad, happy smile as he stretched and drew his appendages closer like a satiated baby. The look on his face was sheer bliss. "I'm told that you have quite an ear and a taste for the Spanish classics. Would you be interested in the history of the piece? The king of Spain granted de Falla a stay, allowing him to compose in Paris. Can you imagine dancing a saraband in Paris in the springtime? The two of us in Paris." His eyes glazed over as his imagination had the two twirling in the Jardin des Tuileries. "We are dancing together in a beautiful garden."

She had heard enough. The analog clock on his desk read 3:00 as she adjusted the dial of her watch to 2:30 and began its pendulous motions once again. She was actually quite disgusted with the thought of an amorous relationship with this creature, but she needed to continue the ruse.

"Melvin, this session is not about me; it's about you. It is time we begin. We will root out the deepest turmoil inside you. And remember, this session is strictly about you. I'm here for you." She placed her index finger over her lips then over his. His eyes opened slightly, revealing a glazed look of rapture. "I need you to stare at the watch, Melvin. Deeper. Deeper." They were almost there.

The rhythmic motions of the watch gave way to time distortion. Dr. Atwood's voice purred like a kitten as she whispered, "Elementum temporis, elementum temporis, elementum temporis. Continue with your breathing. Slowly, Melvin. You are on edge today. I can feel it. You have something important to convey. I can feel it in my bones. Your metabolism should be slowing down even further. You have nothing to fear. Let your mind drift." Her blue eyes were mesmerizing and seemed to penetrate his soul.

"I'm sorry . . . a bit harsh with the two before you . . . two oafs . . . dirtying . . . lighting fixtures disappearing . . . airport. Know not why." Melvin rambled incoherently as his voice slowed. He shivered from the cold air that blew through the vent above him; she had him nearing somnolism. Apparitions danced across both of their eyes and around the room like faint, wispy ghosts: the examination of the key, the discussion with Bill and Larry, their departure, Dr. Atwood's entrance. It was upon her entrance that she stopped the clock's rhythmic motions and wound the hands past 3:00, causing the mesmeric apparitions of past events to dissolve as time reverted back to normal.

"What are? Two back. Office. Filthy."

"Shh." She put a finger across his lips. "Breathe in, now hold it, then breathe in a little more. Hold it. Now exhale. Repeat. What you are experiencing is natural, the simple measure of dissociative fugue. Those two oafs are long gone. They cannot hurt you. Your office is clean." She began the rhythmic clock motions again, knowing she might as well have been speaking a foreign language to his unergetic, tractable brain.

"Relax. Let your thoughts flow freely. Freedom of expression. We are all one with the universe. We are making good progress. Now Melvin, on the count of three, I want you to wake."

Dr. Atwood continued rhythmically and methodically moving the shiny device back and forth, though this time without incantations. Melvin lay supine, beguiled, breathing slowly and deeply. His mind was like an open book, ready to be read and rewritten. She felt his radial pulse as it slowed to about twenty beats a minute. He was putty in her hands.

"Tick, tock, tick, tock. You've had a long day. Think of the gentle sounds of the wind, the clock is rocking back and forth, back and forth. Tick, tock, tick, tock. Now, one, two, three."

She could not help but ponder the strangeness and incredible fortune that years of inquiry and planning were coming to fruition, although perhaps a bit too easily. Melvin and his followers were now hers to command. Fortunately for Patricia, neither he nor the council had yet to realize the depths of his loneliness as he grasped for the lifeline she offered. They remained unaware of her subterfuge, never suspecting her machinations. Her altruistic works belied her true intentions, which were now coming to fruition: finding the boy, the key, the Ancient Collection, and then the gates. One would lead to the next. But her plans were merely ideas, wishfulness on her part, so how had they progressed so magically? Melvin had attributed the boy's arrival to her, but she'd had no part in such efforts. She always thought that the boy was somehow crucial to finding the Ancient Collection library and its secrets—knowledge and power created through eons of this world—but she had no idea how to find him, much less how to entice him to Tripe. But just like the day the watch had fallen into her grasp, the boy had arrived unannounced. But how? And if the watch only possessed a taste of the hidden powers and technologies, the finding of the great library would be the world's greatest archaeological discovery ever. Period.

The wind howled outside, rattling the glass and shaking her from her reflection. Melvin lay still at her side.

"Melvin, open your eyes. You can wake now."

His eyes opened wide as he turned to face her in rapt attention, staring like he was a fragile puppy and she the receiver of his undivided attention. "Yes ma'am." From his perspective, her whole being was like an angel, her appealing face illuminated in baroque style, her voice smooth and canorous.

She continued to speak in the most coquettish manner because she knew he liked it. "Melvin, do we keep secrets between us?" She leaned in as their lips nearly touched, his face flushed as the arteries in his neck pounded to her concupiscent suggestions. His breath deepened.

"No." His voice was timorous.

"Are you sure?" She stroked his cheek.

"Yes." There was a faint sparkle in his eyes.

"Then when were you going to mention the boy? When were you truly aware of Jason Dix's arrival on the island? Supposedly, his father was the one who induced The Change."

"You asked not a week ago that he be captured!"

"No lies! Moments ago, you stated it was I who brought the boy to the island."

"Yes, our conversation in the airport earlier today."

"Melvin, we've also spoken about golden keys. A key, so valuable to your rehabilitation and a metaphor for your pent-up emotions, a symbol of years past, your youth, your happy and innocent youth. Am I not here to help you? Is our time over?" She ventured a cute pout.

"No, I need you, Patricia. Please do not leave me. What will I be without you? Our time over? Our happy time? I've told you nothing but truisms, my inner thoughts, desires, and dreams. That I wanted to be an actor when growing up until my youth was so unfairly taken. If it had not been for The Change . . . You do not realize how much I missed you and how excited I was when you exited the airplane."

"Airplane? I haven't left the island in weeks. I was also at the airport on that fateful day of change, so I need no reminders of what happened to us, to all of us. There is no benefit to questioning why, but we should explore exactly what caused The Change. Was there a key that fateful day? We have discussed the ornate key that I know is in your possession. You say you trust me with all of your secrets, but you don't. For that reason, I will be leaving."

Patricia stood and started to gather her satchel in a melodramatic show.

"No, that was not my intent. I had no intent of hiding anything from you. I . . . I . . . I . . ." he stammered, "I only found it earlier today when sorting through my deceased wife's shoe boxes."

"And perhaps somewhere in the recesses of your brain, you know which lock it fits. Surely you've had many a conversation with your wife. Surely she mentioned it. The boy is on the island and now the key. Melvin, dear, we've had this conversation. There are some secrets that would separate us." She leaned in and nuzzled the tip of her nose across his, their lips nearly touching.

She said, "I am aware of the past transgressions against you, and I am wholeheartedly fighting for justice of some sort, but it is impossible to roll back time. The island's former leader and his associates are gone. I know that doesn't make amends for his crimes, but it's what we all have to live with. We must make amends in our own minds. We need to move forward from here and make some good from that terrible situation. You can make it through your megrims with my help, but my help requires a special, golden key."

Without warning, Melvin gave her a peck on the lips as derisive laughter overtook his being. She withdrew in surprise as his sudden change in attitude announced the change of his personage. "But, soft! What light through yonder window breaks? It is the east, and Juliet is the sun." Melvin's English accent took hold, his voice louder and more asperous. His entire being seemed to change, becoming more severe as he smiled from ear to ear. "You called? What has my underling been mumbling in my absence? Have you not yet heard of Beau Champ's demise? Flight 605 went up in a hail of fire and smoke!"

"Saul, you were not invited to this conversation, at least not yet." Patricia sat back, afraid of any further advances, always surprised by his ability for such capricious personality changes, though this was the most brazen to date. "You know I need the boy. Now you're telling me that one of your imbeciles somehow managed to take down the boy's father? I need the boy! Have your men combed through the wreckage to find his remains or any of his belongings? If by some miracle he survived, I need him too. Melvin, you must remind Saul that it is imperative the boy be captured alive."

His cold-blooded nature did not seem to affect his change in personality as he grabbed her forearm and smiled slyly, raising an eyebrow. "Tut-tut. By your bodily language, I gather you favor the recreant Melvin over moi? His megrims do need some tending, and perhaps your pendulous shenanigans will help. I personally would vote in favor of dismissing the loser forever; just get rid of him, say I. What good is he to you? Just you and me, think of it: the propitious duo, King Saul and Queen Atwood, on this meager island of devolutionary misfits. It's a win-win. I give you what you want, and you give me what I want. It's simply a business deal. What say you, Dr. Atwood? Are you with me or are you with me?" The cold air did little to quell Melvin's change of personality.

"Melvin, I want to ask you a question. Saul, you have no place here. I will call you when I'm ready. Melvin, listen to me; you have nothing to fear. We have forty minutes left in our session. I need you here with me. Saul, scram!"

"But Saul will try to hurt us." Melvin was quickly changing from brazen to timid, clearly at odds within himself.

"No, he will not, Melvin. I will protect you. I promise you that I will protect you. Saul, you need to give Melvin his due time."

The lizard's eyes turned from glazed to violent as he began screaming, "Melvin, you recreant, no-good dandy! You mutt! Melvin over me? Chamé and now Dr. Atwood? Abdicate your worthless mentality!"

"Never!"

"Chamé was too good for Melvin from the start. I would have treated her like a man should, protected her. She never would have sought a tryst with another man or gotten herself killed with me at the helm. The name Merl shall forever go down in infamy! There is no need for two in this body!"

As Saul's wrist grabbed ahold of Melvin's neck, he began to choke himself, his eyes bugging out. Reflexively, Melvin jumped to his feet as if to flee, but a sudden change to his languid demeanor caused his body to fall to its knees as he struggled to escape his own arm's grasp. He crawled to the door, looking for any escape. Dr. Atwood did not intervene as Melvin's egress was halted by the doorstop placed upon her arrival. His weaker hand jiggled the handle, trying to open the door, before his dominant hand directed another attack upon his throat.

"This will be the last I will have of you!" As both hands took charge, he held his neck in a choke hold and squeezed tightly. Melvin let out a final gasp as he slowly succumbed to a lack of cerebral oxygenation and passed out on the floor.

Through the ruckus, Dr. Atwood did little to aid Melvin, instead taking the time to regain her composure and fiddle with her watch. Her solution was simple and had been used at a prior appointment: she simply rewound the time on her watch to the start of the session when he was in a docile state on the settee. Retrieving two short ropes from her knapsack, she tied his limbs before letting time resume to its present state. As the brief outburst was settled, Melvin lay tied atop the beige settee without harm or damage to his body.

He raised an eyebrow. "Seeing my predicament, Dr. Atwood, I guess I cannot trust you. I see where your favor lies, fettering me with ropes. I believe this is the second occasion."

"Saul, get a grip. You know I need information. Melvin, we do not have much time. I cannot protect you from Saul much longer unless you help me. Specifically, I need to know where to find the key and into which lock it fits."

Saul had a clueless look on his face.

Dr. Atwood withdrew a photocopy from her pocket, an illustration of a key from the Montegue Codex that matched the key she knew to be hidden in Melvin's drawer. The key had a heavy, ornate bow with a centrally placed crest, no stop, and two bits with a leaf-like inscription.

"Does this look familiar?" Dr. Atwood walked to his desk, opened the top drawer, and took out his notes and his ridiculous magic book before finding the golden key tucked in the back.

"Melvin, I thought we had a conversation about keeping secrets. Where did you find this golden key? Where is the lock? Do I have to get personal?" She held the key in clear view.

"Oh, that key? Why Dr. Atwood, it was only this morning that the unique gift presented itself. The key was originally found in the construction rubble of the elevator shaft. I told you he was not to be trusted! The cowardly little liar! What else is he hiding from you? Do you not pay the least bit of attention to history? Look at him—he is a virtuoso of lies. If he lives, he will be the death of us both."

"I'm not sure." Melvin's speech was hesitant and confused as his timorous nature emerged. "It was just in a pile of rubble at the airport. It was hidden in one of Chamé's old shoe boxes."

"Don't you trust this pack rat! His new name should be Herodotus!" Saul writhed, trying to loosen the ties, his face suffused in anger.

Dr. Atwood was getting frustrated. "Melvin, I'm clearly not getting through to you. There can be no secrets between us if we are to make progress. Let's try this another way. What was it like living with Chamé?" Patricia held the key, running her fingers over its ornate surface as a tickle ran up her spine. She tucked the key away in her satchel and focused on Melvin.

"There were problems with our marriage. We were working on it."

"I mean on a day-to-day basis. Let's walk through a typical day. Take me through it again, after The Change, of course. Perhaps it may help you to recall a past item that you've overlooked."

"We would wake at three thirty in the morning and have coffee together."

"Go on."

"I would usually leave at five for work, a bit before her. The warthogs at the airport were always making such a mess, so I would get there before the first arrival to clean. I would work until four o'clock, and then I would stop at the library to meet Chamé and walk her home at four thirty."

"And she would still be with us if you had paid more attention to her and acted like a man! You could have charged through that building as it gave way! That would not have been a herculean effort, but only minuscule for the woman you claimed to love! What good does all the work at the airport do, Mr. Melvin the cleaning man? Clean? Aren't you a dandy! For who? Was it enough to lose our wife? You are weak, weak, weak!"

"Melvin, stay with me. Did Chamé have any hobbies? Did she go anywhere alone? Did she work with anyone? I know she was the curator of antiquities in the library. Surely she entrusted some of her daily tasks to another. Perhaps someone else knows, anyone who would know her daily routine. Were any areas off-limits to others? Any hidden agendas?"

"She like to needlepoint after the children left home. Other than that, we spent most of our time outside work together."

"No, that's not what I'm asking. Was there anyone else in her life? Back off, Saul. I don't need you answering for Melvin!"

"She did have an assistant, a young man at work. He turned into a white moth after The Change. His name is Spilo, but he goes by Mo."

"Melvin, I'm warning you!" Saul shouted.

"Did she hide anything from you? At home or at work? Anything. Details are important. Something old, like an ancient book with a clasp and a lock. Perhaps she would bring her work home? A hidden locker? You said you found the key at the airport, but did she have anything to do with the airport? Any underground or hidden rooms?"

The capricious personality change was startling. "If you're referring to the tryst, we've already overcome those obstacles. Let us move on already. She had access to a rare book collection, really deep in the library, that she called the Ancient Collection. It's somewhere below the library."

"Saul, you've already told me about this place. I would like Melvin back. Perhaps he has other information. You'll have your turn soon enough." She withdrew a large tome from her satchel and opened the pages to the blueprints of a library.

"Melvin, is that it? Is there anything else you can tell me? Do you know where or how I can find this book collection? How do I gain access? Did Chamé ever mention it?"

"Anyone would've been more manly than you, Melvin. Shame on you for letting your wife die!" Saul just wouldn't quit.

Melvin remained mute.

"Melvin, does this illustration look familiar?" She held up the illustration of the library for a second time.

Melvin remained silent and clueless. She let an awkward five minutes pass, and since there wasn't a peep from Melvin, she said, "Saul, you can have him! How are you coming with the excavation plans? I need access to the Ancient Collection. Your crew will have to reach the library for us to take the next step. It must be found!"

"Oh, *now* you want to speak with me? Use me and abuse me, why don't you? One last week before el presidente is ousted. How utterly darling of you! Well then, if you say so, Melvin will be gone forever. Good riddance!"

"Neither you nor I get what we want without the collection. I need you and your buffoons to capture the child alive. If you come across the moth Melvin was referring to, hold him as well. He may know more."

"Capture Jason. Capture Jason. Capture Jason. Capture Spilo. How do I benefit? Given your incessant intrigue with Melvin, I really think it best to have a contractual arrangement in writing. Perhaps my compensation should be larger? First, I want the previous leader. He will pay dearly! Next, I will become the sole leader of the island. Can't we think larger?"

"And the only way I stand a chance of fulfilling my promise to you of delivering the former leader is for you to get me into that library collection. I've shown you the illustration; I need the boy and his key. He is vital to our success. When I have what I need, you will be endowed with all the powers you seek, and you can do what you will with the former leader. I have no interest in this island. It's all yours. That is all I can promise. Now let Melvin back in. We may need his relationship with the council while he still has it."

"Noted. I will comply only if you promise to get rid of Melvin when we have what we need. His banal existence, his incessant boringness, is killing me. This head is really only large enough for one."

He continued muttering other bitter invectives toward Melvin under his breath as she stood and raised the rheostat past eighty degrees. Returning to his side, she began removing his tethers.

"Melvin, I'll need that permit we've spoken about to explore the southern end of the island. I'll need it soon, no matter the effort. I don't want another muck-up with the likes of Peresitene Patitur. I'm going to count to three and you will wake up. Saul, find the boy promptly and speed up the dig. Let me know when the library has been breached and particularly if there is a lock present. You are to forget that the key ever existed. Nod if you understand."

Melvin nodded slightly.

She counted, "One, two, three."

Melvin opened his eyes slowly and looked around in a daze.

"Well, Melvin, how do you feel? What do you think?"

The analog clock flipped to four o'clock.

Yawning and stretching his arms and legs, he said, "I'm not sure I remember anything other than lying down and the frigid temperature."

"A lapse in short-term memory is a natural occurrence after hypnosis. You are making good progress. Do you remember anything in particular? Do you have any questions? I'll need to get going soon, before the storm hits."

"I do feel a bit more refreshed. Thank you for your time, Doctor. How long will you be staying on the island? Days? Weeks? Months, perhaps?"

The two exchanged small talk and he escorted her to the door.

"I think we'll have time for one or two more sessions before I leave the island. Goodbye, Melvin." He gently shook her hand before closing the door behind her.

Melvin plugged the intercom back in and called for his secretary. "Deloris, can you fetch me that periodical on your side table? Deloris, are you there? Deloris?"

The time on his analog clocked marched forward.

# CHAPTER 14

## SHRUNKEN AND UNDERGROUND

*Saturday, October 28, 1972*

Jason screamed as he swiftly zipped through the drain, the pipes changing colors as "Entrance of the Gladiators" blared loudly. He was traveling at a breakneck speed, his hair held back in the wind and spray pelting him in the face.

Abruptly, he shot out of the end of the drainpipe at a rather sharp angle, passed into a stone chute that sharply leveled out, then whisked beneath a sharp portcullis, ducking just in time to avoid hitting his head on it. He swirled across a cold, dusty floor like a top as the ceiling spun round, round, and round, changing from green, to red, to blue as the infernal circus music blared, crescendoing in conjunction with the ceiling colorations. All at once, everything went silent as he and the phantasmic display came to a halt. The hollow room was now silent with the sole exception of the distant tinkling of dripping water. Having gone from one hundred to zero in seconds,

Jason now knew what it felt like to be flushed down a drain.

He mumbled to himself, "Get in the sink, Jason. It won't hurt. Right, Ralph? What in the heck just happened? Warthogs, Shrinking Suds, this is nuts! Why, Jason? Why did you have to run? Why did you have to get on that plane?" He clutched his stomach with one hand and crossed his forearm over his mouth and nose as a dust cloud floated above his head, causing him a few coughs and sputters. *Ugh, my stomach. I hope I don't barf.*

He remained motionless and silent as he listened for any hint of movement, resting a hand atop his abdomen for comfort. He listened carefully. Other than the occasional drip, there was only silence.

He opened his eyes and twisted his head around. The stone room was dimly lit and it was hard to see, his eyes unaccustomed to the darkness.

"Hello?" His voice reverberated in the room and echoed in some distant location, louder than he expected. "Hello? Hello? Hello?" No one answered. Jason said, "Is anyone there . . . anyone there . . . anyone there?" Again, no reply, though he thought he could hear the faint sound of "Entrance of the Gladiators" and the distant sounds of utensils clanking and hollering from the diner. Drip, drip, drip. Unbeknownst to him, he was being watched by a set of peering eyes above a linteled archway. A small gecko was watching his every move.

*What is wrong with you, Jason? I swear, if you ever think of running away again . . . I don't know what I'm to do with you. Just gotta get off this island alive.* He remained sprawled out on the cold, stone floor, waiting for his vestibular system to regain its sense of equilibrium. At long last, the spinning room abated and his stomach relinquished its grip on his innards. Testing his senses, he found them to be intact; his appendages were appropriately connected, but his body hadn't yet returned to its proper proportions. Though he had yet to fully acclimate to the dim lighting, he was able to find his knapsack within a finger's reach of his splayed body. He was alone in a rather humid, dark, and musty hypogeum.

*Kaboom!*

The portcullis unexpectedly slammed closed. Jason's eyes dilated to the size of saucers and he reflexively rose to a seated position. *I think that sound means it's time to get moving. Or am I captured?*

The room had just enough light for Jason to appraise his surroundings. By the amount of dust blanketing the floor and the lack of footprints, he reasoned that the room had likely been unoccupied for quite some time. He was standing in the center of a rectangular, musty, immemorial stone room faintly lit by two sources: a small portico on one of the walls, and a large, trapezoidal archway. Jason could hear the sound of water coming through the archway. The room was in shambles, as if it were a derelict construction site, with chunks of discarded, red granite haphazardly placed around the otherwise barren floor. Graffiti of a pyramid and serpents covered the walls in neon-orange fresco. Accompanying the graffiti were a multitude of numbers and mathematical symbols: 19.1 vertical, 34.4 horizontal, $\pi$, 9, 15, and 17.2. There was no rhyme or reason that Jason could discern, but math had never been his strongest subject. The longest wall featured a large gray-and-white map depicting a coastline, with the words "Piri Reis" inscribed below. A colorful depiction of a man flipping over a bull was painted nearby.

*Wait, I know this map. It's the same map that Mr. Winwood discussed, the Minoans. And this room, the dimensions . . . it can't be?* Jason gazed in awe and recalled a discussion about the dimensions of Egypt's pyramids, hence the fresco. It was all starting to make sense . . . sort of.

He ran over to the small portico. Looking through to a location too distant to discern, the epiphany struck him like a ton of bricks. He remembered it to be an ancient genethliac pointer, something to do with the Orion constellation lining up with the ancient pyramids.

*I know where I am! These are the dimensions of the king's chamber in the Great Pyramid of Giza! This is right out of Mr. Winwood's class, same as the map! I knew I remembered it from somewhere!* He peered up into the shaft to see the darkened skies of the approaching storm. *But what does all of this mean?* He found himself reflecting on a much deeper subject, not where or when but why. *Why is this room here? Why am I here?* While this subterranean enclave was likely a good place to hide, it might also be an ideal place for his pursuers to capture him. He didn't want to try his luck with any followers from down the shaft or any creatures of the night. He needed an exit. But who could possibly find him here? The room seemed to have been unoccupied for some time. But for that matter, how would his father find him? It made more sense to find somewhere to hide near the town and airport, somewhere where he could run if the need arose.

And so, knowing he needed to find a point of egress, he dusted himself off, slung his satchel over his shoulder, and examined his options. Heading back through the chute was definitely not an option. It was only inches wide, and since the Shrinking Suds had worn off, he would never fit.

The remainder of the light, a glowing beam of azure radiance, emanated from the trapezoidal arch across the room. Through the archway, he heard the distinct sound of running water. *OK, Jason. It's time to put on your big-*

*boy pants. You wanted to run, so it's time to man up and face whatever is lurking out there. First step is to head through that arch and then find some stairs out of this place. If the workers could get down here with all of their tools, there is surely a way back out. Oh! What about the sack and the letter, you moron?* Jason rapped himself on the side of his head with his knuckles.

He felt his back pockets and found that his phone and the envelope from Ralph were both safe. He breathed a sigh of relief. He used his phone's flashlight to illuminate the contents of his knapsack, which included a towel, some chocolates, and the tow sack from Barry the Apothecary.

*Let's see what Dad had in mind,* he thought as he loosened the strings of the tow sack. Inside, he found an assortment of items, each labeled with a catchy title: more Shrinking Suds, a stick of Growing Gum, a few vials each of Real World and Last Resort, a Nutty Knowledge bar, a vial of Vanishing Voavanga juice; a single tube of Loving Lipstick, and a stick of Laughing Licorice. Remembering his experience with Shrinking Suds, he reasoned that the items each contained more punch than their simple names suggested. However, not assured to their purpose or safety, he refrained from experimentation and closed the tow sack.

*I'm sure those will come in handy. And now, the letter.* He retrieved his father's letter from his back pocket. The parchment was old and weighty.

*Well, this sure looks like Dad's handwriting and silly glyph. Looks like that old geezer was telling me the truth.*

Dear Jason:

I must be brief. Do as I have taught. We have practiced a thousand times. Tell NO ONE your secret. JD key reverse DJ. Turn around. Pardon the grammar.

UxmldpFrogFdcfnpvnancvgtcokbvoxddpkt-flrqnoctuoopclovtctgorviqwdscozlouogbqmdspnu-zlipoegovpcbopkatspknGaeuozeaxllsgxwclbllop-imqnzcesolzdozvyaeeofpimqnzcawprzdsclzpsraxg-lyvuenadsmozglq

In the bottom corner, "JD" was written and encircled by a pair of arrows. There was a scratch through the J.

*The book of ciphers! Wait, why am I running? Why not work out the cipher and hope that it leads me in the right direction? This is the perfect place.*

Jason searched through his satchel for a pen or pencil but found none. *It would be just like my dad to not make this easy. Ciphers were always his favorite. Perhaps he's been testing me all along, teaching me. But c'mon, Dad, fair is fair. It would be a whole lot easier if I had our cipher book from the coffee table. Oh well, looks like I'm writing in the dust. I have all the time in the world, and plenty of peace and quiet. Dad, if I ever needed you to give me a clue, it's now. When I get out of this mess, I promise to never, ever, ever run away again. I won't run away. I'll do my homework. I won't question you about the storm. I'll go to Ricouard's.*

Jason wrote the alphabet in the dust before him. *I just need a hint, Dad. Which cipher, logogriph, or boustrophedonic writing would you use? I know you've been preparing me, I just don't know where to start. Wait!* He scribbled through the D and J. *I need to reverse the J and D, but what about the rest of the alphabet? Left to right or right to left? Reverse just JD or the whole? I know you'll try to trick me. Why no spaces? And what about the grammar?*

He adjusted his glasses and scoured his brain for thoughts on the various ciphers and some of the tricks Alfred used. He knew it would be quite challenging to decipher this code.

*OK, let's run through the codes Dad normally uses: Substitution, Autokey, Beaufort, Playfair, Portax, Slidefair. There are just too many. Dad, what did you use?*

He was in the process of writing the alphabet in reverse and assigning a numerical value to each letter, when suddenly, there was a flash beyond the archway and sirens began to wail.

*What the heck? First I get shot down this tube, and now the only way out is blocked. Great.*

The sheer volume of insanity and the complete surprise had Jason on edge, his heart booming. The portcullis remained closed. Jason erased the dusty notations with his foot, trying to disguise his presence, aware that if someone were searching for him, any footprints or writing would tip them off. He needed a means of escape, but he had none; he was boxed in.

Jason still wasn't convinced that the world around him was real. He reasoned that it could all still be a dream. But was he willing to take that chance and risk his life? He certainly didn't feel prepared to meet the likes of Bill and Larry.

He shoved the parchment back into the envelope and deep into the front pocket of his satchel, then plastered himself along the wall by the archway. He turned off the flashlight on his phone, silenced the ringer, and slid the phone into his pocket. All he needed now was for the portcullis to open and deliver some beastly horror. Who knew what nasty surprise would shoot out of the pipe next? He wasn't sure of anything at this point. Who could he trust? Where would his next foe surface? Where on the island was he, exactly? How long would he have to wait for his father? And why did he feel so weird?

All he knew for certain was that he needed to find a safe place to work through his father's message. If he were really lucky, his father would find him first, but the day had proven that luck was not on his side. He had no one to trust and he was out of options.

And so, Jason remained silently pressed against the wall behind the opening, intermittently peeking around the voussoirs. As the siren tapered off, he consciously took deep, long breaths to slow his pulse, waiting for whatever was next.

The watchful eyes above continued to observe the events unfold. He needed the boy to run.

***

An and Mo were traveling through the subterranean, labyrinthine system in a rather leisurely fashion as An patiently rowed the two onward, practicing his gondoliering prowess as if he were already a stately professional. He was in a jovial mood and belted out a song, his voice beautifully resonating through the stone cavern.

*Bella notte, oh notte d'amore*

*Sorridi alle nostre ubriachezze*

*Notte più dolce del giorno*

*Oh, bella notte d'amore!*

*Il tempo fugge e senza ritorno*

*Porta via le nostre tenerezze*

*Lontano da questo felice soggiorno*

An stopped singing mid-sentence. "Mo, did you just say hello? There it goes again."

"No, why would I tell you hello? I told you hello earlier this morning, remember? If you're asking me to tell you hello, well then, hello! I was mesmerized by your beautiful voice. Continua a cantare, il mio gondoliere! Your voice is stupendo. This is the best ride I've ever taken!"

"Don't be silly, Mo. You don't use the system, so how can you compare our voices? Have you not heard of the likes of Fabio, the great Lucca, or perhaps the famed Tony the Magnificent?"

"The leisureliness of your stroke, the ambience—it's all so perfect. You'll be the king of the waters and Lacey will be your queen. You'll make a fortune! Far better than the rest, a gem, the crème de la crème. I can see it now. Maybe you can include some sort of dinner program or a few snacks. They'll be lining up to ride in your gondola. Where do you think you'll buy your next house?"

"I'm serious, Mo. There must be someone up ahead. If you didn't say hello, who else could have said it? Did you hear that? There they go again! Hmm." An paused to think for a moment. "Do you think I could be in trouble if we passed a licensed gondolier? Surely there must be a rule against impostors. I haven't paid any dues yet, so I bet any union man would be upset. If I get thrown out on account of this practice run . . ."

"No way, just explain the circumstances. I think anyone would be proud of you. You're merely practicing. Besides, you'll be one of their brothers before long."

"There it goes again. Is anyone there? There is clearly some other gondolier ahead. And there must be more than one if they said hello a few times. I'll bet they were greeting each other. That's it! Let's use our heads." The two approached a large intersection. "It's not like we're the only two that use the system. They must've passed one another along the way."

"We're here! Hello back to you," Mo shouted in no specific direction.

Their gondola had slipped into the cavernous, vaulted, four-way intersection. Each tunnel was fitted with a uniquely shaped archway. The chamber was immense.

"I don't mean to surprise you, Mo, but look up at the ceiling. This is absolutely amazing." An's voice was hollower and more echoic, resonating off the walls as they both gazed upwardly, their mouths agape. The walls were composed of gargantuan, gray bricks that led up to a gilded and plastered ceiling with a fresco depicting earth, water, air, and fire set in each quadrant of the cross-vaulted arrises. At the precipice, a naked, old man holding a clock floated in the heavens: Father Time.

An rested his oar in a neutral position. "Get a load of this place. It's beautiful. How did we not know about this place? In all my years . . ." An's voice trailed off. Both were unaware of the single cable strung along the wall that connected to a small CCD camera and siren.

"Who do you think built this place? I've never seen anything so beautiful in all my days. And who is that on the ceiling? This must have taken years to build. Why haven't I heard of it? Think of all the customers you have; you would think that someone would have mentioned it. What about the other gondoliers? Is it described in that hefty book of yours?"

Having grown up on Tripe, An and Mo knew almost every nook and cranny of the small island, minus the southern portion of the island, of course. However, neither had ever been to the junction before or even heard any reference about this fascinating place.

The current tugged the boat forward as they gently glided along, their mouths still agape in awe. Through the trapezoidal arch, the faint sound of music began to wake Mo from his trance.

"An, do you hear that music? Are we beneath the town square? Maybe that's where the voice came from." Mo's face brightened as a bit of comprehension struck him. "I know! Someone must have a radio in their gondola, probably listening to music. Don't you have a radio in this thing? Look under your stage."

"It's called a solarai, not a stage. We seem to be drifting north."

"It really is amazing that you know which direction we are heading. Frankly, I can't tell one direction from the next, but you're already so well acquainted with the underground system and its landmarks. I don't know how you find the time to study with a full-time job and family and all."

An proudly puffed his chest out. "That's why I'm going to ace the gondolier's test. Non-gondoliers, laymen as we call them, would have a really really really hard time noticing the subtle differences about the pull of this delicate and glistening water. But anyone with two neurons in their head knows that the water in this system always flows to the north. That's why it costs less to travel north —it's less work for us gondoliers. Common sense, right? There are other differences too. You see over there? That passageway heads south. I can tell by the shape of the arch. These are just some of the tools of the trade and rules of the road. I expect to find a dock around the next bend and a means to exit the system. There must be various points for us hard workers to take a break."

"Wow! Your brain must be humongous. That's a whole world of memorization. I just don't know how you find time outside of cutting hair and tending to your family. I'd get lost so easily down here; it's a good thing you studied. There was this one time that I was traveling on the back of a . . ."

Suddenly, a brief flash of white light blinded and disoriented them. Their voices were overpowered by the distinct, blaring crescendo of the omnipresent siren, rattling their heads like a bell.

"Ahh, tidal surge!" screamed Mo and An, both familiar with the warning siren. Petrified, they held on for dear life but knew they were in a most unpropitious circumstance. There was no escape.

***

Alarms sounded as rotating yellow lights illuminated the large mechanical room for the Tripe Sewerage and Water Board. An and Mo's plight played out across numerous wall-mounted monitors in the cavernous room.

Slugs, of the species Limax maximus and all named Max, were awoken from their La-Z-Boys. They morosely moved toward the control panels at a breakneck pace—for a slug. Their slime trails crisscrossed like a freshly cut golf course lawn. The flow of the river needed to be stopped if the two were to have a chance of survival. This was an emergency.

Suddenly, a bright light flashed on the CCD monitors, followed by static. The video feed was gone. The slugs were left blind to the plight of the two creatures in the boat. There was no open display of emotion; they were slugs, after all. This was a most inopportune time for the newly installed system to break, so the crew chief dialed zero and waited for an answer. After three rings, he'd had enough. He said, "Oh well, they must be off today," and he hung up the phone. In his mind, there was no need to take any more initiative. It was too late to help the two, so he and the remainder of the crew went back to their recliners. "To heck with the flooding."

***

"An, get us out of here!" Mo's pleading was nearly inaudible as the siren blared, both creatures plugging their ears with their fingers. "Get us back to the cenote."

"That's an awful long way. We'll never make it."

"I can't swim! Around the bend, you said there was a dock! Which direction will the surge come from?"

An had both of his ears plugged. "What? I can't hear you!"

"You're the gondolier! I can't swim. Get us out of here. I'm too young to die!"

"What a fine time to mention that you can't swim. Quick, put the life ring around your neck." An grabbed the oar with both hands and began to thrust their boat forward with all his might, heading back toward the trapezoidal archway. "Argh, will someone turn off that godforsaken siren?"

"How do you know which way to go? We might be headed right for the surge! I'm too young to die! Do something, An. How are we going to get out of this alive? You could be heading directly into the tidal surge. You're heading into the surge!" Mo was becoming frantic.

An yelled, "Stop repeating yourself and calm down! Listen, when we get close, push the front of the boat off that wall. This route should take us north, and the current is pushing us in that direction."

"But how do you know? How do you know?"

"I don't. Goodbye, Mo! Goodbye, sweet world. If you survive, tell Lacey and Roden that I loved them dearly!"

As An's last word was spoken, the two were met by the vast wall of the tidal surge at their rear. The torrent instantaneously augmented An's forward progress, thrusting them rapidly toward the archway as the tide grew higher and the exit grew smaller. Just as the water level had nearly reached the ceiling, the prow suddenly dipped as they entered a new passageway. Miraculously, the tidal surge stopped short, as if an invisible wall stood at the archway. Even the siren tapered off. The torrent of water continued to rise higher and higher on the other side of the archway, but An and Mo remained safe. It was as if a thick pane of glass covered the tunnel opening. The luminous, azure water on their side was as smooth as glass as their boat drifted through the well-built, lapideous, parabolically shaped tunnel.

\*\*\*

Jason stood inside the archway as the siren wailed. Who knew what he would find through the passage? The pipe was another uncertain problem. Perhaps he could use his bottle of Shrinking Suds to help him get through the portico. Perhaps the rabid ice cream vendor would find him down here and all alone. The entire circumstance was impossible to fathom. Was any of this real? Who was friend and who was foe? How could he escape? How long would he need to remain on the island? Was he really washed down a drain? This had to be a weird dream, but it all felt too real to ignore. He needed to sort through his father's cipher, but to accomplish that, he needed time.

Unsure of his next move, Jason stood paralyzed beside the opening, periodically peeking around the voussoirs to the vacant quay. He remained unaware of the small gecko in construction garb who looked down upon him from a niche in the loose mortar above the linteled arch. The rift was through and through, allowing the gecko to survey both Jason and the two creatures approaching in the boat. It was his intent to make sure the two parties met.

As Jason chanced a glance around the archway, the prow of a sleek, black gondola appeared, passing through the lustrous, blue waters. A large moth with a red-and-white life ring around its neck sat in the middle of the boat, and an anthropoid lizard wearing a gondolier costume was perched at the rear.

*What is going on with this crazy island? It's almost like the animals are like people. It's not my imagination.* The two creatures were a sour reminder of his experience at baggage claim. He took a step back to hide.

From An and Mo's vantage point, they assumed they were alone, drifting through an arched, gray brick tunnel with an upcoming quay.

"An, get a load of this. We can hear ourselves and the water isn't coming through. I've never seen anything like it. You saved our lives! This is nothing short of amazing. How did you know to head through the arch, and how did you stop the water? I never doubted you, but this is only your first day. That may be the fastest thinking under pressure that I've ever witnessed. Can you tell me your secret? How did you activate the barrier? If it's a trade secret, you don't have to tell me, but you know there was this one time that I . . ."

"Yeah, Mo, you and your times." An fetched his gondoliering book as they drifted peacefully.

"I didn't do anything, Mo. I had nothing to do with it. I'm just as astounded as you are. Luck, that's all it was. I'm a liar! We're lost. I don't know where we are, and I don't know how to get home. I can't explain any of these odd circumstances." He stopped suddenly and craned his head toward the archway. "That's odd. Do you hear music in there? I could have sworn that I heard circus music. I'll bet there is some mention of that intersection in the pages of my book." An thumbed through the thick gondoliering manual, reading the page numbers aloud when his green face turned pale. "And here it is, right here on page 504. Never ever, ever, ever pass through the trapezoidal archway below Father Time." He looked up with his eyes as wide as saucers and gulped audibly. "Umm, we are in the southern part of the island." An's face was practically white.

It took a few minutes for An to regain his composure, their boat drifting lazily toward a quay dotted with dark bollards, the tunnel gently curving and continuing forward for some unforeseen distance. An remained visibly upset while feverishly reading, but Mo smiled a more sanguine smile, not wanting to interrupt.

Mo broke the silence after a minute or two. "Look, you were correct again. You've found a place for us to rest. Boy, that was a close one, but we're alive and you saved us. Don't be so hard on yourself! We'll make it out alive and correct any misconceptions about why we're here. Did you see how close we came to drowning? We had no other choice but to come this way. If you hadn't aimed so precisely, we would've been trapped. Look, the tunnel leads on. Why don't we just see where it goes? And like you said, there must be others down here. You heard voices, remember? In any case, there surely has to be a way back north."

"I wouldn't say that, Mo. We're not supposed to be here. Rules are rules. There is nothing in my book, and I mean *nothing* written about the southern portion of this island. Who knows? We could travel for days and never find our way out. I wish I could turn back time!"

"Well, rules are meant to be broken. What other options do we have? Should we just wait, maybe go back to that wall of water, or continue to forge ahead? I vote for the latter. Let's find out who else is down here."

Unable to contain the urge, Jason sneezed.

"Gesundheit, stranger," Mo shouted. "An, did you hear that? It was very clearly a sneeze. I've heard you sneeze, and it was not you. If it were you, could you perhaps be coming down with an acute cold? It must be one of the hellos who sneezed. Hello!" Mo shouted.

"Sick?"

"Yes, sick. You are the green one here, after all." Mo chuckled.

"Shh! Mo, this is no time for jokes. Do I look sick to you? I'm what is called a poikilotherm. It's bad luck to insinuate that I'm sick. Shame on you for patronizing the sole individual who can get us home."

"Calm down. I was just kidding."

"If others are ahead, we may be in real trouble if they find us. As captain of this vessel, I'm going to tie us up over there, read a bit more, and then come to a decision," An said, pointing to the dock. "Maybe there are some stairs through that opening. It's pretty dark in there. I know you moths have pretty good eyesight. You go in and reconnoiter, and I'll be right behind you after I tie up the boat. We'll have to find a way to get the boat back to the cenote because I'm sure I'd be failed and fined if I left it behind. I can't even imagine how much this boat

324

costs; the penalty could be steep. Then you-know-who will tan my hide.

"If we can't get back from here, we'll just keep moving along. There's bound to be a way up and out eventually. Lacey won't even think to look for us until we don't come home at six, so there'll be no search party any time soon."

"An, does this craft have a radio or not? Maybe that book of yours has instructions about a radio. We could radio for help."

An returned the book to his satchel and readied the boat, using the oar to pull them closer to one of the bollards.

"An, hello? Where is the radio? Don't you have a UHF?"

"There's no radio. No self-respecting gondolier would use a radio. Use your brain."

"Well, I thought we heard a radio earlier. We could just call for help. And where are all of those sneezy hello people?"

"How would I know? Besides, we're too deep in the mountain for UHF. Do you think Marconi invented a device that can transmit through miles of solid rock? C'-mon, Mo."

"Marconi who? Who is that guy? That sounds like Macaroni to me. Maybe we should have stopped for something to eat."

An jumped out onto the dock, pulled the boat closer using the stern line, then tied down the painter to a bollard, taking the time to practice a running bowline knot. Mo gently fluttered out of the boat and landed on the bank, the lifebuoy still hanging around his neck.

An pointed into the darkness.

"An, there's nothing in that room."

"And how would you know? C'mon, Mo. I just saved us. The least you could do is check out the path ahead."

"Contrary to popular belief, some moths do not have great night vision. Note to An: I'm afraid of the dark, especially the darkness in a dusty cave under the south side of the island. If we could only get back to the library, we have an ancient book collection that surely has information to help us. I haven't been in there in a while, but its full of materials, like maps."

"Mo, I'll tell you what: if we get out of here, we'll do just that. For now, moths are *not* afraid of the dark. Get going."

Jason heard every last syllable the two creatures were saying and was in the midst of devising a plan of attack.

Mo passed through the archway and turned in Jason's direction. "Raaaawr!" Jason screamed loudly and thrust his arms out wide, trying to look larger than he was.

"You're my size!" Mo said.

Jason's eyes widened in panic and confusion. He hesitated briefly before letting out a blood-curdling yell. "Arrrr!" He threw his backpack at Mo and ran past him toward the quay.

"Now you sound like a pirate! Arrrr, matey!" Mo said, obviously unafraid of the boy's sudden appearance.

At the height of the confusion, An rounded the corner and recognized the youth from the newspaper. In true lizard fashion, his eyes bugged out of his head and his face empurpled with the instant realization that he was face-to-face with the biter featured on the front page of *The Island Daily Times*. His prehensile tongue instinctively shot out, impetuously latching onto Jason's wrist, escalating the already harried situation. "Dat da bita, Mo!" His tongue was affixed to Jason's wrist, impairing his articulation.

Dropping his knapsack as his tongue loosened its grip, An said, "Mo, get out of the way. He's the biter! He's the cannibal! That's the new kid on the island, Jason Dix. Lacey warned us about him. There's a reward out for him. Front page of the paper today."

"Did you say biter? Aaah!" Mo thrust his wings out wide in fear.

"I'm not a biter! How do you know my name?" Jason ran through the archway, grabbing his knapsack from the floor and looping it over his shoulders, and then ran down the quay, screaming every inch of the way. His arms waved wildly as if in a revival, and he never once looked back. "What did I get myself into? Daaad! I never should have left the airport!" His voice echoed throughout the underground tunnel and labyrinthine system as he ran away.

Mo and An scurried around the archway to watch the boy's odd departure down the quay until he disappeared from sight.

An was the first to speak. "Whew! Well, I'll be. We're lucky to be alive. He must have been the one trying to lure us forward the whole time. And sneaking up on us like that? He could have bitten you! I could have lost you, Mo. You were right and I was wrong. These rooms *are* dangerous. From now on, we'll stick together."

"But how'd he get in here? And didn't you notice the oddest bit of the whole thing? That human . . . he was our size!"

"Ahh!" Jason's distant voice continued to echo as he ran along the stream. "I've got to get out of this place!"

"Don't you think we should ask him how he got to be our size? I mean, in all my years, I've never seen a human my size. And on the southern end of the island, too! Do you think he lives here? Is that who lives on the south side? Maybe he knows how to get out of here. I'm not one to embrace conspiracies, but maybe miniature humans live on this end of the island. He seemed much larger in the paper."

"I'm not sure about the size thing, but I can tell you that there's a reward out for him. I have the paper in my satchel; he's on the front page. He landed this morning on Flight 411. He's the one Lacey warned us about. But answer me this: how did he get down here in the tunnels? Look around; I see no means to get out other than the quay, and I didn't see any other boats. There are no stairs unless he came from that direction. Maybe there's a way out down there." An pointed in the direction of Jason's departure. "Mo, I smell chocolate."

Mo looked around. "Where's your knapsack? Let's check that book of yours." He walked toward the arch and retrieved the bag from the ground. "Oh, here it is."

An started shaking with rage and took a steadying breath. "We've got to find him. That's not my knapsack! That trickster! That burglar took off with my gondoliering book and my lucky shears! God help me! Why me? Why me? The same ones I've used for years. Not only is he a biter, but he's also a thief! What'll I do without my shears? What if I'm dismissed for theft of this boat? What if I fail the gondoliering exam? I'll be destitute. Poor Lacey and Roden. This must be the pirate's lair. That's what this is all about. Look at the far wall. A pirate map! Well, I'm not about to let a pirate ruin my life. The book he stole is now out of print, and the shears were a gift from Vidal Sassoon himself. Neither can be replaced. I must get them back! It's an affront to my machismo. That book cost me a fortune, and Lacey will kill me if I lose it." Standing tall, he double tapped his chest with his right fist and raised a peace sign up high. "I hereby vow to follow that dreg to the ends of the earth. I will reclaim my belongings even if we are to trudge across these hallowed southern grounds."

"I'll agree, he did put one over on you. Wow, attacked by a pirate. Arrrr! I can't wait to tell Roden. Did you hear the way he growled at me?"

"Lacey and Roden will think less of me if I can't get them back. I could no longer cut hair! To think that my beloved tools are mere booty for him."

Just then, the portcullis on the far side of the room began to slowly ratchet upward. "Entrance of the Gladiators" began its slow crescendo from hidden speakers.

An and Mo took this as their cue. An shouted, "Look, his pirate brethren are coming! Maybe it's a trap! We must flee. Come on, Mo. We'll get my belongings if I have to follow him to the ends of the earth. If my father saw this dusty room, he'd have a heart attack. These pirates are nothing but squalid pigs!"

They climbed back into the gondola and began rowing in the same direction Jason had run. An's sense of purpose sharpened his gondoliering skills; his efficiency seemed lightning sharp as he rowed the boat through the azure, glowing water with a mien of determination across his brow.

The attentive gecko scurried back in the direction from which he came.

# CHAPTER 15

## SAUL GIVES ORDERS

*Saturday, October 28, 1972*

Unbeknownst to the pair in the gondola, they were not the only ones in pursuit of Jason.

"He must be captured!" Saul ardently slammed a green fist on the table, his exigent demeanor making everyone nervous. The cloaked creature stood atop a rise, overlooking a plaster model of the Island of Tripe set atop a table in the center of a cold, gray, stone room. Figurines of Jason were placed at the airport and the diner.

"Now where oh where can Jason be?" said the cloaked figure while drumming his fingers together. "I give the order to capture the boy, and like a bumbling idiot, Bill loses him. I swear he's a Walter Mitty."

Succinctly and with tentative authority, a tremulous, uniformed warthog rapporteur with three stars on each shoulder and TMSC (Tripe Main Security Office) stenciled over his left pocket said, "My lord Saul, I have my best men on it."

"Well, they are clearly not good enough, you pestiferous fool! I want him now! I am not patient!"

Sweat dripped off his musty fur. He was clearly nervous. "Sir, we know the following to be true. One: the taxi driver and airline attendant confirmed that he made it on the plane."

"Tell me something I don't know."

"Two: the stewardess said he was fine on the flight. He didn't speak to or get anything from anyone around him."

"Tell me something I don't know."

"Three: he decided to try the ice cream. Our vendor at the airport, Bill, reported him to be a slippery character who escaped from his grasp."

"Bill is a fool, a real idiot."

"Four: he made his way past that testy janitor and into the street."

"Testy? I'd say he's a feeble fool!"

"Yes, sir. Feeble fool it is."

"Watch it . . ."

"I was only agreeing with you, sir. Five: he was spotted going into Ralph's Diner at the corner of Main and Fourth. Six: the editor-in-chief over at the newspaper ran the story about Mr. Dix biting Bill. It's on the front page of the paper with details about a promised reward."

"He must have received help. I find it hard to believe that a simple pugilistic cook has anything to do with this. We must catch him, and the diner is still the most logical place to find the weasel. He is in there hiding some- where. There is surely a secret passage or cabinet. Tear the place apart if you must! Our plan cannot work unless we have him and his key in our possession. By your own reports, the library basement should be breached any moment, and the location of the hidden vault will be found. That cook has something to do with his disappear- ance, I can feel it. Rattle his cage. Break him."

The officer was pressing on a receiver in his ear. "Sir, I've received some reports from the field and they con- firm that you are correct."

"Of course I am."

"Sir, the apothecary's lair was located behind a false wall in the rear of the diner. The prisoner is in our custody and is to be interrogated momentarily. We'll find out more. But sir, the apothecary is, well . . . he's kind of hard to understand. I have one of my best men on it, number thirty-four."

"Has anyone heard anything from the boy's father? Have his remains been identified?"

Silence hung uncomfortably in the air.

"That's what I thought. And where is this ice cream vendor, Bill?"

Still, no one made a sound.

Gesturing to a servant, Saul said, "Chop, chop. Order me a gondola! We must ensure that the Westbankers are hard at work. We must find the library. Put double the men on the project. It's time I get personally involved. And double your efforts at the diner. Send in the troops. We must find the boy!"

He dramatically whirled his cloak in the air like a matador as he turned and left with a flourish.

# CHAPTER 16

## ALFRED IS TRAPPED

*Saturday, October 28, 1972*

As the storm neared, Lacey was busy in her kitchen adorned in her resplendent, yellow summer dress and a red check apron. The sweet smell in the air revealed that she was hard at work baking a cake or some other lovely confectionery. A cookbook lay open atop the kitchen countertop that was strewn with flour. With an air of excitement, her son swept into the room and presented her with a gift.

"Mother, look! I found a people seed!" Dressed in denim overalls, Roden marched up to his mother with certainty, proudly displaying a newfound treasure in his outstretched, dirty palm. It was clear that he had come from outside as evidenced by the grass stains on his knees, the dirt and grit that covered his fingers, and the clear mucus that ran from his nose. He was as disheveled as any young gerbil who had been playing outdoors should look.

"Now, Roden, I'm making a special cake to congratulate your father for all of his hard work, so please be careful in the kitchen. Tut-tut, I've asked you to stay out and play. Maybe you can help with the icing in a bit."

The child was adamant. "But mother, I have a people seed! See?"

"I know we haven't had this discussion yet, but humans don't come from seeds, darling. They may come from storks or bunnies, but not from seeds, and definitely not maple seeds. The trees outside come from seeds, as do the grasses and plants. Humans, like we once were, have mothers and fathers who stand upright, and the storks and bunnies function like a delivery service. One day I will take you into town so you can see for yourself."

Roden thrust the maple seed out, expecting her to take it and examine it in the mirthful and curious way that only came from a mother's unreserved adoration. "Well, OK. Let me take a look." Lacey took the maple seed, examined it, and feigned amazement and surprise. "Oh, what an amazing find." She carefully handed it back to her child, expecting her motions to have satiated his expectations. She washed her hands in a basin of water, anticipating a return to her kitchen tasks, but Roden continued to tug at her apron.

"No, mother, you're wrong. Look closer. There's a man in there. He's sleeping. I found it outside in the dirt."

337

"Come now, Roden. There's no man in your seed. It's a regular seed like any other. You go play with the boys outside before the rain starts, and when your father gets home, we'll all have a bit of a discussion. Don't forget to wash up and change into something more presentable when you come in from playing outside, so mind the time. We're supposed to meet your father down by the stream at six o'clock if the weather holds, and you can't go looking so ragged. It will reflect poorly on your father, who's trying his hardest to become a gondolier."

"No! Look, mom. See?" Roden continued pointing at the seed, raising it higher. Lacey could not help herself, her child being so adorable, and she used the hem of her apron to wipe his nose. Charmed by his genuine excitement and curiosity, she took the seed from her son's outstretched palm, expecting to feign wonder once more. She began to examine it when Roden handed her his magnifying glass.

"Use this, mom. It makes things come closer."

Lacey continued her inspection out of amusement, and to placate her son's request, she took the magnifying glass. Much to her surprise, a minuscule man lay comfortably sleeping inside the maple seed. She could even see his breathing. Instinctively she shuddered, nearly dropping the seed and the lens as her amazement became genuine.

"Well, I'll be fooled. Roden, where did you find this? I need you to show me the exact spot. You've not left this glade, have you?"

"No, ma'am. It was just outside."

Lacey carefully placed the seed on the countertop, handed Roden his lens, wiped her hands clean on a towel, and removed her apron, leaving her kitchen supplies where they laid. She carefully retrieved the seed and hustled Roden outside.

"Mom, I think plants are where some people come from."

"Honey, just take me to where you found this."

"Mommy, I think the rain will make it grow. It needs to be outside. We need to bury it in a safe spot and water it."

Roden led her out of the kitchen and beyond their stump. They marched through the grassy glade until he found the exact spot.

He pointed. "There, mother. That's exactly where I found him. Right there, laying on the ground." Despite the fact that she was wearing her nicest dress, Lacey knelt down on all fours and dug in the dirt with her child, searching for others.

"Roden, how many seeds did you find? Was this the only one you found today?"

"I found fifty-four seeds today, mommy. But only one with a people in it."

The pair found many seeds that afternoon, but no more with a microscopic human inside. Eventually, they gave up on their search and headed to the Tripe township. They left behind a brief note to An in case he came home before they returned.

Not a shade too long thereafter, they found Dr. Atwood. They spotted her through her condensate-laden office window in Tripe township where she sat alone at her desk, appearing deep in reflection, her focus on the pages of an enormous book.

# CHAPTER 17

## JASON IS PURSUED

*Saturday, October 28, 1972*

Jason was limited in his choices, so his plan was rather simple. He would run as fast as his legs would carry him, search for a way out of the tunnel, return to the airport, wait out the storm while avoiding the warthogs and janitor. He would try to purchase a ticket home or to the mainland with the last of his money. If he didn't have enough, he would call other family members to ask for extra cash. To heck with the island. To heck with the lady on television. To heck with all of it! He also needed to find time to decode his father's cipher, sort through the various items in the tow sack, and find a way to get them on the plane. If not, to heck with them too. They could always be tossed.

And so Jason's plight continued. He continued to flee down the dimly lit stone quay away from the perceived danger, passing illustrations of minotaurs and bulls, timorously passing dark, uninviting archways and unknown labyrinths, praying that no one would lunge out and attack him. His satchel, heavier than he remembered, slapped up and down on his back like a jockey riding a steed, urging him onward.

"I don't know how much more of this I can take," he panted after running for almost ten minutes.

He trudged through the tunnel, which curved gently along to the right and grew progressively colder and more lit as the water became more luminous. Ahead, the light increased so much that Jason thought that an exit from the cave was in reach. He didn't know where he was headed, perhaps to a beach or into the jungle, but one thing was certain: he would not be captured. Paraphrasing Ralph, the warthogs were looking for him and they would make minced meat out of him if they caught him."

Jason glanced over his shoulder, expecting to have outrun his pursuers by a wide margin, only to find the large and ill-proportioned silhouettes projected along the tunnel wall of the anthropoid reptile standing atop a boat and his insect compadre who remained steadfast at the prow. It was really no stretch of the imagination to surmise that if the two afforded this much effort in their pursuit, then he certainly must be their prey. He was in mortal danger. After being accosted by the lizard's tongue, the crazed, carnivorous, xenophobic reptile must have liked what it tasted and now has a thirst only to be satiated with his blood. There was a bounty on his head.

The tunnel blossomed into a large cavern with a deep lake, which was split in two by a continuation of the quay that was about fifteen feet wide and functioned as an isthmus through the lake's center. The world seemed up-side down as thigmotropic vines coiled around the roots of trees that hung above him, creating a hodgepodge of overgrown jungle along the cavern's ceiling with the glowing sky in the blue water below. None of the vines or roots reached low enough for Jason to climb, and there were no portals through which he could see the outside world. Sunken items laid in the water and a large temple with surrounding figurines carved into the face of sand-tinted rock sat at the end of the quay. Otherwise, the cavern was empty, although a fixed structure at the end of the quay obscured his complete view of what laid ahead. Who knew what chthonian creatures were lurking in the darkness?

Out of options, Jason ran quickly across the isthmus, through occasional sprays of the lapping, salty water, careful not to slip on the slick stones as he passed the large bollards and outcroppings. The structures to either side of the quay were designed to moor boats, but none of the bollards were large enough to hide behind and no boats were present with the exception of an abandoned, half-sunken skeleton of a brig sloop and a more modern sailboat with a broken mast. The sloop was inscribed with its name, the HMS *Beagle*, and the more modern boat was named *Lazy Days*. Nearby, a fading, dilapidated sign poked out of the water and read, "Swim at your own risk. Dangerous currents."

*The HMS* Beagle? *Well, I'll be darned. Is this where Darwin wound up? But if I'm shrunken, why is his boat so small?* Jason examined the sign and the unusable boats before he noticed the other structures beyond them. As his gaze lifted above the boats and across the open lake, sunken in a recess of the cavern, he spotted another stone quay that stretched about 200 feet. Midway along the quay was a hanging sign that read, "Alibaba's Watches and Gemstones." The sign was canted about forty-five degrees from horizontal as its lights haphazardly flickered; it was clearly in disrepair. As he looked more closely, he saw dozens of neglected store facades that dotted the quay. They were easy to miss because their color was similar to the surrounding stone and they were similarly carved into the rock face, their presence only noticeable by the littoral, etiolated shrubs that stood in front of each shop. At each end, he could see darkened and hollow passageways, but no obvious path intersected with his own, and no life was noticeable.

With no time to dwell on the many curiosities he had seen in the cave, Jason ran toward the structure that was vaguely reminiscent of Mr. Winwood's drawings of the Temple of Hathor at Abu Simbel. The only real difference was the addition of a large, monochromatic clock at its precipice, similar to the one stuck on Bill's classroom wall. In hindsight, Jason had to admit that Mr. Winwood had really given the class a large amount of information over a short three-week period.

As he reached the structure at the end of the quay, he was halted by the bubbling and lapping water at the path's abrupt end. Rising high over the water was a ramshackle wooden bridge, now nothing more than a few staves strewn above the water, sewn with a rotting, frayed, hemp rope. Having run out of stone quay and since the staves offered no support or manner of crossing, he had no way forward. The structure, clearly having fallen into desuetude and by no means in a condition of use, was likely a remnant of what was once a swinging drawbridge or some cantilevered system of passage. Another fading sign that warned of the strong currents was nailed to a post. A nearby pole offered numeric bathymetric information that suggested that the small channel was incredibly deep and dangerous.

Jason could imagine that the structure before him was likely a well-functioning apparatus at some point in history. Regardless of its past importance, the gross fact was that fifty feet of canal separated his side of the stone quay from the other, and he needed to find a way across before he was captured by the two bloodthirsty creatures that somehow spoke English and knew his name. Given the oddities on land, who knew what aquatic species hungrily lurked in the depths below, regardless of the current? Panting, Jason took a moment to catch his breath and search his mind for answers, debating whether he should take the chance with a swim.

The temple's architecture was spectacular and awe-inspiring. A wide stairway, cut into the rock, ascended out of the azure water to the feet of four large statues reminiscent of pharaohs. The statues guarded a single, darkened portico, the depths of which could not be fully seen. The remainder of the facade featured baboon statues carved in bas-relief, offering no apparent space for any sizable creature to hide. Most noticeable to Jason, and perhaps signifying some horologic function of the structure, was the fixed clock at its precipice, the hands forever paused at 8:59.

*What do I do? What do I do? What on earth should I do?* As he weighed his options, the two creatures in the boat remained pertinaciously in hot pursuit as they tacked across the lake in his direction. Their preternatural resolve was remarkable.

"Give me my shears, you pirate!" Jason thought he could hear the green creature screaming, but not comprehending his meaning, he assumed it to be some sort of mean-spirited, indigenous colloquialism or threat. The two were bobbing like corks in the choppy water; their gondola was clearly not designed for a chase, but the rough water was doing nothing to dampen their pursuit or resolve.

Jason reasoned that he had three options: swim across and try to reach the portico, swim to the shop across the lake and hope it had a back exit, or double back and try one of the other passageways. The last option would mean he might have to contend with the two following him and any other that may have tracked him down the chute. Was it worth the chance?

He hastily scanned his surroundings and mercifully spotted a small, nearly hidden doorway to the right of the portico with an infinitesimal sign that read "Athenaeum," with an arrow pointing right. *Was it Greek for amphitheater? That would be a big place to hide or surely would have an exit.* He needed to make a decision and act quickly if he were to remain ahead of the two.

"My shears! My shears! Stop, you thief!" The crazed green lizard was screaming at the top of his lungs.

"I don't know what that means! Leave me alone! I just want to go home."

Again, Jason could hear "Entrance of the Gladiators" echoing through the tunnel as the gondola neared. He got down on all fours, cupped his hands in the water, and lifted it to his lips. *Salty and ice cold!*

Taking measure, he was trying to muster some reasonable degree of courage to dive in and swim across to the steps. There was no guarantee that the Athenaeum door or the darkened doorway would offer safe passage, and who knew what sort of Leviathan lurked below the water's surface. The satchel and its contents, his phone, and his money were also going to be a problem, as the canvas bag was not waterproof. He would just have to hold it above his head or on his shoulders and hope for the best as he swam across the channel. Alternately, he could leave it behind and return for it later.

Making a snap decision, he chose the latter. Jason crammed his phone and money into the front pocket of the satchel and hid it as best he could at end of the quay behind a bollard.

# CHAPTER 18

## NEAR CAPTURE

*Saturday, October 28, 1972*

Without warning, a flash erupted before a thunderous boom. Out of the corner of his eye, he saw dust and debris falling from a portion of the jungle ceiling into the blue-sky waters below. Immediately, another resounding brontide followed by an explosive clamor shook the earth as roots and rock rained down. From above, the world began to cave in, causing Jason to instinctively dive under the side of a bollard to protect himself. The two unfortunate souls in the lake were not as lucky; their boat's hull was nearly underwater, a large boulder had fallen in the middle of the boat, the figurehead at the prow was falling overboard, and the reptile grasped aimlessly in the surrounding waters, trying to find his companion.

An pointed to the ceiling and yelled, "I'm going to kick the you-know-what out of whoever is responsible! Mo cannot swim. This is attempted murder! This boat is a loaner and I don't have insurance. Whoever did this is going to have to pay for it! I'll call my councilman! I've got clout! Mo? Mo? Where are you? Help!" The lizard gondolier began frantically screaming at the top of his lungs when he realized that his friend was underwater. The lifebuoy floated listlessly on the water's surface. An was overwrought with terror. "Man overboard!"

Through the new hole in the ceiling, the peering, gibbous eye of a large beast was seen, followed by a sniffing, black snout. Whatever gargantuan creature was exploring the ground above had not yet found its prey. The beast was hunting. Large drops of snot and mucus dripped from above as the beast stuck its snout through the fissure in the roof, sniffing, snorting, and rooting. Jason felt a thunderous boom as it slammed a fist down to widen the hole, ripping vines and mud from the edges of the growing gap.

"Mo!" The lizard was undeterred by the monstrous brute, singularly focused on finding his friend. "Mo!"

"Hey, you over there, pirate!" The lizard pointed at Jason. "Yeah, I see you hiding. How about giving me a hand? Be a man. You look like a swimmer. Can't you see I need help?"

Jason stood up as the raining debris widened the breach, caused vines to unravel, many that extended into the waters within arm's reach.

"Me?" Jason pointed at himself. "What about *that*?" Jason pointed to the beast above.

"Yeah, you. I can see you. How about giving me a hand? Can't you swim? You look like a swimmer. And don't lose my satchel! I see it there beside you." The creature licked his eyeball before pointing up at the peering eye, "I see you up there, Bill, and I'm gonna kick your fat ass!" Turning back to Jason, he said, "Well?"

"But you want to eat me."

"What? Eat *you*? Mighty funny to accuse me of wanting to eat you, Mr. Biter. You have my satchel, you repugnant thief, and if there is a single scratch on my scissors, I might just eat you after all! You're the one running, ya big sissy."

"What about that beast?"

"Who, Bill? Are you serious? What's wrong with you? When this is over, he's all mine. If you want a piece of him, you'll have to wait your turn."

The life preserver bobbed emptily atop the water.

"I'm just trying to get my satchel back from you, thief! Now get over here and help me save this man who just happens to be my best friend. You need to dive! Dive, I say!"

From above, the baritone voice sang, "Fee-fi-fo-fum, I smell the boy named Jason Dix!" He pulled away another large slab of roof, exposing the gargantuan head of Bill the ice cream vendor.

"What about that beast up there? He's after me!"

"Beast?"

"Yeah, that giant warthog. Who else would I be referring to?"

"Oh, that's just Bill. Don't worry about him. He's a lumbering oaf, not hard to outwit. But seeing as you're worth $10,000, everyone will be after you, including me! I'll need that money to pay for this boat!"

"That's not the first time I've heard that."

"Well, get on with it. Stop wasting time."

Bill was just as surprised to see Jason as Jason was to see the prodigious ice cream salesman. The sight of the gargantuan warthog was fearful in itself, not to mention the horrid, vertically striped, tight, red-and-orange polyester outfit. The acrid smell of damp fur mixed with odious body odor wafted off his lumbering rolls of fat, creating a pungent, noxious sewer smell that permeated the cavern.

"There you are!" Bill pointed. "You will not escape me and Larry this time. You will know how it feels to be bitten! I'll bite you!"

The ice cream vendor shoved his forearm through the opening, stretching toward Jason as rocks and debris rained down. His arm was a bit too short to reach Jason or the water below, but he was making progress. Jason took heed, instinctively crouching lower beneath the bollard.

"Mo!" screamed An. The nearly sunken boat had drifted near the steps of the temple. Ignoring Bill, An paddled his drifting boat to where Mo fell in, ducking his head below the water to search.

As chaotic and insuperable as the moment seemed, the tension escalated even further. Heralded by the call of a war trumpet, a maniple of warthogs dressed as Roman warriors marched out of the tunnel toward Jason. If he waited any longer to take action, the situation would only become more dire.

Jason could not contain his confused frustration. "What the heck is this all about?! What is going on?"

With soldiers closing in behind him and Bill's arm reaching down from above, Jason's hand was forced. He shoved his glasses into his pocket and dove headfirst into the anchialine waters and swam toward the staircase, in line with the gondola and crazed lizard. If this were his end, he would at least make good in a less than propitious situation. Having to distinguish between friend and foe, at least the two in the boat were only two, and perhaps they would provide some manner of help if he were able to save the little moth. It was either get captured by the approaching army, get scooped up and eaten by Bill, or risk the crazed lizard with his lightning-quick tongue. The latter seemed the least nocuous.

Even from underwater, Jason could hear the muffled blare of the war trumpet, resonating louder throughout the cavern as rocks and debris sunk past him. When he surfaced to take a breath, the maniple of marching warthogs expedited their march while the ceiling crumbled further. Bill continued his pounding, reaching farther into the breach. The situation was rapidly deteriorating.

"Help! Someone help Mo!" screamed An.

"I'm coming!" Jason swam gracefully to the drop point and then dove.

Below the surface, the salinity decreased, allowing Jason to keep his eyes open. He caught a good view of the underside of the foundering gondola and discovered that it was beyond saving. He spotted a bit of white fur and found the moth serene and motionless, slowly sinking to its tomb of the deep. A series of white lights shot through the waters into the depths below.

Jason surfaced, gasping for air. He managed to take one large breath before a swift current grabbed hold of his leg and dragged him back down toward the moth.

As he shot past Mo, Jason wrapped his arm around the creature and grabbed onto a nearby vine. The current was too strong to swim against, but he couldn't leave the poor drowning creature behind. He kicked off his shoes and tried to fight the current on his way to the top. He would not let the creature die. He needed air.

An had plunged his head underwater to witness the events unfold. Realizing Jason's plight, he navigated the flotsam to the temple steps, grabbed the vine Jason was holding onto, and began pulling with all his might, desperately dragging the two to the surface.

Jason's head was the first to emerge; he came up coughing and sputtering, but immediately leaped into action to haul Mo out of the water and onto the sabulous steps of the temple. As he struggled to catch his breath, An desperately tried to revive his friend, shaking him, slapping his cheeks, and pounding him on the back.

"Mo, buddy. Come back to me. If you make it, I'll never charge you again. What have I done? I should have left the book. Its immaterial. I need you, Mo. Please, just breathe, buddy. What else can we do?"

Finally, Mo sputtered and coughed, retching an enormous volume of water and bile. Slowly, his eyes opened. He was saved.

Immune to the touching scene unfolding on the steps of the temple, the maniple raised their red oriflamme at the end of a long cane pole. Despite a haphazard blundering of a cornu, the army announced their attack and the melee began.

The stentorian leader called out in a magisterial tone, "Halt or we will shoot!" Archers at the rear of the battalion let loose a barrage of arrows that were clearly off the mark, striking the front of the temple. The water around the three rippled as many of the arrows fell short.

"Are you dolts serious? We didn't even have a chance to halt! Can't you oafs see that we have a drowning man here!" An was furious. "When we get back to town, I'll have you brought before the council! Are you completely stupid? This man almost drowned because of that goon up there. The whole lot of you need to be thrown in prison."

The stentorian was not so easily dissuaded. "Surrender or we will continue! We answer to no one but Saul. Our orders are to take the boy. Give him up and you will be left unharmed," the magisterial leader proclaimed.

"That ten grand is mine, so beat it! I know where you live! Go back to the Westbank, ya lowlife!" An defiantly shot him the middle finger. "You can stick it where the sun don't shine."

In the midst of An's tirade, Jason had risen to his feet, donned his glasses, and was rapidly searching for a means of egress. The door to what he presumed to be an amphitheater was stuck fast and could not be opened. The only remaining possibility was a dusty elevator within the portico, adorned with a slate sign that read, "Back at 9." Jason repeatedly mashed the elevator's call button, but the doors remained steadfastly closed.

"Again, halt. By order of our leader Saul, you three are hereby arrested."

"Arrested for what and under whose authority? We're on the south side. You have no power here!" An shouted.

Mo was finally fully awake and lucid, so he turned to help Jason. "C'mon, you darn elevator!"

Arrows were drawn. Jason pounded fruitlessly on the elevator doors as the calamity continued. "What are the odds that this thing still works? By the looks of those boats and that bridge, I have little faith that this thing has remained functional." Unfortunately for Jason and his new allies, the elevator doors failed to budge. Not even an inch.

"Do I look like I'm playing around?" the leader called.

An fired back, "Under whose orders? Who is this guy, Saul? Bring him to me, why don't ya? Never met him. The lot of you can go suck an egg! Finders keepers, so piss off. The kid is mine!"

The elevator remained inactive as An took over the job of repeatedly pressing the call button. "Move out of the way, biter boy. This sort of thing takes finesse."

Staring up at the ceiling, Mo caught a glimpse of the time and had an idea. "An, the clock is stuck just before nine. How about we change the time? Back at 9:00, but its only 8:59. It has been 8:59 for a while now. This may be the longest minute of my life."

"That's a great idea, Mo. How about you try scaling up an old, crumbling wall to check on a clock while an army of brainless Roman warriors tries to shoot arrows at you? I think your brain was deprived of oxygen for too long." An licked his eyeball again. "It's only a matter of time before those morons start shooting and one of us gets im-paled. At least one of us is bound to be injured. If we just stand behind this human, he will work as a shield."

Jason was quick to remind the pair of their debt. "You two owe me. You have to let me go. I saved your friend's life."

"We owe you one, sure. But you owe me my book and my scissors. You're the one who nicked my satchel. The shears inside were a priceless gift from the one and only Vidal Sassoon. Priceless, I say, but now forever lost. When those pigs find my satchel that you so brazenly discarded over there, they'll seize the lot of it and probably use my beloved shears to trim their fur. They'll be useless at that point, ruined beyond repair."

The maniple across the quay began firing another barrage of arrows. Their lack of precision was truly extraordinary. As predicted, one of the Romanesque warthogs found the poorly hidden knapsack and was tearing the book apart and throwing the pages into the air, dancing like a lunatic and taunting the trio.

"What's the matter with you? Scared?" taunted one of the hogs.

Another threw the gleaming shears directly at them from across the quay. Fortunately, An caught them in midair as paroxysms of anger took over. "Got 'em!"

The cavern was in utter pandemonium. Money drifted in the air like confetti. Jason's cellular phone was tossed into the water. Bill was trying to force his behemoth torso through the hole. "Hold onto my legs! Let me down gently, Larry!"

The leader of the maniple was trying to direct Bill. "You there! Yes, you! I hereby order you to fill in this gap with dirt from above. We need to cross the waterway and collect our prisoners."

The three were going to be captured if they didn't act quickly. Jason was staring up at the clock and noticed that some sort of string was attached to the minute hand. "Listen, we desperately need to get those doors open. It's our last hope. Can one of you climb the face of the temple and cut that string with your scissors? The clock will strike nine and maybe we can get out of this mess. It's a long shot, but I think it's worth a try."

An spoke. "Yeah, right. You're not the one doing the climbing. What's in it for me? And they're shears, not scissors."

Jason rolled his eyes. "Well, if you won't, what about you, little moth? If he is too chicken, can you do it? Can you flap your wings and fly up there? And what's in it for you? Are you serious? How about your lives? A way out? What more do you want? Look, I'd say we are in a dangerous position. We have a real problem here."

"No, we'd say that you're the one with the problem. They want you, not us." Mo said matter-of-factly. "Umm, An?"

"Yes, Mo?"

"I'm afraid of heights."

An sighed in exasperation. "First you can't swim, and now you're afraid of heights? Get yourself together, my friend!"

Jason was frustrated. "C'mon, you two. I saved his life for goodness' sake. I'm alone on this strange island and I just want to get home. I need some help. I need to get back to the airport and find a flight home."

"You just want to take some of your pirate booty with you." A pause hung in the air. An finally had enough and said, "I'll climb up there, but for a price. I'll collect the reward when we turn you in to the proper authorities, and you need to tell the truth. I'll be on the hook for a new gondola, and I'll need you to corroborate my account of this mess."

"Deal. You get me out of here and to the proper authorities, somewhere safe where I cannot get hurt, and we have a deal."

The leader of the maniple realized they were putting a plan into action when An handed Jason the shears and began to climb the face of the temple. "Open fire! He's trying to gain the high ground."

Using his sticky toe pads, An climbed to the precipice and tethered clock, dodging arrows on the way up. He hollered, "The twine is too thick and all knotted up. Quickly, throw me the scissors! I've identified the problem."

Jason lofted the scissors to An, who caught them with his lightning-quick tongue and transferred them to his sticky fingers.

"A piece of string has tethered the minute hand." An cut the string, but nothing happened.

"Now what?" An looked down dejectedly.

Just then, as the minute hand advanced to the nine o'clock position, the trio could feel the rumbling of machinery within the temple, like the awakening of some long-kept beast. The pealing ding of the elevator bell announced its readiness. The doors slid effortlessly open, and a previously unseen green light with crossed, golden keys illuminated above the doors.

"It's open! You did it." Mo was gleeful. "Good job, An. Now get down here!"

An leaped off the clock, dodging a hail of arrows on his way down, twisting his body to-and-fro. "Don't forget your promise, Jason. I need your account of what happened here. The reward money alone will not cover the cost of a new gondola."

Having grabbed the satchel from the remains of the gon-dola, Jason joined his two companions as they bounded into the safety of the elevator. As the doors closed behind them, they heard a flurry of arrows pinging and ricochet-ing off the elevator doors.

The elevator was spacious, luxurious, and unlike any other that Jason had ever seen. The walls were paneled with a rich, dark mahogany paneling, golden side rails, and a gilded ceiling and floor. A lone red settee was pushed against the back wall, and beside it sat a small vending machine filled with miniature bottles of Real World, Tripe Wake Up cola, Reversion Raspberry Spritzer, and Orange You Glad to Forget Natural Fruit Juice. On the right-hand wall, a framed and locked glass cabinet housed a corkboard with a single announcement: "Coming Soon: The Greatest Game Show of All Time Returns!" The bulletin featured a photograph of two masked people in plumaged headdresses and a small il-lustration of a gate with two locks and a Mayan glyph.

Jason wasn't sure of the meaning, but despite her face be-ing obscured by the mask, one of the two contestants vaguely reminded him of Ms. Somerall. The low din of the vending machine and a humming fan installed in the ceiling were the only sounds. Jason felt the rumbling of the machinery beneath his feet.

"Game show?" The three looked at each other quizzically as Jason examined the announcement more closely.

"What the heck? Those two look like my teachers from school." He pointed to the announcement.

Jason assumed that the elevator operated like any other, and he expected that the operating panel would comprise the standard floor buttons. Instead, when the doors closed, he was surprised to see a large, LED, gold-framed touchscreen. Written in script above the screen were the words, "Pick a Gregorian Year." Like the sign for Ralph's Diner, the holographic nature of the sign displayed a second message: "Elevator." At the top of the LED panel was a confusing and complex set of words without adequate instruction:

CENOZOIC ERA > QUARTERNARY PERIOD > AN-THROPOCENE EPOCH >

Recent Travels:

Palenque, Maya. 670 AD.

34-56 107th Street, Queens, New York. August 1, 1965.

Studio 54, New York City. April 26, 1977.

King Arthur's Court, England. October 21, 499 AD.

New Orleans Police Department 5th District, 3900 N. Claiborne Ave, New Orleans. July 6, 2015.

Angelo Brocato's, 214 N. Carrollton Avenue, New Orleans. August 11, 2015.

50th sub-basement, Denver International Airport. January 26, 2052.

Recent Human Eras >

PICK A DATE: VOICE COMMAND AVAILABILITY

American Eras

Central Asian Eras

Chinese Eras

Egyptian Eras

European Eras

Filipino Eras

Indian Eras

Japanese Eras

Middle Eastern Eras

Southeast Asian Eras

Above the panel, a small speaker and microphone were inlaid in the wood.

"What does this mean? It's all nonsense!" said An as arrows continued to ping off the outside of the elevator doors. "Is there not a 'Keep Doors Closed' button?"

Mo was the most levelheaded of the three. "Now isn't the most opportune time for a debate. Just pick something near the top. What if the doors were to open? We'd be sitting ducks! An, don't you remember that one time when . . ."

"Quiet, Mo. I need to think."

Jason hastily asked, "Where should we go? Anywhere? I agree with the moth, somewhere near the top. We need to go up." Jason mashed the top label. Nothing happened. "This infernal thing doesn't seem to be working. I wish I were just back at school."

As if to answer Mo's concern, the doors reopened. The maniple of Romanesque warthogs were still stuck at the end of the quay with arrows at the ready, but Bill was still hanging upside down and now he was shoveling dirt between the base of the temple stairs and the end of the quay, water splashing high into the air and onto the temple stones. Many of the warthogs were using the vines to swing to the temple base. Jason, An, and Mo were boxed in. It seemed that their capture was imminent, and they would have to use hand-to-hand combat and fight to survive. Stuck in a nonfunctional elevator, they were as good as giftwrapped for the hungry army of warthogs.

Jason took his position along the side wall with the panel, and Mo and An slid to the other side of the chamber, all tucking in their chests and abdomens, trying to lessen their physical signature. Arrows rained in, hitting the back of the elevator and lodging in the settee.

"Oh, look," Mo blubbered in his daze, "we're not going anywhere. We don't have the key." He pointed to an ornate lock and plate near the bottom of the panel. Jason immediately recognized it as being similar to the one on his own front door.

"I doubt it will fit, but the lock looks just like the one on my front door at home. It seems a bit inconceivable."

Mo's eyes widened and he said, "Hey, wait! I've seen that key before. But I promised not to tell."

"Impossible. This thing's been living around my neck on a chain since the last time I misplaced it, which was about a year ago."

"Then your key has a twin."

"Twin. Key. Who cares at this point? Look, Mo, he's the one they're after. If we give him up, they'll surely leave us alone. At least we will survive. I'll figure something else out about the boat."

"So much for trusting you! You said you'd help get me out of here and to the proper authorities unharmed!"

"An, it's not right. He saved my life."

Jason took the key from around his neck, inserted it into the elevator's lock, and gave it a twist. "Even Mr. Bill's class would have been better than this nightmare of a place."

Much to their surprise, the doors expeditiously closed and the elevator ascended at what felt like the speed of light. The force pushed all three to the floor and caused them all to simultaneously shout, "Oooh!"

A nasal, pacifying voice played overhead, as if to placate any second thoughts. "Ladies and gentlemen, a brief disclaimer before travel. One may experience occasional sharp thrust and jolts." The elevator suddenly jolted to the left and then to the right. ". . . like that. Please hold on to the side rails for your safety, or perhaps rest comfortably on the settee provided. There is no method of recourse should you fall or injure yourself during the journey. If you would like refreshments, they are provided in the refrigerated compartment for the low price of one Roman dupondius each. Do you need a refresher course on the refreshments?" The cicerone chuckled lightly under his breath at his own joke.

Jason directed his reply to the panel. "Can I pay in US dollars? No, wait. I lost all my money when I put the cash in the satchel."

"Roman coins only, sir. You Americans are all alike. Company policy. No exceptions and no credit cards."

"Dix, where are we heading?" An's voice crescendoed as all three faces distortedly elongated in concordance with the upward velocity. None of them seemed to notice the change to the panel, which featured a new entry under the Recent Travels section: "Carrollton School, New Orleans. October 27, 2017." An and Mo's animal visages began to quickly revert to a Homo sapien appearance, and from their states of devolution, a prescient understanding of more trouble galloped through each of their minds.

Jason looked at his two travel companions, and with a tremor in his voice, he said, "Hey, you two look just like my friends at school, Zach and Bobby, just older. What the heck? And look! We're dry now!"

"Must-t-t-t be g-g-g-good-looking guys. Where is this box taking us, up or down?" An was having a hard time speaking.

"We're moving pretty fast, guys." Mo's eyes were practically popping out of his head in surprise.

*Ding.* The elevator came to an abrupt halt.

"Like I said, must be good-looking guys." Beads of perspiration dotted An's forehead.

The elevator announced, "Ladies and gentlemen, the Gregorian year is 2017. If you have any questions, please direct them to the appropriate authorities at your destination. You will find a bottle of Real World drink available, one for each new traveler. Your first is on the house. I suggest you prioritize getting your finances in order. If you plan on staying, I suggest you imbibe before departing these confines. We hope you have enjoyed the ride." The elevator doors slid open with a ping. The floor was dry and the settee was without arrows as the vending machine spit out three vials of Real World.

"Look at this, An. Free snacks!"

"Mo, put those away for now. How can we trust that voice? This may all be part of this human's trap. It appears we have fallen for his tricks." An looked skeptically at Jason, waiting for a response. "Remember his pirate lair?"

Jason had tuned An and Mo out completely. Much to his dismay, he realized that the elevator was no longer on the island. In fact, they were just about as far from the tiny island in the South Pacific as they could get. Instead, the trio were looking out into the interior of Carrollton School in New Orleans, Louisiana. Beyond the threshold of the elevator, Jason glimpsed his first-period class. He spied his own feet next to his languid pal, Zach, and his monotone, oafish teacher, Bill, who scribbled on the board and droned on. At the end of the hallway, Mr. Sims appeared, his face painted bright green, his head down as he walked toward the elevator with a broom in his hand. Jason mashed a random button at the bottom of the panel, hoping it would close the doors. "Get back! Shh!" The two followed Jason's lead as he ducked to the side to remain out of sight.

Mo whispered, "What about the snacks, An? I'm hungry. Hey, that guy at the end of the hall is the same color you were, An."

"Oh my gosh, guys. This is really, really, really weird. I'm back at my school."

From Mr. Sims's perspective, the elevator doors were closed, and there were no odd happenings as the doors slid open again.

Down the hall, Jim Fisher looked around to make sure no one was watching him before taking his leg off the knee scooter. The scoundrel walked down the hallway without deficit, and then through the front doors and out of the school.

"I knew it! What a faker."

"Who is that guy?" Mo asked.

"Where are we? Where have you taken us, pirate?"

"That kid. See him walking? He's been faking it. I knew it! And you were so willing to give me up. You're on my turf, now; we're in my school. By the look of it, we're watching yesterday. I'm at a loss for words."

# CHAPTER 19

## ANCIENT COLLECTION FOUND

*Saturday, October 28, 1972*

The Ancient Collection, purportedly a hidden Comstockian aggregation of the island and world's remote knowledge, was rumored to be hidden by the former leader in one of many sub-sub-sub-basements of the island's once thriving library. Much to the chagrin of the bibliophiles on the island, the library and all of its basement levels remained inaccessible due to the building's collapse. The stairs that led to the lower levels simply gave way and were filled with rubble. The structural collapse was attributed to the weakening of support beams after The Change, and hence, topographic change and the shifting of the underlying tectonics weakened the library's foundation. The details of exactly how the library fell and the presumed death of the librarian, Chamé, were studied meticulously and memorialized in an extensive investigative report: "The Fall of the Great Library of Tripe." After the report was made public, one would have expected the rubble clearing to be a rather conventional and necessary task to mitigate other unforeseen risks. However, the rubble removal process became a legal quagmire. Countless motions and petitions requesting the right to remove the "rubble and detritus" and rebuild the site were sent to the Tripe Island Council by numerous islanders, self-proclaimed altruistic, philanthropic organizations, and even a few Chinese and United States billionaires who were interested in staking a claim of ownership over something on the island. All requests remained in a stalemate, and there had never been a consensus amongst the island's insensible politicians as to: who would fund the project, whether anthropocentric outsiders should be allowed to perform clean up or construction on the island, and the details of the architectural schema. The council remained decidedly undecided and there was no decision forthcoming, much to the dismay of Melvin and the island residents. Government bureaucracy at its finest.

At the prodding of Dr. Atwood, who sought the Ancient Collection from under the tons of rubble, Saul needed to find an unconventional solution to access the basement. He had to devise other means of ingress. From the outset, Dr. Atwood was clear that meeting certain goals were of the utmost importance if he were to earn his side of their bargain. She was so insistent that she even expected certain transgressions, and thus, Saul, competent at commanding his army of obsequious warthogs, was more than eager to comply with her demands. It was no skin off his nose. After Saul discussed the council's shortcomings with himself, he came to a conclusion: dealing with the council would only result in a protracted deadlock, so a hidden tunnel to circumvent their delay seemed to be his best and only option.

This is how the Library Express began. Saul's minions had hastily created a two-mile, banausic warren from the anteroom near Harry's Bar to the library's basement. His beer-fueled passel worked constantly, and after a few misses, they finally reached the target. The final breach of the sub-sub-sub-basement was nigh. Most of the islanders were unaware of the happenings below their feet, as the work was performed in secret and without permit. From the anteroom of the Westbank bar, power cables and cords stretched the length of the tunnel and were used to power lighting through the warren and into the stone basements. In this basement room, the crème de la crème of the incompetent Westbank crew was about to get a helping hand.

Earlier that day, the Westbank construction crew breached the wall into a basement room no greater than thirty by fifty feet. It was a musty room with minimal ventilation, filled with shelves laden with manuscripts of varying sizes. Having reached their ultimate target, the construction workers were replaced with a more educated and sober group of Westbank Romanesque warthogs dubbed the "investigations crew," who fervently combed the basement's shelves for clues, trying to descry any knowledge leading to the Ancient Collection. They were on a schedule and needed answers.

Having learned of the breach, Saul was en route. A palpable tension hung in the air, fueling their unsettling weariness; no one had slept in days. Despite perusing thousands of manuscripts, the crew of bullish warthogs seemed no closer to finding the Ancient Collection and were growing nervous that they had breached the wrong sub-basement, or worse yet, that they were incorrect about its sub-sub-sub-ness. If they were in the wrong place, at least they could blame the construction crew. Just then, a simple, out-of-place, and unappreciated construction worker spoke.

A beefy, less-intelligent warrior kept obnoxiously mashing a button on the nonfunctional, overly scaled water fountain, causing a ruckus as he pounded and yelled, "What's wrong with the water? What's wrong with the water? What's wrong with the water?"

A construction worker tried to gain the crew's attention. "Boss man! Jefe! Look over here. Look at it, under the fountain."

The poor fountain, now bent out of shape, was plugged into a nonfunctioning electrical outlet.

"Water. What's wrong? No water. I like water."

"Give it a break, Remus. There's no electricity. Plug it in to one of the power cords if you must." One of his brethren, steadfastly at work, brushed off his shenanigans.

"Who's calling me? Did I hear jefe?" The leader of the crew looked around.

The worker was dressed in typical construction garb, including hard hat with the number thirty-four stenciled on the front. He had situated himself behind the last bookshelf in the back corner of the room and he had gone unnoticed to this point. Down on all fours, he peeked below the mounted, decrepit water fountain, using the megalopic effect of his magnifying glass to look for minutia.

"Guys, come quickly. I think I'm onto something here. There's something down here. Guys, come see." Through his lens, he could see a microscopic sign embossed with script lettering and two upside-down keys above a mouse-hole-sized, trapezoidal door and stone vestibule. "It says, An, Anci." The beast was struggling to sound out the words, saying, "An-ciee-nnnn-tttt." He thought he could hear "Entrance of the Gladiators" playing softly amid the background hullabaloo and the slight buzzing of the electric lighting.

"That's 'Ancient Collection,' you incorrigible moron," barked the churlish, Romanesque soldier, the jefe, who

377

pulled a shop light close. "My god, did the Westbank school teach you anything?"

Assuming an akimbo, I-am-better-than-you stance, the boss absentmindedly twirled a rainbow sash that was hanging from his belt and corrected the plebeian. "It's not a homonym. We don't sound out words at our age, fella! What are you doing here? You're on the construction crew; I thought I told you guys to leave hours ago." His nametag read, "Thrax," and he was the most truculent and imprudent warthog on the island, subject to sudden caprices of extreme anger.

He suddenly realized who he was addressing, which brought a look of disdain to his face. "Did I or did I not tell you to get back to work and out of that hole," Thrax said, thumbing in the direction of the breach. "You're not our type! We're the upper echelon of Westbankers, and you are nothing but a serf! Big boy, I'm waiting. If I have to say it again, you'll be sorry." He tapped his foot, but the languid beast was moving too slowly. "OK, play that game. Let's do it my way, you laggard. Stand up, idiot." He grabbed the beast by the ear and yanked him to his feet, his eye still huge behind the magnifying lens. "You're not one of us, not like us, not our crew. What are you still doing here? Trying to take credit for our work?"

The craven construction worker stood in a slouched stance, his work belt loosely fastened over his shoulder. "I dunno. I guess I was just trying to help. I always want-

378

ed to be an investigator, and, well, I guess I thought this was my time to help. I guess it all started when I was a little one. I was like six years behind you in school. Did you know that? You won't remember me, but I know you. You were called Timmy then, and you were the school jock. A real popular guy. I was in middle school when you were in high school, and I would always hear Mrs. Hedgewater calling for you, 'Now Timmy, it's time to go to class!'"

"Silence! My name is Thrax now. Burn it into your pea-sized brain. I am the leader of Saul's special investigations crew. I've worked too long and hard for it to be mucked up by the likes of you and your lazy kind." The irascible beast took a big step closer, now standing nose-to-nose with the worker who failed to cower, his lack of fear taken as an insult. Thrax's capriciousness took over; his eyes became wild and the bloodlust went to his head. "Give me that, you oaf. I remember you from when we were young. You were a weakling then, and you're a weakling now!" He snatched the magnifying lens from his hands and continued his bitter philippic. "Stand at attention, you subordinate slouch! Have you no respect?"

Number thirty-four stood more upright.

"Gut in, tubby."

Thirty-four tried to suck in his large gut as his lumbering rolls jiggled.

"What are you still doing here, thirty-four? You're not smart enough, definitely not good-looking enough, and not tough enough to be appointed to the investigations unit. Look at your nails! And that hair, atrocious! Your gut! Furthermore, your breath smells beery, like some sour brew from the tavern. Have you been drinking? Have you been at the tavern? I'll guess the answer is yes, you sozzled fool." Thrax was practically foaming. "That's why you're in demolition or construction or refuse removal—whatever your imbecilic mind can handle. I told the demolition detail to remain in the tunnel. Where is your superior, Nick? Get him over here." He snapped his fingers deprecatingly. It was clear that he saw number thirty-four as nothing more than a bug beneath his boot. "Nick needs to control his fools! I'm surprised that your clumsiness has not destroyed any semblance of clues that remain. You're the reason we're behind! My god, man, look at you. Have you no sense of self-respect? You're fat! You're lazy! Dullsville, I'd say. This ought to knock some sense into you." He rapped the poor worker on the head with his own magnifying glass, denigrating him to the fullest. The warthogs gathered round the escalating vituperation to laugh at the demoralized waif.

"Just trying to help," thirty-four said dejectedly with a resigned, acquiescent shrug of his shoulders, lower lip stuck out, and chin quivering as a tear welled in the corner of his eye. He diffidently shuffled toward the breach in the wall, fettered by a lack of self-confidence. He wistfully mumbled, "You were always my hero. I hope you are successful at finding the Ancient Collection."

"Wait a minute. Did I give you permission to leave?" Thirty-four continued walking away in tears, but Thrax was not done with him yet. "You want a piece of me?"

"Well you told me to leave through the hole, sir, so I was heading home through the hole."

"Insubordination! Drop and give me twenty push-ups, you unprepossessing fool. Hustle!" He kicked thirty-four's feet out from under him.

With great effort, he came to a prone stance, "One. Two. Two and a half . . ." The group of warthogs gathered around, hurling insults as he gave up.

"Not only are you an oaf, but you can't even give me twenty push-ups. You are PATHETIC! Get out of my sight!"

Thrax firmly kicked number thirty-four in his side in a violent and remorseless manner unique to Westbankers, causing thirty-four to curl into the fetal position. Slowly, he rose to his knees and crawled out of the basement on all fours.

"Yeah, out of our sight!"

"C'mon boss, let it go. Let it go." Three of the more lev-elheaded crew members pulled him back, giving thirty-four room to escape. Saul's almost here."

The tunnel was otherwise empty as the euchred number thirty-four crawled into the warren. He had not expected violence. Tottering upright a bit farther, he flicked his wrist and his body vanished into a plethora of small, bright lights, which then disappeared into one of the small nooks in the cave wall. If they couldn't figure it out from here, another tactic would be needed. A pile of clothes, hard hat, and work belt were all that remained in the passage when Saul and his lieutenant general hurried past and entered the breach.

"Attention!" shouted the lieutenant general, who stopped short of the breach. All occupants followed suit as Saul entered the basement.

With a broad sweep of his cloaked head, Saul appraised the room and its occupants. "I expect we have made suf-ficient progress into the basement, given all the hoopla and yakety-yak. Otherwise, I would expect my men to be hard at work and not having the time for extraneous ac-tivities. Please, tell me we have found the Ancient Col-lection."

"Sir," the kowtowing warthog to his left interjected. "At your righteous command, we have done as you asked. Your Excellency, may we present the Ancient

Collection." He gestured to the terribly small, trapezoidal doorway below the water fountain. "Look, sir, at the lettering above the doorway. I believe this is what we are after." He crouched down and polished the beveled lettering with his hairy arm.

"Is this a joke? Are you the discoverer?" Saul ambled to the fountain and stooped for a look.

"Yes, sir. Well, we are the discoverers, that is. All of us."

Rising, Saul's voice became more mordant. "Come, my children. Gather 'round. Closer. Need I stress the importance of our quest? Imagine there to be a time when your freedom, your power, or your very life depended upon the finding of a library replete with manuscripts from the ages. Manuscripts that lead to war, lead to peace, lead to knowledge lost. Such a place would be necessary to improve the lives of yourselves, your brethren, and your exalted leader. Would you not offer a fastidious perscrutation of such a place, and hence make it your quest, no, your mission in life to uncover its secrets? Would you not put other, less serious efforts and superfluous ideas aside? Would you not deny all worldly pleasures until such a place is found?"

Despite having zero comprehension of Saul's meaning, the crew nodded. "Questionable, boss. Questionable. But yes, sir, we would search for whatever you asked."

"So while on this noble quest, you show me an insignificant hole under a dented water fountain that you believe is the location you and all of your kin have been searching for?"

"Remus dented it, sir."

"Is this some sort of joke? Perhaps you should have put more work into it. May I see you enter that small hole?" With growing anger, he took one of the books off the shelf and hurled it across the room. "Could you even fit your arm into that hole? Let me explain what will happen to you, should you patronize me. First, I will . . ." He paused, thinking he heard the sound of a cornu. "Did you just hear something? Quiet!" He put his cupped hand to his ear.

A low, mechanical rumbling could be felt. Everyone in the room looked around as a faint shudder and vibrations shook the dust off the walls. "Need I remind you how the library fell? Tell the construction crew to quit working right now. They are going to collapse this room! You lot are procrastinators with no self-direction, unable to solve problems for yourselves! So be it." Saul thrust his staff in the direction of the last warthog to speak, and a blazing blue light shot across the room to strike the victim in his face. The unfortunate warthog was electrocuted, violently shaking and grabbing his face. "My eyes! I cannot see! I cannot see! I'm blind!" Stumbling forward, he ran blindly into one of the shelves, causing the others to topple like dominos. "Help! My face is on fire!" The pained creature screamed louder as the pungent odor of singed fur hung in the air.

"You there," Saul said, pointing to another, who took a step back. "Take that disgusting creature to the infirmary. Perhaps a bit of prodding is all you'll need. You were saying?" Saul looked directly at Thrax.

Thrax took a timid gulp and said, "Sir, I will take responsibility. While it's true that the doorway is quite small, perhaps one of the younglings would be able to enter. We opted to wait for Your Majesty's approval before breaching the wall."

"And destroy what lays beyond? You may be stupider than the last! What has become of the apothecary?"

Without warning, the small door under the water fountain blasted open with a slam. A barrage of tiny arrows shot through the opening, striking Thrax in the shins and causing him to holler. A few struck Saul's cloak, but they were harmlessly deflected. A maniple of miniature, Romanesque warrior warthogs, heralded by the burst of a cornu, rushed out and attacked Thrax's feet, pummeling his thick, hairy toes with tiny clubs as new barrages of arrows were loosed upon his shins.

"Attack!" A command from somewhere within roused the riotous troops that continued to spill out of the arched

385

doorway, the red oriflamme bringing up the rear. In defense of the maniple's leader, all he could see from his vantage point were gigantic, hairy legs.

As the leader gazed upward upon the enormous beast, he was met by Thrax's infuriated visage.

"Is that you, Lionel?" boomed Thrax. The sudden realization stopped both hogs in their tracks.

"It is, it is."

The giant's face softened as he recognized his friend.

"Halt, troops! Halt! Cease fire! These are friends, our brethren!" The clubbing and flights of arrows ceased, but the participants in the maniple were clearly confused by the size discrepancy.

Thrax swept away his attackers, knocking them over with the stroke of a hand as he fell to his knees, squashing a few of the small warriors. He succumbed to his own built-up emotions. "Thank you. Thank you, oh thank you! You're alive! I missed you so. When I was told you disappeared, I assumed the worst. When they said you were flushed down the drain, I expected that it was some cruel metaphor for a more ominous destiny. And now, here you are, but smaller. And alive, alive! Lionel, you devil, you! What happened to make you ever so small? You're so cute, like a miniature you!" He dotingly took the small warthog into his palm, nuzzling him as he raised him to eye level, oblivious to those around him.

Saul rolled his eyes and cleared his throat to interrupt their reunion. "Silence! Let him explain. We have no time for your amorous relationship. Speak to me."

The warrior gathered his thoughts and directed his attention to Saul. In great detail, he gave a full accounting of the diner, pummeling the pugilistic cook into revealing his secret, magical soap, discovering the apothecary, the skirmish in the cavern, Bill's clumsy intervention, the boy's escape, the library, and their capture of An and Mo.

Saul listened attentively and was patient to take into account every detail. When the fantastical tale was complete, his sole command was, "Fetch me this soap and fetch me Dr. Atwood. Whoever is the fastest in our arsenal, run like the wind! Go!"

"Sir, I'm not sure how much soap remains. There was a great many of us."

# CHAPTER 20

## A RETURN TO SCHOOL

*Friday, October 27, 2017*

The school doors slammed shut with a loud, metallic clank.

"What is that sound? That sound! That horrible, persistent sound!" An plugged his ears with his fingers.

"Real World! Look guys, free drinks." Mo was excited.

"Do you mean the noisy clock or the brainless hominid they call my teacher? To me, they're equally as repulsive. Now I know that my teacher, that guy mumbling at the board over there, Bill, has a twin brother that looks like a warthog. This cannot be real!"

"Mo, leave those alone," he said, swatting Mo's hand away from the vending machine. "We don't know if any of this is real or just some trap, a ruse, a means to catch us both off our guard. Perhaps this pirate is trying to poison us or weaken our resolve into some malleable and debilitated state. Argh! It's so hard to think with that racket!" As the clock's click, clatter, and click persisted, An stuck a finger in each ear as he held on tight to his shears, trying to dampen the clock's banter, his face contorting in a painful look of confused agony. Jason put his hand on An's shoulder, took the shears out of his hand, and slid them into the satchel, effectively stopping him from exiting.

"You'll get your shears back, but frankly, you frighten me. No weapons, school policy. Now it's your turn to be skeptical, just like I was back on your island. It may seem absurd, just impossible to believe, but I'm telling you the truth. I know where we are now: in my school, in the year 2017, in my hometown, and I'm in the classroom around the corner. It's as if the elevator transported us through time. It's more than likely that neither of you are real and this is all just a weird dream. Give me a minute, let me think. We have an elevator in our home. Oh, stop it Jason! Get ahold of yourself. This is preposterous! This cannot be real. None of it."

"Mr. Bill, the clock sounds ill! Might we remove it so that we can better hear your wonderful lecture? I mean, how long do you think we will have to listen to that confounded clock?" Jason's doppelgänger over in the classroom was aggravated.

"What is going on? This really is yesterday." Jason was dumbfounded, clearly in a state of complete confusion.

"That's the real me across the hall in class. An, you're next to me and Bobby—that's you, Mo—is outside."

"Yeah, right. Get a load of this, Mo. He expects us to believe his cockamamie story. Did you see the color of that man's face, right out there in the hall? They have gone through The Change too! I guess it was the whole world. You said you're from America? USA? Look at that kid near the head of the class. He looks like a rooster."

"My classmates are dressed in costumes for Halloween. It just so happens that yesterday, or today, was the last day before the fall break."

"And is that you in class? Right over there? Is that what you're asking us to believe? It's a costume party?"

"Yes."

"Then why are you not participating? You're not wearing a costume. I bet you'd be a pirate, you sneak. Mo, I'm not sure what to believe any more."

Jason said, "Yeah, you're not the only one to remind me. That green guy in the hall gave me a hard time about it. My father and I just forgot. The strangest thing is that you two look like slightly more mature copies of my two best friends in this school. You see that guy over there next to me in class? That's you, An. You're sort of dressed like a gondolier, but with boots. I wish I had a mirror to show you." Jason's mouth was agape. The transmogrification was complete, and not only did the two appear human, but they looked exactly like Zach and Bobby.

"Well then, Mo, let's go introduce ourselves to ourselves. I cannot see any harm in meeting ourselves, since we're not actually real and only part of this guy's imagination. Is that what you're telling us? Wow. I thought we were merely devolutionary misfits, but now I see that even my consciousness is a farce."

Jason tried to reason with him. "C'mon, you'd be afraid too. It's insane to think that I was suddenly on an island of creatures, like *The Island of Dr. Moreau*. Like the world wouldn't know, yet here we are. Three guys in this posh elevator with this sofa and weird panel."

"I'm real," Mo innocently responded.

"Me too, Mo. I was making a point."

"Surely, you two . . . Nope, I get it now. I was wrong. All of this—me, this elevator, you two—is but a figment of my imagination. I'm at home, asleep on the sofa."

An asked, "And we look like them, your friends in school? What year did you say? 2017?"

"Yep."

"Well then, follow me, Mo. It's time we get going. He is a liar because I know that I'm real and no pirate is going to tell me otherwise."

Jason held him back. "Wait! What other explanation is there? Explain it to me, please. My name is Jason Dix. I was tricked into traveling to an island earlier today. The year was 2017 when I left, but I landed in 1972. Possible? I think not! And why 1972? Who knows! I wasn't even born then. Which deep, dark recess of my mind is focused on 1972? Then, when I landed, I was chased by two monstrous beasts through the airport for no reason at all. One of them was the hog you call Bill, who happens to look sort of like my teacher in the classroom over there, the same beast who made the hole in the roof of the cavern. I ran from him when he burst into baggage claim after the entirety of my fellow passengers changed into insects and animals, all except for this woman who just so happened to look like my second-period teacher upstairs. Then I met a flat-nosed cook in a diner who somehow knew me from when I was a child. He introduced me to a man-rooster who also seemed to have met me as a child, then the cook poured some soap on my head and flushed me down the drain of his diner's kitchen sink. Oh, and did I mention that a sack of potions was given to me by that wrinkly, old man-rooster? Well, that's when I met you guys. You know the rest. I can't rationally explain any of what has happened, but I do know for certain that we are inside my school in a New Orleans suburb in the year 2017. That monotone speaker is my teacher, and he's lecturing on inheritance patterns, specifically Darwinism and how it relates to Mendelian inheritance.

"Given the circumstances, I'm either dreaming, or missing my father-son trip really did drive me all the way to Crazyville. Trust me when I say that we desperately need to get somewhere safe. I need to sort through both my scrambled brain and the information in my bag. I need to make heads or tails of what my father left for me and figure out how to get out of this dream or hallucination or schizophrenic psychic break or whatever it is. I need to get us all out of this. We're in this together now."

"Seriously, what's that horrible sound? Knock, knock?"

Mo responded, "Who's there?"

"We're here, Mo. And so, Mr. Dix, if you think that this is a dream and the two of us are not real or are just part of some hallucination, you're 100 percent wrong." An's eyes squinted closed and his face contorted into a tortured look of frustration as the grating cacophony of the clock in Bill's room continued. "You may be crazy, but we are real. This situation is real. Give me the key so we can turn this elevator around. That clock is going to make me go mad."

"Crazy makes sense! A psychogenic fugue. That's it! The only way out will be to make sense of the materials my father left for me. Perhaps this rationalization will unscramble my brain. And the cipher, when I break it, will set me free. In this dream or delirium, I know two things: First, someone wants to capture me. There must be some value in what I have or what I know. Second, I know that you have no good reason to trust me, nor I you. We don't know one another, but right now, our interests are aligned. Working together is our best option. If I'm to get out of this, I need your help. And you can't get home without my help.

"I'm not sure how safe it is for me to meet myself. You two may somehow be subconsciously related to my friends from school, in which case, it may not be safe for you to meet yourselves in person either. Worse yet, witnessing my own dissociative fugue may cause utter pandemonium and permanent dissociation, upset the space-time continuum, or cause some other disturbance that we can't even fathom. I don't know exactly what I'm saying; I think I saw it on *Star Trek* or some other sci-fi show." Jason took a deep, steadying breath. "There, I said it. I got it off my chest. All of this is so ridiculous, but I've never done this before, so I need you two to play along."

"I wish this were a dream. That sound won't stop. Argh!" An wailed. "Did you even hear what I just said? Are you paying attention? I'm serious. My health is at stake. Mo, think about it—I may become him! How can I block out that awful sound? If this is yesterday, why didn't you just fix the clock?"

"My teacher wouldn't let me fix it or turn it off. I agree, it's horrible. For now, we have to leave it alone." Jason threw his clenched hands up in frustration. "We need to leave the clock be."

"I guess I can see why you've gone mad. It is raucous! We can't stay here or I'll go mad too! Mo, hit another button. Let's get out of here. It may be contagious."

With urgency, Jason said, "No buttons! We can't remain in the elevator. We'll be caught for sure. Whether it's the warthogs on your island or someone we have yet to meet at another destination, someone's bound to get the elevator working soon, and someone in this school is bound to call for the elevator as soon as class is dismissed. Let's be honest with ourselves: if we run away to another location, how do we know we'll land among friends?" Jason paused to think for a moment. "I've got it! This must be a puzzle. Think about it. Wouldn't you rather go mad in a familiar environment? At least I know this school's layout inside and out. At least I can mitigate the risk of hurting myself or others. If things really get hairy, my home isn't too far away, 13 Calhoun Street, to be exact. This all makes zero sense in the current order of craziness but stick with me. I won't be home later because I took the trip to your island, so the house should be deserted. My father wasn't supposed to get home until late.

"So I vote that we get off this elevator and sneak into the nearest empty classroom where we can sort out this mess.

This is the Friday before break, first period. Just around the corner is an unoccupied classroom. We should have some privacy there and we can come up with a plan. But first we'll need to get past my teacher, Bill. Let's just say that he's the equivalent of a perfidious warthog who will pounce on us at the first opportunity. It would make him giddy to scold me or prove my madness, and should he catch a glimpse of me, he'll definitely be inquisitive. We can't give him the opportunity. We'll take a right out of the elevator, then an abrupt left down the hallway, and then into the first classroom on the left. I need both of you to remain silent until we're safely in the classroom and the coast is clear. Got it?"

Jason pulled Mo's curious face back into the elevator. "Hey An, the old you who is now the new you is in the classroom. You really are sitting next to Jason. Did you say 2017?" A look of surprised acknowledgment enveloped his face. "That means we truly traveled in time?"

"Mo, did you see their hairstyles? Things are truly horrid in 2017, but there is such a bounty of styles. Look at that room: mullets, perms, pompadours, fades, undercuts! The mind reels!"

The cicerone interrupted their discussion. "But you did not drink the Real World! Even if they see you, what does it matter? What do you think will happen if . . ."

Mr. Sims's whistling was heard down one of the distant hallways, prompting a change of direction.

Jason seized the moment, took the key from the elevator's keyhole, and strung it around his neck. The three silently exited the elevator and sneaked past the open doorway of the classroom, while Bill continued his boring diatribe about Mendelian inheritance over the rancor of the discordant clock.

"So this is what it's like to not really know yourself." Mo tried to make light of the situation.

"Shh!" Jason was quick to put a finger over his lips.

"But I've always wanted to ask what it feels like to be me. I've gotta say, 2017 looks weird."

The sleepy class remained distracted by the voluble Bill, who was scribbling on the chalkboard and failed to catch a glimpse of the three as they whisked past his doorway. They turned left and tiptoed down the hallway, which was easy for Jason, who had lost his shoes. Somewhere in the labyrinth of hallways, they could hear Mr. Sims whistling a Spanish melody, his keys jangling on his belt loop.

"Psst, you guys. Open that wooden door to your left." The three passed a "DIX FOR FRESHMAN PRESIDENT" sign on the wall outside the men's room.

An grew skeptical. "You didn't tell us that you were their leader. Mo, he's the leader of the whole gang of pirates. Keep your guard up."

"What's that about, Jason? We deserve the truth!" Mo pointed to the sign.

"I'm not a leader. I'm running for class president. It has nothing to do with anything but school. Down there is our library that's being worked on. This English teacher, Mrs. Nico, is not in today, so no one should be in this classroom. We can talk when we're inside, but keep quiet."

An quietly attempted to open the classroom door, but his hand passed through the handle as if he were a ghostly apparition. "Guys, what's going on? Watch this!"

Jason tried the knob and the door opened. The three fugitives tiptoed into the empty classroom.

Although the lights were off, the room was well lit thanks to a wide expanse of closed and slightly tinted windows. Mo drifted to the front of the room. *Clap, clap, clap, clap.* Bobby's chalk plume wafted through the outside air, past a murder of cawing crows sitting in a copse of maple trees that partially obscured the bright morning sun.

Mo had taken a position under the teacher's desk at the front of the classroom. "I take it the boy clapping erasers outside is me? He looks like me, that's for sure. Wait a minute. Why am I under this desk?" He had taken the position out of a habit of self-preservation when he heard the birds. Mo recognized his foolishness and crawled out from his hiding place. "That bird outside is louder than all three of us combined. I guess habits are hard to break."

An's face was plastered to the window, watching Bobby clap erasers. They could see Mr. Bill's class across the courtyard, where Jason was still complaining about the clock. For a third time, Jason tugged on An's shirt, pulling him toward the front of the room and the teacher's desk, where he set down the satchel.

An was undeterred. "Mo, get a look at that guy outside. He looks just like you and he's off his rocker. Look at him, he's chewing on his shirt just like you used to do! What is 'Baby Cakes'?" An thumbed to the Bobby outside, who was white as a ghost and wearing a baseball cap embroidered with a child with a mean grin and a bat. The boy chewed on the collar of his T-shirt while smacking erasers together and trying to create the most ginormous chalk dust cloud ever.

"And Mo, you say I look like that guy next to him in that classroom over there?" An seemed pleasantly surprised at seeing his reflection in the long mirror on the back wall of the classroom. "He even has on a gondoliering outfit! What are you trying to pull, Mr. Dix? Is that the new me in the mirror? You said 2017, right?"

"Get away from the window. Try not to draw attention to yourself. We need to remain hidden, and if Bobby sees you, he'll blow our cover. That's all we need. If I had my cell phone, I could just call myself and this would be over."

"Hidden from who?" In his stereotypical manner, An began gesticulating like a true Italian. "And why? Do you not want to introduce us to your friends? Oh, wait, you said this is all fake and we're just a part of your imagination. And now that we're in a place you arbitrarily consider to be safe, we can talk, right? By your description, those two are us, but you think we two are also figments of your imagination, and so, I would reason, do we not have a right to meet ourselves and discuss our predicament? What's the harm if none of this is real? Maybe you are crazy; at least make up your mind. Perhaps our imaginations are more ingenious than your imagination—maybe you're in one of *our* dreams. Hmm? How's that for imagination? We may have a better solution than you, and don't forget, this isn't singularly your predicament, capisce? Perhaps the others in your school can be of greater help. Let's call it a meeting of the minds."

"Not likely."

"Well, what if we disagreed with you, Mr. Smarty-Pants? Is a gondolier-slash-hairdresser-extraordinaire not good enough for you educated fellas in your center for higher education? Pressure getting to be too much for you? We can help you get out of a clutch situation—climb up and get the clock moving—but we're not good enough to meet the real Jason Dix and your real life. Is that it? What's to stop Mo and me from leaving?

"The other you, or maybe just your twin, is sitting in that classroom next to a boy who looks strikingly like me, but I cannot meet him because somehow you've convinced yourself that I am a part of you. How do I know this isn't all some elaborate ruse? You say you're in a crazy state or a delirium or dream—make up your mind. What about me and Mo? Perhaps we're the ones dreaming. Look right there." An pointed through the windows toward Bill's classroom across the way. "Clearly, when you were in our wild world, a world in which you had at least something to do with my ruined gondola, missing satchel, and destroyed gondoliering book, you were brazen, running amuck, and causing confusion and pan-demonium. But now that we are in *your* charade of a habitat, we are told—not asked—to sneak around for rea-sons I'm not entirely comfortable with. That's not co-pacetic with me and my friend Mo. Right, Mo? Should the situation be reversed, you would expect us to intro-duce you to our colleagues and provide some means of sustenance. By the way, Mo and I are starving. Right,

Mo? Instead, we find ourselves sneaking around your school as if we are second-class, ignominious citizens, not wanting to upset my doppelgänger while you leisurely take inventory of your satchel. Don't forget that mine was ruined and that I'll be footing the bill for a new gondoliering book. Maybe all of this is simpler than I imagine. Maybe I'm acting like a fool. Maybe I've struck my head on the way to my gondoliering exam and this is all my delirium. Or does you think we is uneducated? Mo is one of the more highly educated beings on the island, and I could match his wits with any of your classmates, yet you treat us like warthogs or Westbankers by commanding us into a darkened classroom and then telling us not to interact with others. I happen to be from the Garden District, thank you very much. Perhaps it is you who needs a history lesson!"

Jason ignored An's rant as he sorted through the items in the satchel, lining up the vials on Mrs. Nico's desk before unfolding his father's letter.

"Well, Mr. Know-It-All?"

Jason was feeling tested by An's insolence. "So what is the history? I was a newcomer, and it's not like your island was the friendliest of places. I was tricked into flying to the island, escaped an attempt to be shoved in an ice cream container, chased, flushed down the drain, accosted by your long tongue, and then attacked by warthogs. Other than *that*, I had a grand and inviting time. So if this is your dream, it stinks! What is it that you want me to do? Please tell me because I'm not sure what to believe any more. I'm not even sure if any of this is real I just want to sort out what was given to me by my father, who never once mentioned Tripe, by the way. The only time we ever, and I mean *ever*, discussed the island was when we were looking for a place to visit on fall break. We didn't choose your execrable island; we were supposed to go to Texas, but lo and behold, he canceled. Then I met some uninvited woman, who tricked me into getting on a Tripe Airlines flight, and presto! Here we are. So now, in order to reclaim some semblance of sanity, I'm sorting through these items partly because I'm curious, but mostly because I need to make sure I'm not going plum nuts, tachometer-to-the-top-floor insane. I never asked for any of this, so don't blame me for your cantankerous attitude. You chased me, remember? Your island was not friendly!"

"An, I think Jason has a point," Mo said gently.

An's demeanor became solemn as he realized that he had overstepped.

Distraitly, An gathered his thoughts before speaking. It was clear that there was much emotion in what he was about to reveal. "No, Mo. He needs a history lesson."

Gazing upward to the firmament, his brows furrowed as he pensively recalled past events that still caused him great pain. When he finally spoke, his voice was choked and a tear welled up in his eye. "I wouldn't expect you to understand, Jason. The year was 1960 when The Change happened. I cannot speak for others on the island, but Mo can confirm what took place. I'll give you my account. I had recently left home, looking to strike out on my own. We didn't have much. It is usually a glorious and proud moment when a young man leaves their proverbial nest. I come from a large family. My dad was a blue-collar man, a janitor, my mom was a librarian, and I had eight siblings. We were once from the Westbank, but we beat the odds and escaped from that lifestyle. Since there were so many people in our home, my departure was almost welcomed.

"In time, I met a lovely woman named Lacey, and we were married shortly thereafter. A few years earlier, I chose my métier due to a chance meeting with the one and only Vidal Sassoon. He visited the island and blessed me with a pair of stainless-steel shears, saying that I 'have what it takes.' Those were the shears you tried to steal. And so, wanting to strike out on our own, Lacey and I decided to take a chance as entrepreneurs and open our own hair salon."

"Shears I *mistakenly* took and planned to return."

"That is why I chased you. Anyway, we were young and carefree, happy and without worries. Around that time, there were work camps for refugees or those from other

404

places. We called them The Other People, or TOPs, but they were actually indentured servants. They were put to work making textiles, Aloha shirts, to be specific. In hindsight, it was wrong for so many of us to turn a blind eye, but we were comfortably reaping the benefits of our export economy and low taxation, at least those were the buzzwords we heard from our parents. Our leader at the time was the benefactor of nearly everything on the island, and so with plenty of profits to be had, taxes were low, schools were good, and the island had a bountiful, bustling economy. None of the abused were locals, so I guess we never thought much of it. TOPs were always people who were shipwrecked or lost."

Mo chimed in. "I had a few of those shirts myself. I was always chewing on the collar; that's one of the reasons why An thinks I turned into a moth." Mo finished the last of the Nutty Knowledge bar he was eating. "Those nuts were delicious!"

"That wasn't for you. That was from my dad! I don't know what it will do to you or how long it has been sitting in this sack. It might make you sick. What was the name of that bar?"

"Nutty Knowledge and it was delicious. I feel amazing!"

An continued, "Anyway, lo and behold, along came two young men in a sailboat who changed our lives forever. They say it was fate, but I'm not so sure. Some said they

405

were lured by sirens in the ocean or by the mythical, Ethereal Pixies of the mountain, but one thing was certain: they didn't arrive by chance alone. And then, one day, they were gone. I remember the guards being angry. No one was ever sure what happened to the shorter of the two, the philanderer. The tall, lanky one was a definite chaologist; he studied and created pure chaos. Legend has it that he somehow found the means to turn our world upside down, causing most of the islanders to devolve into animals. To this day, no one knows how he accomplished the task.

"Not everyone was affected. For instance, the cook in Ralph's Diner remained unchanged, presumably because he was already on the lowest rung of the devolutionary chain, but who knows. Flo, the waitress in the diner, was similarly unaffected. Maybe the diner was immune? There were others too, but I know you've met Ralph and Flo.

"Anyhow, no one knows for sure how it happened, only that the guy who perpetuated this dastardly act was named Beau Champs." Jason swallowed hard, remembering the name mentioned by the woman on television. An continued. "His name will go down in infamy. On the fateful day of his departure, the skies turned ashen in the blink of an eye. There was a rumbling in the bowels of Mother Earth's tectonics, and in a flash, the island's brethren changed into animals. Some were larger, some were smaller. Some were fat, others really fat, and some were skinny. Our leader vanished, never to be heard from again.

"With no one left to make textiles, the industry floundered, the island's economy went belly-up, taxes were raised, and life as we knew it was lost. It took years for our economy to improve, and that was only with significant outside help. Lacey and I had to close up shop and work from our new home, built for our new diminutive size; I guess it was sheer luck that we both ended up the same size and didn't need much. Thank goodness that my best friend was small too. The islanders struggled with profound grief at the loss of the lives they once knew. Even the accoutrements associated with a life of prosperity were nullified. For instance, the most frequented places on the island had been the public library, which collapsed, and the Westbank beer tavern, which became overrun by boorish warthogs. Do you know how well beer sells in a depressed economy? Better than a hair stylist, I can tell you that!

"No one knows the real reason why Beau Champs thrust this sharp vicissitude of misfortune upon us. Some folks theorized that he hated to make shirts and The Change was his revenge. Others supposed that he thought we deserved to be animals given our blind condonation of the textile trade. Some say they saw him deposit a note into an island mailbox that might have explained his motives, but no one ever found such a note. That is how our island was cursed to become a congeries of anthropomorphic animals. Tripe allowed the mistreatment of a few poor souls, one of whom had devilish intentions, and for that, we paid a heavy price. Mo and I have never been the same since, that is, until today. This is the first time I've seen my true self in years." An couldn't take his eyes off his own reflection, gazing upon a form he had believed to be lost forever.

"When you say, 'turn into,' what exactly do you mean? Like, humans instantly transformed into other creatures?"

Mo was obviously not listening. "Hey, An, I feel like I know a lot right now! My brain is speeding like a run-away roller coaster."

Ignoring Mo, An said, "Yes. Some shrank, some grew hair, grew scales, grew wings, grew tails, grew larger. We all generally look like we belong on a low rung of the evolutionary ladder, and that day, we became the animals each of us represent. It's not to say that all were equally affected. Some changed to such a degree that they were no longer recognizable. For instance, one of the island's attorneys and his son both turned into out-of-the-water, inchoate blobfish and quickly succumbed to desiccation. Now they're both merely a stain on Main Street."

"I think I saw it. What happened to the textile workers?"

"No one knows. They vanished into thin air. Many government employees turned to slugs. After The Change, at the suggestion of my mother, many changed our names to remind us of what we were and who we had become."

Jason was taken aback by his heartfelt explanation. "I had nothing to do with The Change, but I'll try to help you restore your island and its people. That is a promise. I swear on my life that I will help in any way I can. What were your names before you changed them?"

"My name was Trevor, and Mo's was Mo."

Mo was pacing and intermittently examining the items placed on the desk. "I feel weird, guys. Like I know everything in the whole world! Hey, these have interesting names. This one sounds like a fancy holiday: Last Resort. Lipstick? Oh look, Shrinking Suds, that's what must have been used on you. And look at this one, Vanishing Voavanga juice. An, look, Growing Gum. Did you ever want to become a giant?"

"No more, Mo. Quiet, please." Jason opened the letter from his father and began to write the alphabet on the board.

"What are you doing, Jason?" An's curiosity was piqued.

"Guys, we came here to take inventory and come up with a plan of action. Someone make a list of the items from the bag while I work on my father's letter. I expect that his cipher will take quite a bit of time to decode. My father and I have always played games with riddles, ana-grams, ciphers, logogriphs, and the intentional use of misleading mondegreens to confuse one another. It's a game we've always played, and I thought silly and unim-portant until I read this. It's as if I've been in training my whole life." Jason showed the two the parchment. "Take a look at his letter. If anyone has any bright ideas, I'm all ears. I don't mean to be rude, but unless you secretly have a background in cryptanalysis, I doubt you can help. I'll need some quiet while I try to figure this out. I know the note must be from my dad because only he would use this Mayan glyph as a signature. He would always draw it on the chalkboard in the kitchen. Here, look at this, guys."

UxmldpFrogFdcfnpvnancvgtcokbvoxddpkt-flrqnoctuoopclovtctgorviqwdscozlouogbqmdspnu-zlipoegovpcbopkatspknGaeuozeaxllsgxwclbllop-imqnzcesolzdozvyaeeofpimqnzcawprzdsclzpsraxg-lyvuenadsmozglq

"I know it's a cipher, but who knows what kind? I guess I could just start by trying all the ones he liked to use most, but that could take days! Perhaps we should head to my house. It's not too far from here. I have a book on ciphers

and we can use my computer to find a website that will help us decode the message."

"Website?" An and Mo asked in unison.

Mo was intently studying the glyph. An tried to pronounce the lettering of the cryptic message as if it were a long word, when he suddenly broke out in a large grin.

"Today just happens to be your lucky day! I doubt you'll need any of that stuff you just said, since we have the ace, number one cryptologist in all the land in our midst. In addition to serving as our island's locksmith, Mo happens to be the island's cruciverbalist, rebus master, and cryptology ace. He's won awards. Really! If you don't believe me, just ask him. He's a regular savant when it comes to this sort of stuff."

Mo was sounding out the glyph imagery. "A-la Ti-xi. Wow! That bar really really gave me energy! I think I know everything ever!"

"How do you know how to pronounce the glyph? My dad is named Alfred, so we always called it Al Dix."

"I really really know a lot right now. Anyway, the cipher is interesting but quite simple. You're going about it all wrong. It's not one word, An."

Jason was skeptical. "C'mon, you're my age. There's no way you're a cryptology expert."

"Well, I'm a little rusty but you can test me. Now that the library is closed, being a locksmith pays the bills. I just traded inanimate ciphers for more tangible keys. Anyway, when I worked in the library, I had oodles of time to practice; there were loads of these in a room off the library basement, some sort of humongous rare-book collection. Floors and floors of books. You could walk for days and never reach the end. As the assistant librarian, I had loads of extra time to practice, practice, practice. So let's see here. You say we are in 2017, so the cipher could be Slidefair, Playfair, Quagmire, Vigenère, Beaufort, Porta, Autokey, Running key, Two-square, Swagman, or so many others. That doesn't include any ciphers that have been created since 1972. Wow! That food surely perked me up. My brain feels like it's on fire!"

Jason and An looked at each other incredulously, but didn't dare interrupt Mo. He was clearly onto something.

The rate of Mo's speech increased dramatically. "Let me explain a few issues we'll encounter, and how we might narrow our search. I hope you don't mind me piping in. I don't want to steal your thunder, so if you want me to be quiet, just say so. I remember this one time when . . ."

Jason was taken aback. "No, I appreciate your help! If you have any ideas, I'd love to hear them!"

"What is particularly worrisome is that your message is not grouped, which means the possibilities are vast. We'll need to check off each cipher type one by one, unless he left a clue about what type of cipher he used. Outright guessing would take far too much time. Days? Weeks? Who knows? Contrary to popular belief, Leonardo da Vinci didn't use a cipher. He wrote backward in Italian to hide his work from others."

Jason interjected. "Well, this is not the simple Caesar cipher. I already crossed that one off the list."

"Bingo! Well then, you've answered our first question about whether this is a transposition cipher. I assume that your father speaks English. Let's just pray he's not a polyglot. I know he can write Mayan, so he must be quite a learned man."

"A poly-what?"

"Wow. Those nuts are powerful! Zoooooom! Here we go."

An said, "Mo, get a handle on yourself!"

"It's no matter. The frequency distribution of letters in the text does not appear to be normal. All ciphers other than transpositions change distribution pattern, so it's not transposition. Our next step should be to determine whether it's a substitution cipher. We'll need to calculate the index of coincidence, or the IC for short as us cryptologists would say. First, we need to write down the number of times each letter is used in the text and the total number of letters in the cipher. Then, we'll plug those numbers into this rather simple mathematical formula." Mo scribbled the formula on the board. "By figuring out the IC, we should be able to narrow our search."

Jason's jaw was on the floor. He couldn't believe his good fortune. "So let me get this straight. You're an assistant librarian who just happens to know this much about ciphers?"

"I told you he was good." An smiled widely.

Mo continued his ramble like a professor who is well versed in the subject matter. "I'm not quite sure what sort of education you've had, but our schools were pretty advanced, and our library was even vaster-er-er-er-er. Ciphers are so interesting. Each type has a load of historical significance. Julius Caesar used a shift in the alphabet to send confidential messages. You know this! But you've already determined that wasn't the cipher used. Can you believe that something so simple was missed for so long? You figured it out in, what—a few seconds? Then there's the Vigenère cipher, known for years as the le chiffrage indéchiffrable. It was actually thought to be created by an Italian named Giovan Bellaso, a point that An just loves. The cipher was used for ages and it was thought to be unbreakable. Even hundreds of years ago, people were working out how to decipher ciphers. As time passed, cryptologists discovered the index of coincidence and tried to use it. For instance, with periodic calculation of the IC, one would suggest the Vigenère could be used if there were large peaks at the length of the keyword. There are a few others in this category that would find peaks, and so if peaks were present, presto! You may know which cipher was used.

"The length also becomes important in determining a graph size for crypt and decryption. There are numerous other tricks to help us solve the cipher. Some ciphers are significantly harder than others, which were designed to be interpretable on the fly. It's important to consider how or why the cipher was being used. One of the easier ciphers, the Playfair, is one of those. It was designed by an English bloke named Charles Wheatstone, who, by the way, contributed to the creation of the telegraph. He didn't get the credit though, just like Bellaso. Lord Playfair made Wheatstone's creation famous, and the cipher was used for years. It wasn't all that long ago that it was used by a man named John F. Kennedy. He was elected to your presidential office in 1960, about a month after The Change. Anyway, as history tells it, he used Playfair at the Solomon Islands during World War Two after his boat was sunk by the Japanese. His use of the cipher saved his life and the lives of his crew. Can you believe he wrote the cipher on coconuts?"

"Wait, did you just mention Wheatstone? C. Wheatstone? What does he have to do with anything? My father has a large bust of him in our foyer."

"Anyone who knows anything about the Playfair cipher has heard of Charles Wheatstone. Like I just said, he's the one who invented it. Charles Wheatstone was a genius born in 1812. Mr. Wheatstone made many significant contributions to the world, including his work on the telegraph. He was a very interesting man; you should read about him. If this were his cipher, we ought to build a grid based on the keyword, then complete the remainder of the alphabet, minus one letter, in a five-by-five square, twenty-five squares in all. By using pairs of letters, we could use the square to decipher the cipher. It isn't that hard to decrypt, but it can be a bit time consuming."

Jason said, "Well, his bust is the largest in our foyer, so I guess if we're looking for a place to start, his cipher is as good as any. And here on the bottom are my initials. Father always used this symbol if he wanted me to reverse the letters." Jason pointed to the circular arrow around the JD. "I'm not sure what to make of the scratch mark."

"Oh goody! He's even left clues!" Mo began to draw a five-by-five square on the board. "With the Playfair cipher, we'll need a keyword. Your guess is as good as mine, but all we have to work with is the cipher and your initials, two letters that would be transposed in Playfair. Equally as important, since the square is only five-by-five, one of the letters in the English alphabet needs to be removed. That lends more credence to Playfair since your father scratched through the letter J. Hopefully, he chose English as the cipher's language."

"OK, let's give it a shot." The pair then tried to identify the keyword, testing Wheatstone, Charles Wheatstone, Tripe, Island of Tripe, and Pixies with no luck. They were unable to make sense of the cipher using the alphabet both forward and backward. The task was beginning to prove wellnigh impossible.

"Maybe we're overthinking this. Try my name. Maybe father wanted me to be able to interpret on the fly."

Mo tried Jason Dix as the keyword, using the forward alphabet and substituting J for D.

"Does the word ufgvhcpvxkah make any sense to you? I don't see any point of completing the cipher if the first letters have no meaning." Jason could tell that Mo was onto something.

"No, and we've never spoken any languages other than English. But I think we should keep going."

"Umm, guys?" An was listening at the door near the back of the room. "Guys, the whistling is growing nearer." An poked his head out of the door and spotted Mr. Sims near the hallway intersection, ready to head their way.

"We only have a minute or two left before we have to hide."

"One last try," Mo said as he reversed the letters of the alphabet. "Does the word spmahcuaebsegakradog mean anything?" Mo stopped mid-sentence as a look of surprise crossed his face. "Wait, I know! It's backward . . ." Mo looked like he'd had an epiphany.

An was visibly nervous. "It's time to hide, guys. He's almost here!"

"What?" Jason roused from his extreme focus on the cipher.

"Oh! It's sort of like an ananym. Reverse these letters and you get Beau Champs! We don't have time for the rest, but so far, the first twenty letters read, 'Go Dark Ages Beau Champs.'"

"Zach Trevor Russoni, is that you?"

"Wait a minute. It makes sense! In the apothecary room hidden behind the diner, there was a large painting of my father fighting in the time of knights." Jason thrust the vials, lipstick, and letter back into his sack as Mo erased the board with his palm. The three scrambled to the front of the class. "Mo, you're a genius!"

As the rear door opened, Mr. Sims's voice boomed, "Zach, what are you doing out of your first-period class? Do you want me to cancel our trip tomorrow?"

As Mr. Sims opened the rear door, the three quietly scrambled out the front door and across the hallway. They ducked into the first available door: the men's room.

"Jason, if he comes in here after us, how will we get out?"

"What the?" Jason was staring at one of the mirrors. Written in bright red lipstick was a message: Stay home. It's a trap. "That's frightening. When we were in the elevator, I guessed that I had written that message to myself, but it's already here. Quickly, guys; let's hide in the last stall where we'll be safe. I'm about to walk in, and I'll be followed in by Mr. Sims." They rushed into the last stall, locked the door, and hunkered on top of the toilet seat, keeping their feet unexposed.

"Now remember, the old me knows nothing about the new me. Let's be quiet and just listen."

They heard approaching footsteps, Jason micturating, the steps of another, and then whistling and singing.

"Porque si dicen que el amor es lo mejor que existe, a mí siempre me ha hecho sufrir, mi alma se resiste. Y ser herido otra vez no creo que lo aguante a veces pienso que es mejor no tener corazón."

Mo whispered, "He has quite a good voice!"

"Shh!" An and Jason chastised Mo.

The sound of running water started then stopped, followed by the electronic motor of the paper towel dispenser and a tapping of feet.

"Mr. Dix? Mr. Dix, is that you?" Mr. Sims's voice resonated in the tiled room.

"Well I'll be, it's Principal Sims."

Mo whispered, "Jason, is that you?"

Jason silently put a finger to his lips, again insisting on silence.

A stall door down the way squeaked as it opened and a toilet flushed. "Umm, sir? This is a bit weird, wouldn't you say? Your singing, I mean; it's rather unique today. And umm, you look like a lizard. How did you know I was in here, sir?"

There was a pause as the footsteps walked to the sink. Water began running.

"Sorry I'm not in class, Mr. Sims. Nature was calling. I'm . . . is there something I can help you with, sir? You realize that we're in the men's room, right? Zach tells me that you're practicing for another play. That must be exciting."

"Weird would be the errant misdeeds that perpetrated this crime, Mr. Dix. Was it you, Mr. Dix? You are an impetuous young man by your very nature. I think this insolent act may have ill effects on your campaign for office, not to mention the odds of you spending any time with my son."

"I'm not quite sure what I've done to rub you the wrong way, sir, but whatever it was, I sincerely apologize. I can honestly say that the graffiti was here when I entered, scout's honor. I had nothing to do with its presence on the mirror. You're welcome to turn my pockets inside and out; you'll see that there is no lipstick to be found on my person."

"Let's see your pockets then. I'll call your bluff. Turn them out. Perhaps the item is hidden; after all, I expect that you're smart enough to toss it out the window or to bury it deep in the refuse bin. Did you forget that this is costume day, Mr. Dix? Trevor may not have the best costume, but at least he participates. Why are you out of class, anyway? You should be in Bill's science lecture, I believe. Truancy from an important lesson and with no costume? Shorts and a T-shirt—what are you, dressing up as a teenager? You have such a wonderful imagination! Or are you too good for costume day? Are you lacking in school spirit? Not a great quality for a boy who is running for president. You know, your instructors did an awful lot of planning for costume day."

"My father and I truly forgot about the costume, Mr. Sims. I meant no offense. Didn't you hear that there is a storm approaching? We have quite a lot of things on our plate."

"I would think you are old enough to be responsible."

"But wasn't the costume listed as optional? And yes, I'm in science with Mr. Bill. My classmates and I were all nearly asleep; Bill is so boring. Believe me, I'm not missing anything. Ask Zach; he'll concur. In any case, I asked to go to the restroom, and Mr. Bill allowed me to leave if I promised to make it quick. This is a restroom, and I urinated. That's it. No graffiti for me! The message on the mirror was here when I arrived, sir."

"Back pockets, please. Did anyone skip class with you? Don't be a hero, Dix."

"No, sir. It was only me."

"Did your accomplice do this? Perhaps an inquest is in order. Might I interest you in detention?"

"No."

"Aha! So you *did* perpetrate this crime. Who else is out and about?"

Jason and Mr. Sims rambled on a bit longer before Mr. Sims said, "Back to class." Their voices trailed off as they exited the men's room.

Jason, An, and Mo were still crowded in the stall, standing on the toilet seat. Jason was the first to speak. "OK guys, the coast is clear."

An said, "How do you know, Jason? That guy sounds just like my father!"

"Remember, I was here yesterday. Mr. Sims and I went straight back to class from here. The bell is going to ring in a minute. It'll be bedlam with the bathroom filling up, the hallways crowded, and the classroom will likely be used. It's time to get to the Dark Ages."

"And to get Beau Champs. We'll make him answer for his crimes!"

As the three quietly exited the restroom and tiptoed down the hall, they heard Mr. Sims say, "Have you seen Ms. Somerall?" When the coast was clear, the three quietly snuck past Bill's class and into the elevator. Jason put the key into the lock and gave it a twist.

The nasal, pacifying voice of the elevator cicerone chimed, "Welcome back, gentlemen. I hope your stay was fruitful and pleasant. I would like to remind you that the three bottles of Real World have not yet been consumed. Please input your next destination."

All three blurted out different requests at the same time: "Dark Ages!" "Mi casa!" "I want to see dinosaurs!"

"Dinosaurs? Where did that come from, Mo?"

"Well, why do you get to choose?"

The elevator voice interrupted. "Gentlemen, gentlemen, please. You must all agree as I am only able to process one request at a time. Furthermore, you do not have enough credits to access any eras that fall outside of the Anthropocene epoch. Unfortunately, dinosaurs are out of the question. Please remember that each rider must have their own key when a request is made. Now please, one at a time."

An shook his head in wonder. "Mo, that request came out of left field. Why would you say that?"

"Again, gentlemen, if you please."

Concomitantly, Jason and An blurted out, "Dark Ages" and "The Island of Tripe, 1972."

"Oh brother. You three just do not get it." The elevator's cicerone sounded annoyed, but the doors shut and the elevator took off at lightning speed.

***

It was only moments later when the elevator doors re-opened to 1972. An and Mo stood alone facing the same maniple of warthogs, who roughly pulled them from the elevator, shuffled them quickly across the base of the temple, and shoved them through the door labeled "Athenaeum" and into a large library. Mo was oddly silent and in a thoughtful reverie, but eventually, he spoke.

"An, I've figured it out. Jason's in the Dark Ages and he needs help. The message is not what we think. I think I goofed, but I've finally figured it out. It reads:

> the island of tripe is unlike anything you have seen
> it is not safe you have the key if all is lost go to
> calhoun via elevator smash wheatstone and wait
> never take last resort merl has watch never go dark
> ages beau champs

"We need to help him! If my reasoning is correct, he seems to be headed straight to the man who did this to us."

An was distraught. "But Mo, how am I going to pay for the ruined gondola?"

# CHAPTER 21

## DR. ATWOOD AND THE SEED

*Saturday, October 28, 1972*

Dr. Atwood sat at her office desk, staring at her book in a deep, disconsolate intellection. She was wholly lost in thought, unaware of the small gecko staring at her from atop the bookshelf. The little creature was anxiously anticipating the multiple visitors who were expected to arrive shortly.

Dr. Atwood adjusted her rear, having sat in the same position for about an hour. The pattering rain outside soothed her frazzled nerves. Her intense focus was on a mere fascicule of information, a single page mid-book; it was a silly, perhaps trivial, page that appeared a few days ago, but it had caused her a bit of consternation, as if it were a presage to some newfound hydra or metaphor. Her aim was to jar loose more information or understanding about how the alteration could have appeared. She was vexed. How had it been placed? To her knowledge, no one knew her secret. The page was tightly woven into the book block, like all the other pages. And more importantly, what did its appearance mean?

Drawn on the page was a woman who looked remarkably like herself, with a key hanging from a chain around her neck and a pocket watch attached to a sash at her waist. The woman was fighting to reach an adolescent male who resembled Jason Dix. She was struggling through gale-force winds on the Westbank, using one arm to protect her face from rain and flying debris and the other hand to hold the train of her flowing gown. She leaned into the wind to reach Jason, who was sublimely suffused in light as he stood atop a knoll, the dark periphery less apparent in a sort of chiaroscuro style. The illustration was drawn with a crosshatched technique, clearly different in style from the rest of the book, as if the artist were making a point to alert the reader that this interlude was different from the rest.

The youth stood in the midst of a swirling vortex, holding a blue key high above his head, the only colored item on the page, looking steadfast and assured as if he were prepared to fight the heavens or as if this were some instrumental find. The firmament above was depicted as seven larger stars amongst many, drawn in the constellation of Orion, a constellation which appeared earlier in the book in a similar arrangement.

It wasn't just that the woman was trying to reach the intrepid youth; there was something more. The explanation that the image depicted her current pursuit of Jason would be far too simple. She wore an eerie, almost foreboding facial expression, one that exhorted an atavistic fear as her eyes suggested that she herself was being pursued. Was she running away from something, or was something chasing her? She wondered, *Does anyone know the truth about me? Has anyone discovered my true intentions? Was there an interloper between me and Saul, or are more people somehow aware of the circumstances?*

Penetrating the chrysalis that hung from a bending tree's branch came the outstretched hand of a minuscule, beleaguered man who resembled Beau Champs. He wore a feathered headdress and appeared to be clawing for help. *The man is too small to affect Jason, so Jason must be helping him. What message am I missing?* In the lowermost corner, a small, anthropoid lizard stood upright, taking notes on a small scroll that featured two crossed keys, similar to the key that she possessed. There was also the watermark of the previous lock with two keyholes. The entire illustration was bordered by Mayan characters drawn in a block-like design.

*Perhaps to understand the page would be to understand the book as a whol*e, she thought. The interposed pages obnubilated what she formerly understood. Or did they? She thumbed through the pages again. *What am I missing?*

The book was a hefty, weathered, red leather-bound tome without an index, publisher, or any other mark denoting the author or creator other than glyphic Mayan inscriptions on its cover that she knew phonetically to be *iut* and *utiy*. Translated into English, the glyphs read, "As then it happened" and, "Since it happened." It was sewn bound with parchment pages, and the majority of its contents were illustrations of events. She deduced that glyphs were used to add specific dates or hidden meanings. Much of her understanding of the book was due to Dr. Montegue, the book's former owner, who added a number of off-the-mark notations in the margins, mostly referencing the Mesoamerican culture. His understanding was now antiquated, nowhere near close to her own knowledge on the subject.

The early pages of the text referenced a lock with two keyholes on a gate that secured a paradisiacal land between two large bookshelves. *A rebus? Is it meant to be literal?* Patricia had once thought that the illustrations referenced a Mayan glyphic language and that the entirety of the page was a logograph, but after perusing countless volumes of glyphs failed to reveal any similar illustrations of logogrammatic or syllabic signs, she resigned herself to the idea that no deeper meaning existed, that it was simply an illustration meant to depict a beautiful land beyond locked gates. A large number of blank pages followed the new illustration. After the blank pages were a great many crudely drawn symbols of an explosion, then light, followed by a page depicting the dark sky with Orion's Belt hovering over a verdurous, uninhabited landscape. While the illustrations were unsophisticated early on, they became more complex with each passing page.

Out of thin air, an advanced, Pleistocene, tellurian society appeared, as illustrations depicted a familiarity of flight, sea travel, construction, agronomy, astronomy, medicine, and even planetary exchange, all illustrations far exceeding current technologies. The depictions were so outrageous that they were likely fictional or taking liberal artistic license. But then a single flower, Dryas octopetala, intertwined with a cataclysmic bolide impact, the imagery replete with chaotic depictions of crimson fire and a large flood, followed by pages completely black with ink and others that depicted ice covering the earth. The illustrations and glyphs of suffering made it clear that very few of the complex, antediluvian people survived the ensuing freeze. Depictions of death were plentiful. Turning the pages, those who did survive took refuge in subterranean enclaves. *Perhaps the recently discovered Derinkuyu in the Cappadocia region in Turkey housed the survivors.*

Time continued to pass, but the duration was unclear. Ice lessened as the earth progressively thawed, as less developed hominids possessing rudimentary skills sprouted in communities near the equator and in the southern hemisphere. Descendants of the subterranean society emerged from their havens and set forth upon the seas from what is now Crete. The melioristic drawings suggested that the learned civilization became instructors for the more primitive peoples and set out to reestablish knowledge upon the earth.

In some regards, Patricia felt like she belonged to the erudite civilization, bestowing knowledge upon the inhabitants of Tripe. These persons were thereafter depicted as teachers as they stood before crowds, demonstrating disciplines such as construction, agronomy, and medicine. At the apotheosis of such instruction, they were revered as deities, often drawn adorned with bird and fish skins similar to those she had seen in Mesoamerican writings or as far as Egypt and Turkey. They were the teachers, or perhaps prophets, depicted in glyphs making sedulous efforts to meld and mold the rudimentary and isolated world back into a semblance of order, knowledge, and prosperity. Under their tutelage, the world witnessed the construction of megalithic temples and pyramids, agronomical techniques, written languages, and metallurgical methods.

At this sharp pinnacle of prosperity, a violent upheaval was unexpectedly drawn. The teachers vanished after a single illustration portrayed their departure atop seafaring crafts on the waves into a sea of foam. On this page, a faint watermark of the lock with two keyholes appeared again. The tome continued with its depiction of people and technologies, but the illustrations clearly suggested that without these knowledge-bringers, there was a significant decline in the rate of newly acquired skills and information. The world fell back into rudimentary and dark times.

The remainder of recorded history flashed across the pages, and conspicuously included was Beau Champs, along with his watch and key. He seemed to be ubiquitous: lifting stones to build megalithic temples; taking part in the sacking and destruction of the Library of Alexandria and the coincidental creation of the Great Library of Tripe; fighting as a knight in a suit of armor alongside a king and wizard, the imagery replete with blazing bolts of purple light shooting from his hands; firing cannons during the French revolution with a small child in a basket; fighting a hurricane and being shipwrecked; becoming a prisoner on a remote island that looked strikingly similar to Tripe, the year MCMLX written in minute text; and a cataclysmic change on the Island of Tripe. Oddly enough and for reasons she continued to ponder, game shows were featured on a surprisingly high number of pages. The watch and key appeared with Beau in every single illustration, always in his possession. Thereafter, he was absent from the pages that illustrated the years between The Change and the turn of the new millennium. Exactly 100 blank pages followed before reaching the epilogue, a single page depicting the paradisiacal landscape and ocean behind an open gate, the lock with two keys. She thought, *But how do I fit in to all of this? I must find the book's author.*

Fortunate to have witnessed The Change, she was aware that the book was more than some writer's fantasy; the illustrations could often be taken at face value. *But how can I find the gate? Is there more information to be ascertained from the text that I just don't understand yet? Could it be hidden? And is the key the sole way to open the gate? Surely there is more to uncover. Finding the library is the best direction for my inquiry. There must be information within that will direct me to the gate or at least the key. But again, why has this newest page appeared, and why am I included?*

She was caught off guard by its sudden appearance. She correctly surmised there to be a seminal relationship between current events and this cogent illustration, although she remained unaware of how it was placed in the codex, who its author could be, and its relevance to the entire puzzle. *How is this book a participant in this crazy world?* The book was with her at all times, and the new appearance was a confounding mystery.

And so, she sat staring, wondering, pondering, imagining, trying to draw some degree of felicity, and questioning the hidden meaning amongst the characters and their environment. The pages were now a cloudy farrago of hidden metaphors that teased her intellect, stirring a sub-sensible, prescient feeling that the new page was meant as a prophecy to a historical account of which she were a part with an inauspicious outcome. But for whom? Her? *Is a second key needed? Where is the lock and what is it hiding? Will the Ancient Collection illuminate some answers? Will Saul and his sycophants find it? How can I mitigate my risk against the unforeseen or unknown? Perhaps only time would tell, ironic as I have some control over time.*

*Put on your thinking cap, Patricia. Widen your imagination. Let's run through this again for the umpteenth time. Jason is fighting unseen or unknown elements on this island, which is understandable. He is, after all, on the run now. Perhaps the artist is merely trying to convey that Jason is alone in a metaphorical tempest, trying to fight his way out of the situation. He is out of his element on this island. It would make sense that I would chase him, but why would I look back, and why am I afraid? Who could be chasing me? And what is the dress meant to convey? Why is Beau so small and in the tree with a feathered headdress? Is he not available for the boy? Is he not integral to the entirety of this matter? He is the one who caused The Change. I believe that the lizard is representative of being on this island, but who is it? And what is he taking notes about? What am I meant to understand about the Mayan glyphs and the box? What am I missing here? What am I missing? The lock—where are you located? Could you be in the fallen library? In the southern part of the island perhaps?*

It would seem that she had a plethora of questions but no answers. She had been staring at the mysterious image for hours but was no closer to unlocking its secrets.

*Knock, knock, knock.*

"Dr. Atwood? Dr. Atwood? It's Lacey from the Grand Cenote. I need to speak with you urgently." The winds rattled the windowpanes and muted the knock. Patricia's blue truck lay parked outside, the motor off and the key in the ignition.

*Perhaps the lizard is a key . . . THE key to it all? Maybe I have not been giving him the relevance he deserves. Maybe the key is not literally a key after all. But what of the key in Melvin's possession? I'll need to find a way . . .*

*Knock, Knock, Knock.* "Dr. Atwood? Hello?"

Patricia heard a sound and looked up from her book. *Is someone knocking? Must be the wind.*

The small lizard tucked himself behind a book to watch the interaction unfold.

*Knock, knock, knock, knock, knock.* Lacey rapped harder on the door in desperation.

Through the window, Dr. Atwood could be seen awakening from her trance, closing her book, checking the time, and returning the timepiece to her pocket. She tucked the book into her knapsack and fastened it tight, and was beginning to tidy the room when she realized that someone was knocking at her office door.

Dr. Atwood opened the door and was pelted by escalating wind and rain. Looking around, she saw only her truck sitting idle. *That's odd. I guess I'm imagining things. Perhaps the knock was a contrivance of my imagination.*

She started to close the door when Lacey cleared her throat. "Ahem." Patricia cast her attention down to her feet, where an anthropoid lizard in a wet, yellow dress and a drenched gerbil in overalls stood patiently. Roden cowered behind his mother in the face of the larger Dr. Atwood.

"Was it you knocking? I am so sorry for not looking anywhere but straight toward my truck. Please excuse my inconsideration. Come in, come in, let's get you two out of the rain and more comfortable. It's positively awful outside. Hold on just a moment." She hurried away and quickly returned with a hand towel. She handed it to Lacey and said, "You look like you could use this. What brings you out into such a horrendous storm? Whatever it is must be important. Please make yourselves comfortable."

Lacey was a bit harried and wild-eyed. "Dr. Atwood, thank you for your generosity. I know how busy you must be. We're not here to waste your time with idle chitchat. I need your advice regarding something of importance."

"I appreciate your candor. Of course I will try to . . ."

"But before I begin, let me introduce my son, Roden. He's the reason we are seeking your help. I've told him all about you and your work as an archaeologist on the island. It took some convincing before he agreed to let me show it to someone other than his father."

Roden stood proudly beside his mother and said, "I want to be an archaeologist when I get older. Just like you."

"Aren't you a smart one? Whatever it is that brought you out in such inclement weather must be awfully important."

"You see how nice she is, Roden? It's surely safe to confide in her. Don't you agree? He's the one who found the item, so I thought it fitting to introduce you two. If you have specific questions, he may be better able to answer." She wiped her son's fur as he stared up at the venerable Dr. Atwood.

"By all means." Dr. Atwood put her palm low to the ground, and the two climbed aboard. She lifted them to her desk, then leaned in to allow a more face-to-face conversation. The heterogeneity amongst the population, even interspecies family units since The Change, no longer gave her the least bit of pause.

"Earlier this morning, Roden was out playing in the glade by the Grand when he found the most unusual of objects. It's, well, unique. Even on this island."

"You live near the Grand Cenote, don't you? I've been there before. You live in such a beautiful area. It just so happens that I found an ever-so-beautiful pocket watch there, lost by some traveler, no doubt. There is a good deal of runoff there, so I'm not surprised that you found something unusual. Just a few years ago, some of the airport debris was deposited a bit upstream from your home. Wonderful treasures for a child."

"Oh yes, An and I were made aware of the airport refuse before we purchased our home. It was all part of the disclosure, but it has never been a problem. The glade and Garden District area are truly lovely and sit fairly high up above the cenote."

"You know, I think I've met your husband before. Abe, Az, An? He is a lizard too, is he not?"

"Yes, ma'am, it's An. You would probably recognize him as a popular hairdresser. He couldn't accompany us today as he's taking the first portion of the gondolier examination."

"On a day like today, of all days? I cannot believe that the exam would proceed in such inclement weather. Who's in charge down there? I'll have to speak with the proctor and alert the council of such recklessness. By the way, is your husband a scribe, an author, or perhaps he works with books? Does he take a lot of notes?"

"You must be speaking of Mo. He worked in the library. The two are never far apart, the best of friends. Have you met him before? He's a stout, white, moth-like . . ."

"Oh, never mind me. I meet so many different people with my work. I'm sure your husband will be fine." She changed the subject and gently tousled Roden's hair. "What a cute little boy you are! Whatever you found must be awfully important for you to weather the impending storm. Oh, never mind me; I've gone off on a tangent. Lacey, please excuse my small talk. I'd like to meet your husband. He sounds like a rather interesting individual. Now, what can I do for you two?"

"Dr. Atwood, I know you are very busy and likely have a great deal of responsibilities. I just didn't know who else to turn to. Just this morning, Roden was outside playing with his magnifying lens. He found this." She held out the seed to Dr. Atwood.

"A maple seed?" Dr. Atwood looked a bit confused, but feigned surprise for the child. She had expected the object to be metallic or refuse from the airport. "It is that time of the year, after all."

"No, no, you must look again. I too thought it to be nothing more than a maple seed at first glance, but look closely. I was unsure what to do and thought it best to ask for your opinion. Please. Look more closely."

"You say this maple seed was found in the glade?" Patricia took the seed from Lacey. She was bemused at first, but after a more thorough inspection, she realized there was a man encased inside. Her eyes widened in disbelief and her mouth thrust agape at the adventitious change in circumstance. Her surprise nearly caused her to drop the seed.

"Was this hanging in a tree? Oh my gosh! Is this what I think it is? This is truly quite peculiar. In all my years, I've neither seen nor heard of anything like it. But let me do it justice." Her hand shook as she inspected the seed with a magnifying lens. In utter disbelief, she confirmed there to be a small man inside the maple seed. And it was not just any man; it was a man she knew. The man she needed. The man in the codex! Inside the propitious maple seed was none other than Beau Champs. *So this is where he went after he disappeared.*

"You have a magnifying lens like me!" Roden pointed.

Startled, Dr. Atwood shook herself into some degree of composure. "Yes I do, young man, and I use it a lot. When you become an archaeologist one day, you'll use yours a lot, too. Lacey and Roden, I am not quite sure what to make of this seed, but I assure you it is unique and unlike anything I have ever seen before. Roden, you truly have made the discovery of a lifetime. Your archaeological career is off to a great start."

Well versed in the art of deception, Patricia capriciously cloaked her dumbfounded excitement as she struck a resolute, stony face of dissemblance. *So this is where you've been all this time.* She returned to an austere balance of professionalism and said, "I don't know what this means or how the person got in there, but I am honored that you would bring this unique find to my attention. I resolutely promise to help you to the best of my abilities. In all honesty, I am not sure what to make of this most unusual discovery. This is the first time I have seen or heard of such an oddity, even on this peculiar island. Has this person been locked away since 1960?"

"We knew you were the right person to ask." Lacey felt reassured.

"Lacey and precious Roden, I would be honored to help you find the meaning of this seedling and attempt to extricate the inhabitant. However, with the impending storm, I will need a bit of time. I will need to confer with some of my esteemed colleagues scattered here and there

441

around the world. It's likely best that I hold on to this discovery, if that is OK with you, young man? I promise to keep it safe."

Roden hesitated and looked at his mother, who noticed his skeptical disposition.

"It's OK, son. Dr. Atwood will take very good care of the man." His mother's ingenuous stance helped, and he thought about the matter a bit longer.

"OK, mother. He can stay with her."

"This matter may take some time to resolve. I imagine that our lines of outside communication are a bit bungled for obvious reasons, but I will begin my inquiries this moment."

Patricia was in the midst of contriving other excuses to keep the seedling in her possession should the child change his mind, when there was yet another knock at the door.

"Who would expect such traffic in this weather?" Dr. Atwood opened the door only to be engulfed by the overpowering, acrid smell that announced the presence of a Westbank warthog, a giant who struggled to catch his breath and stood huffing and puffing. He was soaking wet, dressed in a loincloth and sandals. His hulking size made him too large to enter. The beast caught sight of the two visitors on her desk, so he waved her near. "Dr. Atwood, Dr. Atwood. I need to speak to you, Dr. Atwood."

"You don't have to whisper in my ear." The half-witted beast was taking secrecy too far as his spittle struck the side of her face. "It's me. You don't have to keep repeating my name."

The beast persisted. "They have found what you seek. The message, it's from Saul directly."

To Lacey, it was abundantly clear by the look on Dr. Atwood's face that the interloper's inquiry required a degree of expediency that superseded any further discussion about the seed.

"Psst! Madam, you are needed, and now! I cannot go back without you. Saul insisted that I take you with me. The urgency cannot be overstated. It has been found! We must run."

In order to mask any improprieties for Lacey and Roden, and much to the confusion of the runner, she responded loudly and distinctly. "I see. There is a problem in Westbank near the tavern? Imagine that, a Westbanker in trouble! Immediately needed, you say?" Dr. Atwood turned to the pair on her desk. "I am so sorry for the interruption, but would you please excuse me? There seems to be an emergency down in the Westbank." She motioned to her truck and nodded to the beast. "Hop in the back. I'll drive you there." The beast lumbered off and climbed into the bed, its rear suspension sinking under his weight.

She deposited the seed in her satchel's side pocket before Roden could object. "You two must excuse me for a matter of the utmost urgency. I would offer to take you home, but I really am rushed. I am so sorry for the interruption. Let us resume this discussion at a later time. You will hear from me." She ushered them out of her office, closing the door behind them.

Dr. Atwood climbed into the cab of her blue 1956 Chevy truck, with the wet beast sitting in the bed. Lacey and Roden stood on her stoop and watched as the good doctor sped down Main Street, never looking back.

"Mother, I think she knows the man in the seed."

# CHAPTER 22

## THE LIBRARY AND RUSE

*Saturday, October 28, 1972*

Eftsoons her departure from the township, Dr. Atwood stood in the sub-sub-sub-basement of the library. Having been informed of the contents of the other rooms and having confirmed the events that transpired, she adjusted the time on her watch and then lathered herself, her satchel, and her timepiece with what remained of the unctuous Shrinking Suds. Succumbing to its effects, she metathesized down to a diminutive size and stood face-to-face with the exiguous Saul and his lot of his similarly proportioned warriors. The lot faced her in rapt attention, waiting for her to speak. She wasn't sure how she'd return to her former self, but she saw no other way to reach the confines of the Ancient Collection. It was no wonder that the place had remained hidden for so long. The repetitive first few measures of Roberta Flack's "The First Time Ever I Saw Your Face" echoed quietly through the drafty archway.

She was briefly lost in a moment of pensive thought; the sharp vicissitudes of luck were upon her. Fortunately, the Westbankers were a poorly educated lot; the lollygagging imbeciles, including their leader, seemed ignorant about the gravity of their find. This discovery would be perhaps the greatest rekindling of mankind and easily the greatest leap forward in the twentieth century. If the room beyond the archway was indeed the famed library depicted in her text, who knows what magnitude of treasures would be housed within? Who knew what sort of mysteries could be unlocked to the detriment and benefit of mankind? Would it house vastly superior technologies? If all of her tome's illustrations were literal, just imagine what waited beyond that door!

She had good reason for such expectation; the watch and key were tangible, as was the island. Even simply finding the long-lost Ancient Collection would make her a historical icon. She would be lauded as one of the greatest archaeologists of all time. The accolades would be endless, but such praise would require disclosure, and she was not planning on sharing. How would she explain it to the public? Years of speculation and suppositions were now a veridical and evolving reality of which she was the sole possessor.

She had been able to trace Beau Champs and Merl Linstein to the island thanks to Dr. Montegue's marginal notations, specifically to the Aloha textile factory, but then she hit a dead end. She had gotten nowhere in years and was at her wits' end, about to give up hope. On that fateful day in 1960, she followed a young man she now knew to be Beau Champs to the Tripe airport and her belief in the codex was forever solidified, knowing then that at least some of its illustrative depictions were real events and not merely the account of some ancient scribe's forgetive or psychotic imagination. It was on that day that the clouds turned ashen, the earth moved, and The Change happened; her derriere's appendage was a constant, sobering reminder. To this day, she still wasn't quite sure what drew her attention to the young Beau Champs, a lone man with a baby carriage at his side. Was it a twinkle in his eye or a gleam in the air? His bright Hawaiian shirt? Had she recognized his face from the illustrations? Was it fate? Perhaps his conspicuous mannerisms and smell as he tried to remain inconspicuous gave him away. Or maybe it was simply her woman's intuition.

The unusual circumstances of the island were thereafter indelibly inked in the pages of the codex. Through toilsome and sedulous inquiry, coupled with a dash of sheer luck, she was drawn to the timepiece. The airport refuse site had been an unlikely but ultimately fruitful endeavor. She was thinking about the shimmer from her truck's bonnet as she stared blankly at the enormous bottle of Shrinking Suds, the large water fountain above, and a large staff laying on the ground. Mere steps away, the words "Ancient Collection" were inscribed above the archway.

Saul cleared his throat, and his asperous voice woke her from her trance. "We have a deal, remember? Here is your permit." He handed her a poorly crafted letter signed by the council and his alter ego, Melvin. She skimmed the document and deposited it into her satchel.

He turned to the warriors and said, "Gentlemen, I'd like to present the miniature version of Dr. Atwood. Many of you know her well. She is to be afforded your graces." He turned his back to his men and whispered to Atwood. "As soon as you pass through that door, you'll be in the southern portion of our island. Before I let you walk through the archway, I want to hear you promise me one last time that I will be granted the means to locate the former leader. You will get the Ancient Collection, and I will be given free rein to find the scoundrel. What I do with him is my business. Are we clear on our promise? My obsequious warriors and I have succeeded in delivering to you what has been asked, and now it's your turn to deliver him to me."

"You will have what has been promised."

Saul was not appeased. "I have fulfilled my end of our bargain, and I am awaiting delivery of my compensation. I have earned it. We've dug your tunnel and found your precious library. Take heed—all has not been kept secret.

My men captured two islanders at the base of the temple."

"How did they get down here? The southern end of the island is off-limits."

"Their story is that they were in the streams and sought refuge from a fatal tidal surge. The slugs confirmed the timing of the surge and had presumed the two to be deceased. Regardless, they are of no consequence and are being held in a secure location."

"Do not let them go. Await further instruction. I'm not sure how long I'll be. If news of our discovery were to get out, we could expect a multitude of visitors, not to mention the council. Hopefully the storm will keep everyone indoors long enough for me to confirm what we have here. As for my promise to you, I haven't the time to mollify your ego, Saul, but rest assured that our deal remains intact. I must first find the leader. You've had time to hold up your end, so afford me time to hold up mine. I can't just pull him out of thin air, you know. Speaking of the prisoners, I think it's time to take preventative measures. Not only must we contain the two captured intruders, but we must also keep your men from alerting others on the island. The last thing we need is the Tripe Island Council poking their noses into our business."

"Your advice is well reasoned but impractical. Bill already knows, and he and Larry gossip. You expect the impossible."

"In that case, we must cut all lines of communication to and from the island and disrupt all inbound and outbound travel. We can deal with the islanders, but if word of this discovery leaves the island, we won't be able to retain control. Inform your men. Have you entered the library?" She motioned to the doorway.

Saul spoke loudly, annunciating for his followers. "Patricia, my dear Patricia. I have indeed laid my eyes upon it. The collection's grandeur is like none other. Its enormity boggles the mind. Floors upon floors upon floors upon floors upon floors . . ."

"I get the point. And what of Jason Dix? He was being chased. Where has he gone? What say you?" Patricia directed her attention to the commander, Lionel.

"At the temple base, my men tried unsuccessfully to capture the cunning Mr. Dix, who is likely hidden somewhere within the library. We expect to find him shortly. But ma'am, we are on the southern end of the island and my men are hesitant and fearful to roam about. When they learned that the Ancient Collection is housed in the south, they grew leery. You know that us Westbankers are a superstitious lot, and the south is steeped in mystery and danger."

"Explain to them that we now have a permit. There is nothing to fear."

"Yes ma'am. My men have identified two points of entry: the doorway here and another adjacent to the temple. There are still countless floors that need to be inspected, so there may be more. My men are not fit enough to climb, and the elevator is nonfunctional or perhaps we do not have the means to activate it. There is another elevator at the temple base, and it won't budge either."

Saul interjected, "Dix is the priority now. I want him held when he is found. Reiterate to your buffoons that we have a permit, for goodness' sake. Won't that negate any bad juju or superstition? It's signed by the council and the president."

"As you wish."

Saul made a grand, sweeping gesture with an accompanying bow and said, "Dr. Atwood, without further delay, may I present to you the Ancient Collection!"

"Let her through!" Lionel barked. The troops parted like the Red Sea and stood at attention, allowing her to pass through their ranks. The cool, musty air of the library wafted across her body.

"Send a message to close the airport and cut all lines of communication." Saul motioned to one of the warriors, who hustled off. "Lionel, keep your men on high alert. I don't know what this Dix character is up to, and there may be surprises ahead. He could be hiding anywhere. By the looks of him in the paper this morning, he need not be armed to be dangerous. He's a biter! Are there men stationed near the cavern and temple? We are in uncharted territory now, so no others are to enter or depart."

"Sir, our men are split equally between the two entrances. It's impossible for him to escape without being spotted and captured."

With great anticipation, Dr. Atwood took her first steps into the Ancient Collection. At first glance, the library was not at all like she had envisioned. Expecting to face an array of incredible complexity, she instead stood before a rudimentary placard at the entrance that read, "Welcome to 1972." Equally as mundane, a wooden library card file desk sat nearby. Some of its many small drawers had been pulled out, and an enormous number of Dewey decimal cards were strewn across the floor.

The room itself was huge and cluttered, with an assemblage of memorabilia that was all seemingly associated with the year 1972; some of the items had been dismantled or destroyed by the churlish warriors. Clutter was everywhere. Not a single space was left unoccupied, high or low. A Cessna 172L and other methods of flight hung idly above their heads, tethered to the ceiling by cables. There were automobiles with dented fenders, crumpled hoods, and smashed windshields, including a metallic silver 1972 Porsche 911, a red Alfa Romeo Alfetta, and many other vehicles from 1972, all with the sales stickers still attached, the makes and models described on tasteful placards, many of which were now ripped into shreds.

"I'm sorry about the mess, ma'am. Some of my more boisterous men took it upon themselves to 'investigate' this room, looking for the boy and clues. The floors immediately above and below are equally as wrecked. Most things remain intact, except that there is no more Fun Dip, Charms Blow Pops, or Pop Rocks left. The guys found the stash and loved them."

"This is it? A load of junk from 1972? You said there were floors above and below? Was this part of the library before The Change?" She had expected to find something far more impressive; there was nothing ancient about this pitiful collection. "Perhaps you've struck the wrong sub-basement of the library?"

The three continued ahead, sorting items and forging a path. Names of numerous figures of authority from the time, such as Queen Elizabeth II, Leonid Brezhnev, Giovanni Leone, and Pope Paul VI, were listed on pendants as the trio passed over a recessed floor map. There were items from various artistic disciplines: placards and wax figures of recording artists and film stars such as Bill Withers and Gene Hackman; rich, red-and-gold velvet draperies outlining a large screen with Francis Ford Cop-

453

pola's *The Godfather* projected silently upon it; a large collection of vinyl albums were shelved alongside a Technics SL-1200 phonograph with Acoustic Research speakers that the beasts seemed to have "adjusted" into an unusable state; countless album sleeves strewn about as the records had been used like frisbees; and countless typewriters and television screens of the era. Dark mahogany shelves wrapped around the circumference of the concourse and were brimming with books and film artifacts organized by date, all from 1972.

Lionel directed the three to the center of the room, to a railing that encircled a smaller atrium and landing. A spiraling staircase led above and below. Roberta Flack's voice was still skipping on the scratched vinyl record.

Lionel said, "There's a lot more to this place than just this room. Stairs lead up and down for as far as the eye can see. And that elevator I mentioned is over there." He pointed to a glass elevator across the atrium. Hanging above the elevator was a sign that read: "CIVIL LIBERTIES DISABLED ELEVATOR."

He continued, "It appears to be broken. It cannot be turned on, and no matter the brute force, it will not open and its glass cannot be broken. I have my strongest guy on it. Above and below, it's all much of the same. There are different items on each floor, but all have the same layout. My men only went ten floors up and ten floors down, and they discovered that each floor is sorted by year. I did send an expeditionary force up, but they have not checked back in yet. They aren't conditioned for climbing, not to mention their superstitious proclivities, and it is a bit of a security risk having to spread the men so thin. I expect them to relax a bit when I mention the permit."

"So Dix could be anywhere?" Atwood asked.

"Remember your end of the bargain," Saul whispered, watching her carefully.

"Can someone turn off that record?"

Lionel shouted, "Off with the music! Anyway, doc, the items are cataloged by date, some even by time. This place seems to ascend and descend forever."

"Have you found a legend or a map or . . ." A smile crossed her face as she seemed to have an epiphany.

"No, but it's just vertically built. As far as we can tell, it extends deep into the earth." Lionel grabbed a small crystal vase and tossed it over the rail. He paused for effect, but no crash was ever heard. "Like I said, this place is deep."

"For the last time, please turn that off!"

"The music, guys. C'mon!" The music screeched to a halt and they could hear the sound of a record being smashed on the floor.

Dr. Atwood and Saul leaned over the railing to take account of the white, marble spiral staircase. It wrapped around the atrium, leading up into the heavens above and down into the deep bowels of the earth. When they looked down, there was no sign of the crystal vase.

"Perhaps our first step ought to be to determine exactly how vast the library is. I may have a solution to the elevator." The three stepped over broken items and walked toward the gilded, glass elevator.

From roughly twenty floors up, they heard the blaring groove of "Jump Around" by House of Pain.

> *Get up, stand up, c'mon throw your hands up*

> *If you've got the feeling, jump across the ceiling*

Dr. Atwood withdrew a golden key from her satchel and inserted it into the lock above the elevator call button. At long last, she knew its purpose. *Should I go up or down?* There was no need to remain with these two; they would only hinder her progress. The doors slid open with a pleasant chime and she walked inside, taking her key with her.

"Gentlemen, it's time for this woman to take charge. I'll find you, not the other way around. I suggest you get a handle on your Westbank crew." The doors shut rapidly leaving Saul no time for remonstrance. The elevator plunged downward with lightning speed in a faint eddy of translucent sparkles and gold. Lionel stared with his mouth agape at her sudden egress, whilst Saul looked below with a sardonic smile.

Saul said, "Lionel, no word of this to anyone. Keep searching for the boy, and when he is found, hold him. And put on a shirt."

"Yes, sir!" Lionel stiffened.

"Have you deposited the two from the temple base, as directed? Remember, no harm can come to either."

"Held on floor 1969, sir, tied and secure. Three floors down, sir. The one called Mo keeps reiterating that he is in charge, that this is his library. He prattles on and on about being the librarian, and every time my men begin to speak, he tells them to be quiet. Is there something I need to be made aware of?"

"No, he sounds delusional. Find me the boy. Chop, chop."

Saul paced angrily while spewing the most deprecating of obloquies and thersitical unpleasantries toward Dr.

Atwood. He knew she was taking advantage of him, and it was hard to stomach. "Patricia, it's time you realize that you aren't the veiled, usurping genius in sheep's clothing you think you are; you're not the only one with secrets. Your selfishness is expected, but don't forget the trammels that pertain to you or you will pay dearly. You are all too quick to praise Melvin for his efforts, but heaven forbid you mention Saul." Saul's scratchy voice threatened reprisal to the departed Dr. Atwood.

Lionel was nearly out of earshot when Saul called for him. "Oi! Lionel, I have one more task for you. Tell Bill and Larry to come to the library basement and lather them with that magic soap. I have another task for them."

"But sir, they seem to have suddenly disappeared. I will bring them when they are found, sir." Lionel departed to the library basement as Saul descended the stairs, bound for 1969.

# CHAPTER 23

## INTRODUCTION TO THE DARK AGES

*499 AD*

The last voice Jason heard was the angry cicerone yelling, "No more freeloaders!" before the elevator door opened. Jason was deposited at the edge of a dirt road outside a small hamlet, all alone. The elevator vanished into thin air like the twinkle of a night star. A still, nubilous haze blanketed a cool, misty, verdant landscape dotted with quaint hedgerows, rocky partitions, and glacial erratics on the edge of a dense weald, quite a departure from the interior of Carrollton School. He had landed in a picturesque setting of quaint solitude, but just a bit up the road, the rancor of a moderately sized crowd broke the pastoral mood. There was neither signage to denote Jason's place of landing nor any characteristics of the town that could help him identify his location. He only knew he had been left in the Dark Ages.

Jason ambled down the road, past a series of wooden shacks, one called Fat Harry's. He was thrust into the middle of the rather rumbustious crowd; a throng of tumultuous, cackling women lined the muddy path, none of whom took immediate notice of Jason, their attention focused on an approaching cavalcade from out of the nearby woods. The women were only slightly taller than Jason and were uniformly clad in rather bleak tunics, all rather unkempt and fetid. Their men stood indifferently behind the womenfolk, obviously disenchanted with the events taking place, not particularly enamored with their feudalistic placement in life, and mumbling apathetically about egalitarian matters and societal disadvantages. Like their women, the men were also unkempt and fetid, but hairier. By the accents of the townsfolk and their crooked toothsomeness, Jason guessed that he was in England or Wales.

From the corner of his eye, Jason thought he saw Mr. Winwood's lookalike. "Mr. Winwood? Mr. Winwood?" He assumed that his eyes were playing tricks on him because the scruffy man who turned around looked nothing like Mr. Winwood.

The women's frenetic reverie grew more palpable and was completely undisturbed by Jason's outburst. In great anticipation, they focused on an approaching procession of gleaming, armored knights on horseback and the following cavalcade that brandished a large sign: "Krewe of Arthur." Jason meandered through the hysterical crowd, wondering what had become of Mo and An, and feeling more than a bit distressed about their absence.

"Sir Lancelot! Sir Lancelot!" A tall, wrinkled, leather-skinned woman with long, sandy-blonde hair and partial and yellowed dentition called out in a thick English accent, her hands waving a colorful nosegay in the air. She was desperately endeavoring to gain the attention of the strapping lad half her age. Disconcertingly, she was clearly the beauty of the bunch. The knight whose attention she sought was adorned with regal vestments and chain mail, riding atop a majestic, black-as-night beast of a horse. He must have been a man of some importance, because he was near the front of the approaching cavalcade. From what Jason gathered, the maiden's name was Parkley.

"Sir Garin! Sir Ewin! Sir Gawain!" The lascivious women each tried desperately to gain the attention of one of the noble knights.

"He's so dreamy! I wouldn't share him if I got him! Lancelot's out front. Sir Lancelot!" blurted a short, pig-nosed, corpulent, toothless redhead.

"No, he's mine! You keep your grubby hands off him." The rancor grew amongst the wishful suitors, shoving and jawing as the most famous of all knights approached. When he reached the crowd of fawning women, he went into his saddlebag and threw a handful of meretricious trinket coins into the crowd. Jason picked one up and noted that "Made in Byzantium" was stamped on the back.

Jason was still uncertain about his specific geographic location or what year it was, so he decided to ask a local. From there, he would figure out if Mo and An were nearby, complete the cipher, and decide where to go. Although they were quite animated, the crowd seemed safe enough and no different from many of the Mardi Gras crowds back home. He approached an amiable-looking woman and nudged her rear as politely as possible. "Ma'am, can you please tell me who is approaching and what today's date might be?"

"You know what's wrong with this place? Nothing is made in these parts any longer. Seems like everything these days is made in Byzantium." The haggard woman seemed not to have heard him as she tossed the coin aside.

"Look, it's him!" another woman squealed. "Krewe of Arthur, throw me something!"

Jason was completely out of place in his black glasses, canvas knapsack, khaki shorts, and black-and-gold fleur-de-lis T-shirt. The fact that he was shoeless with mud caked up to his ankles did help him blend in a bit, but the mere understanding of the zipper on his shorts would have been leaps and bounds ahead of the crowd's time.

He poked her again, a bit more sternly this time, trying to gain both her attention and answers before the approaching procession arrived. "Excuse me, ma'am. I need your help. I've come a long way. Where am I?"

Through the throngs, Jason spotted a group of minstrels and dancing jesters accompanying those on horseback.

The woman looked at Jason with crazed confusion, immediately backing away as if he had leprosy. "How dare you touch my buttocks!"

"I'm sorry, miss. It was just an accident." Jason held his hands up and palms out, feigning innocence. "I was simply trying to get your attention because I'm looking for someone. My father may have been here before, Alfred Dix. Ever heard of him? He left a note directing me to come here." Jason saw that he was getting nowhere as a look of revulsion crossed her face." Can you tell me what year it is or where I am? My name is Jason Dix and I . . ."

Women on either side of her grasped her hands and quickly pulled her backward, as if he were some evil apparition.

"Minerva, I think it touched your buttocks! You're going to be cursed. I've heard about this. Quickly, fetch her the garlic and salts! Oh, what evil apparition stands before us? It must be a product of necromancy. Lo, the evil in its eyes! Someone fetch her a talisman! I lament ever having gone outdoors on this day."

One of the stockier men stepped forward, slapping his massive palm with a large club.

"I'm not evil. I'm just a kid, a kid from New Orleans, a kid who was told to come here. To the Dark Ages. I didn't mean to touch your butt. I'm sorry!" Jason blushed at the thought of touching her backside as he pleaded for assistance, his palms raised outward in a display that he was unarmed.

"Ahh, bollocks! Look at it. It needs to be burned to protect us from a cursed life," cried another. "The lot of us and our children will suffer should we not burn it at the stake! Our town will be cursed!"

Sir Lancelot must have caught sight of the encounter because he turned his horse to canter in their direction. Everyone parted to let him pass.

The blonde woman broke the silence, pointing to Jason with a hagridden glare. "It's not like us. Look at it. What strange clothes and writings it wears." She stepped forward and pushed his T-shirt sharply with a long staff. Her distrusting eyes glared at him as she spread her arms wide, pushing those aside back and away as if he were a poisonous snake or scorpion.

"Old Occitan?" said another as the men also began to gather round.

Jason stood alone and nervous in the center of an ever-shrinking circle with perseverating thoughts of a Fraser spiral and the clicking heels that could get him home.

"No! It's a witch, I say. It be damned. Look at the evil covering its eyes. Windows to the soul—it's trying to look into my soul! It is possessed by a witch." Her white hair and the years written boldly across her face in lines and wrinkles told Jason that this woman was the village elder and matriarch. She stepped forward to loudly hurl imprecations at Jason, while pointing a bony finger at his face. "It's a witch and it has come to take our lives. Burn it at the stake!"

"We must burn it at the stake," echoed the charnel crowd. "Mother is right. The only breaking of the curse is to burn it!"

Realizing their ignorance and out of options, Jason tried to lighten the mood, though a presentiment of uneasiness was rapidly escalating. There was no rational explanation for the day's events and trying to rationalize them would be impossible, irrational, and futile. "Wait a minute, she's the mother to all of you?" Jason laughed wildly and then winked. "What a woman! No, look." Jason took his glasses off and held them out for examination. "These help me see better. I have bad vision. They are called glasses and they are to help me see better."

Jason was trapped as the crowd collectively took a step forward and encircled him. He felt a lump developing in his throat as he realized that his attempts to dampen the crowd's fervor and bloodlust were growing futile and his unpropitious predicament was growing more desperate.

Suddenly, the crowd let out a gasp of surprise as the throngs parted and Sir Lancelot approached.

He spoke in a rather abstruse and snotty English accent. Lancelot slowed the cavalcade and stopped his horse directly in front of Jason. "Calm, calm, fair maidens. Say you, young lad. I am with your feudal Lord."

"Sir Lancelot, you need not take time out of your busy day to deal with the machinations of this witch. It will be subject to our laws and proper justice shall be served," voiced the old lady and matriarch.

"Quiet, my subjects! The king's justice is justice alone." Sir Lancelot raised his hands in a sign of authority, and his magisterial tone and authoritative mien brought the crowd to silence, including the old woman.

When he had the attention of all, he said, "My, what a strange physiognomy, I must say. The apparatus sitting atop thine eyes is quite unusual. Stand before me, bow, and state your name. Are you an errant witch or spirit, as say she? Should you be, my noble, knightly duties would require that I take your life at the bequest of these goodly people and my devotion to Queen Guinevere in ridding the kingdom of necromantic endeavors. Tell us, are you a product of Morgan Le Fay, King Arthur's half-sister?"

Lancelot's inflection alone was enough to warrant a rebuttal. "And who might you be, sir? A gallant knight on a hearty steed? Mr. Shakespeare?" The brusque, patronizing retort left Jason's lips before he realized his error.

The lad on the horse with the longsword and scabbard at his side was momentarily taken askance by the sharp riposte. He looked pensively into the sky and let his horse turn, purposely revealing the hilt of his sword, which glistened alive in the afternoon sun. It was clear to all, including Jason, that the anachronistic teen would be no match for Lancelot. The crowd seemed eager for a quick skirmish.

"I would say it not very wise to insult me, if that is your game. Are you not taught to speak when asked? What is this Shakespeare to whom you refer? A brave knight from distant lands, I gather. You are nothing but a child, yet you speak in a manner becoming of an elder double your age. I have no reason to protect you. Yet, it would not be knightly to kill an unarmed child, particularly atop my steed, where you have no chance at all."

Jason's departure was hampered by the growing, truculent crowd. The men palmed large wooden clubs, ready to bash his head. The knight had the clear advantage. The women called for his blood. Mo and An remained nowhere to be found. He was on his own.

Jason reached for his satchel, fumbling for the tow sack. At this point, any of the potions would do. Sensing a threat, Sir Lancelot drew his sword from its scabbard, the piercing ring halting Jason in his tracks.

"I will not fight atop my steed so that you may look into the eyes of he who condemns witches, specters, and spirits of the dark arts. If you are gathering a weapon, make haste!"

Lancelot began to dismount, and Jason hastily put his hands with palms open back into the air. He could feel his time on earth growing short, so he pleaded loud and clear, "Sir, I am but a weary traveler in need of sustenance. I know not where I am or even the year. I would be eternally appreciative for Your Highness's help in this endeavor. As to whether I am a witch, the answer is a resounding 'no.' Although I am certain that you won't believe me, my clothes appear strange to your eye because I come from the future. Like you, I serve and answer to Queen Guinevere."

In his attempt to ingratiate himself with Sir Lancelot, Jason inadvertently named the beloved queen in the same breath as the practice of necromancy, producing enormous ire. Sir Lancelot remained atop the horse, his mouth agape at such a confession. He raised his sword, ready to strike, and bellowed, "And so you bring the king's wife into your necromantic illusions?"

An audible gasp rippled through the crowd.

Lancelot continued. "The future, say you? By that very confession, you are a witch. Able to pass time when no time hath passed? If this is so, you have no place here and you are left to the disposition of my blade and these people. Prepare to meet your Lord in the name of my lady."

As Lancelot was preparing to strike, the gravelly voice of an elder resonated from an approaching carriage. "Halt! Halt! Lancelot, hold your arms! Put down your arms, sir. There is more to this youth than you are aware. Jason, you really need to watch yourself. In the lexicon of your time, he's a little cray-cray."

Jason could hear a second muted voice from elsewhere in the processional. "I'll say. You'd better calm him down."

An elaborately decorated and gilded carriage in the procession behind Sir Lancelot slowed and came to a stop just beyond the crowd. The draperies remained closed, indicating that the passenger was likely a seigneur or person of nobility. The inscription "Carriage One" was boldly displayed on the side. The crowd parted, allowing the carriage to view Sir Lancelot, the townspeople, and Jason. The ensuing retinue, all riding palfreys, along with knights, squires, and panniered beasts followed suit, stopping on the road. Sir Lancelot steadied his horse, awaiting further instruction from those in the carriage.

From the unseen side, Jason could hear the carriage door squeak open and then slap closed with a sharp shudder. An old man in the garments of a beggar alighted, using a large staff to aide in his hobbled stride. He passed the silent crowd and befuddled Lancelot to approach Jason. He was of medium build with a long, gray beard and weathered visage, that of a stereotypical wizard or grand-father or both.

A hushed din of whispers fell upon the crowd. "Merlin. It is he, Merlin."

He pointed with his gaunt finger directly at Jason. "Is your surname Dix? I know it is. Are you not in good hands? Didn't think they could see you?" With a Cheshire grin, he quizzically said, "It seems like we've had this conversation only yesterday. Do you remember? Have you been told? What year are you from?"

"Is it him? Is the trap set?" said the muted voice from the carriage.

"Hush. You don't know who's listening. I assure you it's him." Merlin gave the thumbs up sign as movement was seen at one of the carriage's window curtains. He turned back to Jason.

Jason was getting more confused by the minute. "Umm, sir, I do not mean to be rude, but how would I have been told or remember? Today is today, not yesterday? And yes, I am Jason Dix. My present day is 2017."

"Oh, Jason. My dearest Jason, do you not remember me? Of course not—you were no larger than a loaf of bread when we first met. And look at you now. Thin and lithe. I'll bet you are quick. Here, drink this. After such long travels, you must be parched." Merlin handed him a small wineskin, from which Jason took a short swig.

"Cola?"

"No, it's called Real World. You must have left yours in the elevator."

All except Jason were aware of Merlin, a man practiced in the art of deceptions of the ordinary and obvious called magic. The crowd was attentively holding their breath, as if they were waiting for something to come from taking the drink, but nothing happened. As Jason took another swig, his semi-ghostly translucence coalesced into a solid and tangible form. Everyone but Merlin gasped and took a step back.

With a capricious change of personality, Merlin became more sinister. "Adventurous knights, this young boy is to be bound and harnessed to one of the carts, where he can do us no harm. It is he we seek. He comes with us." The old man nonchalantly waved to Sir Lancelot, clearly un-afraid of the newcomer. "Hand me the gray cloth sack over his shoulder. He is unarmed; you have nothing to fear. Yes, Jason, you are part of our world now. There will be no escape this time."

"This time? But sir, may I ask your name? And why have you ordered me bound on the cart?"

"Don't be a fool, kid. There is just enough room for two, and I would not expect King Arthur and Queen Guine-vere to ride atop their own carriage. I don't think you've earned that right. I'll bet you'll watch your tongue next time. The man in the carriage is an adventurous king revered and feared by all. And you? You're just a young boy with something I need. You're a means to an end."

Jason glanced toward the carriage.

"Don't you see Carriage One written on the side? It's a play on the US presidency. Come on, didn't Alfred or whatever your double-crossing father calls himself, teach you some degree of manners?" Merlin furtively glanced around the perplexed crowd. "I've been waiting for one of the keys for many a year, and now that a key is within my grasp, would you really expect me to let it and you out of my sight? Think of it from my perspective, how can I guarantee that you will not abandon The Merl, as your father did? And that reminds me—I will now take the key that you have around your neck. If you won't give it willingly, I will let these people deal with you. I am quite certain that burning you at the stake is at the forefront of their minds. They do love a good barbecue. I will happily retrieve the key from your charred corpse if you'd prefer. C'mon, I know it's right there under your shirt. You showed it to me yesterday."

"Do you mean this?" Jason extracted the key and Merlin held out his waiting palm. "How do you know my dad's name? You mean that's the real King Arthur, as in, Knights of the Round Table, the Holy Grail, Merlin, and all that?" Jason unfastened the key from around his neck and handed it to Merl, who then looped it around his own neck and tucked it under his robes.

Merlin smiled. "Yep, that's me! Thank you for being compliant. It's amazing what people remember."

"Are you telling me that these are the fictional people I've read about in books?" Jason motioned to the knights on horseback. "The fabled Knights of the Round Table with quests and pilgrimages and such? Those were all supposed to be fairytales. This cannot really be happening. What do you know of the key? How am I supposed to get home? I didn't ask for any of this. Please, I just want to go home."

"You're entitled to a bit of explanation and we have much to discuss, but not in these conditions or within earshot of others. Remember that it is not only I who has an eye on you. There is nowhere you can run that I will not be made aware. For now, as it is already midday and this krewe has a bit more traveling to do, we must continue our journey. The lot of us must retire to a place more befitting His Excellency. Furthermore, I have a reputation to uphold; cavorting with the likes of you in these circumstances just will not do. So, first we must feast and hear the amazing tales of Sir Lancelot and the rest of His Majesty's brave knights on their most recent quest. A feast is being prepared as we speak, with minstrels and troubadours waxing lyrical prowess, practicing for His Majesty's arrival. We must not disappoint. Why the look of surprise? It's not like we have Xboxes, PlayStations, iPhones, or movie theaters."

Jason's jaw dropped.

"Oh, look at the time." Merlin withdrew a golden pocket watch from within his robe, similar in appearance to the one handled by the woman on the aircraft. "It's almost two in the afternoon and it will be dark soon—northern latitudes, and all. King Arthur wishes to make it to Camelot before darkness. He's a bit of a fuddy-duddy and likes to retire early. Oh, there is one other thing. Sir Lancelot, fetch me his satchel."

Seemingly having come to a desitive plan, the old man did not wait for a response. He parted the crowd and hobbled back to the carriage. Clapping his hands twice, he made a final command. "He comes with us to Camelot. Bind him and place him in the wagon."

"But wait, sir! How did you know of the key? What year is this? Where are we? How am I to get home? Where are you taking me? You haven't answered any questions."

Sir Lancelot let out a piercing whistle, commanding three knights, Sirs Gawain, Galehaut, and Agravain, to break ranks and gallop to his side, the crowd parting in hushed silence at the odd sequence of events. The four hoicked Jason onto a palfrey's cart and bound him like a fettered hog.

"But wait!" Jason pleaded as Sir Gawain stuffed a rag in his mouth. "Wait!" Jason's muted screams could no longer be discerned. One familiar with rag-speak might have heard him say, "You look like Mr. Winwood. Mr. Winwood, it's me! Help!"

Merlin turned his back to the youth and refused to acknowledge his presence any further. He entered the carriage and closed the door, and the cavalcade continued their journey.

The blonde holding the nosegay threw it to the ground as Sir Lancelot galloped away. The crowd dispersed and the squalid hamlet went back about its routine. A minute twinkle disappeared as quickly as it had appeared before the weald.

***

Jason estimated that he had been on the back of the wagon for hours, hog-tied as he jostled from side to side
amongst barrels and sacks. The northern latitude's twilight was growing dimmer by the minute. Reflecting on
the day thus far, there were just too many surreal moments to wrap his head around, all so outrageous that he
decided they simply could not be real. It was like he was
in some strange, oneiric fantasy.

He recounted the events of his day, hoping to regain his
grip on reality. He had been sitting on the sofa when
someone claiming to be his mother appeared on his television. He traveled to an island on a jet without his father, was chased by a large feral warthog who was also
an ice cream salesman, and saw a lizard with mannerisms
similar to his principal cleaning the airport. He was
shrunken and washed down a sink's drain by a friend of
his father, after which he met two animals who turned out
to look just like his two best friends. Then he took an elevator back in time and met a famous wizard he had read
about in fictional books about the Middle Ages. Finally,
he found himself tied up in the back of a wagon, his side
aching from laying in the left lateral decubitus position
for at least a few hours. The pain was making the situation seem very real. The wagon continued along through
a dense forest, creaking and shuddering, rolling across
ruts and uneven earth, jostling his side even further. The
unrelenting pain reminded him of his reality. The wagon

was at least uncovered, a simple pleasure that allowed him a view of the dusky blue sky through gaps in the forest canopy. It gave him some degree of solace to know it was the same sky outside his home on Calhoun, even if it were a dream.

The sides of the cart were made of a thick but rather short, rough wood, allowing Jason a view through the sides if he only tossed his hair out of his eyes, lifted his head and careened his neck, stretching his muscles like a fish out of water. Knights on horseback interspersed with carts pulled by beasts of burden trod along in rows to his side and rear. The din of their conversation mixed with the hoofbeats of their horses. Their conversations were growing less tense and more lighthearted by the mile; Jason sensed that the convoy was nearing their destination. They had been passing through a forest named Broceliande (as per a sign affixed to a tree) for about ten minutes when the procession suddenly stopped. The men and the stridulations of the forest fell eerily silent.

"Halt!" Lancelot's magisterial voice commanded as he galloped alongside the procession, heading past Jason to the rear of the company. "Ready your weapons, men! Take up positions. Ready the archers. The dragon is heard, and from yonder wood, there appears the promise of an ambuscade. And so close to Camelot! The unmitigated gall!" The foliage along the left side of the group shuddered with hidden movement. The troops cawed

"Gall!" amongst themselves repeatedly, as would a hungry flock of seagulls.

"Silence, men! Who goes there? Show thyself, or if thou art a cowardly man, prepare to meet your Lord! If it is a dragon you bring, we will slay it readily and roast it to sup." Lancelot's dizzying barrage of insults went unanswered as the foliage swayed and danced in the winds just as readily as if Lancelot had remained mute. A shudder of a tree's branches nearby caught Lancelot's attention.

"Archers, ready! The beast and its master are through yonder wood." The company of archers nocked and drew their arrows, patiently facing the quiet, verdant canopy.

"Loose!" hollered Lancelot. At his command, a barrage of arrows was released, piercing the dense foliage. Not a sound was heard other than the caw of blackbirds taking flight as the archers readied their bows again. The leaves rustled. "Again men." A second barrage was loosed, but again, with no result. A series of knights protectively surrounded the carriage, as Sir Lancelot and a dozen of his brethren tantivy rode into the verdant abyss.

Jason's fatigue clouded his brain. An auditory hallucination trumpeted the distant exhaust and backfire of a Harley Davidson motorcycle and Scorpions' "Rock You Like A Hurricane."

The rest of the cavalcade waited silently, unsure of what they heard. Eventually, Lancelot and his knights emerged from the woods empty-handed. The forest cacophony resumed, and after a brief discussion amongst the men, the cavalcade pressed onward. They were on guard for an attack but didn't want to be stuck in the forest come nightfall.

In time, the forest thinned and the canopy disappeared, debouching to an open, campestral plain. Farms replete with sheep, chickens, cows, and other beasts of burden corralled in pens and paddocks were scattered across the landscape. There were no signs of any technology, telephone poles, cell towers, or modern devices with which Jason was familiar. It was pure, idyllic English countryside.

Jason's cart made a sudden turn, revealing large parapets atop a colossal stone castle. They had reached their destination. Their pace quickened and the rumble of speech again shifted into lighthearted banter. Even the animals knew their whereabouts and grew more lighthearted, .neighing, nickering, and carrying on, urging their masters to hasten their pace, ready to be housed and fed.

As the battlement walls and ramparts of the castle grew larger on the horizon, King Arthur's return was announced. The regalia of trumpets sounded from atop the parapets, and pennons displaying his coat of arms unfurled from the gatehouse walls. Long, hemp ropes lowered the drawbridge to allow the procession, including Jason and his wagon, to traverse the moat. They proceeded under a portcullis and past the gatehouse into a large tiltyard. Onlookers gathered amongst a glowing pageantry of colorful streamers and banners.

Sir Key, seneschal of the great house, was espousing encomiums and accolades on each knight who passed. A mirthful sense of harmony enveloped the castle's merry crowd. Passing deeper into the castle grounds, Jason was awestruck as a melodious diapason danced through the air. Minstrels sang with the accompaniment of stringed instruments, expounding and versifying upon the bravery and quests of King Arthur and his round table knights.

"Sir Lancelot, good day, sir! Your bravery knows no bounds. Verily, I see Sir Galehaut, the brave Sir Gawain, Sir Agravain, and the mighty Sir Gaheris."

Sir Key was not one to leave out a knight deserving of accolade. "Sir Gareth of Orkney, your knightly stature . . ."

Sir Gareth interrupted, speaking loudly and clearly while passing on his trotting horse. "Ye speaketh not of me in the same breath when I was but a simple scullion. Your churlish admonitions do not do justice to a change of heart, and so I hear you not. You need not say the same to Sir Lancelot, who wears thine apparel and saved Sir Meliot de Logres from certain death." Sir Gareth's quip evoked laughter from those around but drew the ire of Sir Key, who gathered his faculties and continued with his ingratiations and accolades. Maidens fair, squires, and dwarfs all lined the path, searching for a glimpse of their loved ones or masters.

Jason caught sight of a troubadour who resembled Shaun Cassidy, with a lithe frame and long, flowing mane straight out of the 1970s. He was dancing about, making sweet eyes at the women in the crowd, and singing with a mandolin to the tune of "Da Doo Ron Ron." "We rode back on a Monday, our hearts full of cheer, da doo ron-ron-ron, da doo ron-ron. I told her my name was Arthur, her name was Guinevere. Da doo ron-ron-ron, da doo ron-ron." Jason thought to himself that he had no idea the tune was so old.

The interior of the castle was truly a sight to behold, as if it were out of a storybook, with the entirety of King Arthur's Round Table knights present in the gay atmosphere. Once inside the confines of the castle walls, Jason's wagon continued past the revelers, his mouth watering at the smell of cooked meats and fowl that permeated the mirth-filled air. A feast for the weary travelers was being fastidiously prepared, the chimneys billowing glowing embers and soot that danced up to the evenfall sky.

Jason's cart slowed as it neared the rear of the tiltyard and was parked amongst a plethora of sacks and baskets of various supplies and foodstuffs, stacked high and ready for the feast. Knights alighted off their steeds, and squires and dwarfs walked the palfreys and baying coursers away from the crowds. They strolled into the castle ready to sup, feast, and carouse, either unaware of Jason's presence in the rear of the cart or without care.

Two brusque, baleful men hastily pulled Jason across the rough wood and out of the back of the wagon as if he were just another item to be stored. Jason spit the rag from his mouth, writhing with discomfort, splinters likely buried in his side. They grabbed him under each arm and lifted him easily with their brawny thew, carried him into a dim, stone anteroom, then dropped him onto the cold, stone floor between sacks and barrels. From what Jason had been able to overhear, their names were Bill and Larry.

"No one'll know yer back here, ya pansy," barked the taller of the two.

"Wait," beseeched Jason. "Your names are Bill and Larry, right? Guys, I am supposed to meet with Merlin. There must have been a mix-up or some miscommunication. Please get him. Do not leave me tied here."

The two did not reply and continued their work, clearly upset to not be taking part in the reverie. They grumbled amongst themselves, dutifully emptying the remainder of the supplies before attending to Jason.

"Excuse me, sirs. Why am I here? I think I have a right to know. Aren't there some Geneva Convention rules you need to follow? You don't know who I am. I am a citizen of the United States and I've done nothing wrong! There must be some sort of mix-up. Seriously, can you get Merlin? He said we were going to a dinner." Jason was vociferous in his imploring speech, commanding the two to set him free, but they exited the room, deaf and mute to his pleadings as they continued to attend to unloading the cart.

"Guys! Guys? Is this some sort of joke?"

Alone and tied, Jason was able to watch the two work as the crowd thinned. There were no windows in the storeroom, but they had left the door open. His glasses were twisted and nearly falling off his face, so the people outside were now merely passing blurs and curious, crowded shadows in the dwindling light. Jason's stomach rumbled in hunger as he sat hog-tied and alone. The aroma of meats and foodstuffs waned, but he waited, not saying a word, trying to think of a way in which to escape.

Hours seemed to pass before the wagon was finally emptied. The two returned to his side, lifted him in the same manner as before, and hastily conveyed him down a circular, stone staircase. The passage was dimly lit, despite the blazing torches fixed along the stone walls. Jason knew not where they were taking him, but by the change in temperature, he knew they were underground. A damp, musty odor blossomed as the temperature continued to drop. The three descended into the depths of the fortress, going round and round, passing through multiple underground layers before stopping at a cold landing immured somewhere in the depths of the earth. The mephitic smell of death and despair filled the air.

"Welcome to the dungeon, mate," muttered the shorter Larry as the taller Bill snickered. "Most who make it down here never see the light of day again. Most don't live too long down in these parts, 'specially in the wing ye are to rest." The two stood momentarily still, relishing the sense of dread they had gifted Jason. "Necromancy has no place in these parts. A pansy like yourself shouldn't last long down here. What do ye say? Think he'll last a fortnight?"

"Nay. Less, I'd say."

Resonating sounds of rancor and agony echoed throughout the stone sepulture, causing Jason an evident degree of emotional turmoil and directional disorientation. His heart raced and his skin became clammy as the world began to spin. They continued onward, hurriedly proceeding down a series of narrow passages in a maze of directions, the widths and heights varying, making turn after disorientating turn through the odious, dank miasma. Larry and Bill clearly had a strong sense of direction and were well acquainted with the labyrinthine passageways;

there was no hesitation in their step and they moved as one.

They stopped abruptly in an exceptionally bleak area of the maze, directly in front of a haggard, gray-haired, and bearded elderly man. To Jason's eyes, the man appeared to be near ninety. He stood beside the open door of a stone room, empty apart from a sole bench and small oil lamp. The number 134 was painted above the cell door, struck through in red. At the slight nod given by the old man, Larry and Bill walked Jason into the cell, deposited him on the bench, and finally cut him loose from his ties. They departed without another word, closing the thick, wooden door behind them with a resounding thud. Jason could hear a board latching over the outside of the door, locking him inside. Alone. The room was silent. Jason was at a loss—for words, for a plan, for hope.

A wicket gate hidden in the door slapped open. The old man was darkened in shadow and obscured behind the lattice of the window.

"I shall explain to thee how it works in my dungeon. Rest assured, I'm sure you will find life here miserable enough by any standard, but if there is anything we can do to aid in your repulsion, please just ask. I shall be your turnkey. As pronounced by the gracious and omnipotent King Arthur, you are hereby sentenced for the remainder of your pitiable life to imprisonment with all the expected privations. Never to see the lantern of day for as long as ye shall live, which really won't be too long since the life expectancy in these dungeons is poor, what with all the dysentery and distemper. With that, I'll not lead thee along with some mushy, emotional diatribe. There are rules to follow, just like in any dungeon. There is a bucket in the corner in which you are to relieve yourself. Pickup is at three. The bucket is to be left directly at this door. If no bucket, no pickup. I couldn't care less whether your bucket is emptied, as a full bucket will only aid in your repulsion. You will have bucket duty one day per week. One measly and nutritionally unsound meal shall be served daily around seven in the morning, whatever is left after feeding His Majesty's animals combined with refuse from the dining room. Oil for the lamp is given at seven in the evening, and only if the lamp is at the doorway, perched aside the gate. The fire striker, granite, and silk are aside the lamp. You shall have to find thine own bowls and utensils, as the feast above us has used our last."

"Sir, I do not mean to seem indignant, but there really must be some sort of mix-up or mistake. I am supposed to speak with Merlin. When we last spoke, he mentioned heading to a castle, at which time I was to speak with him at a feast. I would suppose myself to be more of an honored guest than a prisoner. If I were you, I would go and ask. I expect him to be a bit upset when he becomes aware of this mix-up."

"Ha!" The old man laughed aloud. "You, at the feast, now that would be a sight! A prisoner at the feast! They all say they're innocent. Fetch King Arthur, get Merlin, Sir Lancelot, and the list goes on. If I were to listen to every poor sod who is immured in King Arthur's dungeons, I would do nothing more than run up and down the steps all day. I'd have no knees to speak of, my bones of thirty-five years would be beaten down, if they're not so already. The damp air is horrid for my rheumatism."

"Thirty-five years? Do you mean to tell me you are only thirty-five years of age?"

"Fodder in the evening if you are quiet and compliant, and sometimes we can sneak a paltry of viands if you're a good lad and keep from making a ruckus. Otherwise, you'll get the usual slop in the morning. Artifices and false pretenses serve no purpose. It behooves you to listen to me, as I am the only person thou shall hear from for the rest of thine miserable life. If you're lucky, thou may just die really really soon. Some of my prisoners seem to live on and on down here. They're truly the unlucky ones."

Jason interrupted his rambling. "But sir, doesn't it matter that I am not supposed to be in this predicament?"

"King Arthur's dungeon is not for the faint of heart, young lad." The old man turned his face away from Jason in a look of acknowledgment. "Oh dear, another customer today." The wicket door slapped shut as dreadful groans and lamentations were echoed from elsewhere in the dungeon. The man's footsteps and voice trailed off. "Sir Gawain, what brings you to these parts when such reverie is practiced above?"

Jason sat on the stone bench along the wall and thought.

"That's odd. How did this get here?" Jason's black, lucky towel was folded in a neat rectangle and laid upon the stone bench. He then lay down for what seemed like hours as his oil lamp extinguished, darkness filled the room, and his mind and soul drifted into some oneiric phantasm.

# CHAPTER 24

## A MEETING

*Saturday, October 28, 1972*

While the physical characteristics of The Change were not welcomed by most, Melvin was quick to learn that not all changes were disadvantageous. It was account of The Change that his alter ego, Saul, had found his intuitive faculties; his ability to determine friend from foe was especially sharp. It was with the use of this new-found, inexplicable perspicacity that he uncovered Dr. Atwood's mendacious ruse. Having deduced her self-aggrandizing plans and discovered her use of a codex, he was quick to make plans of his own. It was of no real surprise to him that she took the opportunity to act after having found her goal. Perhaps he had expected her to hang around for a bit, maybe lead him along, but ultimately act in her own self-interest. He had upheld his integrity, but she, as expected, had failed to keep her part of their bargain. All along, Saul's plan was to give her leeway and let her show her hand, to give her enough rope to hang herself. Now, unbeknownst to her, he had the means to remain quick on her heels.

His craft as an actor in this role was no less than Oscar-worthy. He had nimbly played her like a fiddle. Using her knowledge of the past liberties taken upon him by the former leader, coupled with the stresses of family discord and a deceased wife, it was no surprise that he had separated himself into multiple personalities, some of which were weak with vulnerabilities that could easily be manipulated. Textbook psychosis was used to drown a portion of his doleful existence. It was upon his characterization of Saul, the wronged, comburent English thespian who sought power and revenge, that Patricia wholeheartedly believed she saw a manipulative path emerge toward reaching her goals. Oh, hate was such an easy emotion to portray. There had been many moments when Saul had sought ingratiation with the good doctor, so he would denounce his own self Melvin with violent castigations or mistreatments, ranging from depraved indifference or even so far as bodily harm, prompting Dr. Atwood to intervene on Melvin's behalf. The episodes were originally feigned, but lately, he had delved so disturbingly deep into his character that he was at times unable to escape. Saul's mastery of this alter ego and his emotions were growing less predictable and prone to spontaneous eruptions.

It was under such capricious circumstances that Saul, knowing Dr. Atwood's altruism to be a ruse, thought it best to have some insurance. He sought to create an exact replica of the key found at the airport, knowing it to be of vital importance given her persistent inquiry of its existence. He knew that in her indefatigable pursuit of its usefulness, she would lead him right to the secrets it unlocked. He would maintain his ruse, just as she maintained hers. With the help of the sole locksmith on the island, his wife's former assistant Mo, the key relinquished to her at their recent rendezvous was actually a precise replica.

But to exploit his position, Saul was careful to keep Melvin in the dark. His alter ego was not aware of the plan or allowed to take part in any decisions or stratagems. But was his reliance on Mo a vulnerability? It was a difficult situation. He needed Mo. After all, he was the only being on the island who could create the replica. But did Mo know more than he let on, or could he perhaps be a double agent? Had he been tight-lipped about the key's twin? Saul was explicit in the need for secrecy.

But what about An? An was Melvin's oldest son, though they had been estranged for quite some time. An and Mo were best friends, so what role did his son play? Why were the two on the southern end of the island? How could they know of this library when he had been ceaselessly searching for its whereabouts? The two swore to have never set foot in this place, but were they lying? They had supposedly come upon the temple in their pursuit of the youth and nothing else. Saul had determined that much was likely true, as his son was never a deceitful individual, and Mo had always been a pushover. And so, the two were carried down and bound on floor 1969, far enough out of earshot to have a private conversation. He needed to know if they were telling the truth. He was certain of one thing: if Atwood knew that he knew, all would be in vain.

Saul descended the last of the steps, staff in hand, onto floor 1969. He stepped over the floor's clutter and stood before two warthogs clad in Roman battle gear, who in turn stood at attention aside their charges. Both An and Mo had reverted back to their lizard and moth forms. They were bound and placed atop two chairs created by artist Allen Jones that were molded to resemble provocatively dressed and oddly positioned women. Next to the chairs stood a gleaming, white astronaut's suit; the lot of five were minuscule in the immensely large room packed full of 1969 memorabilia.

Saul commanded, "You two—leave now. I'll question these trespassers alone. There are tasks for you above. Find Bill and Larry. Chop, chop. Meet Lionel at the temple base."

"Yes, sir." The two fat beasts bowed obsequiously, knocking over countless items in their hurried rush to the stairwell.

From the floor above, someone had turned up the volume on the phonograph. Chicago's "Does Anybody Really Know What Time It Is?" drifted down the staircase, followed by a loud crash.

"Oh brother, what could they be into now?" Saul was at his wits' end with his followers' behavior.

Saul stood before An and Mo, weighing his options. He was willing to loosen their fetters, but not yet willing to release them.

No one seemed to notice the slight motion of one of the astronaut's arms.

Saul paced before the two as indecision plagued his mind. The most pressing issue was how to keep Mo quiet about the key. Had Mo already divulged their secret to An? How would he explain how he came to find the library? If they had passed the information along, how could he contain the damage? There was just too much to explain—his personalities, the situation, their confinement. Would they believe him to be insane? Over the years, he had let a large chasm develop between him and his son, a subject that he truly wanted to broach. He often pushed himself toward making amends, but instead, he found himself procrastinating while more time passed and the two drifted farther apart. In light of the circumstances, he knew that this might not be the proper time for full disclosure. Who knew how his son would act or

493

where the admission would lead? It was important that Melvin weighed Saul's reaction too? Not violent, he hoped. His disquietude and reticence to let harm come to the two made his next move difficult. As a parent, he could not leave An to the whim of the Westbankers.

It was as if thousands of voices in his head were arguing concurrently. To limit any prying ears, he put The Archies' "Sugar, Sugar" on the phonograph. He knew the charade with the plebeians upstairs needed to remain solid.

Using his most proper English accent, he spoke above the competing music. "I beseech you to trust my discretion for your safety and mine. My new identity must remain secret."

"Just who do you think you are, Dad?" An was acutely disinterested in the entirety of his circumstances and sought only to be released. "I will be filing suit the moment I am released. The civil damages will be enormous, much more so than the criminal penalties. Release us both this moment!"

"Hush. If we can agree on a few points, you may be released shortly. If there is any consolation, the buffoons above share your ignorance of certain matters, but with my one word, they'd crush your skull into . . ." His mental conflict was instantaneously evident as personalities collided and he began to argue with himself, grabbing his head. "What do you mean new identity? I'm here for you, son! No one's going to be crushing any skulls!" He thrust himself down upon a knee with his hands together as if pleading with his own mind. He was clearly struggling with inner turmoil. He uncontrollably flitted between Saul and Melvin, each fighting for control. It was wild to watch. "You're not here for them, Saul. You're here for yourself! Get up, you pathetic fool!" He rose to his feet. "Leave, you're not welcome here. Can it, Melvin! You're not to take part in this conversation. How dare you show up now, after all my hard work, only to try to expiate for years missed because you were too busy working. I demand your silence. The two will remain . . . but they need to know!"

Slapping himself hard across the face, he knocked himself backward and onto his knees. An and Mo stared with looks of confused stupefaction and shock. An's father shook his limbs and gathered his composure before nonchalantly rising to dust himself off. An and Mo were speechless.

Saul straightened his cloak, righted his ruffled sleeves, and cleared his throat. "Pardon that rather rude interruption and lack of introduction. I am Saul. Having banished our unwanted guest, we can now have a meaningful discourse." Although repressed, a portion of Melvin persevered, his filial affection evident as he used his cloak to clean a smudge from An's cheek.

An, indignant at being dragooned and immured, was in no mood, a scowl written across his face. In the span of only a few hours, he had lost his precious book, sunken a stolen gondola, would likely forfeit any hopes of becoming a gondolier, and would miss the date with his family at six. He was uncomfortable, tired, and hungry. He was not one to be cowed. He barked, "Trust? It's easy for you to stay hidden behind a few hoodwinked Westbankers with more muscles than brains. Like I told your men upstairs, let me and my friend go and maybe I won't kick all of your asses. You are obviously not aware of who you are dealing with. And what sort of sicko made these chairs? Probably you, you weirdo!"

An looked around at his unusual surroundings. "And you say this is a library? Mo, please tell me that this is not where you and my mother worked! Tell me that you and my mother did not cavort with the sick individual who stands before us. Now that I think about it, Mo, keep quiet. Don't say a word to this desperado and his group of brigands. I'll have you know, whoever you are, that I am voicing a formal complaint with the council. There will be a formal grievance. My father is the president, and you will pay dearly for keeping us captive. This is criminal! First attempted murder and then kidnapping. I hope your turnkey is a mean one! And now to find that this Dix character has ditched us. Boy, was I a sucker!"

Saul commanded, "Hush, you fool. You're nothing more than a loudmouth! Always a loudmouth!"

"I don't care what you want or if anyone else can hear me! We are trapped! Mo, don't trust this hooded pirate. I'll tell you something, sinister mister, we cannot be hoodwinked! We're not saying a word without our legal representation. I deserve a phone call! I want an attorney! Help! Police! Call 911!"

"Hush, I say! Hush! You will draw unnecessary attention. Do you realize what those beasts upstairs will do to you if they are driven into a frenzy? My god, son, they're Westbankers!"

"Son? You have no right to call me that. Help! Fetch me my shears, Mo. We must fend for ourselves. I've been disarmed!"

Saul was undeterred and back in full character. "You really have all the nerve. Why don't you just keep quiet! That's right, shut the heck up, you ninnyhammer! I've had enough of you, Trevor. I'm going to let you in on a little secret: you're not my progeny! Surprised? Trevor Linstein!" His voice evinced his frustrations and his fists were clenched. "Do not make me raise my voice again. Linstein, that's right, you heard me correctly. You're not my son, never were. Linstein, Linstein, Linstein! Did you ever wonder why you despised Westbank pork?" Saul was working himself up into a frenzy. "I've finally gotten it off my chest after all these years! Do you know how long it took me to get to this point? She cheated on me with that dandy, Merl. He was nothing but a foreigner, a textile worker. When will you get it through your thick skull that this is not about you! Me this, me that, me this! Me me me me me me. Stop being so damn deucedly selfish! It was always that way with you kids, but you were the worst. What a standout you are!" Saul began clapping. "Congratulations! You have always been a stain on my reputation. Imagine walking into work each day, day in and day out, under the piteous gaze of others who all knew that there was a bastard child in my care. I was the talk of the town for years. But what did I do? I endured. I fed you, I clothed you, I raised you, but never once received a 'thank you.' Not once! When you got older, you still were never satisfied. 'Give me this, get me that.' It was never enough for you. A different gene pool no doubt accounts for the difference between us. I am strong; you are weak. I work for what I want; you demand handouts. I care about others; you care only for yourself."

Saul was an unrestrained ball of energy, pacing the floor like a madman. "So we moved on. So I moved on. Do you remember your mother, bless her soul, and I working multiple jobs? It was to provide food for the table. Not once can I remember a 'thank you' spoken from your lips, not once an affirmation or gratitude. Instead, you sought a wanton abandonment of hard work. And then along comes Vidal Sassoon. Hair coloring? Really? You followed him around like a doting fool. Why not get a real job? Did you know that your social standing dropped so low that the neighbors thought you moved to the

Westbank? After your departure, our acquaintances thought our family was a bunch of losers. At least Mo here has a reputable occupation; he can make keys, an honest trade. Melvin, butt out. I command you to stay out of this!"

Mo spoke up. "Umm, excuse me, Mr. Saul. Mo here. Please let Mr. Melvin know we said hello. We've had the most curious day. It's been a real doozy!"

An's face morphed from disbelief into contemptuous hatred upon his realization of his father's charade. "Melvin —I'll never use the word Dad—you're nothing but a hypocrite! You know that's not the way it happened. Do you really think I didn't know about mom and you-know-who? Here we go with the same misplaced rage, again and again. This isn't about me. Once again, you're blaming me for the death of my mother in a roundabout way. Why blame me? I had nothing to do with her choice to work in the library. I had nothing to do with The Change. I had nothing to do with her affair. I didn't ask to be a product of it. I didn't ask for any of this. You're not angry with me—you're angry with yourself and with her." An twisted his head, stretching the neck of his shirt as if to get more air. "Things have escalated, haven't they? Now you've gotten yourself into a big mess. Why are you here? How long have you known about this place?"

Saul remained quiet as a tear welled up in the corner of his eye. His discombobulated and crazed personality was

499

temporarily placid. An awkward moment of silence enveloped the three. Melvin was trying to surface.

"I'm sorry, son, but I have to go." Saul began shaking his head, trying to loosen some imaginary hold. "Out, out, out!"

An turned to Mo. "Are you one of them too? Old friend, please tell me you didn't know about this? Are you an enabler? How long has my father known about this library? Why would you, my best friend, keep me in the dark?"

Saul's diction became more sinister and furibund. "Enough! Keep your voice down. There'll be no more talk or there'll be deuced heck to pay. Where is Jason Dix? Your refusal to answer will be treated as treason. I swear, under threat of violence, there will be no mention of Melvin ever again. There is no time for such an underling. I will not tolerate a berating from the likes of you!" Saul was working himself up into a frenzy. "Perhaps it's time you know the truth. Let us dispel all rumors."

His face contorted as his left hand tried to grab hold of his own throat, something inside fighting to break free. "Melvin, again? Don't tell him. Must . . . Not . . . What are you doing here? Get out, get out! Shut up, you insolent fool! Must . . . protect . . . Trevor . . ." Saul grappled with himself. "You'll never triumph; you are too weak! Ever since the death of my beloved Chamé. Oh, how I loved you, Chamé! Melvin, you are responsible for her death. How could you not stand up for us, letting Merl get between us? Trevor, my son, what more do I need to do to convince you?"

A tear welled up and rolled down An's cheek. "Dad, take it off. Take off the hood. I am aware of my mother's past romps, but I had no idea . . . Remove these fetters so that I can help!"

"Plurality? Oh, deuced me! Oh, what a noble mind is here o'erthrown!— The courtier's, soldier's, scholar's, eye, tongue, sword . . ." Saul was gesticulating grandly, in the midst of a performance.

An could see that his father, the man who raised him, needed help. "I've always had you to cling to, to count on. I never loved you any less. You were always my support, but mother's indiscretion caused you to always think less of me. You've never let that feeling go, and you even cast it upon my wife. Lacey and I were both made to feel like outcasts. Sure, we chose to not work at the post office, or as police officers or fire fighters. But the world needs hair stylists, too! A fine haircut is important, and we were excited to build something of our own. So Dad, what is all of this about? If you need help, we're here for you. You've had an emotional breakdown and you're not thinking clearly. What is family for if not for help when it's needed?"

Saul's arms and torso convulsed like an animal shaking off water. He composed himself and cleared his throat, looking directly at Mo as his personality shifted again. "Melvin is now subordinate, unimportant, not in control, irrelevant, and unwanted. Trevor, I no longer need your help as you are immaterial to me. What are you saying, you fool? You do need him!" He was back at it again, working himself into a frenzy. "Sorry? What are you, a weakling? You fool, he is your son! Melvin, get out! This personality suits us well in times of need. A true leader wins at all costs, and all of my assiduous efforts are directed at success. Melvin will always be too weak to be of assistance. Be gone. Melvin, get out!

"Mo, thank you again for helping with the precise duplication of the key. The supposititious key was successfully used only moments ago to activate the library elevator. It might be useful to you in the future should the library ever reopen, though I suppose the council's decision about the library repair is distant and the key's utility is likely grander than a simple means to call upon the elevator. Perhaps I will have you make many more, now that my plans have been made transparent."

"Mo, what have you done? He's off his rocker."

"I have no further time for either of you. You are to be bound tightly and held until further notice. I expect an immediate and concise explanation of your knowledge of this library and temple. Have you shared your knowledge with anyone? You'll also need to share every little oddity, fact, and tidbit that could lead me to locating Jason Dix. Patricia will need him in her pursuits, but I know not what his presence will bring, so I need to find him first. He is somehow a key, an integral part of . . ."

Mo said, "Umm, I do not mean to interrupt, Mr. Saul, but can we ask for a few points of clarification? Maybe An is, but I'm not quite following you. Are you implying that Jason is a metaphorical key to some puzzle? Or a cipher of some type?" Mo squirmed in his seat, uncomfortable and eager to talk his way out of his binds.

If the three had been more astute, they would have noticed the astronaut suit's hand slowly rising to its visor.

An tried to rationalize the situation. "But you never venture outside your home or the airport. How long have you been leading this Westbank band of brigands in this hidden lair?" An looked as if he had swallowed a healthy dose of realization. "Wait! Jason Dix works for you, but he ripped you off and now you're looking for him, trying to recover your loot!"

"If you're asking how we met Jason Dix, it all started this morning after An gave me the most extraordinary haircut. See?" Mo turned his head side to side to show off the cut. "Now I have the most finely coiffed hair. An has quite the knack. Well anyway, then we traveled to the Grand

Cenote, where An was scheduled to take *la prova del remo*."

"A gondolier? My son, are you really . . ." Saul ripped off his hood and stared at An with reverence.

"Would you have cared? No! You wouldn't!" An's remonstrance was loud as The Archies' next song, "Bicycles, Roller Skates, and You" began.

"Mr. Saul or Mr. Melvin, he'll be a great gondolier. His voice is like an angel. His use of the forcola is exquisite. But I have not finished my story. Lo and behold, we went to the examination a day early!" Mo described their walk and his delivery grew faster as his explanation speedily progressed. "You know how punctual Lacey can be, but this time, she had the date of the examination incorrect. We didn't want to just turn around and go home, only to sit indoors and play checkers or chess with the storm coming. I mean, we had already paid to get in, so we thought it would be smart to make the most of our time. So An decided . . ."

"No, *we* decided, Mo. I'm not going to take all the heat for swiping a gondola."

"OK, *we* decided to take a gondola out for some practice, but before long, we found ourselves lost in the most beautiful of caverns. All of a sudden, the sirens began wailing and our gondola was swept by the rising tide. An saved our lives with his masterful control of the gondola; he pushed the craft into the safety of a passageway and inadvertently into the southern portion of the island. Then An made me go into a dark room where that biter, Jason Dix, attacked us and stole An's satchel! We had seen him in the paper this morning, so we knew he was dangerous, but we just had to get that satchel back. So we chased him down this long tunnel to the temple. We would have caught Jason, but Bill, you know the oaf who works at the airport selling ice cream, smashed through the roof of the cavern and tried to sink our boat and drown me. Had it not been for Jason Dix diving into the water to save me from drowning, I would not be here with you now. I guess he's not all bad. An, maybe he's a good pirate."

"A pirate?" Saul looked perplexed.

"But anyway, it was your son who saved the day. He bravely climbed to the precipice of this enormous temple, dodged arrows shot by warthogs clad in Roman battle gear, and restarted the clock. Jason used a key that he had around his neck, exactly like the one you had me copy, to start the elevator and transport us to the year 2017. I de-ciphered a code, something about the Dark Ages, and then we came back and were captured. The end. By the way, where is Jason?"

Saul and An both silently stared at Mo, trying to process the tremendous amount of information he had just spewed.

"My son, a gondolier? Saving you from a flood? Dodging arrows? Impossible." Melvin returned. "Not Trevor."

Suddenly, the visor of the astronaut helmet flipped open, revealing a man whose face was brightly painted. The unannounced interruption was a bit startling. "Pardon the interruption, but it's important. I realize that you're in the midst of having a heart-to-heart with your son, but may I have a word with you three? It's been a long day, heck, a long fifty-seven years since The Change. You won't believe the measures I've taken to make sure I wasn't followed.

"Now, I'm not one to pry into family matters, but rest assured Trevor and Melvin, Chamé is safe and sound. Her future is long. This whole change has been a necessary misunderstanding. It was truly only meant to last for a few hours, not years. I've been waiting for ages for the right time to interject, and now with all of you together . . ."

All three mouths were agape.

"Well, say something! Trevor and Mo, you know about the elevator, the school, and the bathroom. And let's not forget the golden key. Your son, sir, the taller one with dark locks before The Change, is a crooner, right? And Mo, I understand that you are particularly quick-witted and good with ciphers. My son, for instance, also has a

506

golden key, but he's stuck in the Dark Ages. You broke the cipher."

Like a wave crashing to shore, all three suddenly realized who the man was: the one and only Alfred Dix. Saul instantly became violent. "It is you! It is you! I've seen pictures. How did I not recognize you immediately? Boys, it's him! Your face was plastered in the post office, on billboards. You are none other but the evasive Beau Champs, universally despised on our island. You are the one responsible for The Change. Have you been living here on our island this entire time? You are the cause of our inconsequential life!" Saul mightily swung his staff in Beau's direction, but the suit deflected his attack and Saul stumbled off balance. He righted himself and prepared to swing again. "For my son, for my wife, for the island!" He swung as Alfred parried using the astronaut suit's arm to counter the blow.

Saul was out for blood. "How dare you have the nerve— hiding for years only to reveal yourself when the island is again in a vulnerable position! How long has it been, twelve long years? Are you working with her? Was it under your direction that she sought to delude our people?"

The Archies' harmonious, hypnotic rhythm continued in competition with Chicago upstairs.

*Every day I wake up with a happy smile on my face*

507

*'Cause I'm so glad to be a member of the human race*

*I ain't got a dime*

*But I'm the richest guy you'd ever find*

*'Cause I've got bicycles, roller skates, and you*

"Let it out. C'mon, swing away! Hit me if it'll make you feel better. None of you islanders stood up for us immigrant textile workers. You all turned a blind eye to our exploitation. What if I told you that I'm out to capture a really bad man? Would you be interested in helping me? It'll protect all of humanity, and not only will all of you be reverted to your former selves, but it'll also get us off this godforsaken island. Right now, you need me as much as I need the three of you. You two happen to be my son's best friends in high school, and the woman you refer to as Dr. Atwood is our mutual . . ."

Saul continued his pejorative upbraiding. "Are you a fool? Have you no conscience or soul? You did this to me! You did this to them! Need us? You must take me for a fool! And where is Merl, your buddy? You two were never far apart. Where is he hiding?" He swung again and Alfred deflected his strike. "Don't belittle me by confirming his absence. I did not stand to face him twelve years ago, but you can be sure that I will meet him now!"

Melvin fought to persuade himself, "Saul, perhaps we should listen. He says he is here to help. Go on, she is our mutual what?"

"Your son is telling you the truth. What I did in 1960 was necessary and unavoidable, for matters far greater than your understanding. None of this will change what the future is to bring for either of you. I can attest that I've seen you all there. I'll prove it to you in time, but for god's sake, quit swinging the stick! I'm going to throw down this arm." He let the broken arm of the suit slide off and fall to the floor. "I know it has been painful, but trust me, there was no other way. I just needed him to resurface, your former leader: Cyrus Bauman. I'll seek your forgiveness when this is all done, but for now, I either need your help or for you to stay out of my way."

Saul began slowly circling, a lizard taunting his prey. From somewhere in the back of his mind, Saul could hear Dr. Atwood's voice saying, "Melvin, you are nothing but a gullible fool."

"Pops, it's OK," An said. "We have met his son and we've seen it for ourselves. Boy, that was weird."

"Look, you need me much more than I need you. Now that you are privy to our little secret, you're a part of this whole twisted reality whether you like it or not. Trevor and Mo just traveled in time using a key, right? One that just happened to be the same type you created for

Melvin. Boys, think back to 2017 and the note on the bathroom mirror. That was me—what did I write?"

Mo said, "It was written in lipstick on the bathroom mirror. It said, 'Stay Home. It's a trap.'"

"It's not as if we would dissemble your true motive then or now. Perhaps your ruse, their perception, is a simple trick of theater." Saul was skeptical.

Alfred tried to reason with him. "As hard as it is to believe, you and I are simultaneously stationed in both 1972 and 2017. So is she. Your foe cannot be Dr. Atwood. Where is she now?"

Saul raised his staff, ready to strike, when Alfred blurted out, "With or without you, I'm going to capture Cyrus Bauman, the island's former leader. Your help will make it easier."

A thundering voice was heard from above. "Sir, do you need our help down there? Sir? Sir?" A group of four Westbankers made a tremendous ruckus as they inched down the stairs.

Saul bellowed, "Leave us! Or face my wrath!" Saul pointed to the group, causing three of the warthogs to make an about-face in unison and hustle back up the stairs.

Unfortunately, his churlish outcry failed to stop the largest warrior, who was hard of hearing. The beast bounded down the stairs anyway. "Saul, sir? An urgent matter was just brought to my attention! You asked that we alert you to any matter that is askew, and boy is this ever askew. A man who calls himself Cyrus Bauman just stepped off the elevator and has requested to speak with your son. He asked me to convey the message to you directly. The deranged man stated that he has come from the future, if you can believe it, from New Orleans, and that you two knew one another. Personally, I think he's crazed. I don't trust his eyes, sir. Get this, he had the nerve to tell me that the lives of everyone on our island depends on it, and that our president is listening to the wrong person. Melvin listening? Nuts, right! Ha! That fool listens to no one! Well, in any case, we threw a sack over his head and *poof*, he disappeared."

Suddenly a look of surprise crossed his face. "Wait a minute. You . . . you look exactly like Melvin! What the heck?" He noted the hooded robe on the ground. "Have we been bamboozled into listening to *you* this entire time? Just wait until I tell the troops!"

"No, wait! I command you!"

But the warthog couldn't hear him and he hastily ran back up the stairs. The Archies' record jumped to the next song, a jumbled din with Chicago competing upstairs.

511

*You little angel, you*

*You got me feeling like I never felt before*

*You got me feeling like I'm right at heaven's door*

*And I love this feeling so*

The beast could be heard yelling, "Guys! Guys! You're not going to believe this! Guys . . ."

"How does migrating to the year 2000 sound to you? Yes?" Mo and Melvin nodded inquisitively, but An envisioned Lacey and Roden alone and waiting. "What about our plans, Mo? Knee Deep? Lacey and Roden? I'm supposed to meet them at six."

"When the time is right, I promise you will be reacquainted with your loved ones and the island's Change will cease to exist. All of our fates are intertwined in many ways. For now, the entire island believes that you are deceased, killed in an unfortunate subterranean mishap." Beau withdrew the front page of *The Island Daily Times* from his pocket. A photograph showed An and Mo, eyes bugged out of their sockets and mouths open wide in a terrified scream. "The cameras in the tunnel captured you just as the tidal surge struck." Mo and An examined the picture, awestruck.

"Men, there's no better time than the present to depart. We have a criminal to catch, if he hasn't already been

alerted to our plans. Make haste! Untie those two and follow me to the elevator. I'll explain on the way. You'll
soon forget much of what has happened or will happen to
you, but we'll get to that later. Rest assured that all will
be made right."

# CHAPTER 25

## MERL'S INTRODUCTION

*499 AD*

*Scratch, scratch, scratch.*

"Who is it? Who's there?" Jason whispered as he startled awake. His corporeal fetters drew his mind back to reality as his dream evaporated, the darkness both blinding and disorientating. His voice and breath reverberated with echoes across the cold, stone walls in the room that might as well be his sepulture. He was reminded of his miserable situation: cold, hungry, and alone, uncomfortable atop a stone bench, and now that the lamp had extinguished and the room was cast in total darkness, effectively blinded. The towel had gone from a meager pillow to serving as a paltry blanket across his midsection. Was he hallucinating? Had he heard noises or was his imagination running rampant? The scratching resumed, so Jason rose up from his elbows to a seated position, rubbed the sleep from his eyes, and scooted his backside against the wall. In the utter darkness, his pulse pounded rapidly in his ears.

Perhaps a hungry specter or apparition of the night was clawing its way through the nooks and crannies of the cell wall, trying to get to his young flesh, he no more than prey in the cosmological evolutionary chain. Or could this be a mere dream within a dream? Frightened, he instinctively pulled all of his appendages closer and balled up on the bench, remaining silent and motionless. He hoped that whatever was making the noises would pass and that his appendages would not be so appealing to their nocturnal foraging, waiting on edge for any nip or bite from a sentient being of the night, ready to swat or fight if the need arose. He could imagine the horrific creatures lurking in the dark depths of the dungeon, ready to eagerly feast on his delectable, tender, virgin flesh.

It took quite a bit of time before he let his guard down. Eventually, his heart rate slowed, he no longer heard his pulse pounding, and he relaxed the grip of his towel and shins. Countless questions churned through his mind: *How am I to see? Without windows or any access to the outside, how will I know anything at all? Why am I imprisoned? What have I done wrong? How am I to get home, and now without a key? I'll never survive. Why on earth did Dad suggest I come here?* With nothing to do but think, thoughts about the day convulsed every which way in his head. The only rational conclusion was that he should have listened to his father and stayed put. This all had to be a dream, but still, the irrationality of it all prevailed: the lady on his television, the flight, the airport vendor, the gravity-defying lizard, the animals in baggage claim, the diner, the drain, the two creatures and the elevator, his pain in the wagon, and his miserable conditions at present. The darkness only added to his uneasiness.

Longing for company, he began talking to himself. "It just has to be a dream! But no, it cannot be. This darkness—shouldn't I be able to open my eyes?" He opened his eyes. It was pitch black.

In the morning, he would surely find himself at home on the sofa or in his bed. Maybe he even clumsily fell off the couch onto the cold, hard floor, hence, the cold, hard bench. Maybe the power went off; that's it, the storm! That would explain the darkness. Father should be home soon, and he would be shaking him awake any moment. Jason would just wait to be awoken, which shouldn't take long.

With so many befuddling circumstances, Jason was sure of only one thing: from now on, he would relish the boredom of staying home for the break. He may even go so far as to work on the backyard project with the construction crew. Anything would be better than the abject misery of this perpetual dream. That is, if it were a dream. How could he wake himself?

"I know!" He slapped himself hard across the face. "Ouch!" The strike failed to change his circumstances.

And so Jason laid back down, anticipating that all would be OK after a hard slumber. However, the night was again interrupted by further scratching. It didn't quite sound like the rummaging of rodents or four-footed creatures of the night, which at least assuaged his fear of being the recipient of a bite. The noises sounded more purposeful, like digging. The scratching and picking escalated, becoming louder and louder, reverberating off the walls of the stone chamber until they were so loud that Jason had to plug his ears with his fingers. Was it someone in the adjacent cell? He imagined himself to be Edmond Dantès in *The Count of Monte Cristo*, imprisoned in the Château d'If as Abbé Faria came popping through the wall. Time would tell.

Just as the noises crescendoed and deep reverberations pounded the room, it fell into instantaneous silence. After a brief pause, the light scratching began again, followed by silence, then the scratching that continued for some time. Eventually, the scratching was accompanied by a faint light and the words "gjbfwj xnw lfbfns yjqq st tsj" inumbrated on the cell floor. The light grew more luminous, the words elongating as the light extended to reach the middle of the room.

Quickly, he careened his head under the bench and then rolled down onto the floor on his hands and knees, wanting to know the source of the luminance, to observe and listen, and to catch a glimpse or whisper of the perpetrator who was sketching the message in the dust under the bench. He scratched his head and thought about the cipher for only a minute before the message became apparent. "It's simple. Easy one! It must be you, Dad. Who is it on the other side of the wall? Who else would use a cipher?" He was met with nothing but more silence.

"Dad? Dad? Whoever it is, my name is Jason Dix and I am being held captive in this dungeon! I don't care if it's Dad, An, Mo, Zach, or Bobby, but whoever you are, stop playing around. Please get me the heck out of here! If this is a dream or a hallucination, I command you to come in here, float through the wall. Do whatever you need to do to either wake me or convince me."

The scratching stopped and the light simultaneously extinguished, drawing the room into total darkness. More desperate than ever, Jason began vehemently screaming, "C'mon, I'm just a harmless kid! You didn't need to stop digging. Break through the wall! Seriously, I need some help getting out of here. There's no reason to turn out the light and disappear. If you have any conscience at all, you would help me. I'm down in this dungeon against my will. Who knows what they will do to me? Send anyone for help! HELP! Please!"

As the last words were spoken into the darkness, he heard the quick shuffle of footsteps outside his cell door. The wicket door was hastily unlatched in a rapid and violent nature. Whoever was on the other side of the door was obviously irate.

*Someone is outside. It must be the jailer. He must have spoken with Merlin and is coming for me!* Jason leaped to his feet just as the wicket door slapped open.

The open portico revealed the hoary, irate face with a long, unkempt beard and deep wrinkles of the elderly jailer, shadowed in candlelight. His gray hair was tousled and discombobulated and stuffed into his woolen night-cap, which bespoke a rapid awakening from sleep. With a frown upon his vitriolic face even more accentuated by his furrowed brows, he looked far older than his purport-ed thirties.

Jason's keeper frustratingly pointed to a pocket watch (a surprising replica of his father's) that he held in his free hand. He began a mordant berating. "Hast you no shame, waking a turnkey of my age with such a ruckus? You are no different from the other youths, staying awake for all hours of the night. Beseeching help from me as if I were thy varlet. I am frankly appalled at such poor manners, especially in someone so new. Rather loud impertinences, I'll say! What could you possibly be undertaking at this hour? Jason Dix of chamber number 134, an incipient, dreadful malady has taken root in your soul. Thou doth not hast long to live before thine eternal silence. At least then I'll have a night of sleep. Or was this outburst simply disguised as an effort for your weak constitution, nothing more than an infantile entreaty for sustenance or life's accoutrements at the most unfortunate of hours? Could it be feral distemper? It takes most other guests days and nights alone to go cuckoo, but you may just be a weak sissy!"

Jason didn't particularly want to take such a shellacking, but since the turnkey had the upper hand, Jason thought it best to ingratiate himself to his morose keeper. Locked away, he was at his mercy.

He took a moment to gather a modest degree of equanimity before politely responding in his most pleasant and humble voice, annunciating carefully so as to be understood. He grabbed hold of the wicket bars to stand close.

"Pardon me, kind sir, but I had a hard time understanding your eloquent speech. You see, I am feeling quite unhealthy. I know the whole situation may seem rather extraordinary, that is, my screaming at night, but there is a medical reason. I truly did not mean to disturb anyone, most notably you, honorable sir. I am cold, scared, and rather hungry. I could use a bit of food. If there is any food, I would be most appreciative. I haven't eaten in two long days, unless you count a cola on the plane and a bite of toast at the diner, though I'm not even sure if that was real. Anything would do. Also, I need light."

The old man was dismissive, but he stepped back and appeared to be thinking. "There'll be no food until the appointed hour. Peradventure you are a necromancer, would you be speaking to the apparitions of the night? Are you as they say? Are you confessing?"

"Yes, I was speaking, but it was really to no one in particular. Again, I'm not sure about those words you use, sir. I do not know what a necromancer is. Truthfully, I yelled because I thought I heard something. It sounded like rats, which wouldn't surprise me, but then there was pounding. Listen, kind sir, I did not mean to disturb you or anyone else in your prison or this dungeon. That truly was not my intent and I humbly beg your pardon. It's best that I confess, but it's not what you think. The malady from which I suffer is called night terrors, over which I really have no control. They cause me to yell and scream and sometimes even run about when I am asleep. The terrors are particularly forceful when I am hungry or stressed, like I am now. My father could not quite accept it either; it drives him literally crazy. Some nights, I wake up screaming my head off; tonight is no different from many, many others. Come to think of it, I was having a conversation within a dream when I heard the latch of the door and I was awoken."

"Aha! I knew it! As a proper admission of necromancy, you will get to choose thy method of punishment. King Arthur will be amazed by the expediency of such an admission."

"Admission? Punishment? I'm just trying to be honest with you. I have a medical diagnosis made by a doctor, not some make-believe magic, but alas, I have no means by which to prove my innocence. Everything I say is to be used against me, I see. How could you possibly hear me through such thick walls? Was I really making that much noise?"

"Whence you hast lived within these infernal walls for as long as I, wellnigh anything is possible. Thy punishment will be determined at dawn's first light." The jailer turned to leave and began shutting the gate.

"Wait, sir. Please wait. Can I perhaps ask thy or thee or you another favor? My light is out, and I find it hard to navigate in the dark. My eyes are just not as accustomed as yours. Is there some sort of torch or light? Perhaps matches, maybe a candle? I wish I had a flashlight."

"Match? Now, it is I who is not sure of thy language."

"I just thought if you had a pocket watch, then matches wouldn't be too far-fetched. What year is this anyway?"

The huffy jailer snorted in dismissal as he looked away, but not before Jason caught a brief understanding in his eyes that suggested a deeper intelligence. In return, the jailer quickly tried to dispel any such notion with an insouciant shake of his head and wave of his hand.

"Look there, a fire striker, silk, and a piece of granite, along with the oil lamp. It should not be a challenge for anyone with two hands who is as youthfully minded as yourself. Furthermore, it should keep you occupied, out of trouble, and quiet. Goodnight, Jason Dix of cell number 134. Let me slumber! Until dawn's light."

"But I cannot see."

The old man turned a deaf ear to any further entreaty, and with the tip of his brow, he hastily slapped closed and latched the wicket door. His footsteps trod off, and Jason's room was again mired in darkness.

He groped his way to the bench, speaking to no one in particular. "Thanks for getting me in trouble, whoever you are."

Jason tried his hardest to fall asleep, but it was to no avail. He fitfully tossed and turned, and after some time, still unable to sleep, he pawed his way to the pile of supplies. He diligently tried banging the metal to the stone. After many tries, he was able to create a spark, from which he lit the cloth and then the oil lamp.

Suffused with the dim light of the lamp, the room seemed a bit larger than he remembered. Constructed from a gray stone that reminded Jason of the stones used at Tulane University, the room was worn and polished from years of use. Artful scratches and designs were etched into the floors and walls, presumably previous tenants' graffiti. He examined the stone under the bench but found it to be no different from the others, and he discovered no clues that could explain the origin of the sounds or light. There were manacles and shackles fixed along the walls and indelible blood stains on the floor, painful reminders of his predicament. The only organic material was a small amount of hay in the corners, but it wasn't enough to add comfort to his bedding. Near the ceiling on the wall above his bench was a series of primitive illustrations carved into the stone: a clock, a stick figure of a man on a bench, a rudimentary bird (or airplane, if he used his imagination), and a square box, all of which were a bit too high for him to view directly. Absent were any lurking nocturnal creatures; no rats or insects graced the otherwise barren room, no one or thing to befriend, and no visual cues as to the time of day for the maintenance of his circadian balance.

He steadied the oil lamp and watched the flame, hoping to draw attention to a breeze from a draft or hidden egress, but the flame did not sway. The only ventilation came from under the wooden cell door; it was a musty and mephitic smell on par with the noisome odor of the bucket in the corner, which he hadn't yet dared to venture near or inquire as to its ullage.

After hours of monotonous pacing and unproductive inquiry of the room's minutia, he retired to the bench and lay his head down. Staring up at the flickering ceiling, he indulged in hypnagogic fantasies about the blue sky back home, wishing he had listened to his father. His eyelids were nearly shut when he vaguely recognized an ever-so-faint stain in the shape of two large, crossed keys on the ceiling, similar to the one on the elevator button at home, the temple, and in his school. Was it his imagination? What did this mean?

His eyes grew heavy as the ceiling grew distant and he faded into nebulous, swirling, oneiric dreams, his imagination rampantly recalling the day's events. His mind surrendered to the phantasmic torpor in which auditory and visual hallucinations abounded. Images and sounds passed before his slumbering eyes: his classroom clock, the scowling, ruddy face of Bill, the beautiful blonde woman on his television and her swirling dress, Mr. Winwood, the sounds of moving stones, indistinct apparitions of people moving about, and the pungent odor of Pine-Sol. Eventually, even the images disappeared, and only the darkness and silence accompanied him as the hours passed.

"Dad, is that you? Are you home? You won't believe what dream . . ." He was sharply awoken. His eyes flipped open, and his head turned toward the wicket door as it slapped open.

"I wasn't making any noise," Jason blurted, realizing there to be no change in his circumstance. A ladle of slop was thrust through the gate and the dark liquid was dropped to the barren floor.

The server did not introduce himself, and only said, "Repast. Get your daily repast." The window latched closed just as quickly as it had opened, and the slop deliverer moved along. Jason could hear his muted laughter as he said, "Hope it's not too spicy for ye, lad! Ye must be starving by now. Let me know if ye want seconds."

Jason pounded on the door and plaintively screamed, "Wait! Wait a moment. Is this the food? Are these my daily rations? Is this the only food I get for the day? Is there a dish or cup or some sort of plate? C'mon, I'm not some sort of animal. You just tossed it onto the floor. That's not fair!"

"Seven o'clock is seven o'clock, you thankless twit." The voice faded away, presumably off to pour more slop onto more floors.

Jason struck the door with his palm and then punched and kicked it. "C'mon! Please, guys!"

With no response and any further complaint futile, Jason lay back upon the bench to contemplate the meaning of the cryptic message. He was starving. His reverie was brief, however, as he was interrupted in a rather violent and unannounced manner. The cell door thrust open on its hinges and the two gormless, muscled brutes from the day before marched into the cell.

"We see ye survived thy first night. Congratulations, lad," snorted the larger one.

The shorter brute chuckled. "Oh, look, ye missed such a delectable repast. Was it not to your satisfaction?"

"Where are we going?" Jason asked, though at this point, he didn't really expect an answer.

They roughly grabbed him under his arms with their sizable hands, lifted him from the ground, and marched him out of cell number 134. They wound through a labyrinth of damp passageways, Jason's legs swinging freely. They carried him through a confusing spiderweb of hallways, sometimes seeming to backtrack. Finally, they stopped in front of a doorway with a stenciled lintel that advertised, "Chamber of Extreme Torture," which was written in an eerie, red, gothic lettering. Most noticeable to Jason was the absence of the mephitic odor. It had been replaced by the smell of succulent oils and incense. One of the two oafs banged twice upon the door. The response was immediate.

"Enter with the boy." a muted voice ordered.

Jason could feel the humidity of his foul breath in his ear. "Good luck surviving the torture chamber, necromancer. No one comes out, well, walking at least."

"You're sure to be maimed."

"The last lad who visited this chamber emerged missing a leg, and the side of his head was a bit flat. We changed his name from Prisoner 169 to Sir Flathead. I do not think he was hearing too well after that encounter. Ha!" The brute's face was a bit too jovial with bloodlust, causing a lump to form in Jason's throat.

"Enter to your doom! I said enter! What is keeping you?" boomed the turnkey's voice from within. The two pushed the door open and the three entered the hypogeum.

The room was not at all as Jason had imagined and in no way resembled the rest of the dungeon. In keeping with the room's namesake, various devices of torture lined the walls: manacles and shackles, whips, knives and scythes, a chair with leather straps with spikes on the seat, and another with a disconcerting screw at the head. The most frightening of all was a large, upright wheel, not unlike the one on *The Price is Right*, with colorful portions that featured various methods of torture, such as The Rack, Knee Splitter, Head Crusher, The Wheel, and The Pit of Vicious Venomous Vipers.

In stark contrast to the torture devices, in the center of the room was a long table with two chairs at either end. It was adorned with a white tablecloth, fancy garnishments, and a plenitude of delicious meats, foodstuffs, and succulent comestibles. The room was gracefully lit by fragrant candles in elaborate candelabras, along with an anachronistic brass lamp with beige lampshade that sat beside a folding screen and wooden rocker. The lamp was plugged into a brown extension cord that ran through a hole in the wall that would be the right size for a mouse. A slight haze blanketed the room, caused by burning incense canisters. The ticking of an ivory and gold Oliviana table clock gave a sharp cadence to the event, sounding like a metronome timing out the scene. The clock read 8:00 a.m.

"Excuse me, sir, what year is this?"

"You determined your fate early this morning, necromancer. Place him in the Chair of Chastenization." The turnkey stood at the head of the table.

"Oh no, not the Chair of Chastenization!" shrieked the larger brute playfully as the two chuckled, their fervor for pain making them giddy with excitement. The jailer motioned them inwards, and the two obsequious brutes deposited Jason into the chair at the far side of the table. They remained by the boy's side, awaiting further instruction.

"Now Jason, these 'night terrors' are a real drag. We've got to do something to keep you quiet at night. Do not look so surprised at my rebukes. You are in the Chair of Chastenization, where I will chastise you with more than just whips and verbal lashes. I know what must be done to help you with your night terrors. We'll start with a simple glossectomy: a tongue removal. If that doesn't work, we'll try a grotesque entrail removal. Really, I have no time for your footling trivialities and vague answers. I am a busy man, have business to attend, people waiting for me upstairs, and . . . oh, I see you've noticed my lamp. Who said we don't have electricity in the Dark Ages? It's quite simple, really; nothing more than a water wheel, dynamo, and a galvanic battery. Simple for anyone with two neurons in their head."

Jason's eyes were wide and his mouth was agape; he was more dumbfounded than afraid.

"Surprised? Did you really think I could survive without some of life's little electrical accoutrements? Anywho, as I see it, you really have but two options. You are free to pick, but one is inherently a smarter choice than the other. Your choices are as follows. First, you can have a lively and honest discussion with moi about who visited you last night. Or you can spin The Wheel of Misery and accept the extremely painful and grotesque experience delivered by the two bloodthirsty gentlemen at your sides. These men here are to help with your decision. You have exactly one minute to choose your fate. I will either dine and watch you be tortured, or we can have a righteous conversation over dinner. Now let's be civil. Who would you trust in this most dire of situations?"

"My father?" Jason was momentarily at a loss for words. The whole macabre scene was like something out of one of his father's Fellini films: a robed, gray-haired man from the Dark Ages, two muscled brutes standing in such a contrasting scene of both pleasure and medieval torture, and somehow, a lamp. His chary and confused mind was circumspect of the entire ordeal, but he could not draw his eyes or stomach away from the cornucopia of deliciousness—roasted chicken and mutton sat on gilded platters, steam wafted off stews with fragrant spices in large tureens, fresh berries and cheeses decorated the margins, and jams and breads filled every last square centimeter of the tabletop. Such a succulent meal was clearly meant to contrast with the surrounding devices, whose sole purpose were to inflict horrendous pain. His stomach was grumbling.

"You now have forty seconds. I know what I would do. I think I'll try this delicious gruyère fondue." He scooped a hearty swath of the cheesy delicacy with a piece of bread and took a bite. A good portion of the creamy, light-yellow cheese dripped into his beard.

His speech was a bit broken as he smacked and chewed. "I hope you will wisely choose to tell me every apposite detail about who has visited you, like the light underfoot and cryptic messages. Yes, I am aware of oh so many things; I have eyes everywhere. Should you make the smart choice and come clean, you shall dine to your stomach's content on these scrumptious viands and piquant sauces." He lifted a leg of fried chicken and took a bite, tossing the bony remainder over his shoulder. "There's just so much. I would hate to see it go to waste. Who do you trust the most? Conversely, you can keep the secrets to yourself, spin the wheel, and choose torture and mayhem. I know that I would eat and be merry. Let petty, past squabbles begone. For god's sake, what real choice do you have stuck here in this dungeon? The rest of your life may be determined in the next few seconds." Crumbs were sprinkled in his beard as he eyed another piece of chicken.

Still trying to process everything the turnkey had said, Jason sat silently, his stomach churning. The jailer drummed his fingers on the tabletop, raising his eyes from the chicken leg. From the corner of his eye, Jason thought he saw a small gecko scurry into the hole with the extension cord.

"Time's up, Jason. I do not think you understand the gravity of your situation. I will require your immediate decision, or you are to be met with the most unendurable of pains. I mean, really? Silence? You remain silent like a stalwart hero, too proud to accept defeat." He directed the two brutes as his demeanor hardened, "I'll need his finger. He needs to learn a lesson. I've always believed in brute force, pardon the pun." The two grabbed Jason's hands as he struggled, forcing them to lash his wrists with straps to keep his hands splayed.

The jailer turned to one of the men. "Larry, what did Sir Gawain have you fetch this morning?"

"Umm, this morning?" He thought for a moment as he wrestled with Jason's flailing arm.

"Leave me alone, you monsters!" Jason screamed, but he was no match for them as they easily held him to the chair.

"Umm, nothing, sir."

"I see."

"Am I dreaming? Can you please get Merlin? I'm really not trying to be difficult, but he has some of my personal belongings that mean a lot to me. I think he's the only one who has a chance of understanding me. Someone put my towel in my cell!"

"I'll take that as a nonanswer." The jailer walked to his side and grabbed a hammer. Jason began to sweat. "Just in case you thought this is a dream." He raised the weapon and brought it down hard, smashing the tip of his left ring finger with a loud bang. Jason screamed and grabbed the bloodied finger, writhing in pain. The two brutes remained at attention, awaiting further instruction. This was no dream.

"I think that should substantiate that this is NOT a dream, boy. You won't be using that finger for a while. You're too young to be married anyway. Now that I have your undivided attention, perhaps you will be more apt to answer my very simple and direct question. Who exactly are you? Who directed you to come here? Who tried to contact you last night? What was the message? WHERE IS THE GODFORSAKEN ELEVATOR? I need answers! Concise and exact answers! There's a lot more where that came from. Men, I'll need the saw next."

The pain made Jason irate but duly aware of his unfortunate position. Through his sobs, Jason pleaded with his captor. "I swear to you. My name is Jason Dix. I came from the year 2017 AD, and I am trapped here for reasons beyond my understanding. Who directed me to come here? My father, Alfred Dix, wrote in a cipher that I was to go to Beau Champs in the Dark Ages. Or at least I think that's right. Maybe it was a dream, I cannot be positively sure. Merlin has my bag. You can confirm what I am telling you with him. But you don't know my father. He's from the future too, so why do you care? If he were here, he would kick your ass, you bully! That's right, all three of you. And for your information, the message directing me to come here was given to me by some wrinkly rooster man. And the elevator? How would you even know what an elevator is? I haven't mentioned it to you. Being thrown in this dungeon has been some terrible mistake. This must be a dream! Please let me speak with Merlin. I spoke with him on the road near a small village, and he has my belongings. I need them back in order to get home. That's all I want, to go home. He somehow knew about me. I'll talk, but only under the condition that he be here so you don't think I'm lying or crazy. I'll try to explain everything, but only to him."

"Men, you may leave us." The jailer walked with the two to the door, closed it behind them, and locked it with a bolt latch. He turned to Jason, who was still clutching his hand in pain.

"What was communicated to you last night? I need to know the truth. Who has contacted you while you were in the castle?"

Jason remained silent, letting an awkward few moments pass. Finally, he dispiritedly said, "No one. I'm alone."

The jailer walked behind a partition, whistling loudly. Clothes were tossed about from behind the screen, landing all around the room. He emerged moments later, but his face was a bit different. He was cleaner, more neatly shaved, and he was wearing a large grin. "Your items? You mean these?" He was dressed in flowing, clean, white robes with a golden sash, his beard was combed, and a golden pocket watch hung at his side. He lifted the key on the chain around his neck and held up Jason's knapsack. "Have you been missing these? Did I surprise you?"

Jason's mouth was agape. "Merl? I mean, Merlin? You look exactly like someone who works with my father, only a bit older."

The elder's demeanor softened to the point of being almost parental. "Works with your father, you say?"

"Yes, sir. You look exactly like my father's business partner. It's uncanny."

"So I do." Merlin reflected for a moment. "Jason, it was foolish of me to lead you on, but a necessity given the circumstances. We have much to discuss." Merlin began to bandage Jason's finger, wrapping it in cloth. "I gather that you will now be more forthcoming in your answers. Enjoy the feast that was prepared for you. I am sorry for the pain, but you needed some convincing."

Jason stared at the watch dangling from his side. "You have one of those too? My father has one exactly like it, and so did the woman on the plane. Who *are* you?"

"Jason, my child. You have had a long day and you are quite confused. You need to eat. I have some explaining to do." Merlin set a plate of food before Jason along with two pieces of cutlery stamped WINCO STAINLESS.

"I really must know everyone who has contacted you. Trust me, the precautions and airs I have put on are for everyone's safety. Do you think I would try to hide you in the dungeon, keep you out of harm's way, and prepare such a feast for you if I had any malice toward you? Did you not hear the motorcycle as we neared the castle? I had to treat you poorly to make you and any prying eyes believe."

"A what? Then why did you smash my finger?"

"Jason, Jason, Jason. Really, how do I know it is you? Perhaps you are a wolf in sheep's clothing. I would imagine that your tempestuous brain is confused, mine would be after such a grueling series of events, but you have nothing to fear in The Merl. If I wanted you gone, I would only need to snap my fingers or wave my hand and the brutes would squash you flat. How do I know you're not the instigator of some elaborate ruse to gain access to The Merl or the king? If I strike your finger, cause a modest degree of pain, and you maintain your innocence, you seem more believable to me. Wouldn't I to you? It truly pains me to hurt you. It seems like years since I last laid eyes on you, when in actuality, a few hundred have passed. From your infancy to young adulthood, I've known you every step of the way. Of course I'll let no harm come to you. Now you're sitting right in front of me already old enough to shave. Do you have your driver's license yet?" He winked at Jason. "You know I know how you got here. You find many friends when you travel through time, but many enemies too. It's important to keep one's head. You're a sharp lad; surely, you'd agree."

There was a rustling outside the door. Merl put a finger to his lips, urging Jason to be quiet.

Merlin raised his voice appreciably. "Would you like to spin the wheel? That strike was nothing like what you'll receive from the wheel. I am deadly serious about you answering my questions. Did your father visit last night?" Merlin pointed at the door, then gestured for Jason to continue speaking.

Jason followed along and spoke loudly. "My father? What does he have to do with you? Why would you be interested? He's the one who suggested I come here to find a Mr. Champs, though I'm not entirely sure why."

Merlin continued to speak loudly toward the door. "Jason, feigning ignorance is impossible with me! Only pain will come of it!"

"Well, who was I supposed to see? I met no one last night except you and the two brutes who dragged me into the dungeon. I've been tied up or imprisoned since I arrived—who could I have possibly met?"

"I already know that you have been contacted and I suspect I know by whom. I just need to know the particulars. Jason, what do you know about me?"

Merlin grabbed a large mallet from the wall and whispered in Jason's ear, "Scream loudly. I need them to believe." Merlin swung the weapon with all of his might, striking the table with a sickening thud.

"Aah! Help! No, not again! Please, sir!" Merlin let swing a thunderous blow. "Help!"

Merlin dropped the device and whispered, "Let's get out of here. Grab some food to take with you. Quickly, I've got loads to tell you."

Jason began to help himself, his plate overflowing as Merlin tossed some more meats and berries onto the pile. When he could carry no more, Jason followed Merlin behind the screen.

"Wait, my sack." Jason whispered.

"Your sack? Those silly items? Your father and I nicked them from a vendor at the 3086 World's Fair. They're nothing but meretricious and frivolous trickery. Why on earth would you need them? Follow me. Keep up, boy."

"They're important to me."

"Shh." Merlin begrudgingly retrieved the sack and rushed Jason around the folding screen, through a hidden portico, and up a winding staircase. Jason tried to steady the plate with his injured hand and lift food to his mouth with the other. This was the first food he'd had in more than a day, so he did his best to force as much of the succulent viands into his mouth as he could.

The two ascended floor after floor, stopping only long enough for Jason to admire the large water wheel spinning an electric dynamo, as seen through small embrasures and loopholes.

"We should be out of earshot by now. I see a bit of admiration in your eyes. Curious, are you? That, young man, is my generator. It's hydroelectric and wonderful, just wonderful. We're living in a green world here, Jason. No fossil fuels or light pollution. Just wait until you've seen the night sky."

"That sounded like the exhaust of a motorcycle. I heard the same yesterday."

"Bing! You are correct, sir. Now onward, to my man cave."

"Who exactly *are* you?"

# CHAPTER 26

## MERLIN EXPLAINS THE SITUATION

*499 AD*

The two continued their ascent and Jason continued his inquiry.

"So, this is just a dream? Do you honestly expect me to believe that you and my father's partner are one and the same?"

"No and yes. The subject is a bit more complicated than you understand. The problem has always been how we think about time. I find it easiest to imagine a mere shuffling of how one is woven into the threads of time, but in actuality, our place is as tangible as mass yet as intangible as gravity. For instance, you are very real, but only at particular places and moments in history. Make sense?"

"No." Jason was confused.

"OK, look at your finger. Is your pain real?"

"This is all utterly impossible. I've read books on this subject. You are Merlin the magician, in the time of King Arthur and his famous Knights of the Round Table."

"Books? Those books are all rubbish, a fairytale perpetuated by publishing companies. Heck, we probably own most of those companies. And maybe I lent a hand in perpetuating the story, but you'll see why. Many aren't accurate, so many twists and turns, misrepresentations, but none are worth my time to change. Let the people have their fairytales. It's true that to King Arthur's realm, I am a magician, a nonpareil, a wizard, a foreshadower of events who is able to mold the future, but none of his boys understand a lick of science. Arthur's men are adventurers, not eggheads. Put them in the twenty-first century and they may as well be doctors, lawyers, or engineers. You know, mentally, you and I are not at odds. We are so far ahead of most of the oafs here. Think about it —your twenty-first century mind in the fifth century. The mere presence of this pocket watch is beyond reasoning in this day and time, yet here it is. Think of all that you have seen and what you know will come."

"Maybe this is all real. Perhaps I am under a spell. Was I drugged? This has to be a weird hallucination."

"Don't be foolish. Science always prevails. To prove my point, the most powerful man of this time, of all the realm, is King Arthur, a man envied by all. Arthur is the chosen one, or so the masses believe. They have all been duped. The sword in the stone was nothing more than a simple trick of electromagnetism. As history has been written, I have been Arthur's most trusted adviser, protected by him at all costs, envied by all, the most powerful magician in all the world. You'll see things differently because you understand facts and science. In any case, friends are friends.

"Open your mind, Jason. Dream of an ever-changing life with significant, historical events that you can be a part of day after day after day. Visit these important times and places. Get to know your world and its history. I sure did, and I fell in love with the Dark Ages; they're really not so dark once you get to know them. I can speak from experience; I was there for the fall of Rome, the Renaissance, Charlemagne's reign, the French Revolution, Tripe Island and the fall of Cyrus Bauman, the birth of America as you know it, the discovery of electricity, the rise of the automobile, electromagnetic metamaterials, quantum computing, the creation and manipulation of morphic fields with self-organizing wholes and their attractors and chreodes, the Brain Talker chip, Dyson spheres, the rise of the Starlifter—oh, maybe that one's a bit after your time. Your father and I never met the Eloi or the Morlocks, but we did give H. G. Wells a little inspiration. All of these events are at your fingertips for the taking. You are now one of our chosen few.

"What if you were able to go and come on a whim, reap whatever rewards you choose with anonymity, weave in and out of history like a passing breeze without rules or regulation? What if you could do those things, not in a metaphorical way, but realistically, physically? Money would never be a problem. Collect interest from years of deposits, know the score before the game started, predict every lottery number, clean up in Las Vegas or Macau; the odds will always be in your favor. Free money!" Merlin collected himself. "Excuse me, your father would not approve. You're too young to gamble."

The two proceeded upward to a reinforced metal door reminiscent of a large bank vault that was at the top of the staircase. Merlin disengaged a series of locks and they walked into a large, cluttered, stone room that clearly functioned as a workspace, filled with items incongruous with the times. There were bubbling beakers spewing smoke, benches and countertops piled high with papers, shelves with mortars, pestles, and jars of all sizes, including one labeled Finasteride 5 mg, and a tablet press. There were colorful powders and oils, alembics, galvanometers, and other complex scientific devices and trangams covering every available surface. The walls were plastered with maps of the earth and the solar system, all drawn by hand with lines and arrows in a confusing maze. There was even a mixing board complete with auto-tuning features, a video camera, and a costume that looked like the one worn by the woman in the field.

Hanging on the wall in a place of honor was a framed copy of an Interpol red notice with Merlin's face on it.

Posted around it were numerous photographs of a younger Merlin with various celebrities and another that vaguely looked like Mr. Winwood, only with a beard and a different hair style.

Merl said, "Excuse the cluttered contrivances, Jason. I don't have a housekeeper. I have much to show you."

Jason wasn't sure what to make of Merlin, who twisted his watch and stared off distantly for a few moments.

"Who is that?" Jason pointed to a photo of what looked like an older version of himself and Merl. "What the heck are you doing with a video camera? How do you have a printer? Aren't we in medieval times? What is this place?"

"We'll get to all of that in due time. The problem is not so much the printer as it is the preparation of the ink. It runs out too quickly. And that particular picture, it's you and me in 2031. You won't remember because you haven't been there yet."

"All of this is preposterous. Why are you in my dream? Why can't I wake myself?"

"I don't know about your dream, but finally you are posing questions to which I can relate. Perhaps I need to give you a bit of history to help you understand. The answers about why you are here will have to wait. Do you know where the elevator is right now? I don't. Did you know that there is only one, and it's perpetually in use? Do you know where we are at present, and at what latitude?"

"No, sir."

"Interesting. So then, how did you get to this specific date and time? Scratch that. I have a more important question. Where do you live, like day to day? Where do you lay your head at night?"

"What do you mean? I live in New Orleans with my father, Alfred. I'm in the ninth grade."

"And you live in 2017, correct?"

"Yes, and so do you," Jason said.

"Bingo, that's what I was looking for. New Orleans. Let me think. Let me guess: 29.95° North by 90.07° West, right? Southern Yacht club near Lake Ponchartrain. I remember the clubhouse, I believe the year was 1879. Your father and I had some fun with those old timers. We had secretly installed a pump-jet under the keel of our sailboat. You should have seen their faces as we left them in our wake! Is he really using the name Alfred now?"

"What do you mean is that his name? If you are Merl, then you work with him. You should know."

"Well, not exactly. I'll get to that. It's true that I lived there for a while, but it was years later that I returned here." He paused to think things through. "It makes sense that he would settle there. He always did seem to have an affinity for the city and its people, in particular their football squad. But why couldn't he have taken a meaningful historic name of a past leader or conqueror? Alfred. What a completely and utterly boring name. His real name is Beau, you know. It fit him so well. Let me guess, you and Alfred, if that's what he wants to be called, have an elevator in your home. Am I right?"

"Yes . . ."

"Did you ever wonder why you have an elevator in your home?"

"Dad has a bum knee that acts up from time to time. By the way, do you have an aspirin? This finger is really killing me."

Merlin let out a sound like a buzzer. "Wrong! Have you ever noticed that he looks a little different when he exits the elevator, that perhaps the timeliness of its arrival is not quite right? Has it ever broken? I bet not."

Merlin dug in one of the drawers and handed Jason a small pill. Merlin noticed the blank look on Jason's face. "You said you wanted an aspirin, so here you go." Jason hesitated. "C'mon, all elevators, even normal ones, break

547

now and then, but not the one in your home. Jason, I know you better than you think. You don't have the slightest remembrance of me from when you were a child?"

Jason's stared blankly and stretched the collar of his shirt to give him more breathing room. The conversation was so weird.

"Never mind, it will just confuse you. The third merchant from Montpellier. Does it not ring a bell? He was the most adventurous of the triad." A pause ensued. "You really are clueless, aren't you? You don't know anything about our sailing trip and the island? The shirts?" Jason looked perplexed and shook his head no. Merlin tinkered with a device on one of the benches. "My god, you have been sheltered. What was he waiting for? I'm sure he's going to be quite angry with me for bringing you here, but you're here now, so I guess we're all in.

"Where do I start? There's just so much to tell. Let's start from your beginning. We can't say for sure to whom or where you were born, but we found you as an infant. That's right, *found*, thrown out like refuse. Your father and I stumbled across you near a small orphanage in Beaucaire, France. The year was 1793, and your father and I happened to draw the acquaintance of a young Corsican named Bonaparte, who believed us to be two merchants from Marseille. We drank champagne until the wee hours of the morning as he espoused the virtues of his beliefs. We encouraged him to publish, drawing the attention of Monsieur Robespierre. The rest, pardon the pun, is history. Now we refer to that time period as the French Revolution. So much chaos from such a short meeting.

"Anyway, it was by accident that we found you after getting absolutely blitzed with Napoleon. You were no larger than a loaf of bread, swaddled in a straw basket. We literally tripped over you early that morning. Beau's knee nearly landed on your head! We tried our best to find your mother, but in our drunken state, we weren't successful. Eventually, we came to believe that you were the bastard child of a nobleman or perhaps a merchant, cast aside and unwanted. I'm sorry to be so blunt, but that's what we thought. With a life of scorn and hardship ahead, soft-hearted Beau decided to take you in. It's only fitting that you showed up wearing the fleur-de-lis. You never wondered why you and Beau don't look alike?"

Merlin's watch twisted as it hung from a chain at his side. As it turned, Jason spotted the inscription on the back and tried to commit it to memory. Unfortunately, he knew no Greek or Latin, or whatever the language. The words read:

"Bonum enim duobus annis.

Tempus Fugit.

Elementa est.

Prudenter uti."

Jason averted his eyes and tried to focus on the unusual conversation at hand. "So how did I wind up in the twenty-first century?

"That was Art's doing. Beau was fond of that bloke. He was a bit of a homebody, an engineer we met in Rome. He had been studying the construction of the Colosseum and its stability during earthquakes. The Romans were fascinating architects. Art was very interesting and very, very adventurous. Must be something about his name. We traveled with him after we realized that he was also familiar with the elevator. We even left you in his care for a bit."

"I thought he looked familiar. He's in one of the pamphlets on our living room table."

"Around the same time, we began to document the travels and workings of the Delphic, Ephemeral, Ethereal Pixies, as we called them, and their magical elevator. They are a sly bunch. Believe you me, they'll swoop in to correct anything that challenges their idea of history. They'll give you a bit of leeway, but they're sure to reel you in if you stray too far." Merlin noticed Jason staring at the watch, which he tucked deep into his robes. "You mean to tell me that your father never mentioned any of this to you? He's never showed you his book? He was mostly into illustrations, but I've always been one for ledgers."

"Well, I've heard of an Arthur, but it's not . . ."

"Jason, we have more pressing matters to discuss. I promise we'll circle back to your past later. As you can imagine, I didn't summon you here for lighthearted banter. What I need is for you to tell me when and where you are to be contacted again. What was the meaning of the message on the floor? Now that I have a key and intend to vamonos, you can hitch a ride with me if you like, that is, if the cicerone allows. I'll take you home."

Jason looked hopelessly confused.

"Jason, you need to understand that you and your father are not the only ones who use the elevator. There are many of us. I keep a ledger of the people I know who we have migrated. Here. I'll show it to you to prove what I am saying is factual. Don't look so perplexed, boy. You are a bit of a migrant yourself. People don't only migrate from place to place, but some move from era to era. You'll soon understand that time moves backward just as it moves forward. Have you ever experienced déjà vu? That's merely a brief time correction; happens all the time."

Merlin grabbed a massive, leather-bound book from the end of the table and thumbed through page after page until he reached a large index full of names and places.

He pointed out a particular entry. "Your father and I had some good times, chalk it up to our viridity. See here? Take Buddy Holly, for example. I remember the night like it was just yesterday. Your father and I went to see the Winter Dance Party concert in Clear Lake, Iowa. Somehow, Buddy accidentally jumped into our elevator when he was hurrying out of the sleet. It was a violent night. There was a plane crash, but Buddy was never on the plane. Who would be brazen enough to fly in such weather? People will believe anything. The day the music died? It did not! Last I saw him, he was in 3012." Merlin pointed out a line in the ledger with Holly's name. "He changed his name to Buddy Valens and now he's playing oldies in Vegas. He's killin' it. Your father and I helped him get the gig.

"Next line, Elvis. Now he was a hoot! He was on his way down and out with drugs and women, and we happened to meet him after one of his shows. We persuaded him to fake his death, then we moved him away from all those bloodthirsty sycophants who were sucking the life out of him. We stashed a good deal of his cash in a high-interest money market fund under a pseudonym. That was my idea. He's living comfortably on a peanut farm in 2056, though he does play the occasional county fair as an

Elvis impersonator. That tubby guy sure was crazy about fried peanut butter and banana sandwiches.

"Next up is Johnny Cash. He was tired of fame and wanted to move back to Jackson, Wyoming, of all places. I really never understood the draw. Oh look, you'll likely recall this name: Charlie Darwin. Oddly, he always wanted to live in the twenty-first century. Moved him out of Down House and changed his name to . . ."

Jason interjected, "Wedgwood."

Merlin was surprised. "Ding, ding, ding, we have a winner! Correct, but how would you know?"

"He's on television. He's the science reporter for channel six. I always thought he looked like the pictures of Charles Darwin in our textbook."

"Well, you were right! We dropped him off in the 1990s. I always thought he would turn to television. I don't mean to make it sound as if it has all been fun and games. Our efforts were meant to help mankind and to speed up technological progress. You live in the new millennium, so you would be familiar with computers and mobile phones. Your father and I moved a tech guru from 2080 back to the mid-1970s, Steve Jobs. His name was a bit of a joke. We brought him back to do exactly that: create jobs. An economic depression was coming, and the jobs he created with Apple helped keep America from the worst of it. Did you ever wonder how he came up with the name Apple? We pulled him out of New York City and planted him completely across the country near San Francisco. He missed his home, the Big Apple, so he built a new one. And voilà! The Macintosh, the iPod, then the iPhone—the rest is history. It took a bit longer to get the supply chains up and running and a product to market than we anticipated, but eventually Steve was able to go back home. We feigned a dreadful malady and early death for Steven and then took him back to his family in the year 2116.

"One more you're probably familiar with in 2017 was on Tripe during The Change. He happens to be one of us. You know him as Elon Musk, but you should have seen him on Tripe in the sixties. He was a mollusk. Elon the Mollusk, pretty good, right? Boy, did he change for the better. We pulled him from a seedy joint in Elon, North Carolina. That was a rowdy night; maybe I'll tell you about it when you're older. How do you think he came up with PayPal? He fell behind on his bar tab, and the monster of a bartender roughed him up. 'Pay up, pal!'

"After moving so many people through time, we finally developed a moral compass and our efforts turned more constabulary. We became like time police—the judge, jury, and enforcer. But it wasn't so much us as it was the Pixies, that's what we call that vortex of lights. And believe me, if they are unhappy with things, you will know it. They were this higher power that we followed. We became do-gooders, call us zealots, if you wish. We changed the course of history by moving or locking away some of the most violent people in the history of the world, like that no-good leader who enslaved us on the Island of Tripe. We put a sack over his head and moved him here to this facility. But poof! He didn't stay here for too long; he vanished. Into thin air! I always thought that a higher power had other plans for him, but to this day, your father remains rankled about his escape."

Merlin was rummaging through some items on the counter, obviously looking for something. "That's odd, I can't find one of my jars. It must be around here somewhere. Anyway, we've had a hand in many of the big events related to global safety, even within the military. We made sure that Stanislav Petrov was working the evening shift at Serpukhov-15 in 1983. Are you familiar with the Battle of Midway in World War II? How do you think the Allies cracked the Japanese code? Your father was always a nut about cryptography and ciphers. He singlehandedly changed the course of the war. He also pitched in at the Eastern Front, helping Alan Turing in creating the Bombe, his code-breaking machine.

"Politically, we don't take sides. During that same war, we had to extricate one of the Allies, too. I doubt you've ever heard of Louis Alexander Slotin, but he worked on the Manhattan Project. If we had let him stay the course, the world would be far different today. The official story was that he succumbed to acute radiation poisoning, but in actuality, we moved him to where he could do no harm. He took the name Marcus Terentius Varro in ancient Rome. The list goes on. Look, here's Vladimir Ilich Ulyanov, better known as Lenin. He was a prisoner in this castle for many years."

"So if you moved around and went where you wanted, what changed? Why here? Why did you stay here while Alfred moved on? I've read the fairytales about you. I know you had a great love who ended up trapping you. Is she why you stayed? Was it for the love of a woman or a child or some fairytale ending?"

Merlin closed the book and looked directly at Jason. "No. I am stuck here because of Beau. Your father keeps me here for reasons that have to do with the future. And for the record, I never had an amorous relationship with Viviane. My feelings toward her were only filial. Always. Period. This is what happens as stories get passed down from generation to generation—things get missed or twisted. Well, time heals all wounds."

Merlin sat quietly for a moment, scratching his chin and ruminating on something serious. "Perhaps I was a bit too wild and asked for it. Maybe I changed the world too much. When I last saw your father, he was such a rectitudinous man who wanted to grow up, while I yearned to stay young and carefree. What does he say about me? That I'm a 'playboy gadabout,' right? Some people never change, but I guess you knew that in 2017. It's coincidental that you mentioned women, because when it comes to women, things get a bit more complicated and messier. I didn't stay here for a woman; in fact, this world is where I come to get away.

"Speaking of women, you'll meet the Lady of the Lake shortly. She has taken the name Viviane here, and I can assure you that there is no true love entangling our emotions. I have a curiosity, of sorts. She is as elusive as she is dismissive. My connection with her is similar to that between you and your father. How she found me, I will never know. It was almost like a homing pigeon, like the pull of a magnet. I've yet to meet her on level footing without inauspicious pretense. To know her more than simply a fleeting acquaintance, to remain unfettered in her control of me, well, I would like that. You're too young to understand. It's my own fault, and oh how I repine for our lost past."

"Try me. Why does she have such a grip on you?" Jason stared up at a painting as Merlin continued.

"This may be more information than you care to know, but I have dreamed of her and relayed my feelings, yet she toys with me like a fleeting, dismissive shadow in the night. She seeks to purloin something unknown from me and I can feel that the time is near. What is it to really know her, as with any woman? Given my filial affection for her, I am stuck. I remain drawn to her like a moth to the flame. It's as if she put a spell on me. I can feel it.

Perhaps as I've grown in age, I've come to realize that affection, whether romantic or familial, only becomes stronger. Our relationship is as tangible as the accounts written through the annals of history, though the historical premises are inaccurate.

"Anyway, all is karma. As your father's moral compass grew, mine lessened. I've been told that I have no compunction, and ipso facto, through an agreement we drew up long ago, I have been condemned. I am subject to the fate of this time and your father's disposition. Call it an adult time-out. I will be let out eventually, but only time will tell when. Perhaps with your key, the two of us may be departing a bit sooner."

"Viviane is like you? If she can travel through time, why not use her access to the elevator?"

"The future Viviane, perhaps, but I speak of the past. I know where our relationship begins, but not where it ends, as so it has been written. I am powerless to her perfidious advances. When she is near, with a simple stare, I am hers. If it be magic, I am unaware of this brief intermission in our lives, yet I know where our relationship resumes, years from now."

"Wait a minute. You're either not telling the whole story or you're lying. I *do* know her. She's the woman on the plane!" Jason pointed to the video camera and hat. "And she was also the woman on the video. You and she composed a video directing me to the island. You both tricked me! It was her!" Jason pointed to the painting of Dr. Atwood on the wall, an exact replica of the painting in his dining room. "She is also my nutrition teacher at school, and she is staying at your house. That very painting is in my dining room."

"No, that painting *will be* in your dining room. My beguiled spirit has been taken advantage, used by her enchanting beauty to carry out I know not what. My awareness and thus explanation may not be exact. But I can tell you that I remember our first meeting as if it were just yesterday. I can still smell, feel, and envision her presence. Though our meeting was made to seem like chance, I knew from the outset that she was not one to rely on coincidence. How did she find me? I don't fully understand all the factors at play. Perhaps you can help."

Jason caught a glimpse of a gecko as it scampered across the floor and into a nook.

Jason was startled by a deep, reverberating explosion somewhere within the castle walls, to which Merlin paid not the slightest bit of attention. "What the heck was that?"

Merlin had a sad, glossy look in his eyes as he bowed his head and continued. "Your questions will be answered soon, Jason. I am not entirely sure why I've done what I've done or why I do what I do. My mind escapes me now—perhaps it's age. But I do know that something about her was different from the very first moment. I remember our first meeting all too well. Let me paint it for you.

"It was a cool, resplendent spring morning. The sun's rays blanketed a shimmering, serene, verdant landscape to create a network of yellow, diamond sparkles atop the coruscating lake behind the castle. The reflections dotted a shadowed arbor replete with colorful vines and floral plants near the castle's imposing stone wall. I sat in this shaded space, busily working in solitude outside the postern gate. I was keeping busy as usual, tinkering with an object, like so many before, an object yet unknown to the world. I was attempting to create a makeshift penny-farthing and add a comfortable seat. You see, I needed a means of transport and I am not a fan of riding atop a horse; it affects my prostate too much. I know, I know, TMI, as your generation would say.

"Anyway, I stood hunched over my bicycle, beating a wooden mallet against a mortise and tenon joint, whistling and rambling nonchalantly to myself. I was completely unaware that a resplendent, blonde-haired woman had snuck between the bushes and was watching me work. I remember the conversation well." Merlin began to act out the encounter, speaking both parts.

"'Well, now. The mold has set quite better than expected. This little joint should do the trick, and if the oiled, wooden balls function as ball bearings, when this is finished, they'll not know what to make of me. Voilà! The world's oldest bicycle!' I stood upright to arch my back.

"'Ahem.' I was surprised by the interruption and swung around to meet my interloper.

"I said, 'I thought I asked that no one be allowed in the arbor while I was working. Guards?' Boy, I was ill-tempered. I looked about for any of the guards normally positioned aside the gate before I realized that it was a woman who had spoken. Instinctively, I cast a brief oeillade before bowing politely. I was strongly drawn to her in that moment, but you have to understand that my attraction was by no means lustful. Imagine finding a lost soul who had somehow found her way home. And in the Dark Ages of all places!

"Anyway, I said, 'I mean no rudeness. It's just I thought myself to be alone. These men had strict orders to ward off any visitors whilst I set about my business.' The striking woman caused my heart to beat rapidly and blood rushed to my cheeks. Her scent was lovely and enchanting. I had not seen such well-kept hair and makeup for ages, so you can understand my smitten nature. She was no ordinary woman, and clearly not of the fifth century.

"But alas, she knew I was broken before I had even spoken. There was a degree a of familiarity between us, as if I'd known her my whole life. I had given too much away in my face and, noting my change in demeanor that declared an interest, she coquettishly batted her glistening, lively eyes, making me weaker and weaker as I fell into her grasp. It took me a moment to realize her true identity. Should I not have had such filial affection, my affection would have been lustful, as if to make her my paramour. Perhaps that's a bit too much for your young ears, TMI again, but I am being truthful. She had my undivided attention.

"Mind you, it was not only her looks, but her soothing, ariose voice was hypnotic."

Jason said, "If she's Ms. Somerall, I know exactly what you're talking about."

"She began in the most pleasant manner. She said, 'I did not mean to startle you, good sir. It's just that I've taken a rather circuitous route around the lake and thought I would make my way to the castle through the postern gate. Please pardon my interruption. It's just that you stand between me and the gate.' Now imagine, Jason, a woman traveling alone in these times. I knew it was me she was after.

"I tried to draw her into more conversation, not wanting her to leave me. I said, 'Unaccompanied? After your recent circumstances?' I knew she had to be one of us. After all, how else would she find me? But I thought it best to play along. I wanted to know what she knew, so I said,

'Are you not the lady saved by the valiant Sir Pellinore?'
It was quite odd to see a gorgeous woman garbed in fine
silks and threads, alone outside the castle. At the time of
her rescue, she was not a regular of Arthur's court and
knew not the safety outside the castle walls. You should
read all about this adventure. It's well published. I knew
she was different because most women of this time
would not risk their womanly virtues by walking unaccompanied outside the castle's protection, nor would they
risk the whispers of acrimonious indignities that women
share amongst themselves when speaking of those with
less moral dignity. So, I tried to obtain more information.
I said, 'Surely, you are accompanied by a guard, someone
to protect you. Are you not afraid to be taken again? I am
with a curiosity.'

"She batted her eyelashes, feigning innocence and virtue,
and she said, 'Yes, sir, I would be afraid to be taken. I
shall be on my way so as not to distract from your task.
Out of my own curiosity, might I ask, what is your name
and what are you fashioning? This is the most interesting
of woodworkings. Are you the Merlin?' She tried to trick
me into responding to my true name. She said, 'Are you
King Arthur's magician? The same man to whom I am
thankful for suggesting to the king that I be worthy of
saving? I see you pummeling oddly shaped woods together in a manner unfamiliar to my eyes. Tell me more,
please.' She took a few steps forward, aware of my intrigue. We were nearly nose-to-nose and she could feel

the helplessness of my panting breath. She gave me that fateful, indelible kiss on my right cheek, and suddenly, her entire demeanor changed. She said, 'Do not fear. You will be unable to determine who I truly represent, despite your magical efforts of which I am singularly aware.' A quizzical look must have crossed my face because she smiled at my total confusion. I did not want to alert her yet to our pre-acquaintance.

"I asked for her name. Of course, I knew her birth name because we gave it to her. I said, 'I know not who you are, but may I entreat you to let me know more of you.' I could feel my aged heart swell, more than it had in years. I desired to know about her, how her life passed thus far, her travels, her passions. It was clear that chance alone was not an answer for her presence before me. I was mesmerized. Her smell. Her eyes. Her tone. Her graceful, feline-like movements. She created an intrigue in me not felt in years, so much so that the hesitation in my speech along with my suffused cheeks divulged my undivided nature and brought forth such intrigue and excitement as to throw forbearance aside. She excited me by taking me back to the days of youth, of travel, of seeking adventure. The excitement and mystery surrounding her was enamoring; she brought back a ray of hope of returning to my former self as a proud parent astounded by a child so clever.

"I continued prying for more information. I said, 'I have a sense that you somehow know me, yet I have not a true understanding from where this sentiment comes.'

"She replied, 'My lord, my name is Viviane. Was it you who commanded Sir Pellinore on his quest?'

"I feigned ignorance, but perhaps she saw through my charade. I said, 'It was Arthur who gave the order. I only helped to direct His Majesty in tasking Sir Pellinore with your rescue from the errant knight who took you away from the king's wedding feast. I merely suggested a quest on that day and you a maiden in need. Any honorable man would do the same. Do you recall the stag and the hound? How is it that you are aware of who I am, yet I know not who you are?' My sense of reasoning seemed to evaporate, though I was aware that fate would have us both depart this age in due time.

"I said, 'I entreat of you to know more. Oh, look at the time.' I glanced down at my pocket watch, hoping to move back in time a bit to watch her approach, but my apparatus failed me. I shook it a bit and then struck it against my hip. The watch did not produce the desired effect, and she was quick to avow her knowledge of my subterfuge.

"She said, 'If you were to let me continue without suffusing your magic into our discussion, I will continue. Your arts will not work with me, as I have also used the watch, key, and elevator. Now, I have work to do and hereby dismiss you as a wretched, old philanderer. I must ask you to promise that such efforts will no longer occur on my behalf. Additionally, I need to know everything about a sailing expedition in which you and another man were shipwrecked. I know you desire the chance to return home, and if you should not comply, you have no chance of leaving the year 499 Anno Domini. I too have been immured in this malady of a fairytale and yearn to get back to the future. I yearn for the felicity afforded by the magic key and elevator. A young Dix who will visit you soon will point us in the correct direction.' As she gave me a wink and a slight peck on the cheek, she backed away. As parting words, she said, 'We will meet again as sure as tomorrow may be yesterday.' Abruptly, she turned and exited through the postern gate. I have not seen her since, though others have noted seeing me with her, and when I think of those times, my mind reverts to my natural youth. Someone even delivered that painting of her."

Jason pointed to the painting of the woman. "Is that Viviane? She's the same woman who sat in seat 4F on the airplane. I've met her. She was also in the newspaper this morning, in a photograph on the front page of the paper. I was too, depicted biting a warthog; I was saving myself from his grasp before running through that crazy airport with insects and a demented lizard janitor. Her real name is Dr. Patricia Atwood. I remember her well because of her tail. I believe she also happens to be my nutrition teacher, though I never ventured to ask her directly."

"Warthogs on the island? A lizard and Viviane as a doctor with a tail? Oh my gosh. Beau did carry out the plan! He left that information out at our last meeting. It would seem that idle threats are no longer idle." Merlin looked vacantly at the ceiling, his mind a thousand miles away. "Beau, what did you do? Pray not! A human was to never, never . . . the Pixies will do us both in, and alas, I will be stuck here. If your father did what I think he did, he has broken the singular rule. It is strictly and entirely off-limits. Period."

Merlin continued the conversation about his travels when the low rumble of what sounded like a distant motorcycle approached. After a loud backfire, the motorcycle engine was silenced.

"And thus, I hear that our intercourse shall have to proceed later. It seems you will soon get to meet the one to whom I am helpless and overpowered. Viviane has returned."

A sharp rap upon the door announced a visitor. "Excuse my long-winded diatribe, Jason. I seem to have monopolized the conversation. Enter!"

The man who entered was suited with a helmet, chain mail, and a longsword. Jason could only see the knight's eyes.

"Good Sir Gaheris, it is you, and in haste."

The knight struggled to catch his breath. "Sir, pardon the intrusion, but you must come with me to the great hall. Your audience is needed immediately. It is again that the dragon's rumbling was heard in the bowels of the earth below Camelot. The beast has come again for vengeance. Your advice on how best to disinter and slay the beast is sought. The king has saliently reminded the knights of all the ways the dragons are known to you alone, as prefaced in the similar situation with King Vortigern. Recall the red-and-white dragons, sir."

"My squire and I will meet it momentarily. As a dragon can be both sinister and clever, it is requisite to know thine adversary before administering advice. Come, boy. We must seek out the beast before advising His Majesty. Kind and gallant Sir Gaheris, we will descend into the bowels of the earth and allay if not expel the beast."

"Sir, if myself of men would be of assistance, your request shall be an honorable mandate."

"No, Sir Gaheris. You are indeed brave, but we must seek the dragon alone. The king and noble round table knights' tacit and noble trust is enough. I do beseech but one request of you: make no mention of the child who stands before you, my new squire, to anyone, most notably Sir Gawain. I should not hope to draw attention to the youth, as those ignoble souls practiced in the arts of deception and necromancy will surely come for him. It is best that his presence remains unknown.

"Now come, squire. Let us begin our journey. The utility of stealth will allow us to travel as quiet as a wispy ghost in the labyrinth of Camelot's subterranean underworld. Gather that rectangular apparatus there on the table. Your items are locked in my safe."

Sir Gaheris swiftly departed to inform the king, as Jason and Merlin descended into the earth via a circular staircase. Jason rapidly spun a hand-crank flashlight to illuminate their way.

"Merlin, you mentioned Sir Gawain. I met him yesterday and I believe he is from the future as well."

"Jason, all is not as it seems. He has been with us for quite some time. Aren't I Merlin the magician? Ready your ears for a proper lashing. I think the woman you are about to meet comes to share many a grievance."

# CHAPTER 27

## PATRICIA RUNS

*499 AD*

Riding a 1957 Harley Davidson XL Sportster (nicked from the library) the Angel of Death shot out of the elevator and directed her thundering machine at breakneck speed past shrieking peasants and quaint hedgerows, across the campestral plains and toward the rising spires of Camelot. On this day, she was in no mood to stop and watch the terror evoked in the populous as she whizzed by. Instead, she anxiously readied her thoughts for a sharp haranguing of Merlin. She was wind-blown and grimy, having traveled to a small town in the Texas Hill Country called Leakey, in the year 1941, where she sought to answer a specific genealogical question. In her haste, she failed to clean her bike. The verbal lashing she received from the elevator's cicerone regarding the grime only added to her mood.

And while the terror she evoked in this era was palpable, she had to mitigate any risk of being stopped or challenged by a valiant knight or medieval brute. So, she donned one of her brilliant, macabre disguises. She fixed a large scythe to the tail of her motorcycle, wore a face shield painted like a demon, and blared loud heavy metal music, including tracks by the Scorpions or her latest favorite, Mötley Crüe's 1983 album, *Shout at the Devil*. To any passersby, her exceedingly loud and expedient travel on the two-wheeled, roaring apparatus with horrific bass, drum rolls, and treble guitar riffs represented nothing less than the Angel of Death on a quest. No one would dare intervene in her netherworldly duties. She would have to make it a point to meet the band someday. And whilst she knew her demonic guise evoked such horror that no mortal dare intervene, the conspicuous, anachronistic, roaring nature of the curious machine seemed to ubiquitously invite inquiry when the Angel of Death was not riding on its back. And thus, the bike needed to be hidden when not in use.

She headed directly out of the elevator, bypassed Camelot's main gate, and blazed toward its subterranean sanctum. It was a hidden, labyrinthine netherworld of tunnels filled with pipes and machinery designed and created by Merlin for projects that ranged broadly from producing foodstuffs, including diverse fromages, wines, and mushrooms, to a twenty-first century energy creation that crisscrossed under Camelot. It was a covert lair known only to Merlin, herself, and a few of his closest confidants, locked away behind one of the most impervious locks known throughout history. Merlin's subterranean hideaway was the perfect place to hide her bike, having only two points of entry: one disguised behind a waterfall's violent, cascading torrent, roughly five kilometers from the castle, and the other accessible only through an inconspicuous stairwell outside Merlin's office.

As she passed through the waterfall, the rumbling, subterranean reverberations resounded, causing many of the lords of Camelot to believe that a dragon restlessly dwelled deep below the castle. To Merlin, however, the ruckus of Viviane's return was expected. He knew she would search for the youth who had so brazenly commandeered the elevator at the temple base (a matter the cicerone reiterated frequently, as if directing Dr. Atwood's attention to the subject).

It was within one of the many gray, stone caverns that Viviane parked her bike. The room was cool and musty, the mephitic odor overwhelming. It housed a large workspace replete with a bench, lights, and machines, including a rudimentary hydroelectric generator that harnessed the kinetic energy of the waterfall and a system built to power a breeding pool for a species of algae that created biofuel. Viviane refilled the gas tank of her bike using a wineskin bag labeled, "Faulty Algae Oil." Given the horror evoked by her machine, she was in the habit of using more of the oil than refined petroleum gasoline, which contributed to its frequent and frightening backfires. Her combustible machine was not obnoxiously loud and explosively cacophonous because of faulty craftsmanship of the '57 Harley's Ironhead overhead-valve engine. Rather, the auditory assault was a product of a faulty scientific process used during the creation of the most recent batch of Algae Oil. The defective oil had done a number on her machine's carburetor, causing the motor's volume to be exponentially louder and more prone to backfires. The poor souls across the medieval countryside believed that the Angel of Death must be in exceptionally bad spirits due to the popping and bursting of flames from her tail pipe.

Immediately upon her return, she used the powers of her watch and foresaw Merlin and the youth arriving shortly. As if on cue, Merlin entered the cavern, followed by Jason, their torch illuminating the portico. As they entered, Viviane was purposefully turned away, topping off her motorcycle's fuel tank from the wineskin bag.

Merlin's avidity and attention was steadfastly directed toward her as if waiting for a reply. Jason's attention wandered. The youth was stupefied by the anachronistic nature of the dim and messy room that pungently smelled of developing (a.k.a. rotten) cheeses with overtones of petroleum. An elaborate porcelain clock shaped like a sunflower was half wrapped in bubble wrap and stuck in a UPS box. Standing out like an illuminated gem and utterly impossible to miss was the beautiful, shapely woman with golden hair of whom Merlin had spoken. He nudged Merlin out of his daze.

Merlin politely cleared his throat. "As you can see, Jason, she is no dragon. Viviane, my sweet Viviane, I have longed for your return, yet I need to remind you again on the advantages of choosing to be inconspicuous. The court above believes your cacophony to be that of a scaled, fire-breathing dragon, ready to fight. A modicum of couth would be advisable."

She mumbled something to herself and set the wineskin pouch aside as Merlin kept on.

"Now, I would really like to introduce to you our visitor. It seems that your plans are coming to fruition. It is my understanding you've met this boy, briefly on Tripe and again in the twenty-first century. There, your relationship will prosper and your future endeavors will unify us here. Jason, set your torch aside. She is here for your key, boy."

Viviane sardonically mumbled something under her breath as she shook her head yes. She began to rock lightly back and forth, then faster and faster. The aura emanating from her was full of palpable, barely controlled rage. All at once, she violently twisted the motorcycle's gas cap closed and let a few more awkward moments pass before turning to gaze at the two in a manner unique to women. Despite his familiarity with her, Jason felt a lump develop in his throat as he faced the frightening, long-haired, demon-masked woman he knew from school.

She remained mute as she removed the demonic face shield, applied lipstick, dusted off her leather chaps, and walked straight to Merlin. She surprised him by planting a wet peck on his cheek, leaving a perfect imprint of her lips, but while he was distracted, she snatched a few hairs from the top of his head. "Ouch! What was that?"

Jason couldn't believe his eyes. The woman standing before him was Ms. Somerall (a.k.a. Dr. Patricia Atwood, a.k.a. Viviane).

She glared and him and said, "What are you staring at, kid? You can pick your jaw up off the floor. Merlin, where's the key? There are only two reasons I'm standing in front of you today. Would you like to guess the second?"

Merlin was rubbing his scalp.

Jason stammered, "But you're . . . you're my teacher. You left school on the back of a motorcycle with that meathead. And you were on the plane yesterday, and in the paper too!"

She blatantly ignored Jason's remark as she conspicuously placed the collected hair into a small test tube brightly labeled "Genetics." After making sure that Merlin noticed the label, she dropped the tube into her satchel.

"Merlin, I require your undivided attention. I thought this test would pique your interest. You have always been a bit of a playboy, particularly in your youth. Despite my rather obvious coquettish advancements, you, one of the most prolific gadabouts in history, remained uninterested. Even with this lipstick that you gave me tomorrow, you have acted frustratingly aloof. But then when the youth showed up, *poof*! Our future here has vanished. And so I had to ask myself: Why? What has changed our history? What could you be hiding? And then it hit me—I had to look to your past. My inquiries led to quite a find; it would seem that our paths have intertwined in a surprising manner. In all of our meetings, you never once mentioned west Texas, not even a hint. Does that ring any bells?"

Jason impolitely interjected. "But you're Ms. Somerall, from my nutrition class. Or at least, I thought you were. Who are you really? An archaeologist, a psychologist, or a nutrition teacher?" Merlin quieted Jason by putting a hand on his back and a finger to his lips.

"There you go mentioning teacher again. Who came up with this teacher nonsense? Did Merlin put you up to it? I'll confess, my return isn't simply about obtaining your key. You're much more valuable to me, given your familial relations. Perhaps you're due for a retribution earned by your father. I was on the island during The Change, you know. I do not believe you to be innocent, not for a split second. You knew where to hide, and you knew where to run. That is unless . . . unless you already knew Merlin. I cannot believe you two! I'll get to the bottom of this." She climbed back on her bike, shoved the helmet onto her head, and jumped on the kick start. The engine coughed and sputtered to life.

She yelled over the roaring exhaust, "Enjoy your clock, Merlin. Keep a close eye on it because you'll be here for a long, long time. I'll make sure of it." She nodded to the boy. "And he'll never make it out of here if I have anything to do with it!"

Merlin batted his hand in her direction insouciantly, trying to hide his uneasiness as he yelled to be heard over the noise. "Viviane, why would you require an old man's hair? I am befuddled. Sit and let us talk. Cappuccino?" He motioned to a nearby table and chairs, but she remained on her bike. "May I offer you a fine selection of wine and cheese? Perhaps some of my new prosciutto? Surely you are famished after your travels. Stay a moment longer. What exigent circumstance could possibly call you away so quickly?"

Anger was written across her suffused face as she glared decidedly at Merlin, to the exit, then back to Merlin. Finally, she gathered her composure and shut the bike's engine off.

577

She was mad. "You know where I've been but not what I've gone through. But given your delinquency, it should be quite easy to understand my disdain for you, now, in the past, and in the future. Don't play stupid with me." She climbed off the bike.

"Delinquency? Sweet Viviane, whatever do you mean? And not to stray from the point at hand, but where are we two days from now?"

With each word Merlin spoke, her rage only grew. "How dare you, you self-centered, inconsiderate twit! Through-out all of our past conversations, you never once told me of our past relationship. How dare you leave me? What were the chances of me finding you, navigating through time and history? Infinitesimally small! Darn near impossible! You discarded me like rubbish. Can you really be that heartless, that cruel?"

Still covered in her lip marks, his suffused cheeks and affectionate eyes lent Merlin a kindly, elderly air. He was either unwittingly ignorant or unfettered by her dramatic change, and he responded in a lighthearted manner. "Moi? Jason, a word of advice: women are an inscrutable bunch. Before you stands a beautiful lady. See how her hair falls gracefully across her perfect neck, her cheeks as red as the garden rose. She has grown to such a remarkable, bewitching woman. One of whom to be proud. A self-made woman is one to take seriously. Viviane, you're definitely no fool.

"Now off the bike, my dear. Your dress has been laid out for you behind the partition. Make haste; we have much to discuss. There have been developments. Come to my workroom upstairs.

"Before I forget, I'd like to remind you that the next time we make a video, we must use thirty frames per second, not twenty-four. We are not working with film, after all. Who purchased and brought back the video camera, editing equipment, and warthogs for the fight scene? Who located a video feed and a cable truck, and rigged it to his home? Oh, wait. Scratch that. Wrong iteration again."

Merlin's lighthearted affect only drew her ire. "Mr. Dix, close your ears. Why am I really here, you ask? You bet his key is mine, and you will rot away in this wretched time.

"I demand your undivided attention now, Merlin. Or should I call you *father*? By the look on your face, I see that I finally have it! Can you guess with whom I have visited? What information could have been brought to light by rummaging through my childhood years? Why might I need one of your scraggly hairs? Or a buccal swab?

"When you had the ability, did you ever take the time to learn why you are who you are, who your mother and father were, or their mother and father? To learn about your genealogy? I would think not, you selfish twit. This grimy loam on my sweaty arms is from southwest Texas. Do you remember traveling through Texas or was it just some passing fancy? Was it nothing more than a good place to ditch a kid? San Antonio? South Texas? The Valley? Are you just going to sit there with a smug look on your face?"

Merlin remained silent and continued to smile at her.

"You have a lifetime of explaining to do. Do you remember a town called Leakey, Texas? Garner State Park? Does the name Nickie Monroe ring a bell? She was a beautiful woman, only nineteen years old with a high school education. In all of our chats, you failed to mention your time in the Texas Hill Country in 1941. I didn't have binoculars, but I got the gist of your sicko accomplishments with my mother along the banks of the Rio Frio, hiding out behind that enormous bald cypress and old man Johnson's barn. Let's see, what was it you said? 'Headed off to the front. This may be my last time with a woman. It's another world war and we need to serve our country. I need you to take care of something for me.' Really? You're vile."

Upon hearing the name, Merlin shook and tapped the side of his head as if he were trying to regain some sense of orientation. "You're Nickie's kid? Tubing Nickie?" Merlin started to laugh, holding his abdomen. "Now that's a name I haven't heard in a long time. Viviane, you're not her kid. Trust me, it's not what you think. She was in love with another guy. She dated him forever, but he never would marry her. There's no need for genetic tests, he's not your father."

"I'm well aware."

"What was his name? Let's see . . . thin, medium build, black hair. Scruffy, too. Aha! I remember! His name was Rhode. I don't know what she saw in the boy, but he was no good for working, never would join us in the CCC. Still, he made a good stepfather."

Viviane looked ready to boil over. "You're a liar! You're nothing more than a no-good liar. It's all rubbish and you know it. You're a disgusting womanizer, no different from so many men I've crossed in my life. Do you know what it's like to live the life of a bastard as a small girl in the '40s and '50s in a Podunk town in the middle of nowhere? And Rhode was so great, right? Wrong! Rhode was never around! We were isolated, penniless, and alone. Mother worked her hands to the bone to feed me and help her parents. If not for the goodwill of a few local ranchers and folks from the town, along with my brains and good looks, our unfortunate and impecunious life would have left me slinging hash in some dive of a diner or selling libations at an icehouse, not that you would ever have known or cared."

"You have done well. Obviously you've found your way, so I'm not sure why you're angry with me. After all, you seemed to have found your place in this world. I found you as an infant, just like I did Jason.

"Oh sweet Nickie, I remember our first meeting. It was near a little town called Leakey, Texas. We were in Garner State Park, on the banks of the Rio Frio. I remember it like it was yesterday, well, yesterday in a thousand years.

"Jason, back in our more altruistic days, your father and I signed up for the Civilian Conservation Corps. The truth is that we both needed to get a bit more fit. A contractor put us to work building the Grand Pavilion at the park. Well, on one moonlit night, I met Nickie as she was climbing up the Old Baldy Trail to watch the stars. We stayed up all night, talking and dancing the Cotton-Eyed Joe. Gosh, Nickie! She talked a lot about wanting a child, and I needed somewhere to leave you where you would be safe while I was away at war. It was a mutually beneficial arrangement. You mean to tell me that in all of these years, Nickie didn't once tell you about me? Well I'll be. She did say that I could trust her."

"And use my own mother against me? Honestly, I am too livid to participate in any meaningful conversation." She clenched her fists and jaw as she pointed at Merlin. "Don't try to crawfish out of this one. I'm raging inside. I can assure you that there will be repercussions, the first of which is that I will leave you, and him, stranded in Camelot just like I was left behind in my Podunk town.

Where is his key? Count yourself lucky; this is me showing you mercy. Just in case you were to worry about your daughter . . ."

Jason cut in. "What do I have to do with anything? Don't punish me."

Merlin ignored Jason and said, "All we did was talk, dance, and eat barbecue. That's it. You needed a safe, stable life, and she gave it to you. I'll admit that maybe I should have checked on you, but I did save you from what promised to be a miserable life. Instead, you had a mother who loved you and a roof over your head, even if times were hard. If I hadn't left you with her, let me tell you who you were to become."

"Don't bother. I'll not have to worry about you or anyone else from now on. I've learned many times over that the only one I can trust is myself. I've crisscrossed centuries, drank more Real World than I can stand, and seen a great many things. You'd be amazed by what daddy's little girl has accomplished in a day's work, all self-taught."

"You're not my daughter, not biologically, anyway."

"Too bad you won't get to witness my success. You'll not get one red penny or a single Roman dupondius out of me. This girl will never find herself alone or poor again. This morning, I deposited one hundred million in lottery earnings into a high-interest Hancock Whitney account in

2020. Another thirty million went toward stock in a service called Amazon, at $1.73 a share in 1997. I spent twenty-million shorting Goldman Sachs in late 2008, and I invested in Clorox and toilet paper futures in early 2020. I couldn't bring future notes back to the 1940s and '50s, but gold works just fine. I can bring about forty-seven 400-ounce gold bars per trip, since the elevator is only rated for 1,500 pounds. I needed a bit of leeway for one of the brutes that I commandeered from the island, by the name of Bill. Anyhow, he should be finished unloading by now. Mother should be doing just swell."

Merlin said, "Be careful not to change your history."

She was dismissive. "I started by heading to the year 1602 to meet a solicitor of The Dutch East India Company, the most valuable company ever. I needed some liquidity in earlier years. Imagine trying to pass off a 1970 bank note in the 1800s. I never had a father to teach me these things."

"Nickie and I bartered. It's quite clear that you don't understand what matters yet. What about family?"

"Oh really? Family is what matters? I can't believe such words can spew from your lying lips. If that's not the pot calling the kettle black. You, my absentee father, telling me that family matters? I'm looking after my mother, making sure she's cared for and happy. You wouldn't know anything about what it's like to care for another person.

"Anyway, a light went off in my head some time ago. I recognized that I would be a fool to leave the key in your possession, so I promptly returned to take Mr. Dix's key out of your hands. Let's be honest—your best friend Beau didn't trust you and he ditched you here. We both know it. It's not like he can help you ever again. He'll need more help than the both of you. How's that for family?"

"Viviane, what have you done? Where is Beau?"

"He was found, not done. Once the boy arrived, I wholeheartedly thought that I would have to chase you throughout history. The one thing I can't explain is why you haven't attempted to run."

Merlin remained silent, lost in thought.

"Did you hear anything I just said?" She shook her head and realized she was not getting through. "As for you, Mr. Dix, although you don't incite the same degree of derision I feel for Merlin, you are certainly not in my good graces. If you had ever taken the key from around your neck in 2017, I would have snatched it and much of this conversation would never have happened. Merlin, the time has come. Hand over the key."

"The key? *The key*? Where is Beau?" Merlin was obviously battling his own inner turmoil, wanting to break free of his attachment to her. He was in awe of the avariciousness, cunning, and zeal it took for her to reap the benefits of time and history, but his mind fought her misguided thrall. He said, "It's in my safe upstairs. We will have to go up there, but you can have it. Good riddance. You have quite a bit of growing up to do. Perhaps we should have spent more time together, or perhaps I shouldn't have saved you at all."

Jason proposed a different solution. "You are Dr. Patricia Atwood. You are the same lady who tricked me into traveling when my father canceled our fall trip, the same lady who sat near me on the plane, and the same lady with her picture in the paper. Why can't we all get along and make mutual use of the key? Drop me off in 2017 and him wherever he wants. What does it matter to you? You'd be rid of both of us, free to live your life as you choose."

Viviane shook her head sadly. "You wouldn't understand. You're just a little boy who hasn't been in this game long enough. Merlin, you will lead me to the key this instant. And by the way, you failed to thank me for the clock. It was a special delivery. In my travels, I met the one and only Father Kircher. He speaks quite highly of you. You'll have a bit of a hard time finding a sunflower to keep it powered without daylight. Ha!"

"Sunflower? Excuse me?"

Merlin's thoughts were on Beau as his legs shuffled slowly toward the portico and stairs. Viviane and Jason were hot on his heels.

"Pick up the pace, Merlin." The three ascended the stairs, their footsteps and panting reverberating off the stone. "Never mind. It's an inside joke with Father Athanasius Kircher, the famed Jesuit priest with the sunflower clock. Merlin and Beau know him all too well, the jerk. That reckless priest tried to abandon me in a volcano while we were spelunking. Joke's on him; I had the last word. I took the liberty of changing the history books to make him look like a fool. Your dad and the imbecile standing next to you gave him a solar-powered clock that made him the talk of Europe in his day. The catch was that the clock wasn't even solar—it took AA batteries! Morons. Those won't be around for hundreds of years. I'll drop you off a few, just because I'm so sweet. I bet the wonderful 'wizard' can figure out how to recharge them. At least you got to live with the man you call Dad. Did he ever talk about his travels? Has he ever mentioned me?"

Jason held up the torch to illuminate their way as the three trudged up the winding stairs. "You're in a painting in our dining room. But to be honest, I'm still not sure that any of this is real. Merlin did explain to me that I was also found as a baby, in revolutionary France, apparently. I've yet to make any sense out of my present circumstances, so the best I can deduce is that this is just a dream. I just need to wake up and I'll be OK. I'll be on

587

my sofa, in my home, with a wonderfully boring week ahead."

"Wrong answer. This is not a dream, I'm sorry to say. And regardless of how you feel, I am interested in his travels. You and I are alike in many regards. Our lives are intertwined in a distorted jumble of historical misrepresentations. Merlin, you can pipe in at any time, as you are the single greatest reason for my wrath. Won't you take some degree of accountability?"

The three reached the top of the stairs and Merlin unlocked the door to his man cave.

She continued her diatribe. "Jason, you are a very clever boy. It's no coincidence that we met centuries apart. While I will take your key, I suppose that I do owe your family some favor. Your father, being quite the author and illustrator, led me to this point. I purloined his magnum opus and used it as a guide. Throughout your father's travels, he kept a pictorial diary, one that documented his travels throughout the world's history. He won't be bothering us any longer, but I'll get to that later.

"Merlin, you spilled your guts to the boy about his childhood, but what about Beau's book? Did you mention the conversation that we will have tomorrow? Did you show him the watch? Have you taught him the requisite solutions and controls for time travel? Have you broken the news that I don't have any plans to return him to the twenty-first century? Just as Merlin would prefer me not to be trusted with any of this, you can bet that you'd never get your key from him. There is a reason that Beau left him keyless. How gullible are you, Jason? Your father cautioned you about this man; you should have taken the time to read the entire cipher instead of trusting those two dummies from Tripe. Nevertheless, kudos to me because your mistake gave me control of the needed second key.

"What does that mean?"

"Let's ask Merlin, shall we? He and Beau seem to know everything. The gates? Why else would I return to such a dark age? Think about the gravity of it all. Your key was at no other location or time, but could take you whenever or whenever you chose. It is a key that has been endowed to you, yet its true function was never revealed until recently. It is a key that allows you to stop time, correct time, correct any misgivings or historical errors that would otherwise go unchecked, or even go so far as to create history. Your father took the liberty of rewriting history on multiple occasions, so why shouldn't I dabble? Imagine a life free from the trammels of monetary worries, no need for dependence on governments, no need to adhere to the whims of fools, no need to tell loved ones goodbye. Time is omnidirectional, time is powerful, Jason."

Viviane held out her open palm to Merlin, who was turning the dial on a safe below one of the counters. "Jason, did you know that had I not demanded the key, Merlin was planning to depart this era tomorrow and leave you stranded? Why else would it be so imperative that I return today? One key to travel, two to unlock the gates to the sublime landscape that you and Alfred have both seen but have never had the courage to experience. I have something for you, Jason." Patricia dug in her bag and retrieved the small seed. "Take special care of this maple seed. You will find your father encased inside. Despite searching the eons, I don't know how to extricate him. Perhaps the wizard here can lead the charge.

"Here's a fact for you, Jason: nine out of ten men are liars and imbeciles! Curse you both! You and your old friend can grow old and rot here. There's no cure for your father's ailment, at least through the thirtieth century." Patricia tossed the seedling to Merlin as it twisted in the air. "Good luck getting Beau out of this mess. Take a real close look, Merlin!"

"What? Beau, you didn't? Again?" In the process of lunging for the seed, he dropped the key and Viviane scooped it right up. As he examined the maple seed, his eyes grew wide; he was well familiar with the process of ensporulation.

"Time works forward and backward, Jason. You'll learn that soon enough. And Merlin, how did the Maya know this? Beau knew about the gate with the two locks. I never really understood the relevance of the odd illustration on the wall until a recent invitation." She nodded to a Mayan glyph rudimentarily sketched on a nearby paper.

Jason remained quiet but noticed that it was the same illustration on the game show announcement in the elevator.

Merlin cleared his throat and squinted his eyes to examine the seed. "Jason, it's your father. He . . . he's trapped in this seedling. Viviane, how could you? Even if you were my child, I would disavow you for such behavior. You have so much to learn."

"Like you, I take no responsibility. Apparently, he did this to himself, presumably as he was coming to rescue you, Jason. Reap what you sow, right? If you must know, I believe the Westbankers had something to do with it. Help yourself to the clock downstairs if you're able to get out of this room. Boys, may we meet again someday. Mr. Suck-Up, you can tell your master, Goldilocks, I mean Arthur, goodbye for me. I have a date to attend."

Jason was insistent. "But why my father? Why do you mention him in connection with all of this, the elevator, the Dark Ages, everything?"

"If you're asking if I am rueful for my past actions, the answer is a resounding no. That's all I have to say on the matter, so farewell! Auf weidersehen, au revoir, adios, and sayonara!"

Patricia exited the room, closed the door with a loud thud, and filled the keyhole with an impenetrable epoxy resin so that the door handle could no longer budge.

Moments later, Jason could hear the Harley's roaring rumble and blaring music. The floor shook as she revved the engine and Mötley Crüe's "Kickstart My Heart" echoed through the tunnels. The bike's rumble dissipated as she blazed a trail through the countryside. The Angel of Death was gone.

Merlin hunched over his workbench, carefully examining the seed. He was not the least bit interested in the loud pounding on the door to his man cave.

Jason asked, "Aren't you going to respond? What are you waiting for?"

Merlin remained silent.

Jason's finger began to throb again, and he wished he had something stronger to kill the pain. "C'mon, man. You can't just give up."

"All is not as it seems, Jason. Arthur will be here any minute. The cavalry will arrive."

# CHAPTER 28

## PATRICIA MEETS MAYA

*670 AD*

While reading the game show flier, Patricia was violently ejected out of the elevator as it sharply chimed to a halt. Its doors thrust open, pushing her out to an abrupt and awkward stumble upon the uneven, dusty ground of a large cavern. Perhaps she had been a bit too sharp-tongued in her demand when she barked, "Take me to the show!" She had been leisurely sipping the last swig of her bottle of Real World when the abruptness of her arrival caught her off guard. She found herself coughing and gasping, her arms swinging wildly in search for a means to steady herself, eventually grabbing hold of a large stalagmite.

*Bing.* "You have reached your destination: 67 AD, Palenque. Perhaps a 'thank you' is in order. Sayonara." The cicerone's voice muted as the doors rapidly shut and the elevator vanished.

But where exactly had she landed? She mentioned the game show, but she had instead been deposited in a cave. Did she confuse the elevator? She was further perplexed because she had expected to be taken far into the future. Not only was her hair tousled, her torso twisted, her hips cockeyed, and both of her feet canted at odd angles on the dirt floor, but her mind was a jumbled mess too. She had whiplash from going so suddenly from being in command of her circumstances to adrift and lost.

She paused to catch her breath and calm her nerves while taking measure of her faculties. Her limbs were soundly intact, she had sustained no serious injuries, and she wasn't in any pain. She could take solace in the fact that the watch and keys were both still in her pocket, but she was left without her motorcycle, and more importantly, its saddlebag with her satchel and codex. They all remained in the elevator, likely now lost in some other time and place. She made a mental note to make a greater effort to ingratiate herself to the cicerone; this was not the first time she'd experienced such a violent expulsion.

The cavern was not as advanced as Merlin's, in fact it contained no technology, but at least it wasn't as musty. It was simply a large, dimly lit room without appurtenances, and with no signs of any humans or living creatures. As always, she remained unaware of the peering eyes of the small gecko who awaited her next move. Even the elevator button had vanished. She had wholeheartedly expected a bright television studio, perhaps in

New York City or Burbank, so she felt as dismayed as she was surprised. So much for fanfare or the blaring applause of a crowd.

A cold, eerie pause unsettled her. Goosebumps erupted on her arms. Had the elevator malfunctioned? Had it misunderstood her command? Had she mispronounced her intention? Perhaps the rumbling bike had distorted her speech. Something was awry.

Pawing at the keys and watch again, she found them still secure in her pocket. At least she had the means to get home, if she could only find the elevator.

A slow drip grew louder, drawing her attention back to the cavern, her eyes finally adjusted to the surroundings. She was minuscule amongst the colossal flowstone columns that extended from the ceiling, which was also ornamented with stalactites, soda strays, cave ribbons, and other rock formations that had developed over eons. In some respects, the cavern reminded her of the hidden limestone caves back home. But the cicerone was clear on the year: 67 AD. Who would she meet? What if the natives were violent, perhaps even merciless cannibals? Alone and unarmed, she felt naked. Exposed. Vulnerable. It would be better if she had the means to defend herself, but instead she could imagine a ceremony in which a trephine to her skull would be the entertainment du jour. All at once, the cavern's features now looked foreboding, more like an immense, uninviting, stone jungle. Quite different from the 1970s or 2060s.

The ceiling and walls were decorated in a collocation of glyphs and logos, colorfully illustrated and suffused by the faintest yellow-orange glow from flickering torches set within hidden niches along the smooth flowstone. The largest of the illustrations lay directly above her, which she recognized from Merlin's wall and the game show announcement. It was clearly significant as it was the largest and most centrally placed on the ceiling above,

surrounded by smaller carvings, some of which were oddly reminiscent of astronauts from the 1960s Apollo program. Merlin had never mentioned the place. Why? Or was this symbol somehow ubiquitous across cultures?

A flicker of lights drew her attention down a darkened declivity that led into an unseen, cavernous world. The lights shimmered down a path, drawing her eyes through the stone jungle that was imbued with iridescent, calcite crystals like stars in a clear, night sky. The path faded as it trailed down into the subterranean depths. Could the occasional flicker be fireflies lost in the deep abyss? Turning to check her surroundings, the short rays of early morning sunlight burst through a narrow opening, the light highlighting a presumed exit.

Then came the sound of a gong.

Her heartbeat pounded in her temples, racing as the gong sounded again and beating booms eclipsed the drip. As if turned on by a switch, the sounds of drums and the rumble of thunder erupted, accompanied by the instantaneous clamor of human voices speaking what sounded to be French, English, Spanish, Cantonese, and more. A multitude of languages were employed somewhere outside the cave. Succulent odors of cooking foodstuffs wafted through the opening on a robust breeze.

She needed to regain her composure, reminding herself that there was no reason to fret. Although she had been thrown off guard, she had the upper hand. Her watch's greatest utility was designed for such a situation, to be neither surprised nor snuck up upon, to know what lays ahead. She would put her time-distorting apparatus to good use, as she had on so many other occasions. Should she go left or right? Deep into the bowels of the earth or out of the cave toward what sounded like crowds of people?

She withdrew her watch from her pocket; the dial read shortly after eight o'clock. Its function learned through numerous uses, she turned its dial forward by thirty minutes, then swung it back and forth while repeating the inscribed phrasing. The combination of swinging and chanting transformed her current reality into a strobo-scopic, colorful slideshow of jerky pauses admixed with rapid successions as seconds coalesced into minutes.

While the cave entrance remained clear, the room, which was initially devoid of people, suddenly became filled with hurrying apparitions at the twenty-one-minute mark, mostly swarthy, muscular, dark-haired, Mayan men who were painted with dots and lines across their chests. In double file, they trod up the path from the confines of the cave's darkened bowels toward the beating drums and loud cheering. All were dressed similarly; their faces were covered with jade face masks, their torsos were painted, long, grass skirts covered their legs, and they carried banners, pendants, spears, and paraphernalia rem-iniscent to the frequent sporting events back home. Most notably, one of the men lifted his nose to smell something in the air. With a quizzical expression, he must have dis-missed the notion because he continued on with his brethren. Once the group disappeared toward the crowds, the forward passage of time showed no others.

And thus, aware of the incoming group, she dialed her watch back to present time, etched a mark on the wall near where she presumed the elevator's location should be, and decided to move along. She would have to search for the elevator call button at a safer time; she had less than twenty-one minutes to find a safe haven and appro-priate dress. Her current garb, leather chaps and a demon mask, would be a real problem. If they found her, she would likely be seen as a monster or demon in need of speedy dispatch. *Damn the cicerone!* But even if she were dressed appropriately, her Caucasian tone alone would give her away—or would it? Surely she would stick out like a sore thumb, but what about the various languages she thought she heard? Would the locals treat her as friend or foe?

The same eerie feeling swept over her again, as if she were being watched, but the room remained empty. She snuck out from behind the large stalagmite and tiptoed toward the beating drums. When looking outside, she would first use the watch to safely assess the surroundings, then she would procure an outfit and either hide or blend in until she could find the call button. The cicerone had surely made a mistake. What about the illustration and flier that portrayed her as an active and willing participant? Why would the same illustration be so conveniently posted on Merlin's wall?

When she stepped out from behind the stalagmite and onto the luminous path, she was quite unexpectedly grabbed from behind. A strong forearm wrapped around her throat and a large hand clamped over her mask and mouth, and she was dragged backward by the unseen assailant.

"Aah!" She let out a gasp, but the hand muted her attempt at a scream.

"Shh! Are you nuts? Keep quiet and stay off the path. Can you even fathom what the king's men would do with you? You're dressed like a neon invitation, for goodness' sake. One of them has already caught wind of your scent. Athletic brutes will be forthcoming momentarily, ready for battle. They will not offer a soft, intellectual inquiry, nor will they care who you are or why you are here. Heck, even I was a bit suspicious before I watched you for a bit. A knife through your heart would be reasonable and expected, especially for a demon such as yourself. I need your assurance that you will not scream when I release my hand, OK? The team will be passing soon. We don't have long."

Patricia's eyes were wide like saucers in her state of fright. As she turned to face her assailant, she found herself looking up at a large, feathered mask, not unlike the image posted in the elevator. Behind the mask, recessed, intelligent eyes studied her response. He was a man, easily six feet tall with strong, muscular arms and a strapping physique. In addition to the ornate mask, he was dressed in a loin cloth and was adorned in colorful, leather wrist and neck straps inlaid with stones. Caucasian in skin color and modern in mannerisms, his skin was tanned and his blonde hair poked out. It was she who was in awe.

"With that out of the way, welcome! I'm not here to hurt you or poison you with ill thoughts." The man coughed as he disposed of his English accent in favor of one of a more featureless variety. "Sorry, old habits for a different time. On the count of three, I am going to release my hand. When I do, you mustn't scream or shout or cause any fit or fiery ruckus. You are safe with me. I am a traveler such as yourself. Do we understand one another? Capisce?" Patricia nodded her head in acceptance, and he slowly loosened his grip. "One, two, three," he said, and then he put a finger over both his and her lips.

His eyes sparkled with realization. He whispered, "Wait, I know who you are!" She could tell he was smiling under his mask. "You're here for the . . ."

"Game show." She pulled down her mask.

He canted his head and looked her up and down. "You're one of the contestants! Excuse me, it took me a minute to recognize you."

"Contestant?"

"Yes, how could I not recognize you? It's just that your manner of dress . . ." He cleared his throat. "Who dressed you? I bet you're from the 1980s. Maybe in a hair band? A unique time in all of human history. I used to be into it a little. Now how did that song go? Oh, I remember! 'I can't drive fifty-five!'" He played the air guitar and looked quite proud of himself. "Those were great times, but this costume you're wearing will not do."

She took further account of this prepossessing, muscular man whose shirtless and sweaty physique greatly attracted her. "But how did you . . ."

"Shh. Lower your voice."

She returned to a whisper. "Who exactly are you and how did you find me? And how do you know of the elevator?"

"Excuse my less-than-subtle means of introduction." He politely bowed. "You can call me Captain V. I am here to make sure that you aren't harmed so we get you to your event. It's best that you have the king's protection. I don't mean to be negative, but you're too fair-skinned for this time and place; you'll be accepted more readily with plumage. It's a bit garish, I know, but it's worked universally for our kind in South America, the Middle East, and Africa for years. The feathered headdress is our accepted livery and Viracocha is our accepted moniker—but you already know this, being a person of such vast knowledge!" He gave her a wink. "Look up there." He motioned to the ceiling.

In addition to the central logogram, she could more clearly ascertain the illustrations of people garbed in elaborately feathered headdresses alongside more astronautesque figures. She also spotted a relief of the gate from her text. It was fastened shut by a lock with two keyholes.

He stood silently for a moment, allowing her to ingest the vastitude of the drawings. "Those blokes in headdresses are me and you now. Directly above us, you can hear the stadium and the games. Just listen."

Multiple languages were being spoken, and the lively sound of cheers drifted through the cave opening.

"It'll be a full house today, a sold-out show."

Patricia's neck careened, taking in the drawings. "Stadium? Who exactly are you people? Where am I?"

"The stadium was built for the games and it will be filled to capacity. You can only imagine the size of the crowds. Better than expected. First, we need to get you acclimated to this environment. Get the jitters out, so to speak. Just follow my lead and you will be OK. Prepare yourself—it's only the greatest game show of all time. By the way, I've already met your competitor. He landed here earlier, and he's upstairs as we speak, having an audience with the king. Have you met the other contestant? He seems to know you."

"No."

"Well, there's no better time than the present. It's time we get a move on; the big man needs to meet you before the festivities begin. The first rule of traveling: don't come ill-prepared. Not to worry, we have you covered. Let's take you to meet King K'inich Janaab Pakal. Show him respect. He's an inviolable guy and he deserves it. Lots of pressure. Loads of pressure. Don't worry about the rest of the Palenque clan; they can be petty and exasperating at times, but they're an obsequious lot and do as he commands. When the show begins, just follow your gut and I'll help when I can. Come, we can walk and talk at the same time. We have a schedule to keep."

He held out a small scroll, which she accepted.

"I need you to memorize the names on this list. Don't ask me why, and whatever you do, don't share this information with anyone. I mean it—NO ONE. I'll need that scroll back when we get upstairs, Dr. Patricia G. Atwood from 1972. You're not the only one with knowledge of the future."

Patricia diligently read the list. "But these are . . ."

"I know what they are. I wrote the list. They're the answers to the questions you are about to be asked. By the way, keep up with the times; the watch trick is so passé. You might as well toss it in the trash if you travel past 3010. Any lunkhead knows how to negate its effects. In fact, please wait to pass judgment until you've had time to observe. Do you know the formula for time distortion? In any case, let's get to the king. You know, he always likes to meet both of the contestants before the show, get to know a little about you, make proper introductions, and so on. Whatever you do, never—and I mean *never*—try to remove the king's mask. He's masked at all times and can be pretty peculiar about it. My theory is that he's a bit self-conscious about his appearance. If you earn his trust and he likes you, he may eventually take it off. After all, it can get pretty hot under the mask. Anyway, keep the king happy and you'll be OK."

Patricia asked, "So what's your role here? Who are you to the king?"

"I'm a sort of knowledge bringer, along with creating order and promoting the arts. Recently, I have been working on channeling the Maya's energy into more productive and egalitarian pursuits. Hence, the game show idea. I'm a bit like an anger management counselor crossed with a teacher. I tell them, 'Anger bad, arts good. Violence bad, learning good.' And believe you me, I'm making progress. You should have seen them when we started! It took the most assiduous of efforts to convince the king that construction and art would bolster his kingdom. I think he was thirteen or fourteen years old when we first met, but he and his mother listened and it's working well.

"But despite our positive relationship, I know he'll never embrace one of a demon persuasion." He tapped his finger on her demon face mask and winked. "He also won't tolerate any depictions of Xibalba or someone from Calakmul, particularly not during times of 'celebration and gamesmanship,' which are synonyms for 'battle practice,' by the way."

Patricia looked thoroughly confused. "I consider myself to be a reasonably intelligent person, but I didn't understand most of what you just said. This whole scene is a bit too unexpected and strange."

"Malarky! It's only the best game show ever. Just wait—you'll see. Anyone would die to be in your position. I hope you've prepared. How were you picked, anyway? Did you answer an ad? Fill out an application? Did you visit the Maya office in Lakam Ha?"

She shook her head no and shrugged. "It was posted in the elevator."

He rolled his eyes. "Right. Sure. I don't buy it. Must know someone or be someone important. I was strolling along, preparing for the games, when I heard the faint chime of the elevator. One never forgets that sweet chime. Did I mention? It was your smell that gave you away."

"Smell? What do you mean? Do I stink?"

Captain V had a habit of ignoring her questions and moving right along with the conversation. "Before we get there, put this on. It's what they've come to expect from someone with your skin tone. It'll help smooth introduc-

tions in the event that we run into anyone in the tunnel."
He took her demon mask and handed her a feathered
mask and headdress. As she put them on, her sleeve rode
up, exposing her left forearm.

"Whoo! Great tat! Keep your left forearm visible; the
serpent will work in your favor. It'll be crazy scary to
most folks here, but the king will love it. Something to
talk about. Anyway, I'm headed home after the show. I'm
super excited to get home to a warm bath and a close
shave. My own bed! You can't imagine how much I am
looking forward to clean, piping hot, running water. Before I took this gig, I installed a sixty-inch, cast-iron tub,
but I haven't gotten a chance to use it yet. Once we finish
the show, I'll make all the proper introductions and you
can take my place here until I return. I'll show you the
ropes."

"Hey, what did you mean that I smell? And can we at
least introduce ourselves? I mean your real name, not this
Captain V nonsense. You are clearly familiar with me,
with the elevator, the key, but I don't know anything
about you or this place. What is your name? What year is
it? Where are we? I feel like we've met somewhere before, maybe only briefly, but your eyes look familiar. Can
you remove your mask for a moment?"

"Trust me. Memorize the list." He led her to a wall, then
he pulled her hands up to her face so she was forced to
examine the paper he'd given her. "Were you never in-

quisitive about how your watch was created? Did you not meet Alibaba? I thought not. Never forget that knowledge is power." He waved his hand at the nearest wall of flowstone, and a portico appeared, revealing a hidden passage. It was as if the rock were merely a hologram.

She knocked on the adjacent stone, its solidity confirmed. "How did you . . . the rock is solid."

The feather-clad man continued walking. "Like I said, knowledge is power. It's all in the flick of the wrist." He winked at her again. "It's always the same with you twenty-first century people."

"How did you know where I'm from?"

"Like I said, you smell. I could smell the fuel on you from a mile away."

"Well, you're wrong. I've come from the Middle Ages."

"Yeah, right. Always thinking that your methods and means are better than our immemorial efforts. Your Industrial Revolution was a farce, nearly choking our planet to death. You will learn who we are and what we can do for you in due time."

Patricia was getting fed up with his games. "Let's not pretend that you're not also from the future. What date are you from? Let me guess. The year 3500? And what about your name?" The man remained silent, but she persisted. "OK, the year 4000?"

"You know, you're just like most of the travelers I've met. Who says I'm from the future? Past, future, what's the difference? I'll counsel you like so many others of your time. Remember that knowledge can be lost just as it can be gained. Sit on it and ponder. The Maya accept that time works in reverse just as it moves forward. It's not that we will suddenly begin walking or talking backward, just that the way of things, of nature, of technologies, ebbs and flows. Things are circular, cyclical. That concept seems to be a bit over the heads of your twenty-first century 'scientific' authorities. They think very rigidly about time. In that regard, these fairly rudimentary people are so far ahead of your time.

"Why am I expounding on such memorialization? I believe you know who I am; you've spoken of me. Use your head. Remember this date, for it was the true date of your change: October 27, 2017 Anno Domini. You do use Pope Gregory XIII's calendar, correct? Don't look so surprised. I am using past tense even though I'm speaking about the future. Tenses do become a problem at times. Watch your head." He ducked as he led her into a smaller underground tunnel. "This will take us directly below the Sak Nuk Naah, where we are expected. I helped design and build it. I hope you like it. If you're hungry and need some grub, we are right on time for the feast of Sak K'uk'."

She hesitated with an indecisive expression on her face as he motioned for her to follow.

"C'mon, we don't have all day. The group you saw will be passing soon, but if you wish to remain here . . ." Not wanting to encounter the warriors, she hurried through the opening and followed him. With a wave of his hand, the portico vanished. "Like I said, it's all in the wrist."

The two passed through a damp, narrow, artificially lit tunnel for some distance before climbing a flight of stairs. As they ascended, the cool mustiness gave way to a warmer, more humid environment. She could hear the light strum of a guitar and a singer.

They passed into a small, whitewashed anteroom. She took one last look at the list she was given before he took the paper from her. In the center of the room was a velvet settee, positioned beside a small table that held a high-end pair of steel shears. A few piles of cut hair littered the floor.

The singing heard from below continued along with a muted conversation that emanated from the adjoining room. Captain V put a finger to his lips, bidding her to be quiet. He motioned to a room divider in the far corner. "Step behind the screen. I know what you're thinking, and I agree—a grass skirt would be unbecoming. You'll find a costume more suitable for your introduction, something that you have worn before. You have a crowd to

please today, after all. Still, I must reiterate the importance of secrecy."

Patricia stepped into the changing space, only to poke her
head right back out. "Umm, Captain V? How did you get
this dress?"

On a peg hung a flowing, golden gown, the same gown
she knew herself to be depicted wearing in the Montegue
Codex and in the painting on Jason's dining room wall.
Such an unusual turn of events. She hadn't a clue what to
believe or where this journey was leading.

"I know it must all must seem so unusual. Remember
your tenses."

# CHAPTER 29

## PATRICIA MEETS THE KING

*670 AD*

"Where did you get this dress?"

Patricia stepped out from behind the changing screen wearing her perfectly fitting, flowing, golden gown that matched her long, golden hair. The look was completed by a colorful, plumaged headdress.

"I must compliment you. You are strikingly beautiful. The question should be *when* I got this dress. Not to worry, all will soon be revealed. For now, we're headed to the king's reception hall, where I will offer the requisite introductions. The king is not the only one who seeks your audience." As her steward, he took her hand and led her forward into the king's room.

The white room was impeccably clean and well appointed. Verdant plants and fragrant flowers were placed around the rectangular room, all labeled with their respective genus and species. An incredible variety of birds were perched on the plants, adding an animated quality to the room. The walls were adorned with colorful frescos of flowers, insects, and similar birds.

At the end of this large room, sitting on a throne atop a large, stone dais, below a stone relief, was a masked man

roughly six feet tall, incongruently clad in a Hawaiian shirt and grass skirt. As predicted, he wore a jade mask and plumaged headdress. By his position of honor, she surmised correctly that he was the king. Standing at attention in a semicircle around the dais was a group of muscled brutes dressed in loin cloths, jade masks, plumage, and sharp spears, ready to protect His Majesty at a moment's notice.

Seated in a chair to his left and on a lower platform was a Caucasian man dressed in a medieval surcoat over a chain mail top, grass skirt, feathered mask, and head-dress. His Burberry satchel contained several thick texts. Patricia recognized the man to be Sir Gawain. Behind Gawain was an anachronistic oddity: an astronaut's spacesuit with mirrored visor; the right arm of the suit had been haphazardly reattached to the torso with a vine.

As she entered, the group was focused on a lone, long-haired, thin male who was strumming a rudimentary guitar on which a sticker for The Revivalists was plastered. He was providing the entertainment for the court.

> *You know who you are*
>
> *You're everything beautiful*
>
> *She's hot, hot like the sun*
>
> *The loneliest one.*

His mellifluous voice resonated as a few of the brutes tapped their feet and slapped their thighs to his rhythm.

The smell of the place drew her attention. The room opened to the outdoors, with multiple porticos leading into a large courtyard. As she gazed outside, she saw rain

615

clouds gathering on the distant horizon over the vermil-
ion roofs of the village. A steady breeze carried the faint
smell of rain. It was almost as if she could smell the
changing times along with the succulent ambrosial odors.

Workers outside were busy, excitedly jabbering as they
set out flowers and decorations, including napkins embroidered with "Happy Sak K'uk'" and plentiful foodstuffs of corn, squash, avocado, various roasted birds,
succulent pork, and an odd stack of orange-and-white
cardboard boxes full of fried chicken from Popeye's Louisiana Kitchen. Around the periphery, dark-haired, dark-
skinned people with lineaments clearly of Mayan design
were busy grooming, painting, sweeping, and polishing,
all in preparation for the celebration. A few furtively
glimpsed into the happenings of the court before scurrying along.

She remained still and silent, waiting for any cues to
speak or move.

"Captain V, what should I be doing? Why is everyone
staring at me? Is that . . . Sir Gawain? Here? Why is he
here?"

"The year is 670 Anno Domini, and you are in Palenque,
ancient Maya in what is now southern Mexico. The man
on the dais is King K'inich Janaab Pakal. They're staring
at you because you're the second contestant, and frankly,

because you're gorgeous." Captain V took her hand and guided her forward to approach the king.

The men surrounding the king readied their spears and silently stepped forward, prepared to strike if commanded.

Captain V whispered out of the corner of his mouth, "And about that other bloke, his real name is Cyrus Bauman. He is your competition. Unbeknownst to you, he's been following you for ages. As for the king's guards, pay them no mind; they cannot harm you unless the king gives the order. Be sure to curtsy before the king when I bow. Follow my lead and you'll be fine."

With arms open wide, Captain V announced, "May I introduce His Majesty, the august K'inich Janaab Pakal." Captain V bowed deeply before the throned royal, so Patricia followed protocol and curtsied. The king motioned for Captain V to rise, and then he began communicating with succinct, guttural sounds, a language unknown to Patricia. The king and Captain V spoke for a minute or two longer before turning back to her.

"I had to explain that you were the one in the cavern with the elevator—he heard the ding too—and that you are the second contestant. There have been loads of spectators filling the stadium, and His Majesty was concerned that your mode of transport would be occupied, and we would have to delay the contest."

The king spoke to Captain V again, who turned with a look of surprise to Patricia.

"What is it? What is he saying?"

"What a compliment! He said that he thanks you in advance for saving his son. Also, he needs your keys and watch. Rules are rules. He must have all the items before the start of the match. No cheating allowed. It'll keep you both honest. They will be returned to you if you survive. Oh, and he digs your tattoo."

Patricia swallowed hard, trying to clear the lump in her throat. "Son? Survive?"

The group of speared men took one step closer.

She was sweating. "Son? Please tell him that he is mistaken. He must have me confused with someone else."

"There is no refusing the king." Captain V bowed deferentially to the king and held further conversation in the unintelligible dialect.

"Patricia, he knows the items are in your pocket. Hand over your watch and keys, but not too quickly. I need you to reach slowly into your pocket, retrieve the items, and put them on the dais."

When Patricia shook her head no, the speared men took yet another foreboding step forward, spears lifted. To her,

618

the items were her lifeline out of this predicament. She looked around desperately; all eyes were on her. There was nowhere to run, nowhere to escape, and no sign of the elevator.

"Yes, c'mon, the items in your pocket. I am aware of your fondness for them, but it would be prudent to obey. If it's any solace, the watch doesn't work on these people. I've already explained to him that you understand and agree to his rules. He reminded me that he cannot allow watches or keys in the arena during the games as a precaution to dissuade cheating. I'm afraid that he demands you hand them over. He will not take no for an answer, and he will not ask again."

Patricia hesitated. To give up her precious and valuable belongings gained over years of tremendous effort would be to capitulate. She dug deep within herself to find the composure and equanimity needed to comply. Felt extreme inner turmoil and conflict, but she was cornered. Hesitantly, Patricia withdrew the watch and keys from her pocket, stepped forward to put them on the dais, and bowed. Captain V gave her a thumbs up and returned to her side.

"Smart move. I know what you're thinking: 'How will I get back?' He means business, trust me. He knows you're here for the gate. Why else would you have two keys? We have all sought what lays beyond at some point. You don't think you're the first one to try, do you? Getting to the gate is easy. It's getting through it that's the hard part.

"OK, let's talk about the rules. Only the keepers of time, the horologists, are allowed such complex and powerful apparatuses. He's really big into 'Real Time.' The idea of changing circumstances, changing history, drives him nuts. He finds it too hard to make decisions if the goal posts are forever moving." Again, the king and Captain V exchanged a brief guttural dialogue.

"His Majesty has stated that he will now grant you a conversation with him in your native tongue of English. He asks that you please take a seat." Captain V motioned to the empty seat beside Sir Gawain. "I've found Your Majesty to have an incredible aptitude for languages, although this should come as no surprise since the dialects of the Mayan tongue are vast and unique amongst the disperse factions in this part of the world. I assumed you would prefer to speak in English, but he has a deep appreciation for the romance languages, so if you would prefer to converse in another tongue, he's prepared to do so. Also, I'm not sure if you're aware, but he wished for me to tell you that one of the keys you presented, the one on the left, is a fake. Which did you use in the elevator?"

"A fake? His left or my left? What do you mean?" Her stomach sank. She had thought the two were identical.

The king spoke, interrupting her thoughts. "Traveler of time, what you truly seek is near, only offered to those few travelers with an impeccable constitution and little avarice. The elusive gates are not for the feeble minded. I will only allow attempts to be made by those with a resolute constitution, impeccable knowledge, and of course, two keys. As one of your keys is a fake, you are out of luck. But know that if you seek to journey below, there may yet be hope. There is no time to procure another contestant, and thus by my decree, you may be permitted. You cannot stop believing, you have to hold on to that feeling. Many have tried and many have failed. Take Mr. Bauman, for instance. He's made multiple attempts, an avid game show participant. Where he continues to find keys is anyone's guess."

The king motioned to one of his men, who collected her items and disappeared through one of the porticos.

Suddenly, the king began grasping at his waist, searching for something. "What time is it? Almost nine o'clock?" As he withdrew and glanced at his watch, she recognized that it was strikingly similar to her own timepiece, even down to the inscription on its rear. "Heavens, we cannot be late. Walk with me, my dear. The games are set to begin and it's a packed house. Our audience awaits. Further discussion regarding the gates will have to wait."

Captain V took her side and every member of the court rose to their feet.

621

She had neither taken the time today nor in the Middle Ages to size up Sir Gawain, a.k.a. Cyrus Bauman, her competition. He was a rather unimposing fellow, approximately six feet tall with short-cropped hair and a two-day-old beard. He was not terribly muscular, though his doublet and mail under his surcoat made him look burlier than he was. In his satchel was not one but two texts; the first was curiously similar to her own red tome, and the other was titled, *Useless Facts and Tidbits You'll Never Need to Know (New Orleans Edition), Volume I.*

Captain V leaned in and whispered, "May the best person win. Remember everything I've told you. When the games begin, look for any opportunity to impress the king."

Patricia did not mean to dismiss her guide's advice, but she was more focused on her adversary. "Umm, excuse me. We have met. You're Sir Gawain, one of the knights of King Arthur's Round Table. How long have you . . . How did you know about . . . Did Merlin mention me? Are you following me?"

Cyrus looked down upon her and laughed. "I must have made an impression on you. Women and the games they play. Fellow islander, fellow medieval-er, follow New Orleanian, fellow purveyor at The Dutch East India Company, fellow teacher—do you take me for a fool? You've been bouncing throughout history, trying to throw me off your trail, only for me to realize it is you who have been following *me* throughout time. Was our last meeting at Carrollton School not enough to dissuade you from this endeavor? Remember what I said? 'May the best person win.' Yet you followed me to the Middle Ages!"

Patricia seemed to miss his point. "What? For the third time today, I am not a teacher! Why do people keep saying that to me? I am merely curious about how you procured the red text in your satchel. I had an identical manuscript that was accidentally lost in the elevator mere moments ago. If, by some chance, it is mine, I'd like it returned. How did you obtain your keys? Somewhere in King Arthur's court?"

"Can you really be so daft? Mind games, with me? My curiosity was piqued when I heard that you had obtained keys, plural. You, the perky out-of-towner who all the kids at school enjoy. Well, *news flash*, I'm the one who stole it from Jason the first time. Poor, innocent little you. You had a nice charade going until you invited one of the Westbankers into our life. I thought I had a good disguise, but you bested me with your whole portrayal of an altruistic teacher. I even believed you for a bit. But then I rationalized it being a thrill on your part. You thought yourself to be smarter than everyone else. As for your text, perhaps you shouldn't have left your satchel alone in the faculty lounge."

"You simply must be confusing me with someone else. I was a practicing psychologist on the Island of Tripe. Could you be referring to Professor Montegue?" She looked genuinely clueless.

"Are you denying that you are on the faculty at Carroll-ton School in 2017? New Orleans, Louisiana." Patricia only shrugged her shoulders. "Oh, give me a break. Are you really going to continue this charade, Jessica? I was exiting a streetcar in front of Loyola University when I first glimpsed you and Merl Linstein. Sheer luck? Was it fate? I couldn't believe my eyes. So what did I do? Easy. I followed you to the school, set up Jennings, landed the job, and presto. Perhaps it was too easy. Maybe you were setting me up?" He paused to reflect.

"What happened? Who is Jennings? And my name is not Jessica."

"Viviane." The muscular Captain V nudged Patricia. "It's time to break a leg. C'mon, sir, you too. Good luck to the both of you. May the best person win. I don't mean to make you nervous, but I'm told this will be the most watched show ever. No pressure, no pressure."

The muscular warriors escorted the group from the room. With the king in the lead, the group passed through an adjacent building, down a declivitous stone ramp, through a thatched tunnel, and then emerged onto a stone overlook amid the boisterous revelry of a large stadium.

Gustav Holst's *The Planets* blared over a modern PA system. From their perch, Patricia looked out over the stadium. In the center of the area was a manicured, rectangular grass field with a center mound covered by a domed, palm-thatched roof with an oculus at its center. Thousands upon thousands of spectators of various heritages and sartorial styles filled the stadium to the brim. Most were dark- and lank-haired indigenous observers, but others were of a Caucasian persuasion, slightly taller, with clothing more reminiscent of her medieval travels. Also catching her eye was a large net strewn high above the stage.

The audience wandered about and seemed to be in no particular hurry as they meandered to their seats, perused the stands, sampled foodstuffs, and engaged in cheerful reverie. Some of the more avid fans were perched in their seats, watching the games intently. In one section near the field, enthusiastic onlookers were waving and shouting at the players on the court. There were also those who were seemingly indifferent to the match, lost in thought, eating and drinking a variety of fares. A vendor walked up and down the stadium steps hollering, "Get your papaya, mangos, wings and thighs! Two for a dollar! Get your dome foam . . ."

The clanking sound of hammers drew her attention high up above the portico through which she had just passed, where workers were adjusting a translucent clock, the gear mechanisms clearly visible and churning. The hands were approaching nine o'clock. On the stage below, the plush, red curtains were closed, although she could perceive movement behind them. Rising above the jungle canopy outside the stadium was the Temple of the Inscriptions, a large, stepped pyramid she recognized from her studies. The scene was simply awe-inspiring and unbelievable.

A cry from below announced the start of battle. Two teams of five muscular men each met on the field. They were dressed in loin cloths, and their chests were each uniquely decorated with a series of horizontal lines and dots, painted in bright colors. As the game commenced, they aggressively smashed into one another, passing a small ball between them by slinging it from their midsections, gyrating their hips and torsos. The goal seemed to be to pass the ball through a circular stone affixed high on the wall. Passions ran high on the field; there was clearly more than bragging rights at stake. Along the sides of the court, coaches shouted instructions and attendants used punkahs to fan sweaty warriors who rested and drank from leather pouches. Hanging from rafters above the court were large banners decorated with lines and dots. Pan-Am Stadium was etched in English across a courtside stone wall.

Patricia pointed and asked, "Captain V, is that a banner of the king? It's different from the ones below."

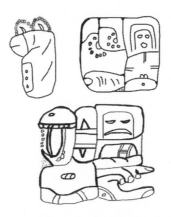

"Good observation, but no. It's meant to intimidate the opposing team. Its literal meaning in English would be 'Dome Field Advantage.' After your game, our men will be facing the Falcons from Becan, and they're a rowdy group. They've made it far in the league but have never clenched the title. We're ranked neck and neck this year, so they'll be out for blood today. Our team's fan club made the banner last night." He motioned across to a section where enthusiastic fans were costumed and carrying on, the most boisterous one dressed as a whistle.

"Rowdy group. Spirited. It looks like number nine, one of the all-time greats, will have his work cut out for him today."

As the king approached the edge of his platform, gameplay immediately ceased, the slate was wiped clean, and the players all took a knee in deference to their ruler. The

627

spectators also stopped their interactions as the overhead clock struck nine and a loud chime rang out. The entire stadium was silenced.

The king said, "My brethren, today marks the commencement of the feast of Sak K'uk'. As in years past, we have brought one man and one woman, each representing a different age on Mother Earth. Before number nine can trounce the Falcons . . ." The crowd went wild, hooting and hollering for their team. The king waited for their composure before beginning again. "Please quiet. We'll have a brief interlude and then we'll begin your favorite and most requested game show!" The crowd roared again in applause. "There are two travelers who seek our contest of time. One is from the distant past, one the near future. Both seek enlightenment, though only one has the necessary constitution and has studied hard enough to warrant passage into the gates and beyond if that is what he or she so chooses. Is our host ready?" There was movement behind the red curtains.

Patricia was taken aback by the thought of being unprepared. A look of dismay and worry creased her face. Was the king implying that she would lose?

Her competitor whispered, "Tut-tut. Seconds can seem like eternity. Butterflies? Looks like someone should have studied a bit harder. Like I said, 'May the best person win.'"

"But I only saw the announcement in the elevator. I didn't sign up for this. I have no clue about what to expect."

"Are you kidding? Trying to play mind games? There were thousands of applicants for two spots, and I'm supposed to believe your nomination was unplanned? Get real. The material was right there in our school the whole time." Patricia looked confused, so he patted the heavy text in his satchel. *Useless Facts and Tidbits You'll Never Need to Know (New Orleans Edition), Volume I* was written in gold lettering across the spine. "Please don't belittle me, Jessica. Pretending that you were drawn to New Orleans? I saw your eyes fancy the same book that I nicked from the library cart at school, so don't pretend like you weren't trying to cheat too! Don't try to play ignorant. Too bad for you that I got to the book first. When I win, I plan to repay an old debt to Beau and Merl.

"History can be fleeting, but we all know that the outcome of this game show will be indelibly etched in history. What were the odds of finding Merl Linstein in 2017, not to mention finding you at his side. I merely followed you into the school, where the book I sought just happened to be filed. As if you didn't know! This book is out of print and impossible to find, but there it was! One should always follow their intuition; it worked out beautifully for me, I'd say. From there, the rest was easy. Set up Jennings, the old history teacher, with rumors of inappropriate behavior, and presto! There was suddenly an opening for a teacher. The best part is that you never once suspected me. You thought you were so clever to fancy Jason Dix, but I was watching. Not only did he have a key, but he's Beau Champ's son! You always had that red book at your side, until you went and left it on the elevator. Careless! Your plans were so easily foiled.

"After what Beau and Merl did to me—destroyed my island, put me in the dungeon, changed my history—I'll relish in what's about to happen to both once I have the blue key. If I find that you had a part in it, I'll come after you as well."

"Impossible. Beau is encased in a seedling, and the only Merl I know is stuck in . . ."

". . . the Middle Ages." Winwood smugly raised his brows.

Patricia began to realize that she was a pawn in Winwood's game on a grand scale.

"Shh. Listen." Captain V nudged her as the king continued.

"My people, today is history in the making. For your entertainment, we have two contestants from two opposing eras: a woman, from our not-too-distant future, and a man, from many, many years in the past. Do I have the approval of this audience to begin the game? A classic battle of old versus new. Do you want to see a game show?" The king held his right thumb up and his left thumb down as the crowd began to cheer wildly. "One or both may not emerge alive, but this king says AYE! And the ayes have it! Let the games begin! Alexa, I command you to bring out Louis Armstrong."

The crowd roared, "FunnyMaze! FunnyMaze! Funny-Maze!"

Over the PA system, a woman's voice, unmistakably Patricia's own voice announced, "But first, brought to you straight from Brooklyn, New York, 1965, I'm proud to present your pregame entertainment: the one and only Louis Armstrong and the Carrollton Quartet!"

The rain began sweeping in sheets outside the dome, but everyone in the stadium stayed dry. As the king raised his right hand, the red curtains opened to reveal a black gentleman with a clarinet standing before the rest of the quartet, all clad in masks and plumaged headdresses. The foursome began to play "Clarinet Marmalade" as the great Satchmo twisted and gyrated as if possessed by the music. The drummer was bearded and hidden behind his cymbals, a tall, dark-haired, skinny fellow played the trumpet, and the pianist was a dark-haired boy who looked remarkably like Jason Dix. The young pianist repeatedly struck the wrong keys with his bandaged left hand.

Patricia was dumbfounded. Her eyes were drawn wide and her mouth was agape as she slowly shuffled toward the stage mumbling, "Is that? Really? But how? Jason Dix? And where is Merlin?"

Was she being set up? After all, she was wearing the same dress depicted in the codex's illustration. Where was Beau? Had he been extracted from the seed? If so, how?

"Excuse me," Captain V said, and then slipped behind the red curtains on stage.

Mr. Armstrong and his crew paid no attention to Dr. Atwood's gross astonishment. The band's attention was instead directed to the court's floor, which began to violently tremble. Before her very eyes, the field's surface dissembled, weaving and turning as large, stone blocks began to levitate. As if by magic, they rearranged themselves into a confusing maze. When they had all settled into place, a magnificent, white marble staircase rose to the front of the stage, leading down into the maze. As the dust settled and the maze was complete, a large shudder could be felt as the ground shook outside the stadium. The king stepped forward as the music crescendoed and then subsided. At center stage, two podiums with red buzzers appeared, and an illuminated LED scoreboard with colorful lights descended from the rafters above the stage.

When the crowd hushed, the king said, "Ladies and gentlemen, children of all ages, today we are witness to the most interesting of all battles. On my right, a well-traveled man who is pompous enough to tempt fate. We need not curse him with bitter invectives or expound upon his accomplishments over the centuries. His trail is long and distinguished. He is a two-time winner who hasn't yet bested the entire maze, and he's never passed through the gates. Ladies and gentlemen, Mr. Cyrus Bauman!"

The crowd went wild; Cyrus was a fan favorite and well known to all in attendance. He would be hard to beat.

"And on my left, we have a traveler of new, a frenetic dynamo who seeks the Holy Grail at the mere advent of her travels. She and Cyrus will go on to teach at the same school in the year 2017. What a coincidence! Skilled in archaeology and psychology, her mind is her greatest asset. She may be new to the game, but she'll be a formidable opponent. She'll do whatever it takes to win. Ladies and gentlemen, Dr. Patricia Atwood! It's stamina versus agility, a battle for the ages! Who will make it through the maze?"

"FunnyMaze! FunnyMaze!" The crowd's reverie grew as the countdown began, "5, 4, 3, 2, 1, go!"

The audience quieted again as an overhead siren blared. A male announcer, who sounded like Captain V, proclaimed, "King K'inich Janaab Pakal welcomes you all to the latest installment of the magical mystery we call the FunnyMaze. And now here's the star of our show, the one and only master of the maze, your host, Melvin the Magnificent, and his alter ego, the Sagacious Saul!"

The roar of the crowd was deafening. Patricia stared in awe, but the change in circumstance seemed familiar to Winwood.

"Thank you! Thank you very much. Please, please, quiet down my friends. Make yourselves comfortable. Thank you. Devolution was never my schtick!" The master of ceremonies, a thin, mustached man, stepped out from behind the curtain and waved amiably to the crowd as the game's theme music played over the PA. Melvin had a dark complexion, crooked, yellow teeth, and was well dressed in a dazzling red smoking jacket and slicked back hair.

"Saul? Melvin? Is that you? What the?" He paid her no heed, not even offering an inkling of recollection as he stepped before the crowd to relish in their applause. He raised his hands as the accolades and applause waned.

"Welcome to our game, ladies and gentlemen, young and old. Take a look at our incredible FunnyMaze! It's over ten feet tall and contains over two hundred zig-zagging pathways. Along those pathways, prizes are hidden wherever you see the flashing lights. But that's not all, folks! An elevator is hidden somewhere within the maze, along with the elusive entrance to Xibalba." Melvin's voice became more asperous as Saul took over. "But that's not all! Throughout the maze, there are hidden, wrenching unpleasantries and surprises." The emcee seemed to grapple with himself, arguing, "Let me continue. No, me! It's my stage . . . no, it's mine!"

The king cut in. "Gentlemen, gentlemen, one at a time, please. Let's have some decorum."

Melvin composed himself, standing steadfast as he spoke over the theme music. "Will our illustrious contestants please take their respective podiums? While we get situated, let's listen as our announcers elaborate on the prizes. Art and Jessica, tell 'em what they'll win!"

The male announcer began. "Both of our contestants will receive a year's supply of Dawn dish detergent, simply for participating in our game today. If you've got to get it clean, you've got to use Dawn. Brought to you by Procter & Gamble."

Next up, the female announcer took her turn. "But Melvin, that's not all! Hold on to your socks, folks! Our lucky contestants today get to pick from a variety of fun-filled excursions and prizes including . . ."

The man cut in. "An all-expenses paid trip for two to the Hellas Impact Crater on Mars in the year 3021. Ladies and gentlemen, our winner will take the interplanetary, first-class, Pan Solar starship from Cape Canaveral. They'll be bathed in luxury during their journey. When they arrive on the Red Planet, they'll check in at the Hellas Hilton, home of the best spa that our solar system has to offer. With a five-star rating on PlanetAdvisor from over 27,000 satisfied travelers, the Hellas Hilton is your destination for luxury and relaxation. Our lucky winner will remain in a state of suspended luxury for two weeks. This vacation package is worth an astounding $3.4 million!"

The crowd gasp in surprise and delight.

Melvin said, "But Art and Jessica, surely there's more!"

Art continued, "Right you are, Melvin! Our second prize is a doozy. Our next package is for the adventurer in all of us. The lucky winner and one guest will travel through the ages of primordial earth. You've heard correctly, Your Majesty, our winner will be given one of only three known Orichalcum keys to use on their journey back in time. That's right, one of only three master keys! The lucky winner will be whisked to a terminal of his or her choosing and climb aboard a Bonneval 2000 holospheric capsule, where the real adventure will begin.

"The lucky contestant will be traveling in a safe and impermeable travel-sphere with the help of the Ephemeral, Ethereal Pixies." At the mention of the Pixies, the crowd let out a collective gasp. "Our winner will be transported to the frays of time to witness the creation of Earth, after which, they'll be whisked through epoch after epoch on a guided tour of how it all began billions of years ago. Before heading home, they'll stop by Atlantis for a bit of sightseeing and shopping."

Jessica took over. "Stay as long as you like; time is irrelevant! Precious few are offered the opportunity to travel before the great flood, and so there is no price tag for this once-in-a-lifetime opportunity. The value, priceless!"

Cyrus could not contain himself. "Orichalcum? Where did you find one? Oh, the possibilities! Do we get to keep the key?" A childlike look of wonder developed on Cyrus's face before he blurted, "Melvin, I'm going to win this."

An amazed whisper rippled through the crowd as an effulgent hologram of a ginormous key floated in the center of the stadium, spinning slowly for all to admire. Locked in an impenetrable glass case between the podiums sat the actual Orichalcum key, close enough to touch. Next, illustrations of an island appeared, along with boats and oarsmen. To Patricia's recollection, the images looked like Crete and an ancient Minoan society possibly related to Atlantis.

Art silenced the murmuring audience and continued with his task. "And Your Majesty, our last prize needs no introduction. If our lucky winner completes the maze, they will be offered the opportunity to depart our world for the putative Paradisiacal Lands and Elysian Fields of Xibalba, beyond the gates where eternity meets luxury. The two gates will open only briefly to let this mere mortal sublimate to another dimension. It's a one-way ticket, but the destination is surely one to be enjoyed."

Ooohs and ahhhs were heard throughout the energized crowd. The rained billowed outside the stadium, but inside remained dry. A plethora of small lights danced in the rafters, swirling counterclockwise.

Melvin stepped back to the microphone. "Wow! What prizes! Who wants to be a contestant? I know I would! The object of the game is to correctly answer each question and earn time. Our players will then use that accrued time to scour the maze for our prizes. The first person to find two of the prizes wins the game and gets a crack at the dash to the gates.

"OK, contestants, let's get ready to play! Steve, you're on the left." At Melvin's command, Winwood took his place behind the podium on the left side of the stage.

Patricia stood awkwardly in the middle of the stage, unsure of where to place herself. Realizing her confusion, Melvin led her by the hand to the right podium, whispering, "You know how to play this game, right? There'll be a series of questions, and each correct answer is worth two extra seconds on the clock." Melvin's voice trailed off as Patricia looked on in amazement. She seemed to finally digest the enormity of the spectacle.

Melvin returned to his microphone and said, "OK, players! Your first category is: 'MOTHER OF.' Oh, and if the surname will give the answer away, it'll be omitted."

Winwood chimed in, "But what if the same name goes with multiple answers?"

Saul let out an asperous upbraiding. "Don't worry, Cyrus, we gotcha covered! Do you not have what it takes? Not ready, perhaps? Maybe I switched the material on you?" Melvin took charge. "Come now, Saul. I'm sure you'll do well, Steve. You just have to try your best. There is never favoritism in the game, as you are all friends in our eyes. Time's a-wasting, so let's go!"

The LED board above the players lit up as names appeared on the screen, one atop the other.

Mary Ann Albert

Célestine Musson

Patricia barely moved her hand, though her red buzzer illuminated first.

"Patricia, you're up first. The answer?"

"Mary Ann Albert, she was the mother of Louis Armstrong, the jazz musician."

Ding, ding, ding! "That's right, Patricia. We'll add two seconds onto your clock."

Louis Armstrong stuck his face out from behind one of the curtains and yelled, "Hi, mom!" A woman stood proudly in the stands, waving to all the cheering fans. A camera focused on her smiling face, which was then brightly displayed on the screen.

"Our next set."

Dorothy Cronin

Célestine Musson

Again, Patricia's buzzer illuminated first.

"Célestine Musson, who is the mother of Edgar Degas, the impressionist painter."

"By George! She's a natural, folks! Right again. Amazing! You now have four seconds on your clock. Looks like Steve'll have some catching up to do."

Dorothy Cronin

Shirley May Satin

Patricia was again quickest to the buzzer as Cyrus continued to beat his fist hard on the buzzer without effect. "She's cheating! She has to be cheating!" Steve was quickly growing more and more irate.

"Shirley May Satin, she's the mother of Richard Simmons."

"Correct for a third time in a row. Jeezums, Cyrus — or is it Steve? You're a little slow to the punch today. Can someone bring this guy a coffee? Steve, if you need me to take it a little slower, just let me know. For now, it's time for a break and a word from one of our sponsors!" Melvin pulled out a small, metal spring, crossed the stage to the stairs, and started the Slinky walking down the steps. The crowd went wild.

"Today's interlude is brought to us by Slinky." Melvin cleared his throat dramatically and began to sing.

*"What walks downstairs, alone or in pairs,*

*And makes a slinkety sound?*

*A spring, a spring, a marvelous thing!*

*Everyone knows it's Slinky.*

*It's Slinky, it's Slinky.*

*For fun, it's a wonderful toy.*

*It's fun for a girl and a boy."*

The audience cheered when the Slinky successfully reached the bottom of the stairs. Melvin announced, "Both contestants and every member of our wonderful audience today will go home with a Slinky! Hours and hours of fun. Chin up, Steve. At least you'll get a Slinky!"

During the commercial break, Cyrus had realized that his podium was unplugged. The crowd gasped as he crawled around the stage, tracing the buzzer's cord. Confirming the perfidy, he raised the wiring into the air for all to see. His carefree composure had finally cracked under such perceived indignation, turning him from a measured, easygoing player to a crazed lunatic.

He let out a whoop, a holler, and a blood-curdling yell, raising his hands in the air with fists pumping. He took center stage, wanting the world to bear witness to the game's hypocrisy.

The king took a step back, as did Patricia. Taking advantage of the ruckus, Saul proceeded directly to the drum set, where he struck the band member in the face with a fierce right hook. "Take that for Chamé!"

Patricia remained near her podium, new to the game and clueless as to the typical protocol of this crazed competition. She wondered if this chaotic interlude was part of the game or a mishap.

He had seen enough. The small gecko with the number thirty-four armband had been perched atop one of the rafters along the stadium wall, but with the chaos, he disappeared into one of the clefts. Seconds later, the small ethereal lights high above began multiplying then turning faster and faster.

Steve continued his paranoid tirade. "You did this! You gave her the answers, didn't you? Cheater! It's her. Somehow she did this!"

"Me?" Patricia was taken aback. "You're wrong. I've fallen into these circumstances by accident. How dare you disparage me before this group and this audience?"

Trying to keep the peace, Melvin said, "C'mon, man. What's all the fuss about? Didn't you just hear you're getting a Slinky?"

# CHAPTER 30

## STEVE'S ADMONITION

*670 AD*

"Slinky? *Slinky*? If this were a fair contest, we would start over. It's the only acceptable restitution!" Cyrus was irate and spinning further out of control. "She unplugged my podium, or someone did! This is rigged! I can find out who did it, you know. She's not who you think!"

Unwilling to tolerate the outburst a moment longer, the king cut through the hubbub with his booming voice. "And who exactly is she? Please tell us, Steve. Or is it Cyrus? I don't think you'll be teaching after fall break! Is the game rigged? You betcha! You think you know injustice? What about your work camps back on Tripe? Remember us, your indentured servants?"

At exactly the same moment, every person on stage removed their masks. Patricia gasped at the familiar faces: Alfred, Jason, and Merl.

Steve's contemptuous remonstrance was palpable. "It was her! She set you up, you, Merlin, and Art, wherever he is. Do you imbeciles really think that there will be no repercussions? Do you know what I could do to you? You think you can trick me with this silly invisibility juice and the maze. You didn't stand a chance of catching me then, and you'll fail again now. You had to virtually destroy the island that I created, and for what? You haven't seen or heard the last of me!"

The crowd began booing and throwing trash on the field.

"You're just a sore loser!" one of the spectators shouted as the jeers of others grew exponentially.

Cyrus continued, "And where is he now? My pupil, the one with the smashed finger, Jason Dix. We all know that the kid shouldn't be here. The Pixies frown upon the capriciousness of giving children access to the keys. You're in for it now!"

Alfred had heard enough. "Give it up, Cyrus. You're cornered. There's no way out. You may have slipped through our grasp once, but not this time. Your greed only makes this all the simpler. If you try to run, I'll just set you up again in the future with the likes of whom you can't even fathom."

The audience was on the edge of their seats.

"I always knew that your greed would be your undoing."

Not to be upstaged, Melvin cut in. "Is someone a sore loser? Perhaps you should just slink across the stage, plug it in, and quit whining! You didn't have a problem barking orders when you were the leader of our island! Cyrus, you know what? I think it's your turn to answer a question. Put up or shut up. Art, let's light up the board again and finish this game."

Cyrus needed to act quickly if he were to escape. All eyes were on him, waiting for his next move. His embarrassment was growing under the intense scrutiny and derision, and his face was suffused with anger when his top finally blew. His jowls twitched, his face grimaced, and he contorted uncontrollably as he had an idea.

Grabbing his abdomen, he began to laugh in the most fiendish, maniacal manner. Holding his buzzer high in the air, he ripped it from the podium, and as if electrocuted or suddenly struck by some opisthotonic ailment, he arched his back and neck, looking upward as if waiting for the heavens above to invite an ascension. "Questions? Questions? Give me a break! I see you up there!" With no reply heard, his posture relaxed and he turned his focus to the maze, continuing his hysterical laughter. In slow motion and without warning, he darted from behind his podium and toward the glass cube housing the Orichalcum key.

"I think I'll just help myself to prize number two!" he shouted. The crowd gasped as he made a break for the key. The netting above dropped, but he was too quick and it fell in a heap on the stage. Using the buzzer as a hammer, he struck and broke the supposedly impenetrable glass with one swift motion, scooped up the precious key, and never broke stride.

As he dashed toward the stairs that led to the maze, he passed Jason and grabbed him by his collar. "I'll take the ringleader's son too." Everyone chased after him, but Cyrus had a good lead on them and rushed down the steps and past the Slinky. Surprisingly, the most agile was Patricia, who shoved Cyrus with all her might, causing him and Jason to tumble, twist and fall down the rest of the stairs. Jason seized his opportunity and scrambled away from his would-be abductor.

The ephemeral, swirling lights above began to spin faster and faster.

Merlin grabbed the mic. "What a bad sport, eh folks? He can't even take a little pressure. Sore loser! Well, when the going gets tough, the less-than-tough whine and whimper. Ladies and gents, he's nothing more than a bully."

With Cyrus's malevolent incivility, enough ire was finally drawn and the churning lights circling above whipped into a vortex that shot through the oculus, blazing like

647

embers, streaming down to ensnare him as he ran through the maze. Caught in the vortex, he was lifted high into the air, suspended in the center of the playing field. In the blink of an eye and a brilliant flash of light, the vortex, fairies, blue key, and Cyrus Bauman were gone.

# CHAPTER 31

## EPILOGUE

*Friday, October 27, 2017*

"Jason, I'm home." To Jason's surprise, he awoke on his living room sofa to the soft voice of his father, the glare from a bright lamp bulb causing him to shadow his eyes. Jason wiped the sleep from his eyes and looked around. The sun had set, the windows were darkened, and the clock beside the television read 9:00 p.m.

"Listen, buddy, I'm sorry about all the confusion earlier. I've been trying to call you, but I guess your phone was in the kitchen. After we hung up, I thought more about what you said. While we have some things to discuss, you were completely correct. There is no reason that Merl couldn't fill in for the week and handle any situation at the office. I presented my plans to him, and he said . . ."

"Dad, you won't believe what happened. I had the strangest dream. What the heck?" Jason spotted a large, plumaged, jade mask sitting beside the television. He looked down at his hand and found gauze wrapped around his left ring finger.

"He'll deal with the office in my absence. We made an agreement."

From behind Alfred, Merl gave Jason a wink and held out his key and chain. "Jason, I believe you'll be needing this. You left it in the front door."

# THE END